PAYBACKS

PAYBACKS

A Novel by
CHRISTOPHER BRITTON

**DONALD I.
FINE, INC.**

New York

Although the author of this novel has been a Marine and has defended DI's in court martial proceedings, and so this novel may seem very real, the events and persons in Paybacks *are fictional. The events never happened, the people never lived. Any resemblance of any character to any person living or dead is purely coincidental.*

Library of Congress Catalog Card Number: 84-073449
ISBN: 0-917657-20-9
Manufactured in the United States of America
10 9 8 7 6 5 4 3 2 1

This book is printed on acid free paper. The paper in this book meets the guidelines for permanence and durability of the Committee on Production Guidelines for Book Longevity of the Council on Library Resources.

This story is dedicated to
1st LIEUTENANT LEE PETERS, USMCR,
and all the others who were paid back by Viet Nam.

---------------------------------- CHAPTER ----------------------------------

One

STAFF SERGEANT Roger Markey was startled by Johnson, the platoon guide, pounding loudly on the doorsill of the duty office in the prescribed manner for a private requesting to speak to a drill instructor. Dispensing with the usual reporting procedures because of the late hour, Markey growled, "Get your ass in here, Johnson. What do you want? You're supposed to be in your rack."

"Sir," said the private standing at attention in front of the desk in his T-shirt and skivvies, "the private wishes to report that Private Collins is sick, sir."

"Sick?" Markey looked up at Johnson. "Well, get in your rack. I'll go have a look at him." He stood up as Johnson disappeared.

As he entered the squad bay Markey was greeted by all manner of sounds being emitted by the sleeping recruits. "Like walking into a cave full of hibernating bears," Markey thought. However, there was one sound he didn't recognize. It was a soft, high-pitched, mewling sound, and it was coming from Private Collins's rack.

Collins was assigned a lower bunk near the squad bay door. The light from the hallway outside was sufficiently bright so that it was unnecessary to turn on the squad bay lights and wake up the rest of the platoon. Actually Markey smelled Collins before he saw him.

Collins had thrown up, and his bed, depressed in the middle from his own weight as well as from years of prior use, was like a canoe, high on the sides, low in the middle. Collins's starched cloth cover lay on the floor beside his rack, where it had evidently fallen from his head.

He was convulsed in a compact knot, both arms wrapped tight around his stomach. His eyes were shut tight in pain, and he continued to make that soft haunting sound, almost like weeping.

One glance told Markey that Collins needed more help than he could provide. He paused long enough to ask Collins what was wrong, what had happened, and when there was no response or change of any kind in the boy's face he hurried to Private Johnson's rack.

"Get dressed and get down to the battalion aid station and get a corpsman. Tell him where to come and then get the O.D. on the way back. Hurry up. I'll wait here with Collins."

While he was waiting Markey took the towel off the end of Collins's bunk, soaked it with cool water, wrung it out and tried to bathe Collins's contorted face.

At intervals Collins would retch violently, his sides heaving in spasms, and this would cause him to struggle and gasp for breath. In almost two years on the drill field Sergeant Markey had never seen anything like it. He suspected every recruit in the platoon was by now wide awake and listening.

"Don't worry, kid," he said in a low, gentle voice, "help is on its way." There was no sign Collins heard him.

The corpsman appeared now, his kit slung under one arm like a football. He came up the stairs at a dead run. Markey appreciated that.

Like Markey, the corpsman did not bother to turn on the squad bay light. He had spent thirteen months in Viet Nam and was accustomed to repairing people in the dark. He bent over the moaning private, took his pulse and then tried to straighten Collins out in order to examine his stomach, which seemed to be the focus of the pain. Collins let out a sudden high-pitched cry and rolled back into the fetal position as soon as the corpsman released him.

"He needs a doc, sarge. He's in shock, I think, but I haven't got a clue what's caused it. Could be a ruptured appendix, but there's so much blood in his barf...I never heard of that happening with an appendix. I'm afraid to examine him further, might do more damage inside."

The O.D., a lieutenant named Cavanaugh, had joined them along with the platoon guide, Johnson, as the corpsman was examining Collins. He ran to call the base dispensary.

"How come he's still dressed, sarge?" the corpsman asked, nodding in the direction of the suffering recruit. "How long has he been like this?"

"I haven't got any idea," Markey told him. "This is the duty platoon for the weekend and I know he had fire watch tonight right after lights out. That's probably why he's still dressed."

The dispensary was no more than half a mile away from the Hotel Company barracks, but it was at least forty-five minutes before the doctor arrived. He seemed annoyed.

"What's the big problem?" he asked.

He took one look at Collins weakly jerking in agony and spitting blood, went over and turned on the light. Instantly a yell of "Flares" erupted from the platoon, and every bed emptied as their occupants dove for cover under the bunks.

"What the hell?" the doctor gasped in astonishment.

"False alarm, you dumb shits. Get back in your racks and shut up," Markey told them.

Glancing suspiciously from side to side, but finally regaining his wits, the doctor asked, "What's this man's name?"

"Private Collins, sir," Markey said.

"Private Collins . . . Private Collins, can you hear me?" The doctor shook Collins's shoulder. No response. He broke a capsule of ammonia and held it under the private's nose.

Collins recoiled and opened his eyes, still doubled up and lying on his side. He looked up, as if struggling to see where he was. Suddenly the group of men standing over him appeared to come into focus for him and his eyes, tightly shut a moment before, became wide, and he cowered like a frightened animal, trying to retreat into the recesses of his bunk.

"Don't . . . please don't . . ." He was begging in a scarcely audible voice.

9

"Don't what, private? What's happened to you?"

Collins coughed, blood and phlegm dribbling out the corners of his mouth and down his chin.

"Please . . . I'm motivated . . . please . . ." He hardly broke the silence. He was crying.

"Private, I need to examine you. I'm going to straighten out your legs and you've got to help me."

Collins was lying on his right side. The doctor put his hands firmly on the boy's left shoulder and nodded for the corpsman to push on the knees. As they reached for him, Collins cried out, "No, no . . ." At the first bit of pressure, he became hysterical, lashing out, but only for an instant, then passed out.

"Lord's mercy," Markey thought as he watched Collins finally relax. The doctor pushed and pinched the unconscious private's abdomen.

"What's this?" the doctor asked, staring hard at Markey and pointing to several angry red welts, beneath which a deep black spot was beginning to swell just below the navel. "Has this man been struck?"

"Not that I know of—"

"Well, those marks didn't get there by themselves, and I'm sure that he looks even worse on the inside. I've got to get him to a hospital. Where's the nearest phone?"

Cavanaugh, the corpsman, Johnson and the doctor all stayed with Markey until the ambulance arrived. The doctor's concern was obvious. Now and then he would glance up from his patient at Markey with ill-concealed disdain, but he said nothing. They waited in awkward silence. It was no more than twenty minutes but seemed like an hour before the still unconscious Collins was taken away.

After the doctor and the corpsman left and Johnson returned to his rack Markey approached Lieutenant Cavanaugh.

"Sir, that doctor thinks I hit that kid. I'm telling you I didn't hit him. There's gonna be trouble, isn't there?"

The lieutenant stared hard at Markey. "Yeah," he said in a tired voice, "there's going to be trouble, an investigation at least."

"Shit . . . I can't believe this is happening to me . . ."

"Sergeant Markey—"Cavanaugh sounded grim—"just between you

and me, you better think about talking to a lawyer before you answer any questions. Especially if that kid's hurt as bad as he looks."

"I'm leavin' on a jet plane..."

"Viet Namese national anthem," Mike Taggart thought to himself. The clear, haunting words of the song on the car radio gave him goose bumps as he drove along. For a moment he scanned the night sky outside the open window to his left.

"Probably some drunken lieutenants somewhere in I Corps singing along right now." The too-familiar imagined scene seemed both very near and very far away to Taggart as he thought about it, and he shook his head to clear the thought from his mind.

"What's the trouble," murmured his wife, Cathy, who was nestled beside him with her head on his shoulder as they drove along.

"Nothing," Taggart told her, "that song is all. It used to fan the homesick fires in Quang Tri. Everybody'd start singing along and things would start to turn blue."

He was driving beside a small bay, so calm and peaceful that hardly a ripple wrinkled the moon's reflection.

"Well, you're home now," she whispered, giving him a hug. "You're not blue anymore, are you?"

The question surprised Taggart. She was the one he thought was unhappy. Being uprooted from Chicago when he'd joined the Corps, turning down the spot in the reserve unit the law firm had arranged in the process, the succession of moves as he went from one phase of Marine training to the next, her miscarriage, the year's separation while he was in Viet Nam, the prospect of fifteen more months in the Corps before they could return to Chicago... he knew how service life depressed her, but evidently not tonight.

"No, Cath, I'm not blue. It's just that sometimes I get pangs of something, guilt maybe, when something like that song reminds me of what's still going on over there. It's hard to go to parties and wear a lampshade on my head when those thoughts are lurking..."

The thought of the lampshade made them both laugh. Periodically, during the party they'd just left, Nick Margolis, one of the defense counsel stationed with Mike Taggart at the Recruit Depot, had raced through wearing a lampshade, grabbing girls and generally being tritely outrageous behind the anonymity of his headgear. Margolis always had more fun than anyone else at parties, even his own.

Taggart, on the other hand, had spent most of the party watching the Lakers' game on television and drinking beer with Tom Horn, a long-time friend who had just returned from WESPAC, the Western Pacific.

"The world needs a few Margolises to keep things moving," Cathy said as they pulled into the drive and parked. "Are you going to walk Feodot?"

"Probably should. After being cooped up this long she won't be able to bark without gargling."

"I'll go with you. Let's walk back down to the bay."

Once they'd descended the path from the sidewalk to the narrow strip of sand that edged the bay, Mike released the straining cocker spaniel from her leash and watched her zoom across the beach, ears aflap as she ran,

"Seagulls beware," Cathy called in mock warning.

It was a warm night for February, even by San Diego standards, and the lights across the water shimmered as Mike and Cathy Taggart slowly walked, arms around each other.

Halfway down the beach they found a canoe, apparently deserted on the sand.

"Oh, Michael, look. Are there paddles in it? Let's go for a ride."

"'Marine Officer Court-Martialed for Canoe Theft.' Some head-line."

"Oh, don't be silly. It's two A.M., the beach is empty and we don't have to be gone long. C'mon."

Taggart didn't need much persuasion. The moonlit beach was empty in both directions. Besides, he loved canoeing . . . if you knew what you were doing canoes went where you wanted them to. He wished life would do the same, and at once told himself to knock off the banal thought. Or was it self-pity?

"Let's go," he said, kicking off his shoes. "We'll leave our shoes to show we're coming back in case someone does show up. Feodot'll hang in."

They eased the canoe into the shallow water, and Cathy arranged the cushions on the floor near the back and climbed in. When Mike took the rear seat she silently leaned back against him, her head in his lap, and trailed her fingertips in the water.

Taggart headed the craft across the bay into a light breeze with a skill developed over a hundred boyhood canoe trips. He paddled soundlessly, listening to the gurgle where the prow sliced the water's stillness.

The smooth, repetitive feel of the stroke, the instant response to every slight directional adjustment his paddle commanded, the slow rise and fall of Cathy's breasts as she sat before him lulled Taggart, seemed to eclipse the world beyond the water. Neither spoke.

Once across, he turned the canoe and let it drift with the breeze back in the direction they'd come from.

"Remember the boathouse?" Cathy murmured.

Mike remembered. One autumn in college he had worked afternoons renting canoes at the university boathouse on the river that meandered through the campus.

Sometimes on rainy afternoons, when nobody wanted to rent canoes, Cathy came by to keep him company. They would turn the canoe on the topmost rack upright, line it with cushions and lie there listening to the rain drum on the tin roof just above them and watch the torrents blow across the surface of the river. They first made love there.

Ever since, whenever Cathy asked what he wanted for his birthday or for Christmas, Mike asked for a canoe, for the life back when . . .

Reminiscing about the boathouse, Cathy was the most cheerful she'd been since the week after his return from WESPAC the preceding October. Taggart wished they could drift forever. . . .

Feodot was wandering near-by when they beached the canoe and collected their shoes. They walked along, drifting still, making their unhurried way home, unaware of the clock.

"Michael, I think that's our phone."

He had heard the ring at the same time she had and had sprinted

13

around the corner to the door. By the time she came into the apartment Mike was on the line.

"Captain Taggart."

"Captain, this is Lieutenant Cavanaugh. I'm the Officer of the Day at the Third Battalion, Recruit Training Regiment out at the base. I'm sorry to bother you at home, sir, but we've had some trouble out here at the base tonight and I think one of our sergeants needs to talk to a lawyer. He says he wants to talk to you."

"Is it a maltreatment case, lieutenant?"

"Yessir, sort of . . ."

"Well then, charges surely haven't been drawn up. Is it so serious that it can't wait until tomorrow morning?"

"Yes, sir, it's that serious. You see, the recruit died a couple hours ago."

"I'll be there in half an hour," Mike said, regretting the need to leave Cathy on this night. "Will you be in the company area or the battalion offices?"

"I'll be at the battalion offices."

"Holy Mother Marine Corps calls," said Cathy as Mike hung up the phone.

"Take it easy, Cath, this one's serious. A recruit has died and apparently one of the DI's is going to be charged with it."

"But why did they call you, Mike? You've only been at the base a month. You haven't even had a drill-instructor trial yet. Why not call one of the others in the defense office with experience in this sort of case?"

"I guess the sergeant asked for me by name. Don't ask me how he knows me. Anyway, I have to go."

She nodded unhappily.

Few cars were on the streets as Mike drove to the base. Even the neon signs on the topless bars near the gate had been turned out for the night by the time he passed them.

If the kid was beaten so bad he died, there must be a whole platoon full of witnesses who at least had heard something, he thought, and wondered how much of an investigation CID had already done.

The lonely gate guard saluted the blue officer's sticker on the car's bumper and motioned Mike on through without stopping him. Inside the gate, Mike slowed to a crawl. The base was small and pedestrian-oriented. The speed limit was fifteen miles per hour. Passing a warehouse, he caught a glimpse of a solitary figure marching back and forth under an outdoor light, a recruit stationed as a sentry to guard the warehouse. Carrying a rifle at right shoulder arms and wearing a helmet liner and canteen belt to signify that he was on duty, the private walked stiffly to the end of the building, stopped, executed an about-face and marched to the opposite end.

"Warehouse is probably empty or full of some strategic war material, like fart sacks," Mike thought as he parked the car in the area designated for personnel visiting at the Third Battalion area.

Battalion headquarters was a World War II-vintage wooden-frame two-story building painted a light tan. On the way in Mike followed a cinder path lined on both sides with freshly painted white field stones. He passed a brass cannon that gleamed with a high shine even in the dark.

Each footstep echoed in the silence of the narrow corridor as Mike made his way to the Battalion Adjutant's office where he expected to find Lieutenant Cavanaugh. The entire chain of command from President Nixon to Lieutenant Colonel Wickerow, the Third Battalion Commander, stared down at him from their pictures on the wall. Turning left into the second corridor, he spotted a light in the S-1's office, the warren of the battalion adjutant. He knocked lightly as he came through the open door so as not to startle the lieutenant in case he was dozing.

Cavanaugh was not dozing. He was bent over the desk making an entry in the duty log.

"Pete Cavanaugh, sir, pleased to meet you." Cavanaugh stuck out his hand.

Cavanaugh had a blond crew cut; the sides of his head were shaved which was the style preferred by the command at the Recruit Training Regiment. He was tall and lean and tan and had a grip like a steel spring. Mike guessed he might be twenty-three, though he looked younger.

"I guess you've been pretty busy tonight, lieutenant."

15

"Christ, yes. The CO just left about ten minutes ago. He stayed the whole time CID was in the area. The regimental and battalion sergeant majors have been in and talked to Sergeant Markey. Lieutenant Burnquist, the series officer's been in, and I'm still trying to raise Captain Gunderson, the company commander. It's been like Friday night happy hour in here . . . I mean, it's been so crowded."

"Where's the sergeant? Markey, did you say his name was?"

"Yes, sir, Sergeant Roger Markey. He's over in the rec room. I'll go get him."

"Just a minute, lieutenant. Before you do I want to hear what you know about what happened. You were the one the incident was first reported to, right?"

"Yes, sir, but I don't know very much. About 2230 a private came in from Hotel Company, first platoon, and said Sergeant Markey asked that I come down to the platoon area. Private said he'd already sent someone from the battalion aid station over there to see one of the other privates who was real sick. When I got over there all the privates were in their racks except the one Sergeant Markey was using for a runner. Markey was standing by this one private's rack and a corpsman from the aid station was bending over trying to talk to this private, all doubled up tight holding his stomach and breathing real hard and not talking at all."

"What'd you do?"

"I asked Sergeant Markey what the trouble was, and he said he didn't know. The platoon guide, a Private Johnson, had come to the duty hut and told him Collins, that was the private's name, was sick. Well, Sergeant Markey couldn't get Collins to respond to him at all so he sent for me and the corpsman."

"And then?"

"Corpsman didn't have any better luck and said it looked like some kind of convulsions to him, so I called a doctor from the dispensary. The doc half-forced Collins out straight and poked around a little bit, then he looks up at Sergeant Markey and asks the sergeant whether Collins had been hit."

"What did Sergeant Markey say to that?"

"He said not that he was aware of. Then I asked why he thought the private might have been hit, and the doc pointed to some red marks on Collins's stomach."

"Could you see the red marks yourself?"

"Yes, sir."

"Where were they?"

"Right under the private's navel mostly, but other places too. Anyhow, the doctor orders an ambulance and takes Collins back to the dispensary and I go back to the battalion, but before I go Sergeant Markey comes up to me and says, 'Sir, I didn't hit that kid.' Those were his exact words, I think."

"Did he say anything else?"

"No. I was thinking how much I hoped he didn't for his sake, but I didn't say anything else except to tell him to think about getting a lawyer.

"By the time I got back to the battalion it was after midnight. I made my log entry and was reading when I received a call from the dispensary, it was the same doctor reporting that Collins had died. He said he'd reported it to the provost marshall's office.

"I asked him what he died of, and the doc said he thought it was some kind of internal hemorrhage, probably caused by a sharp blow to the stomach, but there'd be an autopsy later to confirm. He said Collins was never able to answer any questions. . . . About the time I was hanging up the phone, here comes the criminal investigation people flashing credentials all over the place and wanting to talk with Hotel-1's duty sergeant. I called the colonel and then I took them down to see Sergeant Markey."

"Were you there while they talked to him?"

"No. But the CO showed up right after they did and he went down to the company area. Later the sergeant majors and Lieutenant Burnquist came in and they went down too. About an hour later the colonel came back up. He told me to relieve Sergeant Markey and post the supernumerary. Apparently CID had got Collins's whole squad up and were interviewing them. And then, a few minutes after I got back down there, they came in and read Markey his rights and told him he was suspected of killing Collins and wanted to question him again, and that's when he said he wanted to see you. Then he came back up here with me after I relieved him."

Mike followed Cavanaugh back down the corridor in the direction he'd entered the building from. Cavanaugh turned and opened a plain wooden door. Inside was a large room furnished with a ping-pong table, a couple of card tables and chairs and several overstuffed couches and chairs. A soft drink machine was in one corner and a battered T.V. In the other. Empty soft drink cans and overloaded ashtrays were everywhere. A marine at the far end of the room stood up as they came in.

"Sergeant Markey, this is Captain Taggart," Cavanaugh said.

Mike was surprised to see that Markey was a staff sergeant. No one had mentioned that fact, preferring instead to use verbal shorthand, calling him only "Sergeant Markey." It made a difference. The distance between sergeant and staff sergeant was the equivalent of the distance between associate and partner at Morgan, Miller, where he'd worked before he entered the Corps. Being a staff sergeant meant making the cut. Markey was no longer just an employee of, as they said, determinate duration; he'd been accepted as a member of the firm who presumably would make his career in the Corps. It was Staff Sergeant Markey's Marine Corps to a much greater degree than it was Mike's, because Mike was getting out as soon as his tour was up.

Mike felt better already. He doubted any charges would be pressed against a staff sergeant unless the prosecution was genuinely convinced it had something very strong to go on.

The man walking across the room toward Mike looked as if he had just stepped out of one of the Corps' recruiting posters. He was about six feet tall, slightly shorter than Taggart, and lean as a hard stare. His high cheekbones, black hair and eyes and deep tan made Mike wonder if he could be part Indian. Markey was wearing his campaign ribbons and badges, and Mike could see at a glance that he'd had two tours in Viet Nam and had been awarded a bronze star along with two purple hearts. When he reached to shake Mike's hand, Mike saw the tattoo—eagle, globe and anchor, the Marine Corps' emblem, accompanied by the legend "Death Before Dishonor."

"Evening, Sergeant Markey. Sounds like you've had a rough night."

"Yes, sir," Markey answered in an emotionless voice with just a trace of southern accent. "From the sound of things, hard times have just begun."

"Let's not jump to conclusions," Mike said. "Lieutenant Cavanaugh, thanks for your help. The sergeant and I will talk in here for a while."

Cavanaugh left. Sergeant Markey declined Mike's offer of a Coke, but Mike decided to have one. They sat down in easy chairs at right angles to each other.

"Do I know you from somewhere, Sergeant Markey?"

"No, sir, I don't think so."

"Well, then how did you decide to ask for me? There are several lawyers on this base with more experience in drill instructor cases than I've got."

"I don't know what kinda lawyer you are, sir, but, well, I watched you play in the base championship basketball game a couple of weeks ago between RTR and the legal office—"

"What the hell does that have to do with it?"

"Well, sir, near the end of the game RTR was way ahead and one of our players stole a pass and went the length of the floor for what looked like an easy layup, but somehow you caught him from behind and stopped him from making the basket. It just looked to me like you refused to give up even though it was a lost cause...." He shrugged. "That stuck in my mind, and when this thing happened I thought I might need a little of that before this is all over..."

Mike decided not to remind the sergeant that he had fouled out on that play, leaving the game having scored three points and having held his man to approximately twenty. No sense in unnecessarily undermining Markey's confidence in his chosen counsel.

"What happened with the platoon tonight, sarge?"

Markey took a deep breath, let it out slowly. He took out a pack of cigarettes and lit one, holding the pack out to Taggart, who shook his head. It was as if Markey was looking for a place to begin.

"Well, I sure as hell don't know everything that went on, captain. The first hint I had of any trouble was when Private Johnson, the guide, knocked on the door of the duty office and reported that Collins, one of the men in the platoon, was sick.

"I went to have a look at him and found him lying on his bunk balled up tight, both arms wrapped around his stomach like he'd been gut-shot. He was making a real low sound in his throat, but it was like he didn't know he was makin' it 'cause when I talked to him he didn't say nothing and sometimes he seemed to be having trouble breathing."

"Did you look at his stomach?"

"I tried to but it was obvious he wasn't gonna straighten out except by force, and I was afraid if I tried to pry him out straight I might really louse him up. So I sent for the corpsman and the OD. They couldn't do nothing with him when they got here, so the lieutenant called the doc. The doc finally got him moved around so he could look at his stomach, but Collins still wasn't answering any questions. When he looked at the private's stomach, the doc asks if he'd been hit there. I told him I wasn't aware of him being hit. Pretty soon they took Collins away in an ambulance and things quieted down. Then a while later here comes Lieutenant Cavanaugh again with CID wanting to know what happened. I told 'em just what I told you. They talked to some of the other privates, mostly others in the first squad that Collins was in. Colonel Wickerow and the sergeant major and Lieutenant Burnquist, the series officer, all showed up. I think it was the colonel who told me Collins had died. . . . Finally this sergeant from CID comes out from where they're interviewing the platoon and talks to the colonel for a minute, then he comes over to me and reads me my rights. He says he wants to talk to me some more but that I should know that I'm suspected of being involved in the death of Private Collins, that's the way he put it. And that's when I figured I needed to know more about what was going on before I did any more talking, and I asked to see you. After that I was relieved."

"Did CID arrest you?"

"No."

"Do you have any idea what moved them to read you your rights? I mean, why they suspected you?"

"No. They were talkin' to the privates, so there's no telling what they heard."

"Tell me about Collins."

"He was a funny one. Funny, peculiar, I mean. He wasn't a non-hacker, but he was low-middle. He always appeared to be trying hard, and he was smart on the knowledge part of the program, but I always felt he could do better when I watched him. He looked bewildered sometimes, like he was real unsure of himself. He was never very aggressive, but he wasn't any problem."

"When was the last time you saw him before finding him doubled up on his rack?"

"The last time I saw him was just after taps. First platoon had weekend duty and Collins had the fire watch in the common area between the duty officer and the squad bay. I'd noticed him on duty on my way into the duty office just after taps, but I didn't say nothing to him. Then, a few minutes later, I was sitting in the office doing some paperwork and I heard a clatter outside. I don't know if you know the sound, sir, but we hear it enough around here. There ain't no other sound like a rifle being dropped on a concrete floor."

Mike winced. Dropping a rifle was one of the worst sins a Marine could commit. When he was in OCS, one of his classmates had dropped his rifle and had had to sleep with it tied to his leg every night for two weeks, among other things.

Sergeant Markey went on: "I couldn't let that one pass, sir, so I made a beeline for the hallway, and there was Collins standin' right across from the head. He'd picked up his piece but hadn't reshouldered it yet. When he seen me coming he just turned to shit. He tried to come to attention and to get his weapon back on his shoulder at the same time. He got so nervous he almost put out his eye with the sight blade."

"You weren't doing anything to make him nervous?" Once in the mess hall Taggart had seen a recruit spill soup on a DI's boots and faint dead away before the sergeant could get the first word of reprimand out.

21

"I just said, 'Gimme that weapon before you drop it again,' and I grabbed it out of his hands. We were standin' there eyeball to eyeball, me with Collins's rifle, and I was pissed on account of, after eight weeks of training, something like this shouldn't be happening."

"What did you do then?"

"Well, I didn't think yelling at him would help none. Eight weeks training only made him act confused, besides it'd wake up the whole platoon. So I said to him real low, kinda between my teeth, 'Collins, you ain't showin' me much, and it ain't because you can't, it's because you ain't bearin' down. Instead you're walking around with your head in the goddamned clouds, and if you think you're gonna graduate without even being able to hold onto your goddamned rifle you better think again. Is that clear?' Of course, he's standing there sweating and he hollers, 'Yessir.' Then I say, 'When you're at shoulder arms, I want this weapon welded to your goddamned shoulder. Is that clear?' And I clamped that rifle onto his right shoulder hard so's he'd have no trouble remembering where it went. I said, 'You got two weeks left here, and you better show me something or I'm movin' you back. Is that clear?' And he says, 'Yessir' and that's all there was to it. I been sittin' here going over the whole thing in my mind again and again, and that's exactly the way it happened. I ain't leaving nothing out. I turned and went back to the duty office and didn't see him again until the guide came and got me."

"Did you tell all that to CID?"

"No, sir, they didn't ask. You're the only one who knows that, but nothing happened, I swear to God."

For the first time since he started talking, Mike thought he detected some emotion in the sergeant's tone. A trace of fear.

"Listen, sarge, I'm not going to tell you not to worry, you can't control how you feel. But I am telling you to relax a little. It's too early to tell where this thing is going, but as far as I can see there isn't any evidence to tie you to whatever happened to Private Collins. When someone gets hurt or killed the command gets real cautious. You being relieved is one of those precautions. But you're going to have to be patient while things sort themselves out. Can you do that?"

"Don't look like there's much choice."

"That's right. Now we don't know much about each other yet, but the rest can wait until Monday. Go home and don't talk to anyone about this, understand? Are you married?"

"Yes, sir."

"You can talk to your wife if you want, but no one else. If anyone starts asking questions, send 'em to me. Also, for the next few weeks I'm the best friend you have. If you have any questions, ask me. Don't ever think I'm too busy, because I'm not. Okay?"

"Yes, sir."

"One more thing. Sometimes drill instructors have a tendency to circle the wagons around one of their own when the command starts pointing fingers. That's fine. But tell your friends to stay away from the privates about this. Sometimes it's hard to believe, but most of the recruits are going to side with the drill instructor, and there's nothing much worse than having their good testimony tarnished by evidence the other DI's have threatened them.

"Okay, that's it. Come see me on Monday about 1100. Meanwhile I'll try to see the privates tomorrow. Is your car out in the lot? I'll walk out with you."

"Yes, sir."

The voice had gone flat again.

First light had appeared on the horizon as Mike arrived home. The paperboy was sitting on the corner folding papers. Not even the joggers were stirring at this hour on a Saturday morning. Taggart threaded his way between the half dozen or so cars clustered around the small apartments where he and Cathy lived.

He'd been trying cases less than two years, but from the first file he'd been assigned, he'd learned no two pair of eyes ever saw things exactly the same. What story was CID getting from those privates? What had triggered Markey's relief and the warning about his suspected involvement?

Taggart moved silently as he could upstairs to the bedroom. Cathy was sleeping. The windows in the room were open and a slight breeze

23

rustled the curtains. The wind chimes Cathy had hung outside the window tinkled.

Feodot jumped off the foot of the bed to greet him, and the motion woke up Cathy.

"Mmmm, what time is it?" she asked from the shadows that still filled the room.

"Six-fifteen." Although Mike had been without sleep for more than twenty-four hours he didn't feel tired. That would come later, he thought, this afternoon as he tried to interview those recruits after five or six hours of sleep. Right now there was still some mileage left in that first rush of adrenaline that had come with his involvement in an intriguing new case. He wanted to talk about it.

"Recruit died with red marks on his stomach," he told Cathy as he crawled into bed, although she hadn't asked. "The sergeant says he didn't hit him."

"Mmmm," she replied, rolling onto her side so that she was facing away from him.

"Could be he fell on the 'O' course," he went on, bringing up the standard drill instructor explanation for every scrape or bruise ever sported by a recruit.

No response from Cathy.

"Probably self-inflicted," he added, "obviously the kid killed himself to frame the DI."

No response.

"Shit," he sighed, looking at the ceiling. Inside his brain one voice told him it was unreasonable to expect her to show any interest in what had happened at that hour on Saturday morning, but it was drowned out by another voice, a frustrated one, that wondered whether this was the domestic scene he'd been so homesick for while in Viet Nam and Okinawa. . . .

She had been waiting for him at the gate as he disembarked. Months of reading and rereading her letters, of poring over the pictures she'd sent, were finally at an end. Tanned and smiling, blond hair shining, she had appeared for his homecoming as the Cathy he'd known since the beginning of tenth grade, the cheerleader, the smartest person in class, the best pianist in school, the girl he'd always loved and who he thought would love him wherever they happened to be. . . .

Now, two months later, lying on his back beside her, watching the sunlight inch its way across their room, Mike knew that those images were the tricks of a selective memory. Cathy, to put it bluntly, hated the Marine Corps, the transient life, and their year apart hadn't reversed the malaise she'd begun to descend into when they'd packed their things and left Chicago, she for her parents' home and Mike for OCS. It was as if part of her had gone into storage with her living room furniture. The succession of bleak furnished apartments where she had waited alone while Mike trained for their inevitable year of separation reinforced her blues. By the time he'd kissed her good-by and walked to the plane that was to take him to the coast it was almost with a sense of relief.

What had been for Mike an act of escape from the legal assembly line of Morgan, Miller & Richardson had been for Cathy a rupture in the life she'd planned for ever since they were married. Once, Mike remembered, she had called herself a glorified camp follower. Even though there had been good reasons, at least by his lights, to discard each of the alternatives to his Marine Corps enlistment on graduation from law school, Mike could see that Cathy saw the decision as a fairly selfish one on his part. . . .

He shook his head. Truth to tell, both of them had less to feel regretful about than a lot of people caught up by the war. Staff Sergeant Markey, for one. Mike didn't yet know the details, but very few of the cases he'd handled were untouched by the war in Viet Nam. Wondering what it would be in Markey's case, Taggart fell into restless daytime sleep.

Joe Steiner was drinking coffee with his wife on their patio. It was Saturday morning and the family was lazing its way into the day. The kids were in their pajamas, Joe was in his bathrobe.

The phone rang in the kitchen and his eldest daughter called out that it was for him. Trying to imagine who might be calling this early on Saturday Joe entered the kitchen, tightening the belt of his robe.

"Hello?"

"Joe, this is Colonel Guinn. Meet me at the office as soon as you can, in uniform. We've just got the case that's going to make us both generals!"

"Uh . . . yes, sir. What's it all about?"

"No time now. I'll tell you when you get here."

Joe found himself staring at a dead phone.

On the way to the base, Joe speculated what sort of case had Go-Go Guinn so worked up. It was a drill instructor maltreatment case, of that much he was sure. In the three months Joe Steiner had been chief trial counsel at the Recruit Depot, the irony of maltreatment cases had become painfully apparent.

Marine Corps regulations prohibited corporal punishment of recruits. Sergeants weren't even supposed to swear at their charges. Now more than ever before, with an unpopular war and news of U.S. atrocities in Viet Nam making daily headlines across the country, brutality toward trainees was a sensitive subject. The slightest complaint brought a swarm of congressional inquiries. Headquarters Marine Corps sensed that the slice of the defense budget allotted to the Corps depended on pissing off as few legislators as possible. The base command prosecuted every reported infraction to the fullest extent possible in the hope of deterring any future departures from the regulations, and loss of congressional appropriations.

But with few resulting convictions, Joe was forced to acknowledge to himself as he drove along. The goddamned noncoms absolutely refused to go along with the program.

Steiner thought he knew the rationale. They'd been beaten when they were in boot camp and it had done them more good than harm. They weren't going to let another NCO burn for what they considered a fine old tradition in the Corps. Steiner had seen the result . . . character witnesses parading to the stand to attest that the defendant was a future sergeant major of the Marine Corps. The defendant would take the stand and deny under oath he'd ever raised a finger against a recruit. Behind the scenes the defendant's fellow platoon staff would terrorize complaining recruits into retracting their stories. Finally, the defendant would exercise his right to have at least one-third of the court, the equivalent of a jury in civilian proceedings, composed of enlisted men. In this way the very segment of the Corps most determined to perpetuate the maltreatment was able in most instances to prevent the prosecution from obtaining the two-thirds majority necessary to convict a defendant of a noncapital offense in military courts.

Why in the hell did I have to get sent here right out of the gate? Joe wondered, chewing his lower lip. . . . Having been a Marine pilot for seven years before going to law school on the Corps' extended leave program, he was the senior captain in the legal office. As such he rated his billet as chief prosecutor, despite that until three months ago he had never been in a courtroom. He was also the only one of the ten captains in the office who intended to make the Corps his career.

If I just could have gone somewhere where the facts determine the outcome, not some moth-eaten fucking tradition . . .

Go-Go Guinn was seated at his desk bent over some documents when Joe came to the door of his office. His glasses were resting on top of his close-cropped, balding head.

"Joe, Joe, come in, have a seat." The colonel was full of beans.

"Good morning, colonel. What's going on?"

"I got a call from the chief of staff this morning, Joe. A recruit was killed down at Third Battalion last night. The doctor who examined him apparently thinks he died as a result of a sharp blow to the stomach."

This will keep the congressional liaison officer busy, Joe thought. "Has there been any investigation?"

"I understand CID took statements from some of the other platoon members last night but I'm not clear whether they came up with anything. The statements are available at the Provost Marshal's office."

"What about the DI?"

"A Staff Sergeant Roger Markey, the platoon commander. He's been relieved. Here's his book." The colonel tossed a brown cardboard folder over to Joe's side of the desk. Emblazoned across the front in black block letters were the words "SERVICE RECORD BOOK."

"Apparently when CID tried to question him he asked to talk to a lawyer, so they didn't get anything."

"Who'd he get?"

"Nobody as far as I know. Not yet anyway."

Steiner thumbed through Markey's SRB while Colonel Guinn went on talking.

"Joe, I want you or someone in your shop to get that CID investigation and get down to that platoon today. Grill 'em. Get everything you can on Markey before the other sergeants or defense counsel are able to put any pressure on them. Pin 'em down. Get written, signed statements. Joe, this could be the break we've been waiting for. All the signs point to the use of a little five-finger discipline, and murder is something a lot of these noncoms who normally would be in Markey's corner may back away from. With a little luck we'll have Staff Sergeant Markey's ass dangling in the wind as an example of what future thumpers can expect. It'll do more good than a thousand regulations."

Joe Steiner decided that he'd take this one himself.

CHAPTER

Two

It was unusual for Mike Taggart to be the last one to arrive at the Defense Hooch, as the five defense counsels who shared the room referred to their office. Even the chronically late Margolis was there when Taggart finally showed up at 0815.

"You just waltz in here whenever you feel like it, Screw," growled Jim Carpenter, mimicking the well-known DI admonition as Mike slipped behind his desk.

"It's okay, sir," Mike said, joining in the game, "I've got a note from my mom."

Margolis was reading the morning sports page. Carpenter and Loring were drinking coffee and shooting the shit about the weekend. Only Beeson, at the other end of the room from where Mike sat, appeared to be busy.

Loring was moaning about weekend duty. He had been the battalion officer of the day on Saturday. It was a tradition everywhere that Mike had been in the Corps for the lawyers to pull weekend and holiday duty. The regular officers resented the fact that law school was treated as time in the Corps for purposes of rank, enabling the lawyers to jump from second lieutenant to captain on graduation from Justice School. They resented even more the increased recognition accorded rights of individuals. No longer was the Corps able to deal with troublemakers entirely as it saw fit. It was the law. Hence, it must be the fault of the lawyers. "Lawyer" was only half a word in the Corps, so the joke ran. The whole word was "Goddamnedlawyer," and with that status went weekend duty, Monday morning inspections and a bushel of other shitty little jobs.

That he was of a lower caste in the eyes of other Marines had become clear to Mike the day he received his orders to Viet Nam. They'd been told that excellence in training would be rewarded with preferences in orders, so Cathy especially had hoped he'd get stateside duty by virtue of his status as class honorman.

Instead Mike and all but two of the other twenty lawyers in the class were selected for WESPAC by an alphabetical process. As each lawyer received his orders his nonlawyer classmates would roar their approval. When Taggart's were announced the lieutenant sitting next to him jumped up and pretended to measure Mike for a body bag. Virtue rewarded. Payback was always a motherfucker, so went the ancient wisdom of the Corps.

"Don't give me any hard cases," Loring told Carpenter, who as chief defense counsel assigned cases. "Saturday destroyed my brain cells. The phone didn't ring all day. No one came in the office all day. When I got sick of reading it was either talk to this seventeen-year-old BAM, who was the duty clerk, or throw cards at a hat. All she did was watch cartoons on T.V."

"Yeah, right," Taggart said as he scribbled something on a piece of scrap paper. "I bet it was more like this." He picked up the paper and began to read:

> Captain Loring hated being Officer of the Day,
> Until he rolled the duty clerk in the hay.
> She thought such fraternization
> An order's violation
> Until he explained, 'for the morale of the troops, it's ok.'

"She probably watched cartoons while you did it," Carpenter said.

Loring took it in stride. "Screw you and your poison pen. Besides, she was a dog."

"Maybe you should have killed yourself in protest," Margolis said. "It would have been an unselfish gesture, and we'd have understood."

"Applauded," Carpenter corrected, then turned to Mike and said, "No, I think Captain Taggart over here gets the hard case of the day."

Mike looked at Carpenter. "What's this?"

"I thought you already knew. They're typing up the charges down in admin right now. Go-Go's got himself a murder case. Steiner told me you'd been requested by the sergeant the night it happened and had been out at battalion to see him."

"Jesus," Mike asked, "when's the trial, this afternoon?" Investigation and referral of charges normally took two weeks. "Yeah, I knew, but I didn't think there were any charges yet. I was down at Third Battalion Saturday and again yesterday afternoon to talk to the recruits, but they wouldn't let me see them. That's where I just came from. They still won't. I figured they were holding off to let the trial hooch get the first crack at them."

"Steiner spent almost all weekend interviewing them," Carpenter told him. "He was carrying on about it at the coffee pot this morning. Mad Dog says this is the one that's going to reverse the trend in the drill instructor cases. Apparently Go-Go's already promised the general a conviction."

"Balls to the wall, huh?" Mike said, and then, hopefully, "Is Mad Dog going to take it himself?"

Steiner was called "Mad Dog" with reason by the defense counsel. He was known to have recommended to the CO of Headquarters Battalion that a lance corporal accused of flashing the peace symbol be referred to a special court-martial. In a trial against Margolis, Mad Dog had asked for a bad conduct discharge, six months confinement at hard labor, forfeiture of all pay and allowances and reduction in rank to private for a defendant with no prior offenses who had pleaded guilty to failing to salute. Larry Kendon, the captain who, as special court-martial judge, was second only to Mad Dog in seniority in the office and who was known as "Hippy Dippy" for his affinity for the civilian world he was about to reenter, had responded by sentencing the man to no punishment and asking Mad Dog how he could live with himself when he did things like that.

"Sure, he's going to take it himself," Carpenter said. "This is the sort of thing careers are made of. So what if he's only three months out of Justice School and has never had a general court-martial before. He smells the roses."

"You don't suppose kindly old Captain Steiner had anything to do with my not being allowed to see those witnesses, do you?" Mike asked.

"Heaven forbid," Margolis said, rolling his eyes.

"Well, I guess I better go down and blow in Mad Dog's ear," Mike said, hauling himself out of his chair. "Maybe he'll at least cough up the CID investigation. Sergeant Markey's coming in here at 1100. This'll sure make his day."

The trial hooch was at the other end of the hall from the defense hooch and next to the staff judge advocate's office, where Go-Go Guinn presided, and the administrative and clerical facilities that supported the lawyers' efforts. Equidistant between the two was the courtroom, which Mike now passed with new misgivings based on the intelligence he had just received from Carpenter.

"Hi ya, Habu," he greeted his friend Tom Horn.

Horn's tall, loose-jointed frame was tilted back in his chair, his feet were on his desk. He was reading and loving *Catch 22*.

At his desk immediately on the other side of the bookcase from Horn's, Steiner looked up. "Get out of here, Taggart, we've got work to do this morning that's no concern of yours."

"At ease, Steiner, you're not a major yet. You'll have plenty of time to practice being an asshole later on." Mike bit his tongue as he said the words. He knew it was stupid to antagonize Steiner unnecessarily. On the other hand he was convinced it would make no difference in their relationship during the case.

Appearing to ignore Steiner, but in a voice loud enough for him to hear, he went on. "Horn, my spies inform me that you guardians of the Marine Corps' integrity at this end of the hall are even now typing up a murder charge against a Staff Sergeant Roger Markey, whom I'm representing. I suppose that as the most experienced prosecutor in the

32

employ of this office you'll be the one to see that justice is done in this matter."

Mike glanced in Mad Dog's direction, to see whether his ploy had had the intended effect of cementing Mad Dog's resolve to handle the case himself. Steiner was flushed, his mouth tight as he stared at Taggart.

"Gee, no," said Horn, "Captain Steiner, our chief trial counsel, handles all the murders in this office."

"Oh, well, then you're the man I need to talk to," Mike turned to Steiner. "Is it true that Staff Sergeant Markey's being charged with murder?"

"Yes."

"How about letting me see the CID investigation that was done?"

Now it was Steiner's turn.

"You know there are certain procedures that have to be followed. You people down in defense don't pay any attention to them unless you can find some technical loophole to get one of your scuzzy clients off the hook, but up here we're a little more restricted. You know the drill, the charges will be typed and reviewed, and then, if everything is in order, they'll be taken to the convening authority. If, after review by the convening authority, they're approved, they'll be signed and returned to this office. Then and *only* then will a copy of the charge sheet and the underlying investigation be forwarded to the chief defense counsel for assignment."

"By the book, huh?" Mike eyed Steiner. "Well, Joe, let me leave you with one thought. My scuzzy client has a bronze star, two purple hearts and two combat tours. Because of what happened to Collins you know this thing's going to be in the spotlight every step of the way. If you win and get reversed because of some edge you took just to be sure of overkill, your big victory's going to lose a lot of its shine. Keep *that* in mind when you're deciding how long you can afford to withhold access to the investigation and witnesses while you're spinning your wonderful web."

Mike walked quickly out of the room. At the drinking fountain he encountered Margolis filling a coffee cup with water.

"I don't see any investigation," Margolis observed.

Mike tried to control himself. "Sometimes Mad Dog can be a very hard person to like. I just have to keep telling myself to keep my own temper so I can at least try to take advantage of his."

"That's it," Margolis said, "although I realize it's not easy with a guy like Joe. . . . You going to be up for some basketball this noon?"

"Don't count on me. I have to talk to Sergeant Markey and I have to be ready to see those privates as soon as they'll let me."

When Staff Sergeant Markey showed up, there were fifteen or twenty recruits who were witnesses in one of Loring's cases standing around the entrance to the office. Taggart had seen Markey coming across the drill field, and paid particular attention as his client made his way through the gaggle of recruits. Naturally the privates gave the DI a wide berth, some of them awkwardly stumbling in their haste to get out of the way of anybody who wore the distinctive Smokey hat or cover signifying duty on the drill field. Markey moved through them with a minimum of commotion. There was no swagger, no apparent need to display his powers over these unknown and apprehensive recruits. It was good to see that he apparently was no bully.

"Good morning, sir."

"Good morning, sergeant. How you holding up?"

"Oh, well as can be expected." Markey smiled. "My wife's pretty upset about it but I told her what you said about the Corps' need to take precautions. She had to admit that made sense to her too."

Yeah, I'm just loaded with good advice, Mike thought to himself, having in mind Mad Dog Steiner down at the other end of the hall getting ready to pave his career right over Markey.

"It's too crowded in here, let's take a walk so we can have some privacy."

Outside, they walked across the drill field, its enormous paved expanse shimmering in the midday sun of San Diego's endless summer. Here and there platoons of recruits marched on the vastness, at least half a mile long. Now and then the singsong cadence of the drill sergeants would echo off the buff-colored Spanish arcade that surrounded the field on three sides, reminding Mike of a cavalry outpost in the Old West.

"I'm going to level with you, sergeant," Mike said, stopping and looking directly at Markey. "They're typing up charges against you at the legal office right now. They intend to charge you with the murder of Private Collins."

Mike had to admire Markey. He didn't flinch.

"They don't waste much time, do they, captain?"

"As far as I know, it's a new world record. We can expect them to act faster than usual because there's a death involved. The command is going to want to meet the inevitable inquiries Collins's death will provoke by appearing to do everything possible to get to the bottom of it. I won't shit you, sarge, it looks like they're out for blood, and you're the most available target."

"I can't figure it out, sir, I just can't figure it out. A man dying of some kind of internal injuries with some kind of red marks on his stomach don't add up to no murder charge. No matter how bad the Corps wants to find a scapegoat, I can't see them tryin' to stick it to me on the basis of that. Is there something I'm not seeing, skipper?"

"The only thing I can even guess at is that one of those privates told them something. I won't get a copy of the investigation or get to talk to the platoon until the charges have been formally preferred, but one of them has to have said something to back up their suspicions . . . How about it, sergeant, how do you read that platoon? Anything unusual happen in training that might make some of them have a score to settle with you?"

"I thought about that all weekend, sir, and I talked to both my assistant DIs about it this morning. It's been a real good platoon for us. They were the honor platoon at the range. Hell, Collins had his problems, but he was one of the best marksmen we had. We got good squad leaders that ain't afraid to take charge, and they work together good. That kid, Johnson, the guide, is just about the toughest kid I ever saw come through here. The real nonhackers washed out a long time ago. None of us could think of a single private that would be lookin' for paybacks."

"Well, something's turned sour, that's for sure, and it's bound to turn up pretty quick. Meanwhile, all we can do is keep our heads down." Mike went on. "Let me fill you in on what you can expect.

35

First, someone will call you in and read the charge to you, probably the first sergeant. After that I'll formally be appointed your counsel and I can start doing some investigating of my own, especially talking to the platoon. In a couple of weeks what's called an Article 32 investigation will be conducted. The command will appoint an investigating officer, doesn't have to be a lawyer, and trial counsel will present its case. The investigating officer will make his recommendations to the general about whether he thinks there's enough evidence to go forward with a general court-martial. If he recommends a court-martial, well then, that's what it'll be. You could get sent to a special without an Article 32 recommendation, but with a murder charge it's either going to be GCM or nothing, I'm fairly sure of that. They could reduce the charge just to maltreatment, but they'd look pretty stupid if they do. As a practical matter, by electing to go with murder they've lost a lot of flexibility. If it turns out they've bitten off more than they can chew, they may choke on it . . ."

He realized he was trying to shore himself up as well as Markey. "One more thing . . . the other night I told you you have a right to civilian counsel and you kind of shrugged it off. I appreciate that, but there's no substitute for experience, sarge, and I'm twenty-seven years old and have never defended a murder case. We're swimming in deep water now, and you can depend on me to knock myself out for you. But there may be things that could be done that I won't even think of, that someone who's been there before would hit on right off. This isn't false modesty talking, you should get every edge you can. Don't, for God's sake, worry about hurting my feelings."

Markey started to say something but Mike cut him off.

"Don't say anything now. Think about it for a couple of days. Talk it over with your wife. Come see me on Wednesday at 1100. If anything happens in the meantime I'll call you."

"Aye, aye, sir."

"Any questions?"

"I guess you've answered 'em all for now. When I think of some more I'll write 'em down for Wednesday."

"Fine, I'll see you then."

Markey saluted sharply and turned to walk back toward RTR as Mike returned the salute.

When Mike got back to the office it was almost 1130.

"Go-Go wants to see you as soon as possible," Beeson told him as he came in.

Mike turned and walked down to the colonel's office.

"Colonel in?" Mike asked the surly Corporal Litzinger, who guarded Go-Go's door like some kind of mythical three-headed dog.

With a sigh of annoyance at being interrupted, Litzinger nodded Taggart through without looking up or speaking. Clearly he shared the view of defense counsel prevailing at this end of the hall.

Go-Go was on his way out the door in his tennis clothes, three racquets cradled under his arm and his dark glasses shoved up on top of his head. Go-Go must think he's a fucking starlet, the way he wears those goddamned glasses, Taggart thought.

"Mike, I've been looking for you," Go-Go said in his raspy voice. "Come in here for a minute."

He shut the door behind Taggart and went over and sat behind his desk. "I hear you've been requested for a big case . . ."

"It's going to be a big case if Steiner has anything to say about it," Mike answered.

The colonel's tone became a little more distant. "It's going to be a big case *regardless* of Captain Steiner, captain. A press release acknowledging Private Collins's death will be issued this afternoon. After that you'll be contacted by persons representing, well, a diversity of interests. I just want to remind you that it's not in the best interest of either you *or* your client to try this case in the newspapers."

Mike didn't say anything.

"I say I don't want this case tried in the newspapers. Understood?"

"Yes, sir, I'm familiar with the ethical responsibilities in that area."

"I'm not talking about what's written in any code of ethics, captain, and you damn well know it. A man's been killed in Marine training. These are sensitive times. We're both lawyers and we're both Marines, and I don't think either of us wants to see the Corps savaged by an

37

unsympathetic press because of the mistakes of a very few."

Mike stood up. "Sir," he said, "I hope you've told Captain Steiner the same thing, because he's the one that's going to have a sympathetic audience, not me. Very few, even in San Diego, will read about this and think poor Staff Sergeant Markey. It's going to be poor Private Collins all the way down the line. If the Corps winds up with egg on its face as a result of this case, it'll be because somebody made some promises they couldn't keep."

"Just see that it isn't you, captain. That'll be all."

"You made the local news," Cathy told Mike as he walked into the apartment.

He kissed her.

"Actually, Private Collins did. They said he died over the weekend and that there's an investigation."

Mike opened a beer and leaned against the kitchen counter as Cathy fixed dinner.

"How'd it go today?" she finally asked.

"Mediocre to piss-poor," he said, and told her about his confrontations with Mad Dog and Go-Go and his conversation with Markey.

"Do you want to go out for dinner with the Moreheads Friday night and then to a play? Ann called today and they have four tickets to the dinner-theater."

"I'd rather have you come down to happy hour at the club and then go to dinner, just the two of us."

"Michael, you know how I feel about that club. It wouldn't be so bad if it was just the guys from your office, but you know what it's like on Friday night. There's nine million little, short, blustering fights swaggering around looking for a place to happen."

It was Cathy's opinion that many, maybe most, Marines were insecure guys trying to prove something, who were attracted by the elitist recruiting pitch used by the Corps. She said she excluded lawyers from her theory, but Mike wasn't always sure she really did.

"We were there just two weeks ago," she said. "Let's go with the Moreheads. Okay?"

Mike's reluctance came more from the Moreheads than from the fact that a play had been suggested or from any special desire to go to the officers' club. What he really wanted was to find some way to melt Cathy's feelings about the Corps and the fact that he was in it, if only for another year. He'd been back from WESPAC for more than two months now, and with few moments of relief, there was a distance between them that definitely hadn't been there before he left. Whenever he'd ask her about it she'd just say she didn't like the Marine Corps and that she couldn't help the way she felt, but it didn't have anything to do with them. That's what she said.

In the end he agreed to go to the play with the Moreheads. He didn't want to get into a two-front battle.

Three

"MR. LOGAN wants to see you in his office right away, Ronnie."

Veronica Rasmussen looked up from her typewriter at the messenger. She debated with herself whether to finish what she was typing, but her curiosity got the better of her and she headed for Ed Logan's office.

"Morning, Ronnie, or is it afternoon? Hell, I don't even know anymore."

"It's three P.M., you're close," she told him. "Did you want to see me?"

"Yeah . . . Ronnie, I want you to go out to Osage City, that's ninety miles southwest of here, over in Kansas, and interview this woman." He tossed a piece of paper with a name and address across the desk.

"She just called and she was crying. It seems she was informed last night that her son died out in San Diego Friday night while he was in Marine training. They told her he died of internal injuries, nothing else. She's tried all morning to get some information but hasn't had any luck. I just finished checking with the base out there and they confirm that a private Loren Collins died of internal injuries while in the eighth week of basic training at 0107 Saturday, 6 February 1971. Nothing more."

"Eddie, don't do this to me. No more widows, orphans and bereaved parents, please. For Christ's sake, it's not even news anymore. Besides, it's snowing like crazy out, and I don't know Osage City from Timbuktu."

"Come on now, Ronnie. You know it's news. Kids usually wait until they get to Viet Nam to get killed. Internal injuries, bull... I'll bet a week's pay some sergeant beat the life out of that kid. Now take Mac to run the cameras. He's sitting out there with nothing to do, botherin' everybody else. He can help you dig out if you get stuck. I told Mrs. Collins somebody'd be out there by this evening."

Mrs. Collins was a short sturdily built woman with dark hair on its way to gray. The most outstanding feature of her appearance was her eyes, which were very large and very dark blue. When she came to the door to greet Ronnie and Mac she was wearing a plain blue dress. She smiled slightly in recognition of Ronnie, whom she had seen on television many times, but Ronnie could tell that she had spent a lot of the day crying.

She ushered them into a large old-fashioned living room, very much like the one in the house where Ronnie had grown up. There was a fire in the fireplace, which made it seem even more homelike to Veronica after her two-hour drive across the arctic Kansas landscape.

"I recognize you from the television," Mrs. Collins said as they sat down. "You're even prettier in real life."

"Thank you ... Mrs. Collins, I'm terribly sorry about what happened to your son. I talked to my editor, Mr. Logan, the man you spoke with over the phone, and he tells me you think there's more to what happened than meets the eye. Is it something your son told you? ... Why did you call the station?"

Mrs. Collins shook her head.

"I don't know what I think, Miss Rasmussen. I know it's probably too soon for the Marine Corps to have found out the cause of Loren's death, but when I spoke to the man who called I sensed a reluctance to discuss any cause.... He wouldn't say if Loren had been feeling sick, he wouldn't say if Loren's group had been in some particularly hard part of the training. He wouldn't say anything except that there would be an investigation."

"Did he say why there would be an investigation?"

"Oh, he said something about the circumstances of Loren's death being unclear... I was too shocked by what he'd told me to think of any more questions to ask. But when my husband called back he couldn't get any more information."

"Who called you, Mrs. Collins?"

"A Captain Gunderson. He said he was Loren's company commander. Loren never mentioned him in any letters. The captain said he would write to us about what happened. I had to argue with myself before I called your station, but this on top of all the other was just more than I could handle in silence. I always watch your evening news and I kept thinking of how you uncovered all those people in the building department who were taking bribes. Loren would hate it that I called. He never wanted me to interfere at school or anything, and I just never did, not with him or his sisters, either one. But, well... this is different. What if I were never to learn what really happened? What if by insisting on knowing I could at least prevent the same thing from happening to some other boy? So many boys are dying in the war now, it might be easy for Loren's death to be ignored, but I don't know anyone in the Marines, only Loren. I don't even know anybody in California. I know my husband didn't want me to call but I was just at such a loss. It was probably foolish of me, but such a loss... lord, such a loss..."

Ronnie could see the muscles in Mrs. Collins's face contract from her effort not to cry. A single tear trickled slowly down her cheek and she was biting her upper lip.

"Mrs. Collins, may I have a cup of coffee or a drink of water or something?"

"Oh, my." She looked embarrassed. "I'm terribly sorry, yes, I put the pot on because I was expecting you, I'll just be a minute." She left the room, obviously welcoming the chance to regain her composure.

It was already after eight, and Veronica didn't want to drive back to Kansas City in the storm in the middle of the night. So while Mrs. Collins was getting the coffee she sent Mac, who did not have to be asked twice, to get them some rooms somewhere, with instructions to call and let her know where he could be reached for a ride.

When Mrs. Collins came back Ronnie was looking at the family photos displayed on the mantle.

"Is this your son?" she asked, indicating what appeared to be a high school graduation portrait of a tall, slender, serious-looking boy with very large, very dark blue eyes.

"Yes, that's Loren," said Mrs. Collins, putting down the tray. "And that's his sister Linda in the picture just to the right of him. She's at Lawrence now, at the university."

Ronnie glanced at Linda Collins's picture. She might have been looking at Loren Collins's twin. There were the same prominent, serious blue eyes; her hair, perhaps slightly more blond than her brother's, of medium length and curling up at the ends. The picture made Ronnie think of some of her own high school portraits, except, she thought, Linda Collins took better pictures than she did.

"I guess it was after I called Linda to tell her Loren died that I decided to call the station." Martha Collins stared at her lap, nervously twisting and untwisting a small white handkerchief as she spoke. The memory of her call to her daughter was so immediate, so dreadful, that it dragged her from the present, forcing her to relive each searing moment of that conversation...

The phone had rung several times, each ring like a high tension line in Martha's brain. She'd prayed no one would answer, that she'd be given a reprieve from delivering her message.

"Hello."

"Hello, Linda...this is mother calling."

"Hi, mom. Gee, this is a surprise—"

"Linda, I have something to tell you..."

"Mom, are you okay? You don't sound too well. What is it?"

"Linda, I got a phone call from San Diego about an hour ago..." She was trying to choose her words carefully, to keep the quaver out of her voice. "...it was from the Marine Corps about Loren..."

"Why are you calling me about that? Is something wrong?"

"Linda, Loren is dead. He died early Saturday morning out in San Diego."

Only silence from Linda's end of the line. Then, from far away, Martha thought she could hear the short, quick gasps of her daughter's breath. The voice she next heard was Linda's, but it wasn't the same voice that had answered the phone. It was a wild imploring voice.

"Oh, mama, oh, no, please, no..."

"We don't know how it happened yet," Martha struggled on. "It was internal injuries of some kind, but that's all we know."

"Mama, it's a mistake, Loren isn't dead, it's a mistake..." Linda said urgently.

"It's true, Linda." Martha sought for the strength that would help brace her daughter, tried to tell Linda how it was going to be up to the two of them to help Linda's father through it, but Linda interrupted, "Mama, please come and get me, I want to come home...."

"Linda and Loren are ... were almost like twins, Miss Rasmussen," Martha Collins said, forcing herself back to the present. "Making that phone call was one of the hardest things I've ever done. That's when I decided I had to do something, that the war and all that goes with it had torn at my family too long."

Veronica was puzzled by what she'd just heard. What did Mrs. Collins mean when she said the war had torn at her family? She watched Martha Collins still fumbling with her handkerchief and knew that she must go slow, the woman was stretched so tight...

As they poured coffee Ronnie explained Mac's departure and then asked, "Mrs. Collins, why did Loren join the Marines in the first place?"

"Please call me Martha, Miss Rasmussen, no one calls me Mrs. Collins. May I call you Veronica?"

"Most people call me Ronnie."

"All right then ... Ronnie ... I think he went in because he was facing the draft and since he would have to go anyway he wanted to make it something special."

"What did he think about Marine training?"

"I think Loren was disappointed in the training, and it made him have a lot of misgivings about himself. You can see that in his letters.

I must get you those and let you read them before you leave."

Outside the wind was whistling. Ronnie shivered, stood up and walked over by the fire.

They talked for another half hour. Martha Collins told how her son had been an average student who got good grades by working hard. Not very good at sports, he always went out for the football team and sat on the bench. His senior year he'd received a varsity letter but had hardly played at all. He liked to go along with his dad when he went hunting, and Frank Collins had taught him to shoot, but Loren rarely shot anything, he just liked to be out with his father. His greatest interest was music. When Linda, who was just fifteen months older than Loren, started to take piano lessons, Loren wanted to take them too, so they'd learned to play the piano together, eventually becoming better than any of the teachers in the county. Talking now about her son, it was as if Martha Collins had forgotten, for the moment, that he was gone, and for the first time that evening she became animated.

"Oh, Miss Rasmussen, you'll like Loren, he's really a kind, gentle person..." And then her voice trailed off as reality once more took hold of her.

A lump was in Veronica's throat as she watched and listened to Martha Collins talk. There were no good words at a time like this. She glanced at her watch. Nine o'clock. Where was Mac? Why didn't he call?

Mrs. Collins, as though reading Veronica's mind, invited her to stay overnight. Actually she didn't just invite, she insisted. Veronica was touched and embarrassed and made every conceivable protest, and then Martha suddenly asked, "Ronnie, did you grow up in Kansas or Missouri?"

"Yes, Missouri."

"Then they probably taught you in school what the Civil War was like in Kansas. You know, families divided, brother against brother, father against son..."

"The Jayhawkers and the bloody hills of Kansas. Yes, I know."

"Well, the Civil War is being relived in homes in Kansas and everywhere else in this country too, I'm sure. Loren and his sister Linda were very close to each other. It wasn't just the music, it was everything. The things those two did together growing up . . . there's not enough time to tell you. If Linda was into something she shouldn't be, well, look for Loren, because he was bound to be there too, and they would never tattle on each other even if it meant taking a licking. If one of them had a job to do, the other pitched in and helped finish without being asked. Everyone around here knew there was some kind of deep bond between them that very few of us ever get to have with any other person. . . . Because of their birthdays falling when they did, Linda was two years ahead of Loren in school. Last year she got very active in the antiwar movement at the university, especially after President Nixon said we were going to fight in Cambodia, when all those young people were killed in Ohio, but even before that too. Well, when Loren enlisted Linda stopped talking to him. She called him awful names, and from then on she treated him as if he was already dead, even though she knew he wasn't enlisting out of any special support for the war or love of fighting. That was never his way, you'll see it in his letters. No, enlisting in the Marines was his first big snip at the apron strings. Linda's behavior hurt Loren, hurt him very much, but neither he nor I could talk her out of it. . . . This hasn't been a very happy family these last six months. My husband Frank can't even talk about what's happened, he doesn't even want to listen to my feelings. I saw him cry Sunday for the first time in the twenty-seven years we've been married. He didn't even do that when his parents died. He's out in his shop now. He's been there all day, but he's not making anything. He's just sitting there. And I just float around this big old house like I was some kind of ghost.

"I don't know if I'm making any sense to you, and I'm sorry to put all this on you, but talking to you has made me feel so much better. Please stay, I guarantee you'll be more comfortable here than at the Hotel Grainbelt, that's the only place in town."

Veronica accepted the invitation. Before Martha showed her upstairs to her room she stopped beside an end table near the front door and took out a thin packet of letters tied with a blue ribbon. She handed the packet to Ronnie.

"Maybe you can understand the things these say better than I."

At the door to the room Mrs. Collins handed Ronnie a flannel nightgown, pointed the way to the bathroom and disappeared down the hall into her own room. Veronica paused with her hand on the knob of the door leading into the room, hoping it wouldn't be Loren's room. It wasn't, she was grateful to see. The room, in fact, typified the Collins family, not any one particular member. Clean, spare, dignified and old-fashioned, there was a hot-water radiator painted white standing against the far wall, above which hung a picture of Christ kneeling at night in Gethsemane. On top of the chest of drawers were some ancient baby pictures, and some more photographs were framed and hanging on walls covered with flowered wallpaper. The low-silled window was bordered with white lace curtains, and on the far side of the high four-poster bed there was a wooden rocking chair with a flat homemade cushion on the seat.

Except for a rag rug beside the bed, there were only hardwood floors, and it was chilly in the room. Veronica had goosebumps as she got ready for bed. The storm window rattled as she turned back the heavy patchwork quilt and fluffed up the pillows against the high headboard.

As she snuggled in to read Loren Collins's letters, the bedside lamp cast a small warm cone of light about her head and shoulders. It reached only halfway down the length of the bed and vanished beyond the foot, leaving the corners of the room to the late winter night, out of which came marching First Platoon, Hotel Company, Third Recruit Training Battalion, as seen through the eyes of Private Loren Collins . . .

16 December 1970

Dear Mom and Dad:

I've been here two days and this is my first chance to write. Sgt. Sanchez says we all have ten minutes to write letters home, so I'll use abbreviations. But if this stops in the middle you'll know why.

The 1st night we were here the DI asked the toughest guy in the platoon to step out to the middle of the room. Some guy did, thinking he was going to impress the Sgt. Then the DI looked around and asked who thought they could whip the guy who just stepped out. A private named Johnson said he

48

could and the DI said go to it. Johnson beat up the first guy
real bad and the Sgt. told us Johnson was the platoon guide
until somebody could take the job away from him.

Ten minutes are up. 'Bye for now, please write.

Love,
Loren

18 December 1970

Dear Mom and Dad:

Mom, whatever you do don't send cookies or candy or
anything. One of the privates got a box of chocolates at mail
call today and Sgt. Sanchez made him eat the whole thing.

Also don't send any letters in fancy envelopes or write
anything but addresses on the envelopes. A couple of
privates have had to eat their letters without even reading
them. Not getting to read them would be the worst part.

I almost feel like asking you to give this letter to Linda.
Maybe if she knows it will get me in trouble, she'll at least
send an envelope with something written on the outside. Say
"hi" to her for me when you talk to her. I know she won't
always be so mad at me. At least I hope not.

I have to stop. I miss you all.

Love,
Loren

Ronnie shook her head in disbelief. Eat their letters? What did that
have to do with military training?

23 December 1970

Dear Mom and Dad:

It's almost Christmas. It won't be like any others for me.
When we drill we can see the headquarters building in the
distance across the drill field. There's a big star on the front
of it. It seems like it's a million miles away. Our platoon is
shrinking. Some privates get hurt and some flunk PT—
that's physical training—and get dropped. There's also
something called motivation platoon. Privates get sent there
if they're doing poorly here. My bunkmate was sent there.

49

He says it's much worse than this and he'll do anything not to have to go back. I guess that's why they call it motivation platoon. I hope I don't have to go. Things around here are hard to understand. It's as if the DIs really hate us no matter how hard we try.

I wish I could just keep writing and writing, because writing to you and getting your letters brings me closer to home for a while.

Bye for now.

Love,
Loren

25 December 1970

Dear Mom and Dad:

Christmas! Today we have a lot of free time, although the DI made us PT for an hour in the sandpits this morning. At noon we had ham and turkey. Not as good as yours, mom, but who expected it would be.

I'm almost too sore to write. Yesterday we fought with pugilsticks, which are long bars with padded ends. We fight with them like Little John did in Robin Hood. I got knocked down by another private's first shot. For a minute I couldn't see, but I could feel him pounding me. I was on my face when my eyes cleared, but all I could see was the boots and legs of the others as they gathered around. They were yelling kill, kill, and cheering and the platoon Sgt. kept yelling go for the gut. Get up, maggot. I was trying but the other guy was standing right over me. I thought I heard the whistle, which is the signal to stop, but he wouldn't stop until the DI pulled him off. Afterwards the Sgt. told me that if I let that happen six months from now my ears are going to be nailed to the wall of some VC hooch. He's probably right.

I imagine right now you're all sitting down to dinner. Did you go to church last night? Did Linda play at the services? I figured out that last night at taps she must be playing at that very moment. I pretended taps was Silent Night and we were playing it together again.

Love,
Loren

Veronica found herself out of bed, staring out the window at the light in the farmyard, across the frozen plains. She thought of the boy who must have so often played at the base of that lightpole, where now eddies of snow curled in and out of the blackness in the night wind. If she, a stranger, could feel his presence from his letters, how must his mother feel, his father, and his sister who'd rejected him? . . . For the first time amid all the oceans of antiwar rhetoric, to most of which she had at least paid lip service, she really felt the tragedy of the war. She felt what letters from Viet Nam must sound like to parents, wives, brothers, sisters, children, even television reporters.

After a while she crawled back into bed and reluctantly started reading again. . . .

14 January 1971

Dear Mom and Dad:

Just got back from motivation platoon. I had to go because I knocked one of the other privates down in a pugilstick fight and didn't go for the kill. I kept thinking what it was like when someone went for the kill on me.

I still don't feel very motivated. Part of one of the chants we sing when we're running goes "Kill VC is the Marine Corps' cry. We'll rip their guts and watch 'em die!" There's a lot of yelling and hollering after songs like that. I knew I'd have to fight when I enlisted but we're being taught to fight for the sake of fighting. I'm beginning to think that Linda is right.

Well, I've got to get ready for an inspection. We're going to the rifle range next week. I don't know what's going to happen. Bye for now.

Love,
Loren

4 February 1971

Dear Mom and Dad:

We just got back from the range and I'm pretty sure I'm going to graduate. I shot expert, which is the best. Thanks for teaching me, dad.

51

While we were at the range some of the others in the
platoon threw a blanket over my bunkmate's head after
lights out and beat him up. It was supposed to motivate him
to shoot better. That's called a blanket party, or EMI—extra
military instruction. Private Johnson, the guide, is behind it.
He's worse than the DI's. Everyone in the platoon's afraid
of him. They kept shouting at Gene to get motivated
because he was holding the whole platoon back. The worst
part is that I lay on the top bunk while it was going on and
didn't do anything to help even though I knew I should.

The DI's keep yelling at us to think of ourselves as killing
machines, and it's working, just like all the talk about pride
and motivation and getting with the program. I can see
others in the platoon toughening up their minds as well as
their bodies, but my mind isn't changing at all. The platoon
has become a team, just like it's supposed to, but I'm not
really part of it. I always seem to keep myself on the
outside.

I'm glad you can come for graduation. I can hardly wait.

Love,
Loren

Martha Collins told Ronnie that the February 4th letter had arrived
the morning after they were told of their son's death.

Early the next morning she and Mac shot some footage of the front
of the Collins house, in which Ronnie observed that America's children
didn't have to go to southeast Asia to die, that there were "killing
machines" right here at home.

Afterward she and Mac went back to Kansas City. They never did
get to see Mr. Collins.

Eddie Logan was hard as an oak knot. He had been in the news
broadcasting business twenty-four years and, although he was acknowledged to be scrupulously honest, he had few remaining ideals.
And no illusions. News, even local news, was not a moneymaker for
the station. Eddie had to fight to protect his department's air time; he
had to fight to protect his lean budget allocation; he had to fight

reporters who let themselves be overcome with crusading zeal every time their jobs took them into the midst of some tragedy. Most news was somebody's tragedy.

"No, no, no. For the last time, *no*. Are you crazy, Ronnie? You didn't even want to go out there. No more widows, orphans and bereaved parents, you said. Now you want me to send you to San Diego so you can launch a one-woman assault on the United States Marine Corps. Who the hell do you think we are, CBS?"

Ronnie was pacing in front of his desk. She had tried sitting but was too upset by her visit with Martha Collins to sit still anywhere for long.

"Damn it, Eddie, open your eyes. This station has been editorializing against the war now for almost two years. We think we're hot stuff, enlightening the public. Well, in this case we're not in the vanguard. Not close. The man on the street right here in good ol' conservative Kansas City is way ahead of us, and little by little the pressure is building so that not even Nixon and Kissinger are going to be able to ignore it. Meanwhile, though, they go on flushing our men down that southeast Asian toilet while they argue about the shape of the conference table. . . . Eddie, one of our viewers has died just getting ready to take his turn over there. Loren Collins isn't the first. Think back. Every once in a while a recruit is killed as a result of boot camp brutality. Everyone shakes their head and says that shouldn't be happening, but it goes right on, just like the war. It's the same disregard of moral and legal restraints by our leaders that got us into this goddamned war and is keeping us there.

"Eddie, if by calling people's attention to what happened and by forcing the Marine Corps to explain what's going to be done about it you can exert one ounce of pressure for more responsible leadership, well, you're going to have done a hell of a lot more for the people of this town than just treating 'em to a human interest story."

Eddie chewed the stubby remnant of the cigar he had never bothered to light. He had never seen her so worked up before.

"How do you know Collins didn't die of a ruptured appendix?"

"Eddie, don't you think that if he died of a ruptured appendix they'd

53

immediately have told that to his parents? It would have saved them a lot of embarrassment. You were awfully damn sure it was the drill instructors when you sent me out there."

"Tell you what, I'll talk to the station manager. If he says okay, then you go."

"Eddie Logan, that's the worst cop-out I ever heard. You've got the authority to send me and you know it. If you go to someone else it'll be to find someone to say no for you, because you can't look me in the eye and say it yourself."

She stormed out of the office, slamming the door and scattering the loose papers on Logan's desk. Her phone was ringing when she arrived at her desk. She was so mad, she was tempted to ignore it.

"What is it?" she snapped.

"Pack your bags," Eddie's voice growled over the line.

For an instant Ronnie thought she'd been fired, then he added, "but I warn you, this better be good or you'll be covering the mothers' tea at the seventh-grade cooking class from now on." He hung up.

Four

At 1000 Tuesday morning Joe Steiner walked into his office. Beeson, whose desk was nearest the door, intoned, "Nevermore," in an ominous tone, just like he always did when Mad Dog came into the defense hooch. Steiner plopped Markey's SRB on Mike Taggart's desk.

"Here's a present for you, Taggart. Read it and weep. The Article 32's a week from today."

Mike couldn't think of anything that needed saying, so he just stared at Steiner as he left the office.

"Caw! Caw," Beeson let out as Steiner walked past on his way out. The whole defense hooch cracked up, including Beeson, who enjoyed his own jokes immensely, especially when they were at Mad Dog Steiner's expense.

Mike looked down at the SRB. He knew that in addition to Sergeant Markey's records it would contain the charge sheet and whatever CID had done by way of investigation. That was where he'd find Steiner's ace.

"I feel like I ought to open this in a bucket of water," he told Margolis, who was watching him.

One by one he read the handwritten statements of the privates in Staff Sergeant Markey's platoon. Generally they were less remarkable for what they said than how they said it. Several were unintelligible and he needed Margolis's and Carpenter's help figuring out a couple others. By the time he had read fifteen of the statements a composite picture of his client as a drill instructor was beginning to emerge. A relatively articulate statement by a Private Bachman seemed to draw the various components together:

6 February 1971

Sgt. Markey is different from the other drill instructors because he don't ever yell much. He's the scariest one though, because he's an Indian and can sneak up on you and you never know what he's going to do next. He's behind every post and wall and when you finally see him there he says he just killed you.

One night he turned on the lights after taps and told us it was a flare and we should take cover. Nobody knew what to do so S/Sgt. Markey started turning over bunks and yelling. Now, when the lights come on we all dive under our racks and stay there til they go off again.

Whenever it rains he makes the platoon go outside, even at night. Nobody understands why he does that.

The private never seen him hit Private Collins or anyone else.

Gordon Bachman, Pvt. U.S.M.C.
Hotel Co.,
1st Plt. 1st Squad
826-11-9912

A couple others read:

6 February 1971

Sgt. Markey is a good DI, except duck soup and when he scares people and won't let us sleep at night. The private didn't see him hit nobody.

Louis Jones, Pvt., U.S.M.C.
Hotel Co.,
1st Plt. 3rd Squad
900-01-4061

Once we was at the range the private called Sergeant
Sanchez a spic when the private was talking to Private
Meister. We was all alone waiting for formation after chow.
Later the private was on the firing line lying in the prone
position and Staff Sergeant Markey kneels down close and
asks why the private called his assistant DI a spic. Then he
bit my ear. Then Sergeant Sanchez came on the other side
and asked if the private called him a spic and he bit my
other ear. They didn't hurt none, but the private was scared.

The private hasn't seen the platoon commander hit
nobody. He does other stuff.

> George Bellof, Pvt., U.S.M.C.
> Hotel Co., 1st Plt., 1st Squad
> 902-14-3619

Buried in the stack he found this one.

6 February 1971

Tonight I had to go to the head after taps. In the hall I
heard a noise, and I looked around the corner by the head
and S/Sgt. Markey had Pvt. Collins's weapon. I couldn't
understand what he said except for Pvt. Collins yelled yes
sir a couple of times. Then S/Sgt. Markey hit Pvt. Collins in
the stomach with the rifle butt.

> William Johnson, Pvt.,
> U.S.M.C. Hotel Co.,
> 1st Plt., Guide
> 873-29-5226

"Jesus Christ, look at this." Taggart handed Johnson's statement to
Margolis.

Margolis read it and shook his head. "The fucking guide," was all
he could say.

The rest of the statements contained echoes of Markey's apparent
stealth, including something indecipherable about a tree, but not a
single other reference to Markey striking or abusing anyone in the
platoon.

When Mike called Third Batallion he found out that Staff Sergeant Markey had gone to Camp Pendleton, thirty-five miles to the north, for the day and could not be reached. However, he was finally able to make arrangements to interview the platoon Wednesday afternoon.

The squad bay was immaculate. Taggart stood in the doorway and surveyed the scene: two rows of bunks, each bunk equidistant from and parallel to the one on either side of it; towels identically folded and hung over the metal bar on the inboard end of each rack, the name of the owner stenciled on each, so no poorly made rack could remain anonymous. The dark concrete floor appeared spotless in the sunshine flowing through the windows, which made up the upper two-thirds of the long walls of the barracks. At the geometric center of the room was the omnipresent fifty-gallon steel can, the barrack's "shit can," receptacle of platoon trash, including, Mike was sure, an occasional private. He grinned, remembering his own experience of standing an OCS inspection in the shit can as an object lesson of his own unworthiness. He knew without looking that the inside of Hotel 1's shit can would shine every bit as much as its glistening exterior, the result of nightly hours of polishing.

On the bulletin board on the wall to Mike's right was a single 8 ½ x 11 sheet of paper containing the order of the day. On the wall to the right was a large piece of white cardboard on which Kipling's poem "IF" was neatly printed in block letters. Otherwise the barracks was bare of adornment.

Mike heard footsteps behind him.

"Good afternoon, sir, I'm Sergeant Warthun. May I help you?"

"I'm Captain Taggart, Staff Sergeant Markey's lawyer. Battalion told me I could talk to your platoon this afternoon."

"Yes, sir. That word was passed. Sergeant Sanchez is with the platoon now. They're scheduled back here any second. Would you like a cup of coffee while you wait?"

"Thanks, yes." Mike followed Warthun toward the duty office. "Who's responsible for the poetry?"

Warthun, looking back over his shoulder, replied, "Staff Sergeant Markey brought that in one day, said he found it in some book and

58

copied it for the platoon. Said the son of a bitch who wrote it should have been a Marine."

Warthun was sitting at his desk sipping his coffee, eyeing Taggart through the steam. "Skipper, is it okay for me to ask how it looks for Staff Sergeant Markey?"

"I'd tell you if I knew," Mike said, "but it's too early to say. How long have you worked with Staff Sergeant Markey?"

"This was our third platoon together."

"Sergeant Warthun, what's your opinion of Sergeant Markey as a DI? I want the truth, not some canned bullshit about how great he is. He's in real trouble and I have to know and understand him if I'm going to defend him."

"Captain, I've been on the drill field just over two years. This is my last platoon. I already got WESPAC orders. At one time or another I worked close with at least twelve other DIs. Staff Sergeant Markey wasn't the best at drill and he wasn't the best at PT. He was squared away, but everybody's got their shit together down here and he didn't stand out. But there is one thing he was better at than anybody I ever seen. He could teach recruits to do things better than he could do 'em himself. I'd be tellin' some private how to go from port arms to shoulder arms and he wouldn't have any idea what I was talkin' about, just stand there like a stone. Then Rog would tell him how to do it and it would be like he drew a curtain open somewhere in the private's brain. It's like that with every part of the program. Markey, he can think of ways to do stuff that ain't in the manual."

"Maltreatment isn't in the manual either, Sergeant Warthun, what about that? Would Sergeant Markey give a kid a thump for emphasis once in a while?"

"Sir, in two years on the field Staff Sergeant Markey is the only DI I ever worked with that didn't, myself included. He'd scare the shit out of 'em but I swear to God he never hit one. Markey was different, he was a spook. Somehow he'd managed to sneak up on 'em. I seen 'em when they turned around and found him standin' there just starin' at 'em silent and grim, I thought they were gonna die of fright. Some of 'em would get to be Indians just like him, just strainin' to always know where he was—"

What sounded like an explosion was followed by thunder as a door slammed against a wall somewhere in the building and fifty pairs of heavy boots moved up the concrete stairs.

"YOU BETTER GET UP THEM STAIRS, GOOFY," a voice sounded.

"Well, the herd is back." Warthun grinned. ,

"Jesus Christ, that goddamn Goofy ain't never gonna learn to march." A short, dark sergeant with a deep two-inch linear scar almost like a brand on his right cheekbone came into the office. He stopped short when he saw Taggart.

"Remy, this is Captain Taggart, Rog's lawyer."

"Oh, beg your pardon, sir." Sanchez, wearing his cover because he was on duty, saluted. "We got this one private that can't walk, let alone march. Eight and a half weeks into the program and he still looks like a fucking penguin out there. . . . You here to talk to the privates?"

"That's right."

"They're out in the squad bay now getting ready for inspection. You taking over now, Mick?" he asked Warthun.

"Yeah, you can take off."

"Sir—" Warthun turned to Taggart. "I'm going to be out with the platoon, you're welcome to use this office if that will do."

"That'll be fine."

"C'mon with me then, and we'll get started."

The first private to see them come around the corner toward the squad bay hollered, "ATTEN-HUT," and everybody in the platoon froze where they were at rigid attention.

"Fall in in front of your racks. Move!" Warthun told them.

Instantly the platoon reacted, aligned as ordered in two files facing each other across the room.

"Right file, left face. Left file, right face."

Both files pivoted to face Warthun and Taggart. Taggart tried to guess which ones were Johnson and Goofy but hadn't a clue. They were just two anonymous rows of green; "picklemen," Beeson called them.

"Listen up. This is Captain Taggart from base legal. He wants to talk to each one of you in the duty office after this formation. Anderson, you go first.

"I'll be in the area to answer any of your questions about the inspection. You may talk to each other if it's to help with preparation for the inspection, but I don't want any grabass or I'll just figure you're ready to be inspected and we'll do something else. Clear?"

"Yes, *sir*."

"Carry on."

The formation dissolved back to the individual assignments begun before Warthun and Taggart entered.

Taggart had not been out of his chair in two hours. He had talked to about twenty privates, none of whom knew anything about the incident that had resulted in Private Collins's death other than what they could see from their racks while the corpsman and doctor were tending to him on the night it happened. None considered himself a particular friend of Collins, each saying he kept to himself most of the time and didn't say much. No one said he disliked Collins but no one seemed to know him.

They affirmed the impression conveyed by their statements to CID, and by Sergeant Warthun, that Staff Sergeant Markey had created almost unbelievable tension in the platoon by being where they least expected him, witnessing all the forbidden things they were careful to do only when they were certain beyond all doubt that there were no DIs in the area.

Taggart's curiosity, aroused by one of the statements to CID about a tree, was satisfied when he met the author. According to Private Morkowski the platoon had been told to fall into formation under a tree near the mess hall after breakfast one morning to go to the rifle range. It was still dark when Sergeant Sanchez emerged from chow and marched the platoon away. The unfortunate Morkowski marched at the very rear of the third squad. As he passed under a large branch of the tree he was suddenly, silently and painlessly pulled to the ground by Staff Sergeant Markey, who had jumped out of the tree. Markey told Morkowski he had just been killed in an ambush. No one in the platoon had even noticed Morkowski was gone. Morkowski was terrified. Morkowski said his nickname in the platoon was "Goofy."

The recruit who followed Morkowski into the office was a giant, a tall and lean black man. He moved easily into the office without hesitancy or apparent apprehension, despite that he had probably never spoken to a captain before in his life.

"Private Johnson reporting as ordered." His eyes were riveted to the spot on the wall behind where Taggart sat, a spot designated for that purpose.

"At ease, Private Johnson. Sit down. Smoke if you like."

Johnson sat erect but relaxed, looking straight at Taggart. He made no move for any smokes.

"Where are you from, Private Johnson?"

"Oakland, California, sir."

"How old are you?"

"Eighteen, sir."

The questions and answers reviewed Johnson's background and education, his reasons for coming into the Corps, his ambitions, his experiences in boot camp, his thoughts about being the platoon guide. They talked about his family, the war in Viet Nam, his opinions of all three of the platoon's drill instructors, and of Private Collins.

Mike was impressed. Poorly educated, Johnson was very bright and, as Sergeant Markey had said, very tough. Mike tried to make the interview a conversation, but Johnson volunteered nothing. He spoke directly, looking Taggart right in the eye as he spoke, but as soon as he had answered Mike's specific question he became silent, waiting for the next question. He was unshakable in his assertion that he had seen Markey hit Collins with a rifle, although he added that he wished he hadn't because he didn't like being a snitch, because he could see the trouble one mistake was causing Markey, because he didn't think the platoon commander really intended to hurt Collins, and he had never seen or heard of Markey hitting any recruit before. Mike could see Steiner trying to slip that little aside into Johnson's testimony to give him added credibility. It was sufficiently out of keeping with Johnson's otherwise noncommital demeanor that Mike suspected Steiner had planted the seed of that testimony in the first place.

"Captain Steiner tell you to say that?"

"No, sir."

"Did he ask you whether you wanted to cause Staff Sergeant Markey any trouble?"

"Yes, sir."

"Did he ask you if you liked being an informant?"

"Yes, sir."

"Did he ask you whether you thought Staff Sergeant Markey intended to hurt Private Collins?"

"Yes, sir."

"Did he ask if you wished you hadn't seen Staff Sergeant Markey hit Private Collins?"

"Yes, sir."

Bingo, thought Taggart, making a note of the exchange.

Johnson had a good grasp of the details of what he claimed to have seen. He described how he had helped Collins after Markey had returned to the duty office and how he had gone to the corporal of the guard to get a replacement for Collins on fire-watch. Johnson showed Mike where he had seen Markey and Collins standing, and he got his rifle and showed Mike how the blow had been struck, pretending Taggart was Collins, pulling his punch. He denied that CID had suggested to him that it had happened as he was claiming.

It was 1730 by the time Mike finished with Johnson. Sergeant Warthun reminded him that the platoon was due at chow shortly. Mike had a headache. He felt he needed to review and organize the notes he had taken so far in the hope he could develop some fresh approach or pick up something he was missing. He made arrangements to finish talking to the rest of the platoon the next afternoon and went straight home without going back to the office.

As he drove out Gate One he noticed a group of people seated on the sidewalk across the street from the base, but it was dark and he was preoccupied with thoughts of the afternoon's events, so he paid no attention.

Five

CATHY WASN'T home when Mike arrived. There was a note on the refrigerator saying that she and Ann Morehead had gone to a bridge tournament in La Mesa.

Grabbing a beer, he trudged upstairs to change clothes. His uniform smelled like a tobacco shed from sitting in the tiny office all afternoon. Cigarettes were usually forbidden in boot camp, and most of the recruits had taken advantage of their time with Mike to smoke as many as possible. He wouldn't have been surprised if some had tried to smoke two at once. He held his shirt at arm's length between his thumb and index finger as he dropped it in the hamper.

Flipping on the news as the doorbell rang, Mike opened the door to find Horn standing there.

"Hello, Tags. What's happening? Margolis said you spent the afternoon down with Markey's platoon. I figured you might need a shoulder to cry on."

Mike had been friends with Tom Horn since law school. They had played on teams, groaned about the workload, drunk beer and, finally, faced with the end of their deferments, they had decided to enlist in the Corps. Since then they had coincidentally received identical assignments.

Cathy liked Tom too, although she sometimes thought his laconic, irreverent tilt tended to fuel Taggart's reluctance "to grow up," as she put it. Still, he was like one of the family, and maybe when he and Michael got out of the Corps they'd both grow up a little, as she said, and tried to smile when she said it.

The fact that they were on opposite sides, Horn prosecuting, Taggart defending, wasn't a problem. Horn considered Mad Dog Joe Steiner an asshole, but he didn't give away anything professionally to his friend. In fact, Horn spoke so seldom that it was often impossible to have a conversation with him on any subject.

The national news was on as they sat down. Films of the war in Viet Nam were followed by reports of protests against the war at home. Automatic weapons fire, artillery, rocks, bottles, fists, dogs. People running back and forth, reporters crouched talking into hand-held microphones to the steady beat of helicopter rotors, while the turbulence from the blades whipped their hair. It was the nightly account of the unraveling of the country.

Horn and Taggart sipped their beers and watched numbly as the anchorman reappeared, looked up from his notes and announced: "Meanwhile, in San Diego, California, today the Marine Corps announced the death of Private Loren Collins of Osage City, Kansas. According to a Corps spokesman, Private Collins died of an internal hemorrhage near the end of his eighth week of recruit training. Private Collins's platoon commander, Staff Sergeant Roger Markey, has been charged with Private Collins's murder. Now, for more on this story, we go to Veronica Rasmussen in San Diego . . ."

Taggart looked at Horn and then back to the screen. Horn said nothing. Veronica Rasmussen appeared. She was standing across from Gate Two. In the background several people carrying signs were marching.

"I'm standing outside the Marine Corps Recruiting Depot in San Diego, California. This is the West Coast training facility where the legendary Marine Corps boot camp training is conducted. Although less well-known than its East Coast counterpart located at Parris Island in South Carolina, the San Diego facility graduates approximately one thousand trainees per week, most of whom will receive orders to Viet Nam after some further training."

As Ronnie spoke, the camera toured the base, showing platoons marching on the drill field and scrambling over the obstacle course. In the background the barrack buildings loomed silently, there was a shot of the Headquarters Building and then the camera returned to Ronnie.

"For Private Loren Collins there will be no graduation, no further training, no orders to WESPAC or anywhere else. Private Collins died last Saturday morning just after midnight, and today the Marine Corps announced that the platoon commander of Private Collins's platoon has been charged with Collins's murder, along with violation of several other regulations having to do with maltreatment of recruits.

"A group that calls itself Veterans in Concert to End Militarism has begun a vigil outside the base that it says is intended to focus attention on the Markey court-martial. I have here with me Mark Levinson, the leader of VICTEM. Mr. Levinson, what do you consider to be the significance of your vigil?"

A tall, gaunt figure appeared. It was impossible to tell where his hair ended and his beard began. He was wearing horn-rimmed glasses and a camouflage utility jacket.

"Miss Rasmussen, the Marine Corps tradition of going through the motions of a court-martial for drill instructors accused of maltreatment is almost as old as the tradition of maltreatment itself. Very few, though, are ever convicted. VICTEM hopes that by keeping the memory of Loren Collins alive outside the walls, a force for accountability and responsible leadership will be created inside the walls of the Marine Corps."

"This is Veronica Rasmussen returning you now to New York."

The last thing to be seen before the anchorman came back was a picture of two marchers carrying signs that read "Murderer Markey" and "The Marine Corps Eats Its Young."

"Well, that was an even-handed, objective treatment," Mike said. "I hope Go-Go and Mad Dog invite Mark to the trial."

Horn was silent for a few minutes, then said, "That reporter, Veronica what's-her-name, was in the office today interviewing Go-Go and Mad Dog. She doesn't, as you just heard, think much of your client."

"I gathered that . . . well, it's sure sporting of her not to let her opinions color her reporting."

Markey had called Taggart first thing Wednesday morning to ask whether it would be all right to postpone their scheduled meeting for one day. He said his wife was sick. Mike had no objection since at that point he still hadn't finished talking to the privates.

At 0730 the next morning when Taggart arrived at the defense hooch Markey was waiting for him. They got some coffee and Mike asked how his wife was feeling.

"Whole thing's hard on her." Markey shrugged but didn't say any more about it.

Markey was the first to raise the subject of the case against him. "Sir, I've thought about your suggestion of a civilian lawyer and I talked about it with my wife, like you said to. The truth is, sir, we ain't got any money for another lawyer. I know you say you're inexperienced, but you know the drill field and the Marine Corps better than any civilian would, and that's where this battle's bein' fought. Besides, I asked around. I know you been to Nam. People down at Battalion know you from WESPAC. Everybody says you're good people, that you got guts and will stand up to command if you have to. What's more, I got a feeling you don't want to see no man, especially another Marine, get hung for something he didn't do. So that's it, skipper, maybe I got a higher opinion of you than you got of yourself."

At that moment it would have been impossible for anyone to have a higher opinion of Staff Sergeant Markey than Michael Taggart's.

Mike stood up and they shook hands. "Okay, then it's settled. Let me bring you up to date. I've found out what has the prosecution so fired up."

Mike slid a copy of Johnson's statement to CID across the desk. Markey read it, shaking his head in growing disbelief.

"I talked to him for two hours Tuesday, and he's pretty sure of himself."

Markey went on staring at the statement for a few moments, then looked up. "What's goin' on?... what's going on?... Well, you warned me to expect something like this, sir, but that don't make it any less of a shock when it happens. And the fact that it's Johnson really hurts. I was so proud of that kid, I've even talked to him about trying for the Enlisted Commissioning Program when he gets out of training. I feel like I been kicked right in the teeth and I don't know why."

"Tell me more about Private Johnson," Taggart said.

"Well, I can tell you that more'n any other kid who come through here in two years, Johnson reminded me of me. I mean, he was hungry, he couldn't get enough of the Corps. He ate it up. He's smart and strong and hard... he didn't have no easy life on the outside..."

"Ever see him hit anybody?"

Markey thought on it. "Pugil sticks, hand-to-hand combat, but never anything like you're driving at, never outside training."

"He was the guide, wasn't he? How did he see to it that the recruits did what he said? How did he enforce his authority?"

"I'd say just lookin' at him was enough most of the time to get across that he could back up what he was saying. But I never saw him slug anybody..."

They talked about what Johnson had told Mike, as well as the other recruit interviews. From there they moved on to a review of Markey's Marine Corps career, each assignment, whom he worked for, highlights, possible character witnesses. Several times the sergeant's mind came back to Johnson.

"Johnson, why Johnson? And why me? What's Johnson wanta fuck me over for?"

"Maybe to divert suspicion from himself," Taggart said. "You're the logical suspect."

By the time Markey left, Mike was feeling a little better about the defense. In particular he was impressed with his client, especially his feeling for the Corps and his ability to convey that feeling. At one point in their conversation, responding to Mike's question about why he had enlisted, Markey told him:

"You know, sir, I was one of nine kids. We were one-quarter Cherokee, so as far as the white folks in south Alabama were concerned, we were niggers, and most of them wouldn't have nothing to do with us. The whole family lived in a three-room shack and we farmed with a mule. More 'n once when the mule was lame I seen my ol' man harness himself to that plow an' inch his way along with my mom or one of us kids wobblin' along behind trying to hold it up. There wasn't much to keep us around when we got older, so, when I was sixteen I figured my turn had come. I quit school, if that's what you could call it, and I enlisted. My first day at Parris Island the DI said he didn't give a shit if we was black, white, red or yellow, 'cause when he looked at us, all he saw was green. When I found out I was gonna get three squares a day and my own bed, I thought I'd died and gone to heaven. If I got thumped a couple of times along the way for fuckin' up it was no different from what I was used to at home..."

As Markey talked on, Mike thought of himself and of how tough it would have been for him if he'd not gone to college and then law school. And at every step there had been encouragement and support...

"Anyway," Markey went on, "I went straight to Nam after ITR. There was only twenty-nine days left before I was supposed to rotate, and I got shot to shit in a rice paddy just east of Da Nang. I couldn't hold my head up and I kept thinkin' I was gonna drown before I got a chance to bleed to death. The next thing I knew I was ridin' outa there on the shoulder of a white lieutenant from the University of Alabama. He took a slug himself gettin' my ass outa there.

"Lyin' in the hospital, all I could think about was how that wouldn't have happened on the outside, and I decided right then that I belonged to this outfit for as long as it would have me."

"What did you think of boot camp, Corporal Litzinger?"

Joe Steiner was leaning back with his feet up on his desk, and Go-Go's clerk, Litzinger, was standing, filing some papers in the dead-case file.

"Hated it."

"Do you think all that five-finger discipline that goes on down there is necessary?"

"No, sir, it's a violation of orders."

"I know it's against orders, corporal, but that's not my question. Orders or not, do you think it's necessary?"

How to attack the unwritten code of boot camp—Joe knew that was his problem, and maybe the first step was to understand it from an NCO's point of view. He'd have to face that as part of the prosecution of Markey, he figured.

"Sir, the book says don't do it. That's enough for me. Maybe getting hit helps some people to get squared away. It didn't help me." Litzinger returned to his filing.

Litzinger might make a good witness, but he obviously wasn't the one to get the other guy's viewpoint from. Well, there was still time . . .

Steiner was getting edgy. He was even beginning to wonder whether taking the Markey case himself had really been such a good idea as it had seemed at the time. The publicity it was getting was more intense than anything he'd ever experienced. The civilians were really pissed off over this one. Good, and bad, for him . . .

Talking about it with his wife, Julie, the night before, the downside had begun to dawn on him for the first time.

"Seems to me," she said, "you've got everything to lose and nothing to gain in Markey."

"What do you mean?"

"Well, what with all the publicity, the command interest, the eyewitness, everybody thinks it's an open-and-shut case for conviction. Obviously Colonel Guinn thinks so. What kind of recognition do you get for winning open-and-shut cases?" She paused. "And what kind of recognition do you get for losing them?"

She could be right . . . there wasn't a man aboard the Depot who didn't know a recruit had died in training and that a DI had been charged. Even the recruits isolated in their platoons away from all newspapers, radio and television knew. "Someone died last night over at Hotel Company, Third Battalion . . ." Steiner was sure the whispers had flashed across the recruit mess hall at breakfast that Saturday morning, hours before he'd heard about it himself.

General Fitzroy had ordered flags aboard the base at half-mast.

Rumors of a command investigation of recruit training, presumably to head off one by the civilians, were flying. Julie was right... you couldn't ask "How can I lose?" without also asking, "What if I do?"

Six

"Boot Hill" her father had always laughingly called it as they drove by on the highway. "There's Boot Hill," he would say. Linda wondered what he would call it now that they weren't driving past but were instead turning and going in. "How tiny we must look to Loren," she thought, looking up at the highness of the immense sky and imagining what the mournful little procession must look like from there as it wound its solitary way across the treeless, snow-covered prairie toward her brother's grave.

Loren's body had lain at James Funeral Parlor for two days while the community stopped by to pay their final respects. In one way or another Loren had touched the lives of nearly everyone in town. He had delivered their papers, been their classmate, their teammate, their student, their patient, their friend. He had shoveled their snow, mowed their grass, baled their hay, dated their daughters. One after another Linda watched them come in and share their sorrowful reminiscences with her parents.

In all this Linda had taken no part. She could not bring herself to step into the room where Loren's body rested. She had begged her mother to close the casket, but her mother had refused. So she sat in the reception area outside the room, numbly acknowledging the presence of people she had known all her life with a silent nod.

73

Martha Collins did agree to close the casket during the memorial service. Just before it was about to begin she approached Linda. "I know how you feel, but the casket is about to be closed for the last time. There's no one in the room but family now. Are you sure you don't want to see Loren at least once? It'll be the last chance any of us have..."

I'll see him every day for the rest of my life, Linda wanted to say as she turned to face her mother. The look that she wore stopped Martha in her tracks and made any further words unnecessary. Linda's face was pinched with the effort, unsuccessful, to keep her swollen eyes from overflowing. Tears rose to the brim and flowed down her cheeks, not in sobs or spasms but in a steady stream. Linda tried to speak, to decline this final invitation; she moved her lips but the words would not come, and she shook her head from side to side.

Martha Collins ached at the sight. How difficult for the young to be reminded that no one lives forever, she thought. Without a word she reached out and laid her hand on Linda's shoulder, then walked inside for a last look at her only son.

The unreality of it all, the phone call from her mother, the trip home from school with her older sister, Marilyn, the two days at the funeral home, the memorial service, the ride to the grave and now the burial, the other-worldliness of the whole ordeal finally began to unravel Linda's ability to focus as she walked toward the grave. Everything around her was moving, shaking, vibrating as if the shock absorbers in her brain had lost their tension, and with each step the world swam before her eyes.

"Jesus, God...don't let this happen!" She clutched at the arm of her brother-in-law who walked beside her, as she came to a stop at the edge of the grave that seemed to undulate in the rippling ground. She felt as if she were being sifted through some kind of fine strainer, cascading formlessly on top of the pile of raw earth beside the hole that was about to consume her brother. From there she watched the pallbearers approach. It was as if she was looking up, not down, at the casket, and as it passed in front of her on its way into the ground, turning unreality into awful reality, she heard someone who sounded like the Linda Collins she used to know say out loud, "Good-bye, Loren . . . I'm sorry . . ."

Linda woke up in her bed with the covers pulled up to her chin. Morning sunlight streamed in through her east window. No sooner had she opened her eyes than the thought hit her—the trip was over. Whatever subconscious trigger had been pulled, its shot had run its course.

She stared first at the ceiling and then at the walls adorned with posters, pennants and pom-poms, relics of another time, another person. A time when there had been no war, when flowers had grown in gardens, not in her drug-expanded consciousness; when flags were flown on holidays, not burned on the steps of administration buildings nor used to drape the box that bore her brother.

Her mother came to the door and knocked softly. "Linda . . . are you awake?" When Linda made no reply, she moved away without looking in.

The words to a presumably forgotten nursery rhyme floated in Linda's brain. "Little Girl Blue, come blow your horn, the sheep's in the meadow, the cow's in the corn. Where is the Little Girl who looks after the sheep? . . ." Where, indeed, was Little Girl Blue? Where had she been? Where was she going? Was there anywhere to go?

It had all seemed so *right* to her. Peace and love, harmony and understanding. The Age of Aquarius had swept her away from her past, from her brother, her friend whom she had so righteously dismissed . . .

Linda wandered about the room. She fingered the crepe paper at the tip of the blue and white pom-poms, looked at the stuffed toy bear Loren had won for her throwing baseballs at milk bottles at their county fair. She stared at the translucent agar tabs of acid, the "windowpanes," in the bottom of her purse. She wanted badly to get lost again and never get found. There were too many things she wanted to hide from . . . it was impossible to know which way to run first, and so she sat in silence all that day and the next and the next, barely touching the food that was offered, not responding to repeated efforts to console her.

75

Seven

VERONICA RASMUSSEN walked into the defense hooch. She had never been on a military post before yesterday. The maleness of the place was overpowering. She figured she'd been eye-fucked about a thousand times during the afternoon. She hadn't had to ask Captain Steiner and the colonel twice when she wanted to interview them, but she doubted Markey's lawyer would be as cooperative, especially if he'd seen the news the previous night. What a break that had been, persuading the network to carry her coverage. She'd better use all her resources to obtain defense counsel Taggart's cooperation.

"Which is Captain Taggart?" she asked.

Unaccustomed to having a female voice in their precinct, every head in the room looked up from its desk. Margolis, the eternal hound, said he wished he was.

"I'm Captain Taggart," Mike quickly told her. Like Martha Collins, he immediately thought that Veronica Rasmussen looked even better in person than on television. Her auburn hair fell in waves to her shoulders, where it dissolved into a velvet pullover of the same color. Her cowl neckline combined with her hair to softly frame the skin of her face and neck. She was altogether stunning.

"I'm Veronica Rasmussen from—"

"I know who you are."

"Well, then, you know I'm here to report on the death of Loren Collins. . . . I was hoping you'd be willing to talk to me about the case, from your perspective—"

"From your news report last night I thought you were here to report on the death of Staff Sergeant Markey," Mike said quietly.

"Please, captain, I don't want to argue with you. Disregard Sergeant Markey for the time being. Just tell me, from your experience here, what you think are the causes of maltreatment of recruits, in spite of all the regulations prohibiting it."

Taggart sighed. "Look, there's no way I can answer that question and expect you or anyone else to disregard the fact that it's the defendant's attorney talking. I'm sure Captain Steiner and the folks down the hall will be glad to explain the infallibility of Marine Corps justice to you, especially where my client is concerned."

Taggart's back was, literally, almost against the back wall of the office. Behind Veronica Rasmussen he could see that everyone in the office had stopped whatever they were doing and were listening intently to the exchange. Margolis was checking out, as he'd put it, Veronica's rear axle.

"Captain, you have no reason to complain of one-sided reporting if one side of the story is all that the reporter can get." Taggart's provocative if matter-of-fact tone set her on edge.

"Miss Rasmussen, I have the impression that one side of the story is all you think there is, and all you want from me are some explanations you can knock down on-camera with your own penetrating analysis."

"Well, I'm sorry you feel that way, Captain Taggart. Up to now I've assumed that Markey might at least have his own side to the story, but based on what you've told me, or rather failed to tell me, I can only conclude that he doesn't."

"Suit yourself," Taggart said to her back as she departed.

On Friday morning Taggart had a short trial defending a private first class against assault and disrespect charges in a special court-martial. It was a relief to think of something other than Markey's predicament for a few hours. By midafternoon, though, he was back at it, heading for the dispensary to find Dr. Nellis, the doctor who had treated Collins the night he died. Several times during the past week he had called and left messages for Nellis. They had not been returned.

At the dispensary he was sent to an office on the second floor. There was no name on the door. Mike knocked. There was no answer, so he opened it and looked inside. A slightly built, shaggy-haired navy lieutenant of about medium height was sitting there. He wore a plastic name tag—"Dr. Nellis." He was reading a novel.

"Yes, you looking for someone?"

"I'm looking for you, Dr. Nellis. I'm Mike Taggart from the legal office. I've been assigned to represent a drill instructor named Roger Markey who's been charged in connection with the death of Private Collins. I understand you treated Collins the night he died."

"Examined was all I could do by the time they bothered to call me."

"I read the autopsy report, doctor, and I'd like to talk to you about what happened last Saturday night."

"Captain, I've no intention of talking to you about this case. All I have to say to you is in that report."

"Hey, take it easy, lieutenant. I'm just trying to do my job—"

"That's what I'm trying to do too," Nellis said, "and I don't see anything in my job description that says I have to have anything to do with spokesmen for murderers. Now, if you'll excuse me, I'm busy." He picked up his novel.

It just came out of him. Thinking about it later Mike was a little surprised at himself, but at that moment it seemed natural and right.

"Put down that book, lieutenant, or I'll shove it up your ass."

Nellis put down his book.

"Doctor, I don't know why you've got your ass in a sling, and I don't really care. All I know is that Staff Sergeant Markey is faced with the end of a career that's at least as important to him as yours is to you or mine to me. Right now he's facing years, maybe life, in prison for a crime he swears he didn't commit. I want to be able to say everything that can be said on his behalf as effectively as I can when the time comes. Now, whether you like it or not, you're involved. All I'm asking of you is that you share your knowledge of the case with me, so the man can at least have a fair shot at defending himself. Let's leave the judgments to the court."

Nellis shrugged. "That's a pretty speech, but have you ever known a drill instructor who admitted hitting a recruit? I've been here two and a half years and I've seen what goes on. Those sons of bitches put on that Smokey hat and suddenly it's as if they've got a license to abuse a bunch of poor, dumb, frightened kids, mentally and physically. And don't make the mistake of thinking I'm some bleeding heart, captain, I've seen the tangible evidence. I've put casts on them, stitched them up, wired their jaws. I've heard all the lies about how it happened. I've seen the fear. I've had recruits beg me not to send them back down to RTR. I saw fear that night, Taggart. That boy was sick with fear, and I know where it came from. Now one of the sergeants has finally managed to kill somebody, and if you think for a minute I'm going to kiss the Corps' ass and say Collins fell off the obstacle course or took an unfortunate blow during training from a pugil stick, you're very mistaken. And that's the end of my speech."

"I'm not asking you to lie, Dr. Nellis," Mike replied quietly. "I know bad things have happened, Collins's death is one of them. But it's by no means clear that Markey's the one who caused it. I have a witness who tells me that in two years Markey is the only DI he's ever worked with who never hit the recruits, including the witness himself. It may be clear that Collins was hit, but it's not clear by what or whom ... that's up to the court. Please don't let your feelings about this system put you in the position of denying an innocent man the opportunity to defend himself."

Nellis was unimpressed. "So innocent that an eyewitness saw him hit Private Collins with a rifle butt? Is that right, captain?"

Goddamn Steiner, Taggart thought.

"You're goddamned right I've got feelings about this system, as you put it. The kind of glorification of war and endurance of pain that's taught around here went out with the Middle Ages, or so I thought till I got here. I didn't ask to get stationed with the Marines, and there's no way the Corps can make me look the other way on this one. . . . As I said, I'm busy," and he picked up his book again.

* * *

The defense hooch was deserted when Mike returned from his encounter with Dr. Nellis. At 1700 on Friday afternoon he was sure most of the others were over at happy hour at the officers' club. He sat at his desk and looked out the window.

Taggart had always thought his major asset as a lawyer, if he had one, was his ability to get along with all kinds of people. He certainly wasn't a great legal mind; law school had quickly disabused him of that notion. Now he was even beginning to have doubts about his ability to win friends and influence people.

What's the matter with me? he wondered. This is no way to help Markey. First I piss-off Mad Dog and Go-Go. That's understandable given the circumstances. Maybe even pissing-off that reporter's forgivable, she was bent out of shape before she ever came in here. But Nellis, that's a different story. Angry or not, I'm not going to get anywhere by antagonizing witnesses, no matter how biased.

He was mulling over this depressing thought when he heard a slight rustling sound. It was Horn, silently leaning against Margolis's desk, which was opposite Taggart's. Mike hadn't even heard him come in.

"Profound thoughts?" Horn asked.

"What else? What's up?"

"I waited around to see if you wanted to go over to the club."

Mike glanced at his watch. He had time for a quick drink before he had to go home and get ready for his night of culture with the Moreheads.

"Better both drive, I've got to leave early to go to a goddamned play."

"Sounds like you're really looking forward to it."

"We're going out with the Moreheads."

Horn emitted a long, low groan. He had met the Moreheads once, when Ann had dropped by to see Cathy on a night when he and Taggart were watching a basketball game on TV. Once was enough.

The bar at the club was going full blast when Horn and Taggart entered. At the far end of the room from the bar a Filipino rock band was blaring.

"Just like Okinawa," Mike said, nodding in the band's direction.

Someone, probably Margolis, had pushed a group of tables and chairs together over by the glass door leading out to the veranda, and nearly the entire legal office was sitting together, having declared an off-duty cease fire.

"Hey, Tom, Tags, over here," Margolis called out across the room, standing and motioning in their direction. He was squinting at them through the smoky haze, and they barely detected the tips of his drooping semiregulation mustache.

"I'm surprised he doesn't have a lampshade on his head," Mike told Horn as they made their way toward the smiling Greek.

A number of the lawyers' wives and girlfriends had joined them, including Margolis's wife Jackie, whom Mike liked very much. Even Go-Go was sitting with his troops on this occasion instead of politicking with the bigwigs at the bar. Beside him sat Veronica Rasmussen, who was flanked by Mad Dog Steiner on her other side. Go-Go's gesture at office solidarity suddenly became clear.

As Tom and Mike sat down Margolis resumed rolling dice for drinks and regaling those at his end of the table with an account of how he had taken the base tennis championship from Go-Go the day before.

Taggart ordered a beer and surveyed the familiar scene. All over the Corps crowds like this were gathered in "O" club bars this Friday, rolling dice, arguing about air power versus infantry, goading any navy personnel unfortunate enough to be in their midst, drinking too much, trying to put the make on any woman in the area. In each, a demure nude, always oriental, would be casting her painted, benign gaze over the scene from her position of honor above the bar. Horn once observed that, based on his experience, all the models for those portraits must have had silicone operations.

The music, the clink of glasses amid a hundred different conversations, the unending rattle of the dice, and the occasional shouts all combined to drive Taggart back inside himself, thinking the anachronisms of the Corps.

"If you buy me a drink I'll promise not to pester you about the Markey case," Veronica Rasmussen said, and settled into the empty chair beside him.

Taggart declared a private truce. For the moment. "It's a deal."

"Is it like this every Friday night?" Ronnie asked.

"Yeah, usually. This is just the prelude to the dance later on. Three hours from now there'll be more than a thousand people here, mostly singles. They call it the body exchange."

"It sort of reminds me of college," Ronnie said. "I bet, though, that these same people would be more buttoned up if they were civilians."

Taggart looked at Veronica. It was plain she was no dummy.

"I suspect you're right. You should have seen the clubs on Okinawa, the intensity on the big nights there is unbelievable. Everybody is on the make. Sometimes the crowds actually seem to throb with the tension or excitement or whatever it is."

"Any theories about why?"

"Who knows? The closeness to the war maybe. Okinawa's the springboard into that shithole, you should forgive the expression. Everyone is either on their way there or on their way back or with someone who is. Why not let it all hang out?"

"Eat, drink and be merry . . . ?" Ronnie smiled, but then stopped when Taggart suddenly looked serious.

"Something like that, I guess," he said, looking directly at her. "But to hear it put that way makes it sound sort of demeaning. People tend to be people wherever they are. They worry about what's going to happen to them, force themselves to be high to cover up their fears. The greater the fear, the greater the put on." He laughed. "So sayeth Dr. Von Taggart."

Now it was Ronnie's turn for appraisal. This was an unexpected side of the man she identified so completely with Loren Collins's killer.

"It sounds like you don't like the war any more than I do," she said.

Taggart just looked at her. He wasn't giving any more away to her. She was there to cook his client. He'd need to remember that.

"Ronnie . . . Ronnie." It was Go-Go calling from the other end of the table. He was standing beside the short, balding, unsmiling figure of Colonel Katkavage, the chief-of-staff, who was bouncing on his toes as if impatient to be free and away from the contagion he knew infected lawyers in general and defense counsel in particular. "Ronnie, can you come over here for a moment, here's someone I'd like you to meet."

Leaving her purse and promising to be right back, Ronnie joined

Guinn and Katkavage. When she returned a minute or so later, Taggart was gone.

"Excuse me," she tapped Horn, who was silently watching the stripper who had begun to perform. "Where did Captain Taggart go?"

"No stay," replied Horn, borrowing the inevitable explanation of Okinawans for the disappearance of anything or anybody.

CHAPTER

Eight

CATHY WAS ready and waiting to go when Mike walked in the door. She glanced at her watch as Mike galloped upstairs. The Moreheads had arrived by the time he came back down.

Harvey was wearing a sport coat over a silk shirt unbuttoned almost to his naval. He was decorated with gold chains and bracelets. Horn referred to Harvey as "Christmas Tree."

"Put some poor devil in jail today?" Harvey asked, although Taggart had told him half a dozen times he was a defense counsel.

As they drove to the restaurant-theater Harvey talked on and on about the San Diego real estate market. In a way Harvey was easy to be with, Mike never had to say anything.

Mike and Harvey were the same age, but Harvey was about thirty years older. Except for his Southern California get-ups, he reminded Mike of some of the associates at Morgan, Miller & Richardson. He would ride up the elevator with them in the mornings on his way in and think to himself that there was really no difference between them and the fifty-five-year-old partners standing next to them. They talked deals all week long, rode hours to and from work on the train, went to brunch at each other's homes on Sunday morning and played golf on the weekend. Mike felt trapped whenever he thought about going back. He felt he'd lost something by opting for the chance at the high salaries and prospects for success that such firms used to recruit the law school graduates they wanted, but he wasn't sure what ... Oh, well, he thought, at least I've had a three-year escape from old age."

Cathy, on the other hand, loved the life in Chicago. She couldn't wait to get back, and he knew it. They were close, had been for so long, that maybe they forgot people could change, and it was nobody's fault ...

During dinner Mike listened to Ann and Cathy talk about their exploits at the bridge table. Taggart preferred the bridge talk to Ann Morehead's other big conversational fixation, the war. Ann considered herself a protector of the downtrodden masses, even though her husband drove a Cadillac at the age of twenty-seven and made his money selling other people's houses for more than they were worth. She talked about circulating petitions, writing letters and going to watch other people demonstrate. Harvey wouldn't let her do any of those things herself—might be bad for business—so mostly Ann played bridge. Mike had thought at first that some of the things she said about the war were calculated to shock her listeners into beginning to think. After a while, though, he concluded that they weren't calculated at all. They were just blatherings.

During dinner Harvey sent his meal back twice for adjustments and finally went back to explain to the chef personally what he wanted.

The play was a musical, *1776*. The actor who played Ben Franklin looked more like the pot-bellied college kid who had waited on their table and poured wine in Mike's lap than he did the elder statesman of the Continental Congress. Nevertheless, Mike enjoyed it.

Afterward they stopped at a cocktail lounge on top of a hotel in Mission Valley, the center of San Diego's civilian night life. After the waitress brought their drinks, Ann said that "It was a good thing the nation's founding fathers weren't alive to see the United States' aggression in Southeast Asia."

Mike made his contribution to what he knew was coming by saying that they probably would have welcomed the war because after two hundred years they would have just about run out of Indians to kill. He said it with a determinedly straight face.

That sailed over Ann's head, and she was off to the races. She ran

86

through a litany of peace-movement slogans with a pugnaciousness that, Mike thought, if it could have been bottled by the war effort might have turned the tide in Nam. The Gulf of Tonkin, Weh, Khe Sanh, Cambodia . . . she covered them all, calling Nixon, Kissinger, Bunker and Westmoreland war criminals. Taggart nursed his beer and tried to ignore her. Then Ann said, "You know, I actually am glad on weeks when our death toll in Viet Nam is up *because* it means the pressure on us to get *out* of there is increased that much more . . ."

Cathy sensed the danger, but it was too late. Taggart had too many dead friends, had written to too many mothers of dead sons, wives of dead husbands to let it go by. He set his beer bottle down on the low table in front of him and leaned over in Ann's direction so she'd be sure to hear him. "I hope you still can say that in the next war when that kid you had to keep Harvey's ass out of this one comes home in a bag with his dog tags jammed between his teeth."

Ann blinked for a moment, as if trying to comprehend, or not comprehend, what Mike had just said to her. Then she pointed at Taggart and started screaming. "You . . . you . . ." and then commenced sobbing on Harvey's shoulder. The other people in the bar all looked around at them.

"What the hell's going on?" asked Harvey, who had not heard what was said.

Cathy said they had all better leave. By the time they were outside, Ann had sufficiently regained control to refuse to get in the same car with Taggart, so he and Cathy ended up taking a cab home.

It was not a very pleasant ride. When they got home Cathy went upstairs without saying a word. By the time Mike let the dog out and then back in and had locked up and gone upstairs, Cathy was in bed with the lights out and was giving forth with what sounded like a snore. It was a sound he had heard too often since his return from overseas, one that he could not remember her ever making before he left.

"Come on," he said to Feodot, "let's take a walk."

Mike was reading the morning paper when Cathy came downstairs. She wordlessly poured a cup of coffee and made toast.

"What's on tap for today, Cath?" he asked, hoping to break the ice.

"I was going shopping with Ann, but you've probably put an end to those plans. Of course I realize they're trivial and meaningless compared to the weighty matters *you* deal with."

"Cathy, I'm sorry about—"

"I don't want to talk about it."

"Well, what are we going to do, walk around here like two armed camps in a cold war? That's really something to look forward to."

Mike realized that if everything had been all right between them what had happened the previous evening wouldn't have upset her so much. . . . He tried again, but wound up asking her if she was mad at Ann too for what she had said, or was he the only culprit.

"Two wrongs . . . what Ann said is no excuse for what you said. Using somebody's child against them is really low. How would you feel if our baby'd lived and . . ."

"There it is," Mike thought to himself. Cathy had been pregnant when they'd left Chicago but had miscarried shortly after Taggart began OCS.

Sometimes it seemed she blamed the Marine Corps and him for her loss. When he'd tried to talk about it all she would say was that he couldn't understand how a mother would feel. Mike knew enough to say nothing about her apparent lack of interest in how he felt. He also knew that any further effort to justify what he'd said to Ann Morehead would be a waste of time now that he knew the real rub. But he also couldn't really blame her. Situation normal, all fucked up . . .

"Besides," Cathy was saying, "if I behaved toward your friends like that, you'd be mad as hell. Well, that's what I am. I'm mad as hell," and she went back upstairs.

When Dave Richardson called to see if he wanted to play handball, Mike was halfway out the door before he'd hung up the phone.

Taggart lay on his back on the lawn alongside Richardson, both exhausted from two hours of trying to kill each other on the handball court. He could feel his body sucking up the bright sunlight as it struggled to rejuvenate. The cares of the preceding days seemed miles away as he stared up at the blue infinity above him and smiled as Richardson went on about the antics of his twin eighteen-month-olds.

"Just a minute . . . wait," he said, putting a hand on Richardson's arm. "Let me get some more cokes, I'm dying."

He got up and walked stiffly toward the soft-drink machine at the corner of the building, throwing their empties in the trash can on the way. As he turned away from the machine he saw Veronica Rasmussen walking down the sidewalk toward him, evidently on her way out the gate. She was wearing white slacks with bell-bottomed cuffs, a white blouse with a button-down collar, a plain navy blue scarf around her neck and carrying a blue plaid madras blazer. She looked like she'd just stepped off a yacht. Taggart wondered who she'd been interviewing this morning but didn't ask.

"Oh, hi . . . Mike, isn't it? I didn't recognize you." She smiled. "Been jogging?"

"Handball. Want a coke?"

"I shouldn't even talk to you after the way you ran out on me last night, but sure, I'll have one." Here was a target of opportunity she hadn't expected to find.

He thought of explaining he had to go to a play with his wife, quickly decided not to as he bought a third coke.

As they walked back across the lawn Veronica looked at Taggart and was forced to admit there weren't many fat marines. She was five feet, seven inches but Taggart was almost a full head taller and very tan. Not thickly built, his muscles were well defined. He seemed more at ease than the other two times she'd seen him. He even smiled once, crinkling his gray eyes at the corners. Ronnie thought of Norm Karocek, a man she dated in Kansas City. Norm wasn't fat, not yet, but Norm's idea of a workout was a three martini lunch. Ronnie didn't think Norm would like the Marine Corps.

Richardson, a black man, was lying with arms outspread, as if he was trying to get them around the sunlight. He had a build like a wrestler. Hearing their footsteps, he called, "Thought I was going to have to send out a search party. Where you been?" But when he saw Ronnie, he got to his feet.

Mike introduced them.

"Please call me Ronnie," she said to Dave, and then turning to Taggart, "you too."

89

Mike nodded and collapsed on the ground.

Richardson went on with his story . . . It seemed one of his kids had been waving his arms around at breakfast and accidently stuck his finger in his eye. To help offset the tears that followed, Dave had suggested that his son have some banana, it would make him feel better. "The kid stopped crying," Dave reported, "and looked at me as if to say, Are you kidding me? When he saw I was serious, he picked up the banana on the plate in front of him and stuck it in his eye."

"Already smarter than his ol' man," Taggart said.

"You live here or just out for a visit?" Richardson asked Ronnie.

"Just for a visit, I live in Kansas City."

"Kansas City. I'm from Kansas City . . . what part of town?"

"I grew up in Independence. Now I have an apartment right in Kansas City."

"Do you know where the ballpark was, where the Blues used to play and then the A's after that? That's my old neighborhood," Richardson said, adding he hadn't been back in ten years.

"Sure, my dad and I used to go to a lot of games."

"You might have parked your car right in my mom's yard. 'Hey, mister, watch your car for fifty cents!'" Dave laughed, remembering the game of blackmail he and his friends used to play.

"So you were one of those guys . . . listen, I've still got a foul ball I caught that Vic Power autographed for me after the game."

"Vic Power . . ." Richardson's thoughts drifted back. "Power, Clete Boyer, Hector Lopez . . . the A's had a few players. Everyone used to say they were a Yankee farm club, and it sure seemed that way sometimes—"

He came to suddenly and asked Ronnie what time it was.

"Oh, oh, I gotta get out of here. Marie's got me babysitting this afternoon. Nice meeting you, Ronnie. Give my regards to K.C. See you later, Tags." He trotted off, throwing his wet gear into the back of a rundown pickup bearing only the gray primer coat.

"Last vehicle on the streets of California with a running board," Mike said as Dave roared away, waving.

"He seems nice," Ronnie said. "And he certainly seems to enjoy being a father."

"Better be careful," Mike said with a straight face, "you might slip and say something nice about one of those savage, uncivilized drill instructors you're so determined to save the world from."

Ronnie was too surprised to even be angry at Taggart's dig at her determination to focus the public's attention on the Markey case.

"You mean *he's* a DI?"

Taggart nodded his head.

"But, he's—" She stopped. Anything she said would sound dopey. Of course drill instructors had wives and families and hometowns. She'd just never thought of it before. She was silent for several moments. She knew Taggart was watching her. She didn't want to ask just then, but suddenly she had to know.

"Does Staff Sergeant Markey have a wife and family?"

"A girl Deborah, six, in first grade, a son six months. Name is Brett."

It was Taggart who changed the subject, saying that her chances of finding a cab on the street outside the gate were poor. "I'll give you a lift back to your hotel, if you don't mind waiting for me to get cleaned up and you don't mind riding a motorcycle. I don't live too far from there."

They walked slowly across the quiet base to the locker room and showers half a mile away.

"Are you a good handball player?"

"Average, I guess."

"Can you beat Richardson?"

"He hands me my lunch."

"Ever play racquetball?"

"A couple of times."

"There are some courts in the apartments where I live in Kansas City. I started to play some in the last year."

Taggart said nothing.

"If I'm around here long enough, will you play some racquetball with me . . . or are you afraid I'll hand you your lunch?"

"Your torpedoing me on the racquetball court is the least of my worries where you're concerned." He didn't smile when he said that.

Ronnie sat on the step outside the Quonset hut while Taggart took a shower and dressed. A dusty road ran just to her right along the west side of the Quonset and disappeared into the distance. Beside it was a series of logs, pipes and ropes in a variety of configurations. It was the obstacle course, Taggart had told her as they approached. Overhead an occasional plane taking off from the adjacent airport left a deafening wake.

There did not appear to be any organized activities going on that hot, lazy Saturday. Now and then lone runners would lope past, most of them wearing combat boots, slowly fading from sight in the distance beyond the obstacle course. A couple of them were scarred, and one was limping badly. He struggled along, his crimson T-shirt darkened all over from his exertions.

As one runner approached the part of the road paralleling the obstacle course, he veered to his left, vaulted a three-foot log hurdle, took two or three short, choppy steps and leaped for a horizontal bar, swinging his feet above his head and jackknifing his body over the top. The momentum of his swing carried him almost to two more low log hurdles, the first of which he cleared like a hurdler and the second of which he leaped onto, gathered himself, sprang forward, grabbing a bar above and swinging his legs up to catch a pipe at right angles to the bar, which he shinnied feet first to a horizontal log at the end. Using his legs to pry himself into an upright position, he balanced about eight feet off the ground. From there he tightroped along one of the logs that ran in the direction of the course to a twelve-by-twelve beam, where he jumped for a chest-high log three feet away. Pivoting over that on his stomach, he dropped about eight feet into a sawdust pit.

He hit the ground running, cleared another low hurdle, muscled himself over a high plank wall, another hurdle, then a shoulder-high horizontal log. The runner's legs proceeded to chop down the space between obstacles like pistons, never fully extending as he ran because of the immediate need to spring in one direction or another as each obstacle was reached in turn. Next came a series of five chest-high horizontal logs about three feet apart. Leading with his left arm and right leg, the runner rolled over the first of the series, spinning as he landed so that he immediately hit the next log the same way. There was a rhythm to his movements as he spun. Although not within earshot, Veronica could readily imagine the sounds of the runner's labored breathing, the pounding of boots on the hard-packed ground, the rasp of fabric being dragged across the wood and steel as he completed his difficult passage.

At the end of the course was a twenty-foot rope, and the runner seemed to gather speed as he approached. Without pause he leaped and seized it at arm's length above his head, climbing hand over hand. At the top he slapped the beam the rope was anchored to and yelled something that Veronica heard faintly but could not understand. The echo of his call had hardly died across the otherwise empty field by the time he finished his sliding descent and ran on. The whole process had taken no more than sixty seconds.

Veronica had the sense of being on another planet. This whole performance was out of any world she knew. She'd also never been on a motorcycle before, and this was a big one. She climbed on behind Taggart and sat rigidly upright on her folded blazer—it was too hot to wear—holding onto Mike's hips. They idled their way back across the base, through the gate where the guard saluted. Turning right they passed the anti-Markey demonstrators and eased into light traffic. After a short distance Mike leaned the bike through a U-turn around a lane divider and headed past the topless bars, fast food joints, used car lots and motels advertising hourly rates that surrounded the base.

Leaving the commercial district behind they crested a hill and a wave of salt air washed over them as the vista of Mission Bay came in view. From the top of the hill Taggart accelerated. The wind in Ronnie's face made her feel good. From the throb of the engine she could feel variations in speed, and the sway of each change of direction communicated itself to her and made her an integral part of the movement forward, not just a passenger. She relaxed and leaned forward into the wind, wrapping her arms tight around Taggart as she did so.

"This is terrific!" she shouted above the drumming of the engine and the rush of the moving air. "You'll have to take me again.

* * *

"No, Eddie, I'm not taking a vacation at the station's expense," Ronnie said emphatically, although she had to admit, as she lay on her bed cradling the phone and looking out at the sparkling bay filled with sailboats, that she had been on vacations she enjoyed a lot less.

"No, Eddie, there's no one here with me. It's just some kids outside down by the water. Yes, my windows are open. This is San Diego, Eddie, not Moscow."

Jesus, she thought smiling at Logan's concern, this is like talking to my mother.

"Yes, that's right. The Article 32 hearing is Tuesday, the day after tomorrow, at 1400, I mean two o'clock. The prosecutor says it's like a preliminary hearing. I've got reservations back that night. I hope I'll have something on Markey between now and then. His counsel's not quite so leery of me as he was at first. Besides, he's . . . oh, never mind . . . Has Mrs. Collins called, did she leave any messages for me? Yeah, yeah, I know, you're not my goddamned secretary. Just check with the switchboard, will you, before we hang up?"

Eddie came on gruff and surly but insisted on her calling him daily, even on Sunday morning, just to make sure she was all right.

"No messages? Okay. Yes, I'll call tomorrow. Good-by, Eddie."

94

Nine

LIEUTENANT COLONEL Kitagawa had been appointed the Article 32 pretrial investigating officer. Kitagawa was partially of Japanese ancestry, but it didn't show. He was short and fat and practically bald, and the remaining hairs on his bumpy scalp stood straight up in a lightly forested crewcut. Thick glasses rode on the south end of his nose and he spoke with a nasal mushiness. He had worked for twenty years in the Bureau of Weights and Measures in Washington, D.C., maintaining his membership in the Marine Corps Reserve and accumulating rank. It was a mystery why he had applied for a return to active duty. Kitagawa wrote the book on going along, getting along . . . his appointment as the investigating officer all but guaranteed that the forthcoming recommendation regarding how the charges should be treated by the command would be as the command wanted. Horn referred to Kitagawa as "Nippon's Revenge."

At the hearing Mad Dog Steiner presented the skeleton of his case, being sure that there was some evidence in the record on every element. There were no surprises. Taggart kept silent for the most part, objecting only that the time for argument came after the questioning, not during it, when Steiner began to call Markey a "murderer" and an "assassin" while framing his questions. He presented no evidence on Markey's behalf, preferring not to show his hand to Steiner.

Steiner had loaded the charge sheet. In addition to the main charge of the murder of Private Collins, Markey's descent on Morkowski from the mess hall tree and Private Bellof's bitten ear showed up as two counts of assault, and there were two counts of "disobedience of the general orders pertaining to the training regimen for recruits." It was alleged Markey had on numerous occasions interfered with the platoon's sleep between taps and reveille and had prevented the privates from eating by ordering them not to take any food when they passed through the chow line. Duck soup!

"Why are the privates so reluctant to testify against Markey?" Veronica whispered to Margolis, who was also watching the proceedings.

She was right. Private Bachman was on the stand, and Steiner was having to chase him all over with his questions to pin him down.

Q. "Private Bachman, you are in Hotel Company, 1st Platoon, correct?"

A. "Yessir."

Q. "Staff Sergeant Roger Markey was your platoon commander, right?"

A. "Yessir."

Q. "Describe the routine followed by your platoon at taps."

A. "Sir?"

Steiner repeated his question.

A. "The private doesn't understand, sir."

Q. "What don't you understand?"

A. "The question, sir," said Bachman, never looking up from his hands twisting nervously in his lap.

Q. "What is it about the question you don't understand, private?"

A. "The private doesn't understand what the captain means by routine, sir."

Q. "ROUTINE," Steiner almost shouted, as if saying it louder was the key to understanding. "What did the platoon do each night at taps?"

A. "Went to bed, sir."

Q. "I know that. I mean, what *else* did you do?"
A. "Went to sleep, sir."

Steiner was fuming.

Q. "What did Staff Sergeant Markey do after taps?"

Taggart objected that the question lacked foundation; there was no evidence the witness ever observed Sergeant Markey after taps. He was overruled.

A. "The private didn't see the platoon commander after taps, sir."
Q. "You saw him sometimes, didn't you?"
A. "During the daytime, yessir."
Q. "You saw him sometimes after taps, didn't you?"
A. "I think once he come in because he left his clipboard, yessir."
Q. "Did you see him any other times after taps?"
A. "The private doesn't remember, sir."

Steiner showed Bachman a copy of his statement from the investigation and asked if that was Bachman's signature.

A. "Yessir."
Q. "Do you recall Sergeant Markey coming into the squadbay after lights out and turning on the lights and knocking over bunks?"

"Objection, leading question—"
"Overruled," Kitagawa ruled.

A. "Sir, will the captain repeat the question?"

Steiner repeated the question.

A. "That was an awful long time ago—"
Q. "But you *do* remember," Steiner quickly interrupted.
A. "Vaguely, yessir," Bachman conceded grudgingly, and then,

brightening, he added, "but the platoon commander, he didn't hurt nobody, I remember nobody was hurt, sir."

So it went. The whole exercise was like pulling teeth. The only exception was the tall black private who testified that he saw Markey hit Collins in the stomach with a rifle the night Collins died. The witness looked directly at Markey as he spoke.

Veronica watched Roger Markey closely throughout the hearing. She could only see his back and once in a while his profile as he turned stiffly to speak to Taggart. Most of the time he sat erect, as unmoved as his "Smokey" campaign hat that lay on the counsel table in front of him.

Everything about him, his bearing, his features, made Veronica think of some marble statue instead of a man. It was obvious to her that he felt he had done nothing wrong. Too bad he didn't have to be the one to explain to Loren Collins's parents how their son had died.

When Taggart's turn came for summation he made two arguments. "The only serious charge on this charge sheet is the murder charge," he said matter-of-factly, speaking directly to Kitagawa. "None of the other charges are general court-martial offenses. As they're presently drafted, Staff Sergeant Markey may be convicted of one of these less serious offenses, but not of murder or any charge relating to the death of Private Collins. If that happens, Sergeant Markey is going to be saddled with a general court-martial conviction for misconduct which, under any other circumstances, would probably be handled by some nonjudicial punishment. The mere act of including charges such as these in a general court-martial amounts to punishing Sergeant Markey for the death of Private Collins before he's ever convicted of it. For this reason I respectfully request that the charges which do not relate to Collins be dropped."

Mike knew he was stretching a point with that argument; he also suspected that with Kitagawa he might as well be standing on his head singing the Marine Corps' Hymn as make any argument at all but he plunged on.

"*Sir,*" he said, jarring the colonel out of his daydreams, "it must be clear that the prosecution has failed to present any evidence that

Staff Sergeant Markey intended Private Collins any serious harm. Even if all the prosecution testimony is believed, there is no evidence of the kind of life-endangering intent that must be present to support a murder charge. I submit that Staff Sergeant Markey should not be forced to face even the remotest possibility of being convicted of murder, based on the evidence offered by the prosecution. I suggest that the appropriate recommendation on the evidence before you is a charge of involuntary manslaughter." That was, of course, for the record. He knew the colonel wouldn't allow it.

Mike sat down, knowing that if Kitagawa heard him at all it was only as the words journeyed in one ear and out the other. He had been mentally preparing for a murder trial ever since he first heard Go-Go and Steiner had made the case their special project. This Article 32 hearing was mostly a pro forma prerequisite. He had told his client not to get his hopes up.

Kitagawa told counsel that his recommendation would be expected by the end of the week and adjourned the hearing.

Veronica was waiting outside the courtroom when Taggart and Markey emerged, heading for the defense hooch. Taggart nodded to her.

"Mike, I have to talk to you, it's important."

"Can it wait a few minutes? I need to talk to Sergeant Markey . . . by the way, Sergeant Markey, I'd like you to meet Veronica Rasmussen."

"How do you do, Miss Rasmussen," Markey said quietly.

His subdued tone took Veronica by surprise. He sounded almost shy. Had he barked or snarled she would not have thought twice about it; perhaps he was more affected by what he had done than she had guessed. Or, more likely, he was affected by what was facing him. . . .

"How about I meet you here in a half hour?" Taggart interrupted her scrutiny of his client.

"Oh . . . fine, see you then," she said, still preoccupied.

Later, outside, Taggart and Veronica walked along the east edge of the drill field. The day had been warm and sunny again, but now the sun was very low and it was getting cool. Here and there a solitary figure walked across the vast, flat asphalt table, melting into its blackness after having gone only a short way. In the distance they could hear the almost musical chant of an unseen DI calling cadence as he marched his not visible platoon to chow.

Suddenly Mike stopped walking and snapped a salute that he continued to hold, even though she was the only other person in the vicinity. She could see from the headlights at the far end of the street back by headquarters that even the cars had stopped. Then she heard the plaintive notes of a bugle far away playing Retreat. Its melancholy call saluted the departing day. The sky was three shades of red in the west, and in the descending gloom Veronica felt for a moment as if she and Taggart were the last people alive on earth. She shivered.

After the last notes had died away they resumed walking. Veronica told him she planned to leave that evening. For a few moments Mike didn't say anything. When he finally did, he made some lame joke about how Go-Go and Mad Dog would miss having a press agent.

"Mike, I learned something about your Sergeant Markey today that I'd like to comment on."

"What's that?" His tone was half-curious, half-suspicious.

"I understand that Markey killed another marine with his fists and was court-martialed for it in Da Nang in 1969. Are you aware of that?"

The way Taggart stopped walking, abruptly, betrayed his ignorance of the fact, even though all he said was, "Say again."

Veronica repeated it.

"Where did you hear that?"

"You know I can't tell you that."

"What was the outcome of—" Taggart stopped. There was no sense in confirming he hadn't been aware of any such thing, although he knew it must be obvious.

"I'm not going to comment about it now," he said stiffly. "I hope you're not going to broadcast that."

"I most certainly am going to broadcast that. I wouldn't be doing my job if I didn't."

"Is your job to hang a man before he steps into the courtroom? Because if you spread that story around, the pressures that exist on this base for a conviction are going to become overwhelming. I could walk into that courtroom and present evidence that on the night Collins died Markey was doing volunteer work in a veteran's hospital and he'd still be convicted—"

"Mike, it's the truth. I don't know the details yet but I have confirmation that it happened. You can't ignore the facts. Once you begin to do that, where are you going to draw the line?"

"Suppose the so-called facts aren't relevant to the question of whether Markey killed Collins? If this Da Nang thing happened, even if it never gets into evidence against him, news of it will go around this base like wildfire. Inevitably some of the court members will have heard of it. It's human nature to believe a man committed an act a second time, if you believe he committed it a first time. Don't do this, Ronnie. Let Markey's guilt or innocence be decided on the facts of this case, not something that happened at a different time and place, in a very different world."

No wonder he's a lawyer, Veronica thought to herself as she listened to Taggart. It was a persuasive plea but her mind was made up.

"To my way of thinking," she said, "one of the facts of this case is that he's killed before, that he has a tendency to react with violence when provoked. The last broadcast I made I neglected to talk to you first. I'm sorry I did that, and I'm giving you the chance now to give me Markey's side of the story. But if all you're going to tell me is that I shouldn't broadcast this information, I'm just wasting my time."

For the second time in the brief period of their acquaintance, Taggart found himself saying, "Suit yourself, Miss Rasmussen." Only this time he was the one who turned and walked away.

In addition to being angry at Veronica, Mike was angry at Markey. They had spent hours covering every aspect, he thought, of the sergeant's career. How could Markey have failed to tell something like that? If true . . .

Instead of going home as he had planned he ran back up to the office and grabbed Markey's SRB. He leafed through it quickly to the pages having to do with disciplinary infractions. They were clean, just as he remembered from his first review.

He quickly called Third Battalion to see if Markey had stopped there after the hearing before going home. They hadn't seen him. He dialed Markey's home. As he listened to it ring he cursed himself for not thinking to ask Veronica to at least hold off until he'd had a chance to talk to his client.

Sergeant Markey answered the phone and told Taggart he was watching his kids while his wife was at the laundromat. He expected her back about 2000. He promised to come down and meet Taggart as soon as she came back. Mike told him something had come up that wouldn't wait until tomorrow and hung up. He wanted to be looking at his client when he asked him about Da Nang.

He next tried to reach Veronica at her hotel, but she had checked out before noon. He called the airport and had her paged. No answer. He called the local affiliate of the network that carried Veronica's station in Kansas City. They said she wasn't there. He left word. Finally he called the Kansas City station and left word.

Then he waited. He reviewed for the thousandth time the file he had accumulated on the case so far. It was so quiet he could hear the defense-hooch clock ticking. He had never noticed that before. Now and then solitary footsteps would wander down the otherwise deserted corridor outside. The admin office was closed, so there was no coffee. Suddenly, after the stampede of events of the last ten days, it seemed like time had stopped.

Roger Markey was in civilian clothes when he walked into the office, wearing a white sport shirt open at the collar, and a sport coat of deep burgundy leather—Taggart recognized the Okinawa tailoring—dark slacks, white socks and loafers. As might have been expected after their phone conversation, he was very subdued. He did not look or act like someone who had beaten a man, or was it two men, to death.

Taggart quickly told Markey exactly what Veronica had told him. "Tell me she's full of shit, sarge, please tell me she's full of shit."

Markey sat leaning forward in the hard wooden chair, his forearms on his knees, his hands together almost as if he was praying. His silence told Taggart Veronica was not full of shit.

After a full minute he said, "It's true, captain. There's more to it than that, but it's true." He did not look up. "I knew what it was as soon as you said it wouldn't wait."

"Why didn't you tell me about it when we talked the other day?" Taggart asked. "If I'm going to represent you I've got to know the worst. What if the prosecution found out about this and I didn't? The best way for me to help you is to prepare to meet whatever the other side comes up with, and this is no way to do it. I can't handle any more surprises."

"I was scared, sir. That's the truth. I was so scared after you called that for a couple of minutes I thought about headin' for Mexico. I know what everybody's gonna think when this gets out. It's the same thing I'd say if I was in their shoes. He did it once, he'll do it again. That's what they'll say, and I'll be fucked. I guess I knew all along that it'd get out. The Corps is like a goddamned small town. Everybody knows everything about everybody, and if they don't there's always someone who's glad to pass the word. I'm sorry for not telling you, sir. I'm sorry for draggin' you into this whole mess. I do trust you. Every time I talk to you I feel better about things. Even though things don't look too good, at least you can explain 'em so I can understand."

Nothing Markey had just said had been said with any spirit. All the snap was gone from his voice. It was obvious his client was in even lower spirits than Taggart was.

"Let's not count ourselves out just yet. Tell me what happened."

It had happened on Christmas Day in 1968. At the time Roger Markey was a buck sergeant, an E-5. He had been in Viet Nam for eight months and had been in continuous action. Looking back, it seemed almost like a dream. The caution and deliberation with which the platoon moved back and forth around the regiment's area of responsibility were obscured by the relentless and crippling heat, by dust billowing up in red clouds, caking their eyes and teeth and food, or by the rain that fell in rich, heavy curtains, warm and steaming, so that it seemed to hang in suspension, neither rising nor falling, a sodden blanket hanging dead in the air through which they moved. It seemed as if the platoon moved languidly like the fat jeweled hand of some long-departed French planter as he ineffectually brushed at a persistent fly while dozing in the afternoon.

They moved in extremes. The boredom of the endless routine, patrolling, digging in, waiting for night to end; the terror that punctuated their days and nights, sudden bursts of fire from unseen weapons, maiming explosions of mines, mementos from vanished enemies, the screams of friends who died or wished they had.

For the last two months Markey had been the platoon sergeant, during which time three lieutenants had been consumed. Late in the afternoon two days before the Christmas holiday, Lieutenant Gagliano had been hit by a single round, straight on, in the bridge of his nose. He died with his bars in his pocket, his .45 in a shoulder holster inside his utilities, carrying a rifle to further disguise his rank from snipers, who preyed on officers, corpsmen and radio operators. When the platoon cautiously got up from the cover of the rice paddy dikes to which it had been momentarily driven by the crack of the shot that killed Gagliano, it belonged to Markey.

It took them a long time to get home from that patrol. Home was a hill a mile and a half or so beyond the treeline from which the shot that had killed the lieutenant had come. The company was moving toward that hill, which overlooked a nameless village, for what seemed to Markey like the hundredth time since his wanderings through the countryside began. Now the platoon resumed its approach toward the trees with new respect, reconnoitering them with rifle fire as they came. Search revealed no sign of the assassin. No one had expected it would.

Once in the cover of the trees they stopped to call in a medevac for Gagliano. Nothing was available for two hours, by which time it would be completely dark. Charlie's time. Markey set the platoon in a make-shift perimeter while the corpsman and a fire team from the third squad fashioned a stretcher out of ponchos to haul the lieutenant's body in to the company. The platoon's last real stretcher had rotted after spending its entire combat life of two months soaked with the platoon's blood and sweat and the constant rain.

The trees grew on a bank that had once been a road built by the French. Emerging from the other side, the platoon had to descend a steep slope that the rains had beaten into thick soup. Markey was over on the extreme right with the third squad, seeing that arrangements were made for relief of the stretcher-bearers at intervals, as the platoon started down the bank. Some members of the third squad directly to his front had already reached the bottom of the bank when there was a tremendous roar that ripped through the rain, a breath of heat on the back of Markey's neck from a distance of more than fifty yards away. It came from his left in what he guessed was Sergeant Delbie's second squad sector. He could see nothing in that direction in the downpour and the gathering gloom, but shouts for him to get the hell over there told him there was trouble.

It was Galecton, the medical corpsman, who had stepped on it, whatever it was. The only evidence to be seen in the slime halfway down the bank was a crumpled, rusty fragment of an old C-ration can, discarded perhaps by his own platoon on an earlier visit to the neighborhood. Whatever calling card it had contained had literally blown itself away along with Galecton. The corpsman no longer existed. Here and there indistinguishable pieces of meat, bone and uniform were found, and these were collected and put in a small pile. Corpsmen rarely stepped on boobytraps; they usually walked on the interior of any formation, and Galecton had been in the midst of a wedge formed by the fire teams from the second squad. Someone in the second squad had probably walked within inches of the device without either seeing it or triggering it in the dusk and mud.

Markey looked up. He could not see where the rain ended and the lead sky began. "No armor against fate," he muttered. He had read that saying once somewhere and always remembered it. It had given him a kind of fatalistic courage. He was immune until his time came. Now, not for the first time, he was seeing the underside of the source of his courage. When his came, there would be no escape.

Fate had not been kind to Sergeant Delbie, the platoon's second squad leader. Markey had first met Dave Delbie in boot camp and they had gone through ITR together, becoming good friends. Markey had gone directly to Viet Nam, and had been medevaced back to the states eleven months later and eventually rejoined Delbie at Camp Pendleton. For several months they had raced all over southern California in Dave's Mustang, chasing girls and getting drunk whenever they were off duty. It was really the first time in his life that Markey had ever been on his own. In boot camp his ass had belonged completely to the Corps, and even in ITR liberty was a rare treat. His first tour in country had been spent entirely with his platoon before he was hit, and that had been followed by his hospitalization. Now he was eighteen and relatively free, and he shared his hard-won freedom with Dave Delbie.

Things changed when Markey met and married Sherill, but Delbie remained his closest friend. He had been the best man at their wedding, and weekends and holidays usually found a third place set at their table for him.

Markey had already reached his decision to try to make a career in the Corps, while someone in the system had passed over Delbie. Dave was now a corporal, perhaps the only corporal in the Marine Corps with an 03 MOS who had not been to Viet Nam. He was disturbed by it; he considered it some kind of insult to his manhood to be a Marine in a time of war and never have set foot in the war zone. When he heard that Markey had decided to volunteer for another tour in Viet Nam to improve his chances of having the career he wanted, Delbie decided he too would volunteer, although it required a nine-month extension of his original enlistment.

Their orders came in at the same time. They were both assigned to the First Marine Division. Arriving in the division replacement pool together, their luck had held and they eventually wound up in the same company and platoon, Markey a sergeant, Dave a corporal who was soon promoted...

Now Dave Delbie's luck had run out. The closest to Galecton when the bomb detonated, his left side had been shredded by the blast. His left leg was off at the knee and the jagged ends of the two bones of his left forearm protruded like some kind of ghoulish tuning fork, stark and bare, from the torn sheath of flesh that ended just below the elbow. The hand was gone. A piece of shrapnel had grazed his left eye, leaving a deep scratch across the cornea, and another fragment had pierced his left cheek and exited through his right one, leaving his mouth and tongue nothing but a pulp from which an occasional fragment of tooth protruded. He was peppered with lesser wounds in a dozen other places.

By the time Markey reached him, Delbie was surrounded by several other members of his squad, who were doing what they could to halt the flow of blood with the meager battle dressings they carried in their packs. Galecton's medical supplies had perished with him. Delbie was conscious, obviously in shock. He was propped up on a poncho liner under a tree so he wouldn't drown in his own blood. He stared un- blinkingly down at the wreck of his body. He groaned from time to time but otherwise was still.

Markey tried again for a medevac and learned there would be nothing now until morning. He briefed the company commander on the situ- ation. There was a distinct risk that even if the platoon made it back to the company position that night, casualties would be taken as a result of being mistaken for the enemy as they tried to pass through the lines in the rain and blackness, despite the radio. Markey was told to take a position where he was, dig in and stay put for the night. The mile and a half between them might as well have been a hundred except for the artillery cover the CO promised to arrange.

Quickly Markey set up the platoon in the treeline. He put LP's out north and south along the former road, ordered a fifty percent alert and settled in to wait until morning. Delbie was made as comfortable as possible at the CP, where Markey and Lance Corporal Kennedy, the radioman, set up a radio watch. No fires or lights of any kind were allowed.

After about three hours, Delbie began to surface from the initial shock of his wounds, and he began to scream and tear at the dressing on his lacerated eye with his remaining hand. Markey had to tie Dave's hand to his side to keep him from doing further damage. The screams were not shrill, high-pitched shrieks. Delbie's mangled mouth pre- vented that. They were hoarse, formless, animallike howls that seemed to be trying to throw Delbie's soul out of the ruin and agony of what was left of him. They penetrated Markey's shield of numbness. They made him frantic to do something to relieve his friend's misery, but he was powerless, the pain-killing morphine had gone up with Galecton. When he wasn't screaming, Delbie gurgled piteously. It was impossible to understand anything he was saying, but it was clear from his tone that he was begging Markey to help him.

Hour after hour the screaming and gurgling went on, until finally subsiding first to groans, then to whimpers. Delbie was plainly insane with pain and fear. At first Markey considered gagging him, but after making the rounds and learning that the rain so deadened the hoarse cries that they could hardly be heard on the platoon perimeter, he decided not to. He was sure Delbie's shouts, if Charlie heard them, weren't telling the VC anything they didn't know already.

Occasionally the drum of the rain would be split by the crump of artillery, as shells were lobbed at random intervals on likely approaches to the platoon's position. Once in a while the horizon far to the east was faintly illuminated by flares from the company position. Otherwise, the world outside the perimeter remained empty until dawn. About 0430 Delbie's soul succeeded in escaping.

Not long after first light, the medevac arrived for the lieutenant, Delbie and the remnants of Galecton. After that the platoon saddled up and rejoined the company around noon. The patrol had lasted about thirty-six hours. Three men, ten percent of those who began it, were now dead, including Roger Markey's greatest friend. They had not seen a single enemy soldier. It was Christmas Eve.

On Christmas morning Markey was flown into Da Nang, which was southeast of their AO. It was to be the beginning of his R and R. He was meeting Sherill in Hawaii.

He was a stone, without any feeling of joy at the approach of this brief respite from horror. He took no part in any of the holiday chatter among the half dozen or so marines being taxied from the battalion back to the air-conditioned, warm-water world of Da Nang. The platoon had received worse hits during his time with it, but none more frustrating, none more maddening. To die without ever seeing the enemy, to die on ground you personally had "secured" at least three times before, to be forced to stifle the urge to explode in retribution because there was no enemy to strike out at. Markey felt as if Delbie's missing hand was wrapped around his heart, squeezing it until every emotion ran through the dead fingers, leaving only a cinder.

Arriving at the air base, Markey reported to the Marine liaison and learned that he had nearly eight hours until his flight was scheduled to depart. He stuffed his valpack into a locker and headed for the NCO Club at the First Marine Air Wing.

He was sorry he came as soon as he walked in the door. A kind of beery revelry prevailed. Smoke was thick in the stale air, obscuring the emblems of the various Marine units in country that studded the walls. Behind the bar someone had pinned a red Santa's hat and white whiskers on the nude who reclined in the portrait there.

The group at the bar was laughing and shouting, sometimes singing along with the Christmas carols being played on the club's stereo. Markey wanted no part of them. He only wanted a corner where he could sit and refuel his numbness. He was edging his way past the revelers when he heard his name being called.

"Markey . . . Roger Markey . . ."

Looking around he saw someone standing up, apparently motioning to him through the haze about four tables away.

"Markey, I thought that was you. Jesus, how long has it been . . . boot camp?"

There were few people on earth Markey would less rather have seen than Leonard Gilpin. Gilpin had been in his platoon in boot camp, where he had been one long, uninterrupted pain in the ass. His constant complaints and second-guessing had been about the only divisive force in an otherwise tight, well-knit unit. Gilpin was a whiner, and now, Markey saw, he had somehow whined his way to the rank of corporal.

Gilpin and Markey had not been friends in basic training, they had coexisted. But now, twelve thousand miles and five years away, Gilpin was acting as though they were old buddies.

"Hey, Markey . . . c'mon over here and join us."

Empty chairs were at a premium, so Markey sat down and ordered from a tiny Vietnamese waitress who looked like she was no more than thirteen. When the drinks arrived Gilpin insisted on paying.

"Here's for the drinks," he said, handing some military currency to the girl, "and here's something for boom boom later on." He winked and added a twenty-five cent tip.

"You number ten hog, Gilpin." The girl giggled. Apparently Gilpin was a regular around there.

"Fucks like a mink," said Gilpin as the girl moved off.

Gilpin was stationed with the airwing in Da Nang. Markey remembered from boot camp how Gilpin had crowed over his assignment to aviation electronics school with those in the platoon who were headed for ITR, the infantry training regiment. "You dumb bastards are gonna be slogging through the mud carrying forty-five pound packs, eatin' C-rats and getting killed, and I'm gonna be pushin' buttons, eatin' steak and drinkin' whiskey." And that was the way it had turned out, Markey thought to himself in disgust.

Gilpin was accompanied by another corporal, whom he introduced only as Jim. The three of them sat drinking for more than an hour, with Gilpin doing most of the talking. He was now feeling very bitter toward the Marine Corps. He said he'd been enticed into reenlisting with a promise of being sent to Officer Candidate School, and then had been turned down. He'd been reading every piece of antiwar literature he could get his hands on for some time, and this, his first tour in Viet Nam, had been an eye-opener. Now, he said, he could see what a bill of goods the leaders had sold the American people. Viet Nam was their gift to the industrialists. It was the place they'd designated for the consumption of their products, it created their markets and in return the manufacturers and bankers lined the campaign coffers of the politicians.

Even in the unpolitical world of the enlisted man's Marine Corps, this stuff was old news. Markey had heard it all a dozen times before, and neither he nor Jim paid much attention to Gilpin's railings. It was just the kind of tired horseshit Markey would have expected Gilpin to be laying down. For all Roger knew, it was true, but he wasn't dumb enough to think he could do anything about it.

But then Gilpin's bite took a new turn. "You," he said, apparently dissociating himself and Jim from Markey, the unwashed grunt, "you're the killers . . ."

At this Markey looked directly at Gilpin. He'd said something that touched a nerve. "Why don't you shut up?" Markey said.

"You go around killing these people, they never asked you to come. You burn their villages, you trample their rice crops so their kids starve . . . You turn their daughters into prostitutes and you kill them. You kill them and kill them and kill them. You fuckers out swaggering through the vills, big-time Bush Marines, just raping an entire people, an entire country, just to line some fucking civilian's pocket . . ." Gilpin was waving his finger in Markey's face now and speaking very loudly. "You dumb fucks, you're the ones who keep the war going for those sons-a-bitches back home. *You're* the real enemy . . ."

Markey was leaning forward with both elbows on the table, staring hard at Gilpin, who seemed hypnotized by his own hate-filled anger. "I'm not gonna tell ya again, Gilpin, shut the fuck up."

"You dumb bastards—" Gilpin ignored Jim's restraining hand on his shoulder and shouted, "—the joke's on you. What jerks you are to keep letting yourselves get killed—"

Markey hit him then, a single punch that punctured the cloud of pain and fear and frustration that had been smothering him for months. Finally he was no longer impotent, finally he was able to do something. Delbie, Galecton, Gagliano, the hundreds of dead and wounded men he had watched filter through the platoon, the company, the battalion, the war went marching through his mind. Markey thought he'd hit Gilpin right between the eyes, but apparently the beer had slowed him enough so Gilpin had time to turn his head a little.

Gilpin went down like he had been shot. A crowd gathered around and another sergeant took the unconscious man's pulse.

"Man, you really fucked him up good," the other sergeant said, holding Gilpin's limp wrist and looking up at Markey from where he was kneeling. "I think this cat's dead, man. You killed him . . ."

Sherill Markey did not spend the week in Hawaii with her husband. After he failed to arrive as scheduled that first night, she went back to the hotel, sick with worry. First thing the next morning she contacted the Marine barracks at Pearl Harbor to try to find out what happened to her husband. They told her to go back to the hotel and wait, which she did. It was not the kind of hotel that had room service, and for two days she ate nothing because she wanted to be there when the phone rang to tell her what was wrong. She imagined all kinds of awful possibilities during those two lonely days, but not in her wildest imaginings did she ever think what she eventually learned on the evening of the second day. Then she went home.

Markey spent the time that was to have been his R and R in the III MAF Brig and later on a legal hold that was to last six weeks. He was charged with something relating to Gilpin's death, but it wasn't murder. He was assigned a lawyer and there had been a court-martial, in which he had been found "not guilty."

III

"That's about all there is to tell, sir," Markey said quietly, looking across the desk at Taggart. "I killed the guy. I didn't mean to, I swear to God I didn't mean to, but I did it, and I skated. But I didn't kill Collins."

Taggart had not once interrupted his client during the narrative. How many times had that same scene been played out among Americans in the last six years with only slightly less tragic results? He wished he had tape recorded the account so he could send it to Veronica Rasmussen.

Mike was heartened by the "not guilty" result. At least Markey had been given one good lawyer by the Corps.

"Who was your lawyer in that one, sarge?"

"Captain Bornholtz, sir."

Mike had never heard of him. "Was it a general or a special court-martial?"

"I dunno, special, I think. I never had nothin' like that Article 32 thing we had today."

Somewhere there was a record of that court-martial lying in a file drawer. Mike desperately wanted to know what it contained. Was it a live bomb ticking, waiting to be detonated somehow under Taggart's defense of this case like the explosion that had killed Galecton and Delbie? Or had the unknown Captain Bornholtz managed to completely defuse it?

"What was the evidence?" he asked. "Did you have a psychiatrist? Did he take the stand? Did you take the stand? What did you say?" The questions came pouring out.

"Hold it, sir, please slow down. I didn't have no psychiatrist. The prosecutor just showed the court some report proving Gilpin died and had this Jim guy testify that I'd hit Gilpin. Then Captain Bornholtz asked Jim a bunch of questions about what Gilpin had been doin' just before I hit him, and Jim told it pretty much the way it happened. Then I was a witness, and I told 'em what I just told you. Then the court members went into another room, and about half an hour later they came out and found me not guilty."

"Is that all the evidence that was presented?"

"Yes, sir. Captain Bornholtz, he wanted me to get some witnesses from the platoon or company that I had worked close with for a long time. You know, like we talked about for this court-martial, to say that I was a good marine and all that, but everybody I'd been in country with for any length of time was either dead or medevaced or rotated, so I didn't get nobody."

"The medical report, an eye witness and you, nothing else, is that right?" Taggart sighed.

"Yes, sir. Captain Bornholtz said afterward that I won with the He-Got-What-He-Had-Coming-Defense."

CHAPTER

Ten

ONCE WHILE wrestling in high school Taggart had stupidly let himself be pinned after piling up a big lead. His loss provided the team's margin of defeat. Long after everyone else had gone home he'd come out of the darkened school to his car in the snowy parking lot, disappointment still oozing. There, bundled up like an Eskimo, stood Cathy, waiting for him. They didn't have a date. He didn't know she'd be there.

"Thought you might need some cheering up," was all she said.

Now, in the wake of Roger Markey's story, Taggart needed cheering up again.

It was after eleven o'clock when Mike finally pulled his motorcycle up outside the apartment. He hadn't called to tell Cathy he'd be late. When he walked in she was watching TV. He was surprised she was still awake. He apologized for not calling, and he detailed the development that had delayed him.

"Why should you apologize, Michael? Why should you let me know where you are or what you're doing? If the Marine Corps had wanted you to have a wife, it would have issued you one. Isn't that the way it goes?"

Taggart put down the piece of cold chicken he had grabbed out of the refrigerator. "Cath, come off it. If you had a nickel for every time

I didn't call and let you know I'd be late in the last five and a half years, you wouldn't have two bits."

She didn't say anything.

"Whenever I raise it, you deny there's anything different between us, but there was a time when you'd never have said something like that. Cath, a man's life is at stake in this case, and you want me to believe you're upset about some cold potatoes. That won't hunt. You've been feeling sorry for yourself ever since we left Chicago. Nothing I do makes you happy... You know, for three years we were really something special. We could touch each other in a thousand ways without ever having to say a word. Making love with you was beautiful ... now it's like you can't wait to get it over with. What's wrong?"

Well, he'd said it. He'd said it without shouting, without cursing. He'd said the things that had been building up ever since his return. He was scared of what might happen, but whatever happened couldn't be worse than the last three months.

She was crying, something she rarely did, but she stuck to her guns. "Michael, think back. Think all the way back to when we first started dating. Even then, what I most wanted was a home, a place to settle down in. I could hardly wait to get out of college and get started. I thought we both wanted it. You never said you didn't. But here we are, married more than five years and still gypsies. Do you know how many times we've moved just in the two years you've been in the Corps? Five. Count 'em, Michael, five times."

Every word was true. But what had been their alternative, Canada? The draft? A reserve unit? Hadn't they agreed that the Corps was the best available choice? Times were tough. At least he'd come back...

"Oh, Michael, don't give me that." She wasn't crying anymore. "Ever since you got out of basic you've loved every minute of it. You even tell war stories about OCS; for God's sake. How many funny stories do you hear me telling about my year on the farm with the folks? Or my wonderful year teaching first graders in the very same grade school *I* went to...? Once you got back to Okinawa from Viet Nam you could jock it up with your friends, drink beer every night, ride motorcycles, go out with those school teachers—Wait, let me finish." She cut off Taggart's attempt to interrupt her at what he thought

116

was her suggestion that he had been dating the American school teachers on Okinawa. "I know you say you were just part of the group at those parties you wrote about, and I believe you. The point is, how many parties do you think I went to? Zero, Michael. It was the same story with friends, I didn't have a single one my own age. The Corps is a one-way deal, Michael."

Mike could grant her some of that, the loneliness and isolation she'd felt during his absence, but many of her friends from high school were still living in her hometown and she'd never called them. Plenty of the same sort of things she liked about life in suburban Chicago had been available in Ames and in San Diego, either inside the Corps or outside it, but she'd shown no interest in them.

"It's not the *same*, Michael. I don't *belong* to any of these places, I'm not... I'm just not at home in them. Home? I'd no more get started putting down some roots than we'd have to pull out and start all over. I'm sorry, but I don't think I can live like that. I may not be liberated, Michael, but at least I think I know what I want. Do you?"

It was long after midnight when they finally went to bed, with nothing resolved. Sleep was a welcome escape for both of them.

"Joe, Joe"—Colonel Guinn was backpedaling despite his seniority in rank—"things are going to work out all right. Take my word for it, this is going to wind up helping us."

Steiner stood in the midst of Go-Go Guinn's office, hands on hips. The doors were closed.

"All the same, colonel, I wish you'd discussed it with me first. I don't care if Taggart knows about Markey's other court-martial, but I'd hoped he wouldn't find out until after I'd decided how to make use of it. That "not guilty" finding's a problem. Besides, by having it broadcast, Taggart's been given a built-in motion for a change of venue. I'd bet anything he'll try to get this trial moved to another base."

Steiner was plainly upset. Go-Go was always trying to play the big man, and he had let Veronica Rasmussen coax the information about the Da Nang court-martial right out of him. He'd even told her where she could get verification.

Guinn couldn't see the harm. "Ah, he'll never win any motion like that, not the way the deck's been stacked around here in favor of drill instructors. Besides, you could never have kept Taggart from knowing. Even if Markey didn't tell him, it's right there in his record book."

"I didn't say I wanted to keep him from knowing," Steiner said, brandishing a sheet of paper he'd been holding. "I just said I wanted to postpone his finding out about it a little longer."

Well, the cat was out and it couldn't be undone. Steiner stalked back into his office, where he found Taggart leaning against his desk talking to Horn. Steiner tried to ignore him, but Taggart was there to see him.

"Joe," Taggart began, "did you happen to see the morning news on Channel 3?"

"What is this, Taggart, twenty questions?"

"You know damn well why I'm here. Markey's got a prior court-martial on homicide-related charges, and there's no mention of it in his book. Why don't you just take a peek in your desk and see if that page accidentally fell out in your rush to deliver the book to me. I'd kind of like to see what it has to say."

"You saying I took it out? Why don't you say what you mean?"

"Okay. That page's absence is no coincidence. Now why don't you try to find what's become of it—"

"Get out of here, Taggart." Steiner walked past him. "That news story was as much a surprise to me as it was to you. If you want to replace a missing record, follow the prescribed procedures, don't bother me with it. Now take off, I've got work to do."

As Taggart left, Steiner dropped the missing page, which he had been holding, into the wastebasket. "Son of a bitch thinks he knows everything."

It was 1000. Lance Corporal Gordon Byrd from Pampa, Texas, stood at ease in the guard shack at Gate 2. The midmorning watch was slow. Everyone was at work so there was no traffic, even Barnett Avenue outside the gate was practically deserted. Across Barnett the demonstrators protesting that recruit's death looked like they were dozing in the sun. Byrd yawned. He wished he could take a nap. Two more hours until his relief was due.

Idly Byrd watched a hippy who was walking slowly along the sidewalk from the west toward the gate. He was making very poor progress. His head was hanging down and he swayed slightly as he walked. "Probably stoned," the lance corporal decided.

As the bearded, long-haired figure finally drew even with the gate, he seemed to list to his right and appeared about to wander unintentionally aboard the base. Byrd stepped out of his booth to stop him.

"Hold it, mister, halt."

The hippy looked up dully but continued to stumble forward onto base property. Byrd hurried over in front of him and stopped.

"Hold it right there. You can't come aboard this base without some identification. Either explain what you're here for or turn around."

"Hey, man, take it easy. I just come in to take a pee. Man, there ain't a tree or a bush or anything out there."

"Well, you can't take a pee in here. Go find a gas station or something. Now get out of here."

"Don't get uptight, man, don't get uptight. Just let me go right over there in those bushes, okay? I'll only be a second," he said, pointing across the lawn to his right, in the direction of the general's quarters.

"For the last time, I'm telling you to leave this base or you'll be put off."

"Hey, man, haven't you ever had to take a pee?" He began to fumble with his zipper. "I'll take a pee right here on your fucking spitshine—"

Byrd sensed more than saw the movement behind him. He whirled to see three more bearded longhairs moving through the gate on the opposite side of the guard shack.

"Hey, what do you think you're doing? *Halt,*" Byrd shouted, and took a quick step in their direction. The three sprinted through the gate and ran off across the base as he spoke, each in a different direction. Behind Byrd the one looking for a place to take a leak set sail for the general's quarters.

The midmorning tranquility in the defense hooch was shattered by

119

the simultaneous wail of at least a dozen sirens.

"INCOMING," Margolis instantly yelled and jumped under his desk.

Taggart, who had just come back from his confrontation with Steiner, looked around at the other defense counsel.

"What the hell do you think's going on?" Loring said.

A military police vehicle rocketed past on the street outside, headed in the direction of the general's quarters.

The base was suddenly on full alert. Warrent Officer Stepp from the Admin Discharge office ran into the defense hooch to ask if they knew what was going on. There was at least a squad of MPs over by Gate 2, he reported.

Taggart was dialing the trial hooch to see if they knew what was happening when there was a tremendous uproar somewhere not far outside the office.

"JESUS CHRIST, WHAT THE BLOODY HELL IS THIS?" came the unmistakable roar of none other than Colonel Katkavage, the chief of staff. Followed by the sound of running feet in the hall as the offices along the corridor emptied to see what had the Kat so upset. The sirens continued to shriek.

The Headquarters Building at MCRD was situated at the north end of the drill field. It was separated into two wings by a large arch in the middle. Two stories high, the faces of the arch were open all year in San Diego's mild weather. Into each side of the arch were built the entrances to the corridors that ran the length of the respective wings. The two wings were connected on the second floor, where the legal offices were located, by walkways that ran around the perimeter of the arch. Both the center and sides were open except for a low rail. The commanding general's flag flew from a pole on the roof above the arch. It was the main entrance to headquarters.

The defense hooch was nestled just off the northwest corner of the arch, so Taggart and the other defense counsel were able to get a ringside position among the crowd that gathered. There on the floor below stood Katkavage in a cold fury. He was staring at two signs freshly spray-painted in large red letters on the buff-colored stucco wall just inside the arch. "MARINES SUCK" and "FUCK KILLER MARKEY."

That explains the sirens, Mike thought as he walked back to his office. He guessed from the ongoing blare that the two signs Katkavage had found wouldn't be the only ones. For any potential court members who might have missed the morning news about Markey's Da Nang court-martial, this sure ought to bring it to their attention.

A neighborhood Italian restaurant straight out of the movies, La Sicilian was tiny, family-owned-and-operated, and the waitresses spoke Italian to each other, not just memorized phrases to the customers. There were red-and-white tablecloths and wax-covered chianti bottles on the tables, knickknacks on the shelves behind the counter, and a short, stout waitress named Lucia who sang beautifully as she waited on tables when things were slow. Now she beamed in friendly recognition as she greeted Mike and Cathy, who had eaten there several times during their two and a half months in San Diego.

They sat near the back, and Lucia let the candle at their table and took Mike's order for a beer. When she came back with it they ordered.

"Well, today was Kendon's last day," Mike said about one of the lawyers in the trial hooch who was getting out.

"Oh, yes, well, I knew he was getting close. I was talking to his wife at Margolis's party. That sounds like a good firm he's joining. They'll loan their associates what they need for a down payment on a house at low interest and postpone principal payments for five years. The Kendons are buying a house right away . . ."

Mike's jaw tightened. He didn't say anything, but Cathy hadn't missed the reaction. "What's so wrong with buying a house? It makes more sense than living in apartments and throwing rent down a rathole all your life."

"I guess so . . . in some circumstances . . ."

"When wouldn't it be?"

"Well, when your employer who's loaning you the money is also telling you which neighborhood they want you to live in."

That seemed to take Cathy by surprise, and Mike knew he should have stopped there, but he didn't. "That outfit where Kendon's going interviewed at Michigan while I was there, and those down-payment loans were part of their bail even then. But the firm tells you the

121

neighborhood where you're supposed to buy. I'm betting that's the deal Kendon's buying into. That same bunch made everybody they were seriously considering take psychological tests to make sure they didn't get anybody who wasn't their type. Horn calls them Big Brother. I asked Kendon the other day if he was ready to be told what color skivvies to wear on Wednesdays. He thinks it's funny now, I wonder how funny he'll think it is a year from now."

"That shouldn't be such a problem for anyone who's spent three years in the Marine Corps," Cathy said quickly. "At least they're out of the Corps and settled down somewhere beginning a career, a life."

Taggart didn't try to control his grimace.

"Well, you better start thinking about it, Michael, because a year from now it's going to be your turn."

He didn't say anything, he didn't have to. His unspoken dread at going back to Chicago, as well as his feeling he wasn't suited for it, had been apparent to her since Quantico. She had hoped that a year away would show him that the things he considered hypocrisy and politics, and hated so much, were pretty much the same everywhere so he might as well make the best of it. Instead he had come back more hostile about it than ever. He wasn't going to change. That seemed obvious . . .

"What're you going to do, Michael, stay in the Corps?"

"No . . . I'd have to start giving a shit about stuff besides the clients, get to be another Mad Dog." Actually he had thought about staying in the Corps, but he knew what he liked about it wouldn't last. Horn, Margolis, Loring, Beeson, the people he'd been drawn to, would all get out, and he'd be left with the Mad Dogs, the Go-Gos, the Kitagawas. As his seniority accumulated he'd be promoted up and out of the courtroom into some damn administrative capacity. The trials, the competition, trying to outsmart, outpersuade the opposition was what he liked. And sometimes you got a Markey to defend that you could care about . . .

"Michael, how do you decide what to give a shit about?"

It was a fair question, though he wasn't in the mood to admit it. He didn't exactly have all the answers either. It was like what they said about obscenity . . . no one could define it but everybody thought they knew it when they saw it.

"You know, Michael, it seems you just have such contempt for practically any kind of authority I can think of . . . the church, the government, the law firm, the command . . . *Somebody's* got to be in charge, don't they? You're not hurting, you've got plenty to eat, a nice place to live, a good job waiting for you. What's wrong with security and success, and they're practically yours for the asking. Or taking. Maybe it's *your* values that are cockeyed."

"Could be, except I wonder if Lynn West would agree. Or Roger Markey."

Lynn West had been a close friend of both Mike and Cathy throughout childhood and had been the best man at their wedding. He too had joined the Corps and become a helicopter pilot. He had been killed trying to extract a Marine platoon from a hot zone not far from An Hoa. Mike and Cathy had learned of Lynn's death their last day in Chicago, the same day Cathy had found out she was pregnant. Mike invoking Lynn, who in many ways had been as close to Cathy as to Mike, really hurt.

"Jesus, Michael, you're going to let this wreck your life, aren't you? You're just going to spend all your time going around being pissed off about things you can't do anything about. Why? What's the *point?*"

Taggart shrugged and went to work on his plate of spaghetti. How could he make her understand, especially when he wasn't sure he really understood himself . . .

"Another thing," she went on, not accepting his silence, "how can you use Lynn's name in the same breath as Markey's? Any trouble Markey's in, he made for himself—"

He looked directly at her. "You really think Markey killed that kid, don't you?"

"I *really* don't give a damn about your precious Markey right now. I'm talking about us . . ."

"Well, think about this. In a way . . . the same kind of thinking that got Lynn killed is trying to kill Markey . . ."

123

CHAPTER

Eleven

THE ANONYMITY of the featureless landscape of eastern Kansas was further masked with snow from a recent storm, but a bright sun was shining, forcing Veronica to put on her dark glasses as she drove. She was happy she had decided to drive out to meet with Martha Collins instead of just talking over the phone. It was Veronica's first day back after eight days in San Diego and her desk was a mess, but maybe a further story would come out of this visit. Even if it didn't, the drive was exhilarating. She so seldom ventured off city streets and urban freeways that it was like discovering new worlds the rare times she did drive to the country. She did not drive fast, preferring to soak up the spaciousness of the almost unbroken horizon speared only occasionally by a solitary grain elevator.

She watched a hawk circling high in the empty sky and took note of an abandoned farmhouse, speculating about the good times some family must once have enjoyed there and wondering about what had reduced it to its present low estate. How could she have groun up in the midwest and know so little about farming? The Collins's farm was the first one she had ever even been on.

Veronica felt there was much she had learned on her trip to San Diego that couldn't be gotten from a newscast. Markey, Steiner, Guinn, Taggart, the demonstrators, their personalities and interrelationships, the background of recruit training, the atmosphere at MCRD—there had been much Martha Collins had wanted to know at the time of their first meeting that she hadn't been able to find out. Would she still want to know the answers Ronnie now had, or would talk about these things only aggravate healing wounds?

Veronica suspected that the wounds left by the death of her son had not begun to close for Martha Collins. Her sad, distant tone over the phone, the reference to her daughter dropping out of college, the fact that she didn't feel she should be away from home for any length of time right now all said that time, the supposed healer, had not yet begun its work...

When she arrived, Mrs. Collins came out of the house to meet her, assuring her that the car would not be in the way of the men working with some huge piece of equipment in the large shed across the farmyard from the house. There seemed none of the melancholy in Martha's voice that Veronica thought she had heard over the phone. She remarked on Ronnie's newly acquired suntan, adding she had never been to California.

Inside the house was as Ronnie remembered it: big, warm, neat and old-fashioned. For almost two hours Ronnie related the things she had seen, the conversations she had had, the overall impression she had gained of the place where Martha Collins's son had died. Martha knew about the pending court-martial, but this was the first she'd heard of Johnson's eyewitness account of the assault or of Markey's earlier court-martial in Viet Nam. She seemed most interested in what Veronica knew least about, the personality and character of Staff Sergeant Markey.

"How could a man with two little children of his own do such a thing?" she said. "I'm sure those men have to be tough and that something just broke inside Loren when that sergeant hit him, but you read his letters, Ronnie, something had broken inside Loren a long time before any of this happened. What kind of a...a system is it that makes people treat each other that way? Maybe if people can be made to see how wrong that is, well then, maybe some good will come out of all this..."

Veronica wanted to reinforce Martha's hope, but years spent watching miles of protest marches and days of demonstrations that didn't seem even to chip at the immunity of the powers-that-be from considerations of right and wrong made it difficult for her to do so with any sincerity. Still, she supposed, she wouldn't have insisted on going to San Diego after their first visit if she didn't share some of Martha's feeling. Seeing Markey convicted would be a step in the right direction...

When Martha began to fix some lunch Ronnie offered to set the table. Martha told her to set two places, but she had prepared three plates and before sitting down took one of them up the stairs. Soon she was back, plate still in hand.

"I don't think my daughter Linda is going to let us forget the past for a long, long time," she said, putting the untouched plate of food down on the counter and sitting down.

Outside the sun was melting the snow on the Collins's roof, and the melted water trickled noiselessly past the kitchen window in a small but steady stream, distorting the sunbeams that shone through in their play on the floor. Now and then the sound of male voices from the yard would penetrate the solitude, but Veronica didn't hear them. There were no interruptions in the sunny farm kitchen as little by little Martha Collins unburdened herself of the story of her daughter's withdrawal since her brother's burial.

The girl who had so attacked her brother over his decision to enlist was now punishing herself terribly. Only fifteen months apart in age, they'd had only each other during the isolation of early childhood on the farm. They liked to make up word games in which one would start a sentence and the other would finish it, spinning together stories from their shared imaginings. The result was an empathy between them that reminded everyone who met them of twins. They had memorized each other's parts in the church Christmas pageant, and Linda had been able to recite Loren's piece in addition to her own when he was struck with stage fright. They played the piano together as if it was being played by one musician with four hands and appeared in many local recitals. Even after both were in school and had other friends, it was obvious that Linda and Loren Collins were a team. Loren earned his first bloody nose trying to keep the Hays kid from picking on her. When Linda

127

was an attendant in the homecoming court during her senior year in high school she chose Loren, only a sophomore by a quirk of birthdays, to escort her, ignoring the teasing of her classmates. When Linda went away to college, Loren was the member of the family she usually wrote to. She took pains to describe campus life for him, and on big college weekends she would invite him to visit, arrange a place for him to stay and find him a date.

It was in the middle of her sophomore year, Loren's senior year in high school, that Linda became involved in the campus antiwar movement. She carried signs and picketed, and twice her passive resistance to the authorities trying to keep order had resulted in her brief arrest. She changed her major from music to journalism to arm herself, she said, for the coming battles and wrote protest letters to the school paper, the Kansas City papers, congressmen, anyone she thought would listen. Her letters to Loren and her parents were filled with angry rhetoric at the widening of the war, rising casualty lists, increased draft calls and daily scenes of death and destruction beamed by satellite from the jungles and rice paddies of Southeast Asia. God, how she hoped Loren wouldn't have to go, or would refuse.

It had been like a slap in the face when he enlisted that summer. He had tried to explain, but there was nothing he could say, nothing she could accept. Her feelings for him were reversed. She screamed at him. He was a pig, a murderer. If he thought he had to do something like killing people and burning their homes to prove his manhood he could expect no support from her. So she gave him the silent treatment. And that was the way it was when she returned to school in the fall. There were no more letters for Loren, no more weekend invitations. Loren waited to go on active duty until after the harvest, and Linda had maintained her disdainful silence at Thanksgiving, the last time she saw her brother alive. When he called her at school ten days later to say good-by on the evening of his departure for San Diego, she refused to talk to him. . . .

"Now," Martha was saying, "I'm afraid she's blaming herself for what happened to Loren. That doesn't make sense but there you are . . . We've tried everything we can think of, our doctor has talked to her, and our pastor and her roommate from school but she just doesn't respond at all. She sits for hours like she's in a daze, hardly moving, and then all of a sudden she'll look like she's about to strangle on something. The muscles of her face go tight and she'll hunch her shoulders and just sit and shiver. She'll go for two or three days without a bite, then we'll hear her going down the stairs in the middle of the night. She hasn't spoken to a soul since the funeral."

By the time Martha's story was told, the kitchen was in midafternoon shadows, and the relief Veronica had felt earlier at what she had interpreted as Martha Collins's resilience had turned to amazement at her strength and ability to endure.

As Veronica drove east back toward Kansas City her spirits no longer soared. She felt cold, although the car heater was all the way on, and the gloom of the eastern sky in the late winter afternoon swallowed her alive.

Friday night. Ronnie walked into her dark apartment, switched on a light, took off her gloves and scarf and hung up her coat. Funny, she thought, what a chore that seems after a week of balmy southern California.

Back only three days and it seemed like three months. Kansas City was cold and snow-swept. The newsroom smelled of stale tobacco and cold coffee; the arguments and shouting at work, even Eddie's semi-benevolent yelling, gave her a headache. Downtown traffic seemed to move at a snail's pace.

It was stupid, she told herself, suddenly to become impatient with weather she had lived in all her life, with sounds and smells she'd considered marks of finally reaching a place in the world of journalism she'd always aspired to. "It's always tough to come back from vacation," she told herself as she leaned back on her couch and went through the day's mail. Bills, ads, a reminder from the landloard not to play televisions and stereos so loud at night.

"I hope they delivered one of these personally to that jerk next door," she said to the notice. Sweeping the discards off the coffee table, she turned on the television on her way to the kitchen, where she began to think about dinner.

She had declined an invitation to dinner from Norm Karocek, the

129

guy she went out with more than any other. Norm had announced big plans for a night at The Rotunda, the most expensive restaurant in town, a "welcome home from the land of the freaks," he'd said. She had begged off, claiming jet lag. She wondered what Taggart or his black DI friend, Dave Richardson, would say if they knew they were considered freaks by Norm Karocek. She wondered what Norm would think if he knew she didn't necessarily share his opinion. Having come of age on the campuses of the midsixties, the word "marine" had always conjured up the image of some bullet-headed thug running through a brick wall just to get to the other side. She was still digesting the thought that they might be people, like anybody else, at least some of them—but *not* Markey. And there were more like Markey, she suspected, than any other kind...

Fishing in her briefcase, she pulled out a paperback book Taggart had given her, the life story of a general named "Chesty" Puller, a sort of living Paul Bunyon of the Marine Corps, according to Taggart. Saying that it was his understanding that a good reporter always did her background research, Taggart had given her the book with the caveat that while much of what she read would seem crazy to her, she should keep in mind that Chesty's business was war, which was insane anyway. It might give her some insight into the values of the world she was reporting.

She thumbed it idly, glancing at the collection of photographs midway through. Ol' Chesty even looks like the Marine Corps' bulldog, she thought.

She was about to take her first bite of the tossed salad that was to be her meal and begin reading about Chesty Puller when the news commentator on the television that had been droning in the background mentioned San Deigo. Ronnie began to listen.

"... defense counsel for Staff Sergeant Roger Markey, the Marine drill instructor charged in the beating death of recruit Loren Collins, at the Marine Recruit Depot in San Diego, responded to earlier reports that his client had previously been court-martialed for beating another marine to death in 1969 by saying that the earlier court-martial had resulted in his client being found not guilty..."

"Damn you, Taggart," Ronnie muttered, "why couldn't you have at least given that to me. It's my story."

Hearing about the Markey case on television upset her. At first she was angry, considering it as she did to be her exclusive province. But after a while her anger turned to disappointment . . . so what if Markey was found not guilty? No doubt that meant he got off on some legal technicality. It didn't mean that he hadn't killed someone with his fists. It didn't mean that he was automatically qualified for duty as a drill instructor, where temptation for brutality was so strong. Somehow she'd thought Taggart would have come up with something better.

Still, word of "her" case piqued her appetite for *Marine,* the title of General Puller's saga. She plunged in.

Twelve

ONE WEEK to the day following the Article 32 hearing, Lieutenant Colonel Kitagawa filed his expected recommendation: "It is recommended that the charges under investigation against Staff Sergeant Roger Markey be referred to general courts-martial without amendment."

Steiner put his chop on it without reading it, nor did the recommendation gather any dust on Katkavage's desk. Within two days the interim fate of Staff Sergeant Markey was squarely in the hands of the commanding general.

General Fitzroy was a member of the clean-desk club. Ordinarily work placed on his desk in the morning was completed before he went home that night. Such was not the case with the charges against Markey. Day after day, silence.

Steiner would walk down to the general's office and inquire of the general's aide whether the Markey case was among the matters being handled by the CG that day. And each time he would walk back gnawing his upper lip, trying to figure out what the delay might mean. As the days passed he became jumpier and even more irritable. He worried that the longer it took for the general to decide, the more likely the decision would go against the prosecution.

Taggart allowed himself to think so too, and kept his fingers crossed

. . . Long before the Markey case Taggart, who had been stationed at several bases, had concluded that being a general was as close as anyone could come to being a king in the United States. Marines saluted generals' cars even when generals weren't in them. The atmosphere aboard a base depended on the personality of its commanding general. If the CG was a tyrannical despot, then the base was administered as a tyrannical despotism with nitpicking regulations, rigidly enforced, often in situations where they were never intended to apply. To Mike, something of an iconoclast and product of a liberal legal education, and a nonmilitary home and family in which most of his discipline had been instilled by his parents' personal example rather than by threats of punitive action, the atmosphere was often oppressive. Mike felt he knew the commanding general personally at each of the bases even though he had never met any of them.

Generals also tended to be isolated by their staffs, each member of which jealously guarded his individual fiefdom of responsibility. Staff recommendations tended to be based on precedent, on the way things had always been done before, as a shield against risking the disapproval of the reigning despot. "One hundred and ninety-five years of tradition, uninterrupted by progress" was how the saying went.

MCRD was the best base Taggart had ever been stationed at. If General Fitzroy was a despot, he seemed a relatively benevolent one. When Mike had reported aboard, the general took time out to meet and welcome him. He tried to do that with all his officers. He had allowed himself to be persuaded to permit motorcycles on base. On occasion he had been known to walk unaccompanied and unannounced around the base in civilian clothes just to see how things were working. He was friendly, if in a detached sort of way. His base was run with common sense. Taggart admired General Fitzroy, thought him a good leader.

Among the papers supporting Kitagawa's recommendation, that had been so hastily forwarded up the chain of command, was a single typewritten page setting forth substance of Mike's summation at the Article 32 hearing, a request that the charges other than murder be dropped and that the murder charge itself be reduced. Taggart had managed to have it included with the connivance of Lance Corporal

Adams, one of the legal clerk-typists that Mad Dog tyrannized.

After two weeks Fitzroy finally took action. It was to be a general court-martial, and murder was to be the only charge. Won one, lost a big one. Sink or swim. Mike leafed through the package of papers returned from the CG's. The insert was nowhere to be found.

Three days after their dinner at La Sicilian, while having dinner at home, Cathy announced that she had decided to go back to Chicago for a visit. All things considered, Mike thought this might be as good a time as any. It was only three months after being reunited, but she made it plain that she was just marking time until he got out of the Corps. Maybe, she said, this would make time seem to pass more quickly for her.

"When do you want to go?"

"Tomorrow morning. I've already got the ticket."

Mike could sense things beginning to fall apart. "You're not visiting Chicago so much as you're escaping this place. Isn't that right?"

She bit her upper lip and didn't say anything.

"Are you coming back?"

"I don't know."

"Cath, do you love me?"

She nodded. "Yes."

"Well, then don't go, not like this. If you want, I'll take some leave after the Markey case is over and we'll go back together. This tour is going to be over in a year—"

"It won't be over, Michael. You'll get out of the Corps, but it won't be over."

"Meaning?" He knew the answer before it came.

"Michael, you were restless even before you left Chicago. The Marine Corps has only made it worse."

"Cath, it was tough to look ahead or think of Morgan, Miller in terms of a career when I had the Corps ahead of me. It'll be different when we go back, it'll change, you'll see..." The words almost stuck in his throat.

"It would be nice if I could believe that. Ever since law school you've wanted to be something *else*. You didn't like law school."

"You can't hold that against me. There must be thousands of—"

"That don't like law school? Maybe so, but I've begun to think there's always going to be something about everything you try that you'll find phony or that will disappoint you or not live up to your exalted standards."

"Not loving law school or being a glorified spear carrier at some law factory seems lousy evidence for your damning conclusions."

"It's not just what turns you off, Michael, but how you react. I can foresee you repeating that scene with Ann and Harvey over and over again. Different issues, different players, the same clash of . . . values. I need to decide if I can live with that." She got up from the table and went upstairs and started packing without touching her food.

The next morning Mike put her on the plane for Chicago. They spoke very little driving to the airport and waiting for the plane. She got her boarding pass and was ready to board as soon as the gate was opened.

"Good-by, Michael, take care of Feodot," was what she said. She also kissed him on the cheek.

They both felt like hell, but they weren't talking.

Taggart didn't go to work that day. He went home and exchanged the car for his cycle and disappeared as fast as he could into the mountains east of San Diego.

One morning, about a week after Colonel Kitagawa made his recommendation about the charges against Staff Sergeant Markey, during the period when Steiner was wearing out the passageway between the CG's office and the trial hooch, Taggart found a letter waiting for him on his desk when he arrived at work. He almost never received mail at work. Lately he hadn't received much at home either. Cathy had handled most of their correspondence with their families. Mike assumed she'd told her folks about her decision, so there'd be no letters from that side, and he hadn't written his mom and sisters since she'd left. He wasn't looking forward to telling them the current state of affairs. There'd been no word from Cathy since she'd left.

Picking up the envelope he immediately saw from the return address that it was from Veronica Rasmussen. He checked the name of the

136

addressee, thinking someone had given him Steiner's mail by mistake, but it was addressed to him. The envelope appeared to be her personal stationery, addressed in longhand. After all those letters he'd so recently gotten from Cathy while he was in WESPAC, after all the times he'd come running when Mail Call was sounded, and the rush of happiness he'd felt whenever his name was called and an envelope in Cathy's handwriting was passed back from hand to hand by the others who crowded around the mail clerk at the law center on Okinawa, after the hours of devouring what she wrote, rereading the lines in an attempt to divine whether they held her real feelings, in the wake of such an ingrained ritual it seemed strange to be receiving a letter from another woman.

March 2, 1971

Dear Mike:

I just finished *Marine*. I'm glad Chesty wasn't my father. Anyway, thanks for the suggestion.

I suspect that your motive for making the suggestion had less to do with your desire to deepen my understanding than it did with your desire to promote your client's point of view. If that's so, I certainly understand, just like I understand your desire that I not report Markey's Da Nang court-martial. I hope you understand that it was something I had to do. We both have our clients, Mike.

Since coming home I've seen two reports of the Markey case on the news. They made me jealous, both of the reporters who are horning in on "my" story and of reporters who are in the San Diego sun while I'm in the Kansas City sleet and snow. I'm trying to persuade my editor to let me come back out for the trial, so you may not have escaped being humiliated by me on the racquet-ball court after all.

Hope your other cases are going well.

Best wishes,
Ronnie

Taggart was tempted to write back that he hoped that with more understanding would come greater tolerance of his client's position but decided against it. It was clear he wasn't going to be able to redeem Staff Sergeant Markey in the eyes of the press.

The letter could not be interpreted as an apology, or even a truce offering. Still, he didn't think she had written just to thank him for the book.

Thirteen

SHE HAD seen Veronica Rasmussen on television. The woman seemed bright and poised and pretty, and she'd gotten things that not long ago Linda Collins had hoped to achieve for herself. But not anymore. Now Linda no more wanted to see Veronica Rasmussen than her pastor or her doctor or her roommate or anyone else her parents lined up to cheer her up. In fact, she wanted to see Veronica least of all. Veronica had been to San Diego to investigate Loren's death, her mother had said so when she told her she'd asked Veronica to come back to talk with her daughter. Linda knew there was nothing the woman could say that could possibly make any difference. She would only make it worse.

She had to get away. But from what? This house? Her family? Osage City? School? Linda had considered getting away from all of it since her brother died. More than once she had packed and unpacked. Yet there she lay on the bed, fully dressed in the dark, staring up at the fixture in the middle of the bedroom ceiling. She couldn't see it in the dark but she knew it was there, just like she knew where everything in her life was. Nowhere. And when someone's nowhere, she thought, there's nowhere to run.

Linda passed the night with such thoughts before Veronica's third trip to the Collins home, this time at Martha Collins's request that

Ronnie try to convince Linda that the way to survive her miseries was to fight to overcome them. Ronnie didn't know if she was up to it, but now rehearsed what she would say as she drove west along the narrow two-lane highway leading to Osage City, early on an overcast March morning.

Sometime long after midnight Linda reread the letters Loren had written from boot camp. For her brother to have died thinking she hated him . . . too profoundly sad for weeping, blank and unseeing, sometime before dawn, Linda ran away from herself.

An hour before Veronica arrived, Martha Collins walked into her daughter's room and found the haunted girl hanging from the light fixture. Neatly arranged on her bed were Loren's letters and a note.

> Dear Mom and Dad,
>
> I have done a terrible thing. I used Loren's love as a weapon against him. And because of that he began to die long before the final blow was stuck. I thought I was protecting Loren. I tried so hard to do the right thing, even though it hurt so much, but all I did was let the one person I loved most die believing I hated him. The love I have always been given I have repaid with scorn. I truly do not deserve to be with you. I do not deserve to be anywhere at all.
>
> Linda

Whatever her mood, in the five years Veronica Rasmussen had worked for Eddie, she had been a spark. There had been no odds she did not believe could be overcome. She had displayed an almost uncanny intuition that put her a step ahead of her competition. Veronica lit fires under people, she made everyone around her more effective. When she was reporting on one of her special projects, the station's ratings soared. Several times, Eddie knew, she had turned down better offers from stations in larger media centers. He didn't quite know why, but he did know it was only a matter of time before the right opportunity would come along and she would be gone. Meanwhile, she was the station's brightest star.

During the three days since she'd been back from her unplanned intrusion into the immediate aftermath of Linda Collins's suicide, Eddie

Logan had watched Veronica prowl morosely around the newsroom. It was like someone had pulled the plug. All of the indignation that she'd shown at the death of the first Collins child seemed to seep out of her with the death of the second. For the time being she appeared to have lost the starch of her original resolve, leaving only grief. But unless Eddie missed his guess, her inherent strength would pull her back before much longer.

On the morning of the fourth day after her return from Osage City, Veronica was waiting outside Eddie's office when he arrived. He looked at her, trying to gauge her mood as he hung up his hat and coat and threw his galoshes in the corner.

"Eddie, I've got to go back to San Diego," she said quietly. Her voice was firm, not angry like a month ago.

Logan had known that it was coming, and he knew what he had to say, although the words nearly stuck in his throat.

"Ronnie, I can't send you, although God knows I wish I could. The story is getting attention, you've achieved your purpose, you stirred up the interest. This one isn't going to be swept under the rug."

"Eddie," she said, "that family . . . I saw them that morning. It's not just a story anymore, I feel like I've been swallowed up by it. Eddie, I've got to follow through on it for myself as well as for the story. It belongs to me . . ."

"Hey, Ronnie, I can see how you feel, it's written all over you, but you don't even know if there's going to be a trial yet. That general's still sitting on it—"

"No, he's not. It was on the late news last night. General court-martial on a single charge, murder, starting April 12th."

"April 12th. Ronnie, that's a *month* from now. Be reasonable. We're just a local station. I'll concede it's a real tragedy, it has strong local flavor, but it doesn't rate sending my best reporter fifteen hundred miles away where she can work on nothing else for a month, to say nothing of the expense."

Veronica knew he was right, knew it but couldn't accept it, not with the still-too-fresh image of Martha Collins sobbing uncontrollably, incapable of being comforted, finally having to be sedated; not with the image of Frank Collins sitting in an almost catatonic stupor, speaking to no one; not with the image of Linda Collins's body, covered with a sheet, being wheeled from her room to the waiting ambulance, her toes, her breasts, her chin, nose and forehead silhouetted in white, ghostly reminders of her recently vanished existence.

"Eddie, there'll be other things I can do out there. I've checked, there's a Cattlemen's Association convention next weekend. I can report that too..."

Logan stared at her. "Ronnie, you don't know a cow from a turnip. I might send you a week before the trial, but not a month. The things that will be happening the next three weeks won't mean anything to anybody but the lawyers."

And to me, Veronica added to herself. But an idea was beginning to take shape. "Eddie, I haven't had a vacation in almost two years. I must have almost three weeks coming. I want it. Now. Tack on the week you're going to give me and you'll get a month's work for what amounts to a week's wages."

The spark was coming back.

"Anybody who'd pull something like that on me needs a vacation," Eddie said, "but under the circumstances you ought to go east, not west."

"C'mon Eddie, don't make jokes. This is *important* to me..."

She was probably already packed, he thought. "All right, for God's sake, go ahead. It's plain enough I'm not gonna get any work out of you until you get this out of your system."

Logan thought he heard a "thank you" shouted back at him as she ran out. He sat there staring after her. Somehow, he felt, they both had known how this conversation was going to turn out before it even began.

Fourteen

TAGGART HAD just been handed three new cases, unauthorized absences, routine stuff. He was leafing through the files when Sergeant Markey walked in.

"Good afternoon, sir, I got that list of character witnesses you asked for." He handed Taggart a piece of paper.

Mike took the paper. "How're things going for you down at battalion?"

"Jesus, captain, I'm goin' crazy down there. It's like I was already convicted as far as some people are concerned. They give me a desk, but they don't give me nothin' to do. Some people I've known for a long time go out of their way to avoid talkin' to me. I guess they're afraid to be seen with a killer."

Taggart hadn't seen Markey this low since the night following the Article 32 hearing. He'd heard what it was like for the drill instructors awaiting courts-martial to handle forced inactivity, now he was learning about it firsthand. Regulations called for a DI charged with maltreatment to be kept from contact with recruits pending resolution, but there was really no place to put them. Most of the men were so conditioned to the rigors of having to outmarch, outrun, out-PT, outsmart and sometimes outfight sixty wild, undisciplined eighteen- and nineteen-year-olds that they were like fish out of water if forced to sit behind a desk for more than an hour between sunup and sundown. Going from being the pride of the Corps, an elite, to excess baggage with an uncertain future while their friends continued on the drill field drove some to drink, destroyed families and made them bad-tempered, restless and irritable. The smarter the man, the greater his sense of the irony of being persecuted and abandoned by the Corps to which he had given so much. And Markey is a smart one, Taggart thought as he watched his client across the desk from him.

"They've got me a job as assistant to the sergeant major," he grumbled, "except the sergeant major don't need no assistant. 01' Prudhomme, he—"

"Wait a minute," Taggart interrupted. "Did you say Prudhomme? Is John Prudhomme the sergeant major down at Third Battalion?"

"Yessir, for the last six months or so, ever since he rotated back from Okinawa."

Prudhomme. The last time Taggart had seen Prudhomme was at Quang Tri. The battalion was coming out of the field, standing down and preparing for withdrawal to Okinawa. Once inside the secure confines of the giant Quang Tri Combat Base the colonel had ordered a day off from the war. Skeleton crews had manned the essential posts. From somewhere steaks had been produced and now sizzled on grills made from fifty-gallon oil drums. The troops from the various companies mingled and milled leisurely around the dusty clearing in front of the battalion command post. No less than ten different kinds of music blared from at least fifty different cassette decks. Someone had come up with a frisbee and a game of catch had quickly become a good-natured free-for-all.

Nursing a beer, Taggart sat on top of a sandbag-reinforced bunker and surveyed the scene. Prudhomme, whom Mike scarcely knew at the time, sauntered past.

"Looks like you got the best seat in the house, lieutenant. Mind if I share your perch?" Prudhomme asked, hoisting himself up with an effortlessness that belied his almost fifty years. "Troops are sure glad to be gettin' the hell outta here," he said as he watched the goings-on.

"How about you?" Taggart had wanted to know. "How do you feel about leaving?"

"It's different for people like me, lieutenant. I can't hardly remember when I wasn't a marine. I've lived in Corps houses, bought groceries at Corps stores, sent my kids to Corps schools, all my friends are Corps people. When you been in as long as I have the Corps gets to be kinda like a family itself. It hurts me to leave, 'cause I know people are gonna say the Corps couldn't get the job done . . . maybe the Marines ain't what they used to be."

"Did you feel the way they do," Taggart asked, nodding in the direction of the troops who were beginning to form a chow line, "when you were their age fighting in other wars?"

"I don't think so." Prudhomme looked out over the low, naked brown hills speckled with the various squat, olive-colored emplacements of the Division. He was trying to recapture the image of the terrified, seasick, eighteen-year-old crouched in the bottom of an assault craft, waiting for the jar and slap of the front ramp dropping into the surf that would trigger his dash across the beach at Peleliu.

"I don't think so," he said again. "There we were fightin' to win, there wasn't much point in survivin' if we didn't win. Those kids—" he gestured "—they're just fightin' to survive. Most of 'em could give a shit less whether we win or lose, even if a person could tell the difference over here, so long as they get home to Suzy in one piece. They're the ones that's being asked to die, the ones the Corps means the least to, and the war nothing at all. I gotta keep remindin' myself of that when I'm tryin' to understand all the problems we got now . . ."

It seemed like yesterday and a million miles away all at the same time. Taggart blinked himself back into the present. Sergeant Markey was still talking about conditions down at the battalion.

"The sergeant major is a good man, sir, and he's tried to help. He makes like he's usin' me for a runner for classified material between him and Top Rhodes up in the G-2, but I know what's in them sealed envelopes—it's nothing but the newspaper. They're just doing it to keep me busy, but that's just make-work, and that's worse than nothin'."

Taggart had no doubt that having too little to do was worse than

145

having too much, especially for people good enough to be DI's in the first place.

"Ahh, what am I doin' bendin' your ear?" Markey finally said with a grin. "Things may get worse, then I'll be wishin' I was the sergeant major's assistant again."

"That's one way of looking at it, but things can get better too. Let's see who you've got on this list of witnesses."

Taggart scanned the list. Both Sergeant Warthun and Sergeant Sanchez, Markey's former assistants with Hotel 1, were there. So was Top Browning, the Hotel Company's first sergeant. Taggart didn't know Browning, but he was glad to see his name on the list. First sergeants were company men of many years' service and their testimony tended to carry a lot of weight, often more than that of less-senior people who might be in better positions to observe. With rank presumably came wisdom; it wasn't taught in any law school but it was a belief as widely held at Morgan, Miller & Richardson as it was in the Corps. To question it was heresy, Taggart had long ago discovered.

"I see you have Staff Sergeant Stovall on your list. He's not in Hotel Company, is he?"

Staff Sergeant Jared "Stonewall" Stovall was a legend in his own time at MCRD. He was in his second tour on the drill field, and rumors of his antics with the recruits continually filtered up to the defense hooch, but, amazingly, he had never been the subject of charges. It was said of Stonewall that he owned no civilian clothes and slept on a cot in an empty duty office when he was between platoons. No one could ever remember him taking any of his leave.

"No, sir, not now he isn't, but about a year ago we were in the same company for a while but we never had a platoon together. I don't even know him real well, but when he heard I was up on charges he looked me up right away and offered to testify, so I put him on the list."

It figures, Taggart thought. Stonewall was the honorary chairman of what the prosecutors referred to as the Drill Instructors' Protective Association. He'd probably taken part in more courts-martial than Taggart.

"Sergeant Markey," Taggart said. "I'm sure you understand what character witnesses are all about. The impression we want to create for the members of the court is that here are three or four excellent marines who have gone out of their way to appear at the trial and go to bat for you because of their firm belief that if you're convicted it will be a miscarriage of justice."

"Yes, sir . . ."

"Well, I've only been here a couple of months so I don't know Staff Sergeant Stovall personally, but he's not exactly an unknown commodity up here. The first question he's going to get asked on cross-examination is how many times has he been a character witness for DI's charged with maltreatment. You see the problem."

"It's kinda like a whore not gettin' any respect."

"That's it, sarge. That, along with Sergeant Stovall's lack of opportunity to observe your work, isn't only going to weaken the impact of his testimony but I'm afraid your other witnesses will be tarred with the same brush. I don't want to use him. Blame it on me when you tell him. It'll be the truth."

"Yessir."

"Now, why aren't there any officers on this list?"

"That's a problem, sir. Lieutenant Burnquist just come aboard right before Collins died, and he don't know me at all. He said he'd do it but he wanted me to talk to you about it first. Captain Gunderson, he just said he wouldn't testify. Said he was too busy. I don't know who else to get."

Too busy. Taggart almost choked. A DI like Markey worked eighty to a hundred hours a week doing his part to keep the company rating high and the CO's ass out of a sling at Battalion, and at the first smell of trouble the CO is suddenly too busy. Taggart made a mental note to ask around about Gunderson.

"Well, what about Burnquist's predecessor? What about someone from one of your other duty stations, preferably Viet Nam. If we can find someone, there's a good chance we can have him brought back at the Corps' expense in a case like this one, but we have to find him and find out if he'll testify."

"Most of the ones I had the last trip to Viet Nam weren't around

147

long enough to shake hands," Markey said flatly. "The one I was closest to was Lieutenant Devlin, on my first tour. Jim was his first name. I was a pfc or a lance corporal then, but he made me his radio operator, even though I hadn't been to Com School. He's the one who recommended me for my Bronze Star. He's the one I told you about, who saved my life."

"Where's he now?"

"I don't know. I got medevaced back to the states when I got hit and never saw him again. I heard later that he got hit bad and got a medical discharge. I suppose he went back to Alabama, that was where he was from. I wrote to him in Nam, while I was in the hospital, to thank him for what he done for me, but the letter come back undelivered."

Taggart wrote down Devlin's name and the word "Alabama" beside it. Probably nothing would come of it, but with their backs to the wall no piece of information was too insignificant to note.

Mike sighed and stood up. "OK, Sergeant Markey, we've still got some time left, we'll come up with something. Let me think about it for a couple of days."

"Yes, sir."

"Listen, I've got a couple of phone calls to make before everybody secures for the day. Thanks for coming up. Just be patient down at the Battalion, okay? You said it yourself, it won't last forever, so hang on."

"Aye, aye, sir. It helped a lot just gettin' it off my chest. I'll handle it, don't worry."

Once Markey was out of the office, Taggart grabbed up the phone and dialed Third Battalion.

"This is Captain Taggart from Base Legal. Let me speak to Sergeant Major Prudhomme." As he waited for Prudhomme to get on the phone, he thought about Markey's last words, "don't worry." The client reassuring the lawyer. Ironic, but right now the lawyer could use all the help he could get.

Fifteen

VERONICA HAD just spent forty-five minutes with Joe Steiner. He had been in an expansive mood, saying he'd offered Taggart a deal . . . he would recommend that the commanding general limit any sentence Markey might receive to a forfeiture of all pay and allowances, reduction to the lowest enlisted rank, a dishonorable discharge and fifteen years imprisonment in exchange for a guilty plea.

Had Taggart approached him about such an offer, Veronica wanted to know.

"No," Steiner said, "but he ought to be glad for his client's sake that he's got it. He and Markey know what's facing them if they gamble and lose. This way Markey can at least cut his losses and be out in three years with good behavior."

"Plea bargaining?"

"Yeah, except this time there's no bargaining, it's take it or leave it."

"What do you think he'll do?"

"What can he do? He's got an eyewitness against him, a quality eyewitness, not some shitbird screw-up. He'll squirm for a couple of weeks, maybe make a couple of counteroffers, but in the end he'll take it. Not even a whole court full of ex-DIs could ignore testimony like Johnson's."

Well, Veronica thought as she walked down the corridor toward the defense hooch, at least Taggart hadn't solicited the offer, so it didn't look like he was waving any white flags quite yet.

"AH'M NOT TAKIN' NO MORE JIVE FUM' THIS GREEN MO'FUCKER—" The defense hooch exploded with shouts as Veronica walked in. At the far end of the room a giant black man in rumpled green utilities shot to his feet beside Taggart's desk, tipping his chair over behind him in the process. "DON' YOU SAY SHIT TO ME 'BOUT NO COURT-MARTIAL, MAN. AH DON' WAN' NO JUDGE. AH DON' WAN' NO JURY. THEY ALL BE NUTHIN' BUT A BUNCHA JIVEASS BEAST MO'FUCKERS ANYWAY. BROS DON'T GIT NO TRIAL BY THEIR P'S, THEIR P'S ALL IN DA BRIG OR GITTIN' FUCKED UP IN DA NAM. AH'LL TELL 'EM WHAT THEY CAN DO WITH THE MO'FUCKIN' *MARINE CORPS*."

Carpenter, Loring, Margolis and Beeson were all watching intently. Veronica thought the man was going to attack Taggart, but he sat leaning back in his chair and stared at the raging figure towering above him. Finally the man stopped for breath.

"Sit down, Private Collinwood. Use your head," Taggart said. Collinwood remained standing. "I'm your lawyer, not the commandant of the Marine Corps. Here, look, would it make it any easier if I took my bars off and put 'em in my pocket?" Taggart began to unpin the captain's bars from his collar.

"Don' bother," Collinwood mumbled as he bent over to pick up his chair and warily sat down in it.

Taggart began to talk to the man quietly, and Veronica could not hear anything further that was being said. Mike had not acknowledged in any way that he had seen her enter the room, although it would have been impossible not to see her in the small office.

"Welcome to your first exposure to Mac's Pack," Beeson said to Veronica, who was standing beside his desk. "Sugar Bear over there is a member in good standing," he added, indicating Private Collinwood.

"Mac's Pack?"

"MacNamara's One Hundred Thousand," Beeson went on. "Somebody, I don't know who, although MacNamara always seems to get the credit . . . somebody decided they could solve all society's woes and the need for military manpower all at once if they took the causes of the woe and put 'em in the military. I don't know how they screened 'em, but they wound up with one hundred thousand uneducated, unemployable, mostly minority troops and tried to ship 'em to Viet Nam. Now don't get all sentimental about this. These guys aren't just poor kids who never had a chance. These are bad dudes, guys who burned their bridges a long, long time ago. Most of them had records of felony convictions, not just nickel-dime but violent stuff. And the recruiters aren't too choosy these days. The grand strategy went sour, though. Most of them, like Sugar Bear, went to the brig instead of Viet Nam."

"What'd Sugar Bear do?" Veronica asked.

"Lady," Beeson said, "you're looking at one of MCRD's living legends. Two years ago, on his second day of boot camp, he attacked one of his drill instructors and put him in traction for months. Sugar Bear split, police picked him up in Detroit in a stolen car a couple weeks ago, and now he's the Corps' problem again."

"The DI was beaten up?" Veronica said. "That's a switch."

"It happens"—Beeson shrugged—"a DI's got to be on his toes, learn to recognize the signs before it's too late and then act quick."

They were interrupted by Taggart calling for Collinwood's chaser. An underfed-looking white marine armed only with a nightstick appeared. He was shorter than Ronnie. It was his job to prevent Sugar Bear from escaping on the walks back and forth from the brig. He was plainly, and properly, terrified of his prisoner.

"Get in here, you albino mo'fucker," said Sugar Bear, thrusting his huge hands out for placement of the handcuffs. Veronica could not entirely suppress her laugh at the ridiculous scene, but was quickly sobered as Sugar Bear brushed past her. "Git outta my way, puss."

Taggart was looking right at her when she turned back in his direction, walked back to his desk and sat down in the chair that was still warm from Private Sugar Bear Collinwood.

"Hello"—Taggart smiled slightly—"Sugar Bear's not too cuddly, is he?"

She shook her head and they began to talk. Taggart did not mention

151

Cathy's departure. Veronica said nothing about Linda Collins's suicide, although she assumed he had heard of the girl's death.

When she asked him about Steiner's offer to try to work out a plea bargain, Taggart was surprised. If Steiner wanted to negotiate, why go public with his offer? He told Veronica he had no comment about the possibility of a successful deal being struck other than to point out the danger to any such possibility resulting from public disclosure. Privately, Taggart thought Mad Dog's talking to her meant he was only fishing for the defense's estimate of the case by its response, rather than achieving any agreement. He didn't say this to Ronnie, but he and Markey had already decided to disappoint Mad Dog with the strength of their rejection.

"Aren't you going to ask me not to report it?" Veronica asked, deadpan.

"After what you did with the Da Nang court-martial story, why should I?"

Which made Veronica's color rise. She was about to tell him not to blame her for the weaknesses in his case when Taggart's phone rang. He answered it, listened for a couple minutes, then agreed to meet at the caller's home in half an hour. As he was about to hang up he glanced at Veronica and spoke hurriedly again to the caller, asking whether there was any objection to bringing Veronica with him if she promised not to report anything she heard at the meeting. He had a reason, he said, and he would discuss it further when they got there.

"Do you want to go with me to visit Mrs. Markey?" he asked as he hung up the phone. "And will you agree to the condition you just heard me mention?"

"Sure I want to go," Veronica said promptly, "and no, I can't agree to stop being a reporter. Why should I?"

"Because I don't want the Markeys' private lives all over the TV screen. Listen, if reporting this case is all you're going to do for the next month, you may as well expose yourself to *another* side of the story."

"I'm sorry, Mike, I'm still a reporter, not a social worker—"

"Then go back down and pump Steiner for more scoops," Taggart said, picking up his cover and disappearing out the door.

Veronica quickly realized she wasn't getting anywhere sitting beside Taggart's empty desk, and obviously he wasn't bothered by her not coming along on his terms.

Mike was halfway down the back steps of the headquarters building when he heard her call out, "Hey, soldier, wait a minute. Got room for a social worker?"

Taggart's car was parked in a lot behind the extreme west wing of headquarters building. As they stepped outside the back exit he gestured at a spot on the light yellow wall that had obviously just been sandblasted.

"There's part of the legacy of your story on the Da Nang court martial."

Ronnie looked where he was pointing. Although the paint had been removed, "FUCK KILLER MARKEY" was still clearly legible in the light-colored stucco.

Mike had visited with Sherill Markey several times since beginning to represent her husband. Early on he made a point to meet with her and describe at least generally what would be happening, and he had met with her and Roger two or three times to explain developments. The last time he had stayed and had dinner with the family.

The Markeys lived in an apartment complex that reminded Mike of the place he and Cathy had lived in in Quantico. Whatever lawn had once existed had long since been erased by the feet of the legions of children and dogs who roamed the premises. The asphalt in the parking lot was in pieces. Numbers were off of doors or hanging upside down by only one of the two original nails that had held them in place. The window in the door leading in to the common stairway was broken.

Following Mike's knock, Veronica heard a deadbolt click and a chain lock being unfastened on the other side of the door. Sherill Markey answered the door and smiled at Mike, a smile she transferred to Veronica on being introduced. In her right hand she steadied a healthy looking infant, resting most of its weight against its hip.

Mike told Mrs. Markey about the prosecution's proposal of a pretrial agreement, saying he would call about it further the next day, then

153

told her the reason for Veronica's visit to San Diego and his thought she ought to see what life was like for a DI and his family away from the drill field and the recruit barracks. He emphasized Veronica would not make specific reference to what she saw or heard and said he hoped Sherill could give Veronica some idea of what life was like for families of career staff NCO's. First, though, he wanted to see Deborah.

"She's in the bedroom, I'll go get her." Sherill went into a room that opened off the living room, and Ronnie could hear her. When Mrs. Markey came back she was accompanied by a slender dark-eyed girl with coal-black hair and dark features. Deborah, a six-year-old, had many of her father's features. Ronnie could see that the girl's cheeks were tear-stained and her eyes red-rimmed.

Taggart slid from the couch where he'd been sitting to the floor, and knelt on one knee. "Deborah, come over here so I can talk to you. You're still my friend, aren't you?"

The girl nodded her head, walked over very solemnly and stood beside Mike.

"Deb, I really came to see you today, not your mom or dad, but we can't talk very much in here with these two ladies gabbing. How about we take a little walk the way we did last time I came to visit, and you can fill me in on some of the things you've been doing . . ."

"Okay."

Mike stood up and Deborah reached up and took his hand. "We won't be gone long," he said as they went out the door, and Ronnie suddenly found herself alone with Sherill Markey and the baby.

Sherill eased the tension right away. "Deborah came home from school crying," she said. "Something she never does. She was crying so hard that it was a long time before I could even find out what was wrong. Finally I pieced together that the kids at school had been teasing her, calling her daddy a murderer and telling her he was going to have to go to jail and that he was never coming back. Nothing I said seemed to help. She was really crushed, kids can be so mean. Rog has duty tonight and won't be home and I didn't know what else to do. Really, I'm kind of glad he's not here. If he'd seen that . . . he's really been down, ever since that came out about the trouble over in Da Nang. He's even beginning to blame himself for volunteering for the drill

154

field, even for staying in the Corps, on account of what he's afraid this new trouble is going to do to the family. . . . Anyway, the only thing I could think of was to call Captain Taggart. Deb was really taken with him the other time he was here. I don't know why, maybe because he listens more than other grownups. Deborah's usually so shy, she'd never go for a walk like that without Rog or me along."

Veronica wondered what Taggart could possibly be telling the child . . . and what would he have said to Martha Collins the morning after her daughter's suicide?

Ronnie was more than a little impressed by Sherill Markey. She sensed no resentment toward her, a little distant maybe, but not hostile, even though the news coverage of her husband's case had been largely unsympathetic, particularly her own. It made Veronica curious, just as she knew Taggart had hoped it would, and she asked Sherill about being a military family.

Sherill sat back and said she didn't know where to begin. No one had ever asked her about her life before. She'd taken so much for granted, she said. What did she think about her life? . . . Well, one thing was for sure, the Marine Corps wasn't exactly ideal for married people. It took the number-one place in a marine's life, and his family and dependents had to go along. The frequent moves and long separations made it hard to have a normal family life. Medical treatment was free, but you never knew if you were going to see the same doctor twice. The commissaries and post exchanges offered groceries and merchandise at a discount, but that was because salaries were low compared to civilian life . . . "Still, what would we have if we hadn't stayed in the Corps? Rog is real smart, but he's only been to the tenth grade. I graduated from high school but the only jobs I've ever had have been as a waitress. We got married during his first hitch, before either one of us was twenty, and we didn't really think about too much except each other and how much fun we were having just being together day to day. The future could take care of itself. Rog thought he wanted to stay in ever since he came back from Viet Nam the first time, but after we got married and the time came to really decide, he said he'd get out if I wanted him to, but I didn't. Staying in seemed like the best thing to do.

"Now we look back and say how lucky we were to have made that decision. Lots of men around here hate their jobs. They move from job to job, they've got nothing to be proud of. The Marine Corps has certainly given us that, and now we've been in long enough so we have lots of friends. At every duty station there's somebody we've known from before. I can't complain. After all, we volunteered."

"What about the courts-martial?" Veronica asked. "Those wouldn't have happened in civilian life."

"The one in Da Nang, I wasn't there . . . and Rog never talks about it. I think the memory of Dave's death still hurts him too much to talk. The fact that he hit and killed that other man because of it only makes it worse."

Who's Dave? Veronica was wondering, but before she could ask, Sherill Markey went on.

"As for this one, I know he didn't do it, and I have to believe Captain Taggart's going to get him off. It's scary, but I guess it's all part of being on the drill field. It's like everything else in the Corps, some good and some bad. Roger's career depends on his fitness reports from his CO's, and that depends on his platoon's performance against the other platoons, so you see, no matter how good you are, if someone else is better, you lose. If he gets a bad fitness report, he may not be allowed to reenlist or may not be promoted when the time comes. Rog is under a lot of pressure, all the DIs are because of that.

"We volunteered for the drill field, just like everything else." Sherill shook her head and gave a shrug. "It was a compliment to be asked, it meant Rog was considered one of the best. It meant more money too. We've been saving for so long, we've almost got enough saved up for a house. With VA financing we think we can swing it. We were going to drive around and look at places for the first time when Rog got off duty the morning after that boy died. Now everything's up in the air. After Brett was born we'd hoped I could stay home with the kids and not go back to work, but now . . . now we don't know if we'll be together for a while, I mean, if Rog gets convicted next month. We just have to wait and see. . . ."

The front door swung open and Taggart entered, all stooped over so Deborah, who was riding on his shoulders, wouldn't hit her head on the door frame. The little girl was smiling and told her mother Taggart had pushed her on the swings. Taggart didn't say much. Mrs. Markey thanked Mike for coming, and Veronica thanked Mrs. Markey for talking to her.

"To be honest," Sherill said as she walked them to the door, "I did it for Rog, so you'll understand that we're people too."

It was well after five and getting dark as they drove north along the freeway. Taggart had said nothing since leaving the Markeys.

Ronnie broke the silence. "What did you say to Deborah?"

He shrugged. "I told her her daddy didn't kill anybody and anyone who says he did is wrong. I told her not to worry about her daddy going away, that he and I were doing everything we could so that wouldn't happen."

Ronnie had a million more questions she wanted to ask. Who's Dave? What did he have to do with the trouble in Da Nang when Gilpin was killed? What kind of sentence could Markey really expect if convicted? She could go on and on, but looking across the seat at Taggart, who appeared to be lost in some dark thoughts of his own as he drove along, she decided there'd be a better time, and place. She had a month, she reminded herself.

Neither of them said anything the rest of the way to the hotel, where Taggart dropped Ronnie off with barely a good-bye. Then he went over to Horn's place to watch the Laker game and got so drunk he passed out and spent the night on the couch.

Sixteen

IN TAGGART'S opinion, Jack Beeson was the best lawyer he had seen in the Corps. He had brass balls. Short, stocky and gravel-voiced, Beeson genuinely thrived on controversy. Covered with hair everywhere except on top of his head, when he stood up to begin a cross-examination and fixed his stare on a witness, with his five o'clock shadow at 0930 in the morning and his ferocious, nonregulation mustache, many a story began to crack. Beeson had challenged the command so many times, Taggart was amazed he hadn't been made a prosecutor. The commanding general and the chief of staff were frequently included on his lists of requested witnesses, in theory because he needed to discover whether any command influence was present, but in reality because he hoped the general would order the charges dropped rather than testify. He drove Mad Dog Steiner, whom he called Nevermore, into a frenzy.

For weeks Beeson had been locked in a running battle about the length of his hair with a lieutenant colonel who occupied a neighboring office. Because he was getting bald, Jack grew his hair long on the side and combed it over the top in a desperate attempt at camouflage. The result was a ghastly departure from the Corps' revered regulation requiring extremely short haircuts. The colonel's mild hints as he walked by Jack in the passageway became caustic insults, followed by complaints to Go Go about the personal appearance of his men. Beeson ignored all.

The dispute had even moved Taggart to write a poem—an un-Marinelike thing to do but he'd always liked writing poetry—joking that the barbarians who conquered Rome undoubtedly had longer hair "...than a legionnaire." Somehow it got published in the base newspaper, which provoked the wrath of Colonel Katkavage. Go Go was still sore about that.

When Taggart arrived at the defense hooch on the morning following his walk with Deborah Markey, he found Beeson had finally gotten a haircut that roughly approximated regulations. Go Go, in a typical chickenshit maneuver, had told Carpenter to get Beeson squared away or failure to do so would show up in Carpenter's fitness report. As the chief defense counsel, Carpenter was nominally Beeson's immediate superior, although they were the same age, had been in the Corps the same length of time, were both captains and had the same date of rank. They were also good friends. Go Go had no leverage over Beeson by way of fitness reports because Jack was getting out and had a job waiting for him. He also had already been to Viet Nam, so that was no threat. Carpenter, on the other hand, hoped to join the FBI when he got out, and Go Go knew that fitness reports would play a part in whether Carpenter was accepted.

When Carpenter explained the situation to Beeson, Jack gave in without having to be asked. But now, as Taggart settled behind his desk, Beeson was taking an oath of vengeance. Braving hoots of skepticism from his colleagues, he vowed to tell the lieutenant colonel who had been the source of the trouble to "get fucked" that very evening before an audience consisting of the entire clientele of the O Club at happy hour. Such audacity rivaled Babe Ruth pointing to where he intended to put Charlie Root's next pitch in the '32 series. Using the military justice system to irritate the military establishment was one thing, at least there Beeson was in his home park, but telling the colonel to get fucked in front of his peers was quite another. It would be an insult, no matter how well deserved, that the colonel could not ignore.

The officer's club was much more the colonel's home park than Beeson's. It was the regular officers' lair, their mess. There, as elsewhere, the lawyers, especially defense counsel, were merely tolerated by the Corps as a necessary evil, ignored for the most part, so long as they didn't stir up trouble. If he carried it out, Beeson would need a lawyer. He might need an undertaker. Quickly, before he could regain his senses and recant, Margolis suggested Beeson "put his money where his mouth was."

By midmorning a book was flourishing in the defense hooch as the odds against Beeson carrying out his insane promise began to climb. Even Lance Corporal Lofton, the woman marine whose misfortune it was to be assigned as a clerk-typist to these pariahs of the Corps, wanted a piece of the action. Beeson covered all takers.

Taggart was replaying the morning's events in his mind as he hurried along the edge of the drill field on his way from the brig to the club. Sugar Bear, in solitary confinement for some infraction of brig rules, could not be brought up to the defense hooch to see him but had been sending messages requesting Taggart to visit him with every one of the brothers brought up from the brig that day. Now it was late. Mike hoped he hadn't missed Beeson's triumph or humiliation. When Mad Dog Steiner had come in to place his bet he'd said he hoped he lost because it'd be worth ten dollars to him to see Beeson in chains.

Mike was nearing the end of the grinder when a bugle blast signaled retreat. He faced the flag on top of the headquarters building and saluted. As he did so he noticed Veronica Rasmussen standing with her back to him, also at attention facing the flag, about fifteen yards away. When the music died away he called to her and walked over.

"Hi, what brings you out here?" he asked.

"Oh, I don't know, that night after the Article 32 hearing I thought that music was so beautiful I wanted to hear it again. How about you?"

"I'm on my way over to the club. Friday night ritual."

"Mind if I tag along?"

They walked together through the dark. Taggart explained that they might arrive in time for her to witness Beeson's death by strangling at the hands of the colonel.

161

At the club it was the usual Happy Hour scene: groups of tables pushed together, field-grade officers concentrated at the rail, cocktail waitresses weaving in and out among the crowd, bartenders a blur behind the bar. Margolis had sheparded the legal office over to its usual spot by the patio door and, as Mike and Ronnie sat down, Horn told Mike that nothing had happened yet but the colonel had just arrived so they shouldn't have long to wait.

The colonel now stood at the bar surveying the lawyers and their companions with disapproval, searching out Beeson. He didn't have far to look, because Jack was sitting at the end of the lawyers' group nearest the bar. When the colonel spotted him he squinted to assure himself his eyes weren't playing tricks on him. No, it was true, Captain Beeson had gotten a haircut. The colonel strolled across the room toward Beeson to rub a little salt in what he knew must be an open wound.

"Well, Captain Beeson, I see you finally got your locks cut." The colonel spoke in a loud voice so as to attract as much attention as possible.

Turning his chair so that he was facing the colonel and leaning back with his hands folded around the beer in his lap, Beeson answered in an even louder voice, "Yessir, you finally had your way with me."

"Who knows, captain, you may even find you enjoy looking like a marine for a change."

Everyone in the room was now listening.

"Colonel, can I ask you a question?"

"Sure."

"Do you have any sons?"

"Yes, I have one son..."

"How old is he?"

"Eight. Why?"

"How often do you make him get his hair cut?" Beeson pressed on.

"What? Oh...once a week, yeah, once a week without fail—"

"What are you going to do when he turns fifteen and tells you to get fucked?"

As the saying goes, the silence was deafening. For a few seconds

162

Taggart thought the colonel would go for Jack. If it had happened in an overseas club where brawling was more common, Mike was sure there would have been a fight.

The colonel stood there staring at Jack. The indirection of Beeson's ploy epitomized everything the colonel detested about lawyers. It was disrespectful, all right, but it wasn't exactly disrespect. He could never make a charge stick. Goddamnedlawyers. For a moment longer he considered his options, including assault, then, deciding against martyrdom, he went back to the bar. Minutes later he was gone.

Before Jack Beeson had even turned his chair back toward the group, Taggart and the others were reaching for their wallets. Move over Babe Ruth.

Not long after Beeson's performance people began to drift away from the bar. When Horn left for the airport to pick up a friend flying in for the weekend, Mike and Ronnie were surrounded by empty chairs. At the far end of the group of tables Loring and Beeson were getting ready to leave.

The prospect of going back to that empty apartment depressed Taggart. There had been no word from Cathy in the time that she had been gone, and when he had tried to call the people she said she'd be staying with there was never any answer. What's more, damn it, he liked Veronica Rasmussen in spite of their opposing positions on what was presently the central fact of his existence—the trial of Roger Markey. She seemed like someone who could take it, as well as dish it out. For certain, she was no phony.

"How about dinner?" he blurted out.

She looked at him ... she'd been hoping he would do something to prevent their evening together from ending there in the half-empty bar. Take it easy, girl, she told herself, this guy's married. No problem ... there were all sorts of ways she could rationalize accepting his invitation. After all, next to Markey himself here was the best possible source of information about the defendant in the case she was there to report, if she could just get him to talk. But, why kid herself, she also wanted to accept because, marine or not, she liked Taggart. Be-

163

sides, he'd made no secret of the fact he was married, although he'd said little about his wife. Nothing Veronica had seen of him made her think he was the type to cheat, if there was such a type.

"Sure," she said, "where shall we go?"

"There's a place called World Famous. It's right on the water down on North Mission Beach."

"Sounds great."

Walking back toward headquarters, where Mike's car was parked, he said he wanted to go home and change into civilian clothes first. He could drop Ronnie off at her hotel and come back for her or she could come over to his place while he changed and they could go from there. It would only take a minute.

"What will your wife think about that?" She immediately wished she hadn't said that.

Taggart kept walking. After a moment he said, "Cathy's gone."

It was clear from the way he said "gone" that he meant for more than just the evening or a visit. She wished she could have seen Mike's face when he'd spoken just then, but it was too dark. Obviously something had gone wrong in Taggart's marriage. He didn't offer any further explanations.

Except for a sidewalk and a low wall there was nothing between World Famous and the Pacific Ocean except sand. People who went there were the people you saw at the beach all year round, not tourists or summer visitors from the eastern part of the city. There were as many sandal-clad, shorts-and-T-shirt-attired customers as there were diners wearing sweaters or sports coats. With good food, a relaxed atmosphere and a great location the tiny restaurant bridged a number of contrasting segments of the beach population.

Mike and Ronnie were standing now in the bar and having a drink waiting for a table. Suddenly Ronnie choked and swallowed hard, as if she had swallowed something from her drink that didn't belong there, or inhaled a bug. The bartender and a couple of patrons exchanged knowing glances.

"Are you all right?" Taggart asked innocently as she stopped coughing and heaved a deep sigh to regain her breath. "What's the matter?"

164

"That flag..." Ronnie, still hoarse from her brief seizure, nodded toward a large flag displayed like a wall hanging across the wall immediately above their heads.

The flag was the California state flag, with a field of white, across which the California golden bear was prowling. Only on this particular banner a second bear was depicted mounting the first in an obvious act of ursine copulation.

"I dont' think the city fathers would go for that in ol' K.C.," she said, laughing.

"It's important to show one's institutions a little disrespect," Taggart said solemnly.

After they were seated and had ordered, the waiter brought some wine. Mike raised his glass. "Here's to justice."

"Yes." Ronnie touched his glass lightly with her own. "Let's hope that this time it's not too blind." A case of opposite sides clearly attracting.

That was the last reference to the trial throughout the evening. They exchanged backgrounds, traded stories for more than two hours. Ronnie described Eddie Logan to Taggart, his truculence and his gruff good will and advice. She made Eddie come alive, imitating but not ridiculing the way he would chew his unlit cigar when listening intently to something.

Mike talked about his visits to Kansas City while a kid growing up. The visits to the American Royal Livestock Show with his father in the fall, the trip to his first major league baseball game as a present on his twelfth birthday, the time he ran away four years later and tried to join the rodeo in Kansas City and after five days finally chickened out and hitchhiked home.

Veronica could sense Taggart reaching inside her with his questions, gently probing but never prying, never seeming to interrogate. She found herself talking about what it was like being an only child and daughter of a sports-crazy father, things she'd previously only half-considered. Taggart's interest in what she had to say seemed genuine, not just from curiosity or probing for probing's sake. She was also getting a deeper look at the Taggart she'd first glimpsed during their

165

encounter at the officers' club during her first trip to San Diego when they had talked briefly about the war.

"Whew," she said at last, pressing her cheek with her fingertips. "Either the wine or your questions has made me warm, let's go outside."

Taggart looked at her, saying nothing.

"What are you thinking?"

"That maybe now you know a little more about how people you interview feel," he said with a smile as he stood up to leave. "Television lady gets dose of own medicine?"

Outside the salt air and the crash of the nearby waves further sharpened her senses, already fine-tuned.

"Let's take a walk on the beach," she said.

Taggart vaulted over the low wall and took hold of Ronnie's hand to steady her as she jumped lightly down to the sand. There was a moment of awkwardness as Mike appeared undecided whether he should continue to hold her hand or let it go. He let it go. They turned and walked toward the waterline, now far out on the beach at low tide. They kicked off their shoes and carried them when they reached the water. The hard, cold sand and icy water felt good on their bare feet and ankles. It filled Veronica with new energy and made her want to run.

"C'mon," she said suddenly, nudging Taggart in the stomach with the back of her hand, "let's run. You desk jockeys need some PT," and she took off.

In an instant Taggart was beside her, moving easily, matching stride for stride as they ran, splashing each other with their footfalls whenever the last of the surf would wash gently into their paths. No race, no competition, just two exuberant people floating through the night. Mike felt as though they were suspended in a crystal ball, like the one his grandmother had kept on her coffeetable when he was a little boy. Only instead of snowflakes there were the distant lights of the beachfront buildings blending into the stars clinging to the sky above the restless black of the sea.

After a while they gradually slowed to a halt. Both were a little out of breath, and Ronnie rested her hand lightly against his shoulder as she paused momentarily to catch her breath.

She turned toward him, suddenly serious. "It's been fun . . . hasn't it, Mike?"

Taggart looked down at her and nodded. "The best time I've had in a long while," he said quietly, and then he slowly turned away and resumed walking, catching up her hand as he did so, and together they continued on down the beach.

The hotel where Ronnie was staying was a number of small individual units, each partially secluded from the rest. It was a resort designed mostly for families. Ronnie's room was on the north side of the man-made island that the hotel complex was situated on, just steps from the bay.

Taggart was able to drive right to her door. It was almost one A.M. and he closed the car door quietly behind her as she fumbled in her purse for the door key. Once she found it, they stood facing each other like a couple of teenagers not knowing how to say good-night.

"I meant what I said back there on the beach, Ronnie, about this being the best time I've had in a long while," Mike said quietly. "Thanks. I guess I'll probably see you around next week. Good night . . ."

Veronica simply nodded and said nothing.

Taggart was halfway back to his car, and Veronica still had neither spoken nor gone inside.

"Mike," she called softly, and he stopped and turned around. "Mike . . . I brought my racquet. How about some racquetball one night next week?"

It sounded to Veronica like a really dumb thing to say at the end of such an evening. Well, it was the best she could manage, to let Taggart know she would like to see him again without coming right out with it, as she might have done if he weren't married.

"Sure," he said quickly. "How about Wednesday?" And then drove away, feeling exhilarated and uneasy all at the same time.

Seventeen

IN THE days following their dinner together Taggart saw nothing of Veronica. He wrote briefs in support of several motions he intended to make in advance of Markey's trial. Not only did he have to write them, but he had to type them himself because Lance Corporal Lofton typed like she had ten thumbs. And Taggart preferred to take every precaution he could against giving Mad Dog Steiner any clue to his plan of attack.

Veronica made it a point to avoid the defense hooch. Normally she was the soul of self-assurance; normally she was the one who controlled any relationship in which she was involved. That was certainly the case with Norm Karocek back in Kansas City. Ronnie had a standing offer of marriage from Norm but couldn't picture herself in that permanent a relationship with him. Nor would she sacrifice her independence by living with him, although she had no moral reluctance about such an arrangement. When it got right down to it, she thought there was more to her than there was to Norm, and she wanted to do nothing to encourage him into believing she felt committed to him in any way. It wasn't snobbery, she told herself, it was just a poor fit for the long term.

Now, with Taggart, she did not feel entirely in control of either herself or the relationship. The ease with which he had made her want to reveal herself to him the other night made her feel vulnerable, in a way she was unused to feeling.

What Taggart had said at the restaurant about how maybe now she'd understand how people felt when she was interviewing them troubled her . . . was that all it was? She hoped not. She wasn't afraid of strong people . . . what she was looking for was someone willing to share her strengths as well as his own. She was willing to share, not be dominated. Was Taggart as genuine as he seemed, or was he just playing some kind of subtle game with her? As she went about the rounds of interviews she had managed to arrange and did her research on the history of drill instructor trials in the Corps in the newspaper graveyard at the public library, she thought about all this, and made up her mind to go slow until she satisfied herself about the real Michael Taggart.

Waiting in her room for Mike to pick her up for their racquetball game she began to wish she'd called him to confirm their date. It had been made so hurriedly and at the last minute, he might have forgotten. She noted wryly that nothing about her reservations of the last four days made her look forward any less to seeing Taggart again. To the contrary, she was intrigued by the combination of how he had made her feel when she was with him and her later thoughts about him. She very much hoped Mike Taggart was all that he seemed, and wasn't so afraid of being disappointed that she was unwilling to find out.

Taggart, of course, had not forgotten. Rather than play at the base, where there were no shower or dressing facilities at the courts, he had made reservations at civilian courts. He knew he would take heat from the guys who hung out there when he showed up to play racquetball. Most of the handball players looked down on racquetball as a profanation of their more perfect game.

Mike's own reservations about it weren't so profound. The two or three times he had played racquetball he hadn't enjoyed it as much as handball and the gouges left by racquets swung wildly against the court walls resulted in bad bounces for handball players who later used the courts. But after all, it was a game, and the fact that it was a good coed sport was a plus as far as he was concerned.

He had rented a racquet and was dressed and waiting when Veronica came out of the dressing room, wearing a deep burgundy colored warm-up suit with a white stripe on the legs and sleeves.

"Well," he said, "if the game went to the best sweatsuit, you'd have a lock on first place." He smiled when he said it.

"Oh, this old thing?" Ronnie replied with an exaggerated nonchalance.

As they walked to their court, Veronica turned heads of players waiting for their games. Once on the court Veronica was all business, and Taggart began to suspect that he'd been sandbagged. She moved lightly through what seemed to be a set routine of preparation. She tested how the ball came off the walls from various angles. She had long legs and her first step to the ball was quick and confident. Her concentration seemed very strong; time after time she would drive her practice shots against the identical spot on the wall. There was no wasted motion in her strokes, and her follow-through and recovery put her in good defensive position. If, as she once said, she was no more than an occasional player of a year's experience, Taggart was the Commandant of the Marine Corps.

His suspicions were confirmed within the first ten points of the game, which were won by her. The score had reached 5-0 while Mike was busy making mental adjustments from handball. The sixth point came on a long volley in which each was struggling to move the other out of center court into a position from which a good shot could not be made. Finally Taggart hit a low backhand that clung to the left wall as it rebounded off the front. Ronnie was barely able to reach it, and her return was weak, resulting in a waist high setup coming right down the middle to Mike's stronger forehand while she was still plastered against the left wall. Seeing the opportunity to break her serve, he waited until the ball was just the height he wanted it and rocketed it low and hard against the front wall so that it hugged the far right as it came off.

He was still in his follow-through when Veronica dove past him, her right arm stretched to the fullest extent of its reach. No more than the top half inch of her racquet reached the ball the instant before she hit the floor, and, unable to swing, she flicked it back toward the front with only her wrist.

The whole play took only a second or two, but it unfolded like time-lapse photography to Mike, who had relaxed his concentration after hitting what he thought was a sure winner. Back on his heels, he watched helplessly as the ball wobbled in a soft arc toward the front wall, kissing it lightly about two inches from the floor as it died.

"Nice shot," he said dryly to Veronica, who had instantly come off the floor into defensive position. Her right knee was sporting an angry strawberry the size of a silver dollar that hadn't been there before. She didn't rub it.

"Six serves zero," was all she said as she lined up for her next serve.

The lead quickly became ten. Taggart hadn't really cared about the match going in, but now he realized that if he didn't pick up, this wouldn't even be a workout for her. Slowly but surely he began to get his game together, salvaging seven points in the first game for a 21-7 loss.

They really went after each other in the second game, Taggart saying little, Veronica nothing other than grimly reciting the score. Bearing down, Mike managed to match her point for point, drawing on his handball experience. It was plain she was too good to be overpowered, and he battled the temptation to try. Instead he concentrated on moving the ball around from side to side, back and forth, hoping to wear her down.

He could see no evidence that she was fading in the second game, although he did manage to squeeze out a 21-20 victory. By the middle of the third game, though, he could see that she'd lost a little, but she more than made up for it with her superior shot-making ability. She had had the serve with the score tied at twenty all, but lost it on a dive by Mike that earned him a strawberry of his own. Now he was serving, and he hit a high lob to the back left corner, the same serve she had been returning the entire match. This time, as Ronnie shifted her feet to meet it, they somehow became tangled and she stumbled and was off balance as she tried to backhand her return. The result was a shot off the ceiling about half-way to the front, which Mike watched drop harmlessly to the floor.

He turned back to her . . . she was sitting on the floor leaning against the back wall, legs sprawled in front of her, racquet dangling from her wrist by its cord.

"Great game." She smiled for the first time since stepping on the court. "I could use a beer."

"Great game, yourself," Taggart said in open admiration. "You said a while ago that you were going to hand it to me, and regardless of the outcome you really did. Next time I can't count on you tripping."

"I told you my dad wanted a boy."

They stopped at La Sicilian for a pizza, and again talked easily for a long time in the almost deserted restaurant. Mostly the subject was the war and what it was doing to the country. Mike told her about a Sunday evening in March of 1968 when he and Cathy had been visiting some friends in married-student housing near the end of his last year of law school. It was at the high-water mark of Eugene McCarthy's presidential primary campaign. L.B.J. was delivering a nationally televised address and had just announced a bombing halt everywhere except the vicinity of the DMZ. Thinking he'd heard everything of substance the President had to say, Mike had gone out to the car for something he'd left there. Just as he was unlocking the car door a tremendous cheer erupted simultaneously from the surrounding apartment buildings. People threw open their windows and just began shouting into the early spring night. Out on the street passing cars began honking their horns. Here and there excited people ran from building to building.

Taggart had hurried back to his friend's apartment, and as he walked in the door he heard the unmistakable pop of a champagne cork. What the hell was going on? Sticking a glass of champagne in his hand, his host told him that Lyndon Johnson had just announced that he wouldn't seek reelection.

"So much for the Great Society," Taggart said. Brought down by a war that had split the nation.

Ronnie had her own story to match. On a sweltering summer afternoon in 1967 she'd been waiting for a bus on her way home from work. It was a typical crowd of commuters, except for a long-haired young couple who stood apart from the crowd talking quietly to each other. They were dressed in old, faded clothes, the girl was braless and the boy had a scruffy beard. The bus was late, the crowd was irritable. Finally the bus that most of the people were waiting for arrived. It wasn't Ronnie's bus, so she leaned against the wall and watched them board. At the back of the group waiting to board was a grandfatherly looking man with a shock of gray hair, with a loosened tie and his suit coat draped over his arm. As he reached the bus door he turned toward the young couple, who were not getting on, and began to shout, "Hey, this is your bus, this is the bus for you, it goes to the *zoo*. That's where freaks like you belong, in the goddamn zoo." Then he hopped aboard the bus as the youngsters stood there open-mouthed. But the old man wasn't finished. As Veronica watched in astonishment he ran down the aisle to an open window, stuck his head out and picked up his tirade. The boy then ran up to the bus as it pulled away from the curb and spit right in the old man's face. The whole episode had made Ronnie want to cry, she said.

"What do you suppose had happened to that old man to make him react that way?" she now wondered aloud. "The loss of a son, maybe?"

"In 1967 . . . maybe." Mike shrugged. "These days it doesn't take nearly that much, and in my opinion the flower children are just as narrow-minded in their own way as the people who support the war. I was in a cab in a traffic jam on my way to the Los Angeles airport when I was coming back from Okinawa last October, and people gave me the finger and yelled at me when they saw my uniform . . ."

Ronnie was getting a side of things she rarely heard.

They were the last customers to leave the restaurant. As they walked to the car, Veronica took his hand. It had been their one physical intimacy that night after leaving World Famous. It seemed to her they could say things to each other with their hands that they were still afraid to speak out loud. An elderly couple walked past them going in the opposite direction, also hand in hand, and smiled, as if the four of them shared some special secret.

Before they said good-night Taggart suggested a picnic the following Saturday. He left her standing alone just inside her door, holding her racquet, feeling less uneasy about Taggart's ability to affect her, but

174

troubled, and wondering about the melancholy note she remembered hearing in his voice when he had told her Cathy was gone.

It was the first cloudy day Veronica had seen during her time in San Diego.

"Weatherman must have known we were having a picnic," Taggart said as they walked out to his cycle. A small yellow backpack was dangling from the handlebars by its straps.

"If you ride in the rear, you carry the gear," he said, helping her put on the pack and adjusting the shoulder straps down from his size to hers.

Once they were on their way she felt again the exhilaration of her earlier ride. Except this time she was relaxed from the beginning, leaning into the turns, feeling the rhythm of the engine's pulse, trusting Taggart as he knifed the bike along the city streets and out onto the freeway.

Rolling down the on-ramp, the high-pitched whine of the engine kept building higher and higher until just when she thought it would fly apart Mike hit the top gear and they seemed to fly over the road. The highway wound among brown, barren hills dotted with housing developments. At times the Pacific would be visible off to their left between the hills as they whisked past the beach towns north of San Diego. Del Mar, Encinitas, Leucadia, Carlsbad, Oceanside, all were left in their wake as they entered the rugged emptiness of Camp Pendleton. On their right were steep hills, peaks still hidden in the overcast, and on the left the green-gray glassy waters of the ocean shone darkly, like obsidian, beyond the surf.

Soon Taggart was slanting toward an exit ramp that curled back beneath an underpass, and suddenly they were at the beach. In a way Ronnie was glad for the clouds. There would be few people to share their sanctuary. This early in the morning it was still deserted. Had Taggart picked this place because of its remoteness?

"That's an interesting blanket," Ronnie said as he stood with his back to the offshore breeze, letting the wind spread a satiny green camouflage cloth in front of him. "What is it?"

175

"A poncho liner. They're good in Viet Nam because they're insulated and dry fast. I once defended a sergeant on Okinawa who stole ten thousand of them. Sold them to the Okinawan tailors, who made jackets out of them. My client was trying to raise money to buy his girlfriend out of the bar her parents had indentured her to . . . and he did. Of course as soon as he was arrested they sold her again, because she was still underage. A real windfall for her parents."

There was nothing to say to that grim story. Its message was clear enough. It was still early as they sat side by side drinking coffee and staring out at the sea.

"Strange," he finally said, "I mean, to be sitting here, with you, and knowing that at this instant on the other side of that ocean people are dying, maybe people I know."

"You're not hardened to it by now?"

Taggart squinted at her through the steam rising from his coffeecup. He shook his head. "I went over there thinking I was going to be what they call a REMF, a Rear Echelon . . . well, you can figure out the rest for yourself. But when I arrived I found out that lawyers had to be infantry platoon commanders for three months first, before they were assigned to the legal office. In those three months I saw enough bone-deep misery, and fear, to last me a lifetime. I saw some heroism too, even if from some very reluctant heroes. Almost no one thought twice about putting everything on the next card, if it was to save another Marine in trouble. It didn't make the news, but it was there . . .

"When my three months were up and I was leaving, the whole platoon gathered around the chopper that was going to haul me out of there. I felt guilty, and grateful, to be going. It was like leaving your friends or your family in the middle of some horseshit job. Except you don't get killed in most jobs, even horseshit ones . . . I could see it in their eyes, how much they envied my leaving, but I doubt they begrudged me my good future. I felt crummy then, and I don't feel any different about it now."

Taggart looked back out toward the west.

"I guess that's a part of it I'll never really be able to share," was all Ronnie said. He didn't answer, but silently suspected she was right.

After a while a couple with a little boy about six or seven set up

176

their blanket and some lawn chairs off to the left and slightly in front of them. The child played for a while, digging in the sand. As they talked Veronica noticed Mike was watching the boy, who had produced a baseball glove and a ball from somewhere and had evidently asked his father, who was reading, to play catch. The father shook his head, and the child began throwing the ball in the air and catching his own throws, and eventually one got away from him and rolled up to the poncho liner. Taggart quickly uncoiled, scooped the ball up before it stopped rolling and tossed it back to the boy, then he raised his hands in front of his chest to signal the boy to throw it back.

Their game went on for some twenty minutes, with Ronnie watching from where she sat. The boy's parents never looked up. Back and forth the ball flew, the boy laughing and shouting when he made a particularly good catch, Taggart silent except for an occasional word of encouragement or compliment. He was the Taggart that Veronica had seen with Deborah Markey, gentle, now feathering each throw so the youngster could handle it. When the game ended, Mike flopped back down beside Ronnie and motioned for his new friend to join them.

"Ronnie, this is Ryan, Ryan, this is my friend Ronnie."

Ryan smiled. Mike asked to see Ryan's glove, and the boy informed them it had been a Christmas present. They talked about gloves for a time, with Mike mentioning that when he was breaking in a glove he would jam some baseballs into where he wanted the pocket and wrap the glove with a cord, demonstrating with Ryan's glove as he talked. Ryan listened intently, and Ronnie would have bet a thousand dollars that the next time that glove went on the shelf it would be jammed with baseballs and wrapped just the way Mike had described.

Before long, Ryan's parents called him. They were already picking up their chairs to leave. Taggart watched the boy trudge off in their direction. When Ryan turned and waved good-bye Mike waved back. As he lowered his arm, Ronnie leaned over and kissed him.

"One of us had to break the ice, Tags. Sometimes I can't believe you're real. C'mon, let's go swimming." With that she began to wiggle out of the light blue denim hip-huggers she was wearing.

"You've got to be kidding. T.V. lady dinky dau, which, f.y.i.,

177

means crazy in the language of our Southeast Asian allies. That water isn't more than sixty degrees."

"Yeah, and the air temperature's twenty degrees back in Kansas City and people still go out in it," she mumbled through the white cotton pullover she was taking off over her head. "C'mon, Jarhead, get with the program."

Shaking his head, Taggart slipped off his shirt and levis and stood beside the bikini-clad Veronica.

"Look," he exhaled, "I can see my breath."

"Only one way to do this, fellow penguin. Last one in has to fix lunch," and she raced toward the water, splashing through the icy surf and throwing herself headfirst into a wave. Taggart was right behind her. The cold almost paralyzed him as he followed her into the wave. As he came to his feet and wiped the water from his eyes, she hugged him tight.

"Oh, T-T-Taggart, w-why didn't you tell me it would be so *cold?*"

"The Corps has a saying for people who do things like this."

"What's that?"

"If you're going to be a prick, you might as well be hard."

"How profound. C'mon, now I can tell my friends back home I went swimming in the ocean. Let's get *out* of here."

Wrapped arm-in-arm they waded out and walked up the otherwise deserted beach toward their belongings. From the seemingly bottomless confines of the backpack Mike produced towels and a hooded sweat-shirt that zipped like a jacket, which he draped around Ronnie's shoulders before she headed off to change.

By the time she came back he had moved the poncho liner over beside a fire-ring and had collected enough driftwood to start a fire. They sat there, watching the tide go out, drinking wine and eating hard crusty bread and cheese.

"Mmm, I don't think I've ever had anything that tasted any better." She smiled with renewed warmth. "You should be a chef instead of a lawyer, Tags."

Her remark struck a strange, discordant note. "Could be that after the court gets done sentencing Markey for what happened in Da Nang that'll be my best option."

A week ago his words would have made her fighting mad, but now ...well, for a man who seemed so understanding, why couldn't he understand why she'd acted as she had on the Da Nang story. She was thinking about trying once more to explain when he took her hand.

"Forget I said that. It sounds like I'm setting up an alibi. ... How about a walk?"

They went on down the beach. The wind had picked up and Veronica was happy to have the hood over her still-wet hair. As they trailed along in the sand, a sandpiper wandered ahead of them, poking here and there with his long needlelike beak.

"No birds in Viet Nam," Taggart said.

"What?"

"I said there aren't any birds in Viet Nam. I didn't see any. That sandpiper made me think of it."

"Why do you suppose that is?"

"Must be a lot smarter than we give 'em credit for."

"Smarter than people?" she said. He shrugged.

Eventually they came to some rock formations. Worn smooth by the ebb and flow of the waves, their hollows and indentations were prisons for the tiny creatures that lived in the margin between land and sea. Sitting quietly on the rocks, they studied these tidal pools, watching their inhabitants scurry about as they awaited rescue by the tide.

"We had joy, we had fun, we had seasons in the sun," she murmured.

"But the stars we could reach were just starfish on the beach." Taggart finished the verse.

She turned and met his stare.

"You like McKuen?"

"Sometimes. It's a dark secret, and would end my career if it got out, but I like poetry. Even write it sometimes. Can you stand it?"

"I think it's terrific." She drew his head down to her and kissed him.

Slowly they retraced their way back to the poncho liner, collected their things and headed south toward San Diego. While they were well north of the city it began to mist, and soon the rain that had been threatening all day was falling steadily. Taggart called back over his shoulder above the wind and rain and roar of the engine to ask if she wanted to stop at a coffeeshop and wait out the storm. Veronica, already well-soaked, said it didn't matter. They went on. Huddled behind Mike to get out of the wind, she wondered how he could see. Whenever she looked over his shoulder, the sting of the rain driving into her face made her turn away.

As Taggart coasted to a stop in front of her room Ronnie slid off the back of the bike and ran for the door. She was already inside by the time he'd jerked the cycle up onto its stand in the semishelter of the lee side of the building and ran back through the rain to the door. As he stepped inside into the twilight of the darkened motel room, Veronica embraced him, shivering, nestling close as she felt his calloused hands beneath her sodden shirt on the bare skin of her back.

Hands. She smiled to herself. Slowly he withdrew one of his arms from behind her and with his thumb and index finger tilted her head up so that she was looking at him. He bent and gently kissed her, a contrast to the tension she sensed in the tautness of the muscles she could feel and see as he held her.

He straightened slightly, and she leaned back, resting on his arm that encircled her waist. Braless since her swim, her nipples were outlined in dark circles beneath the wet white cotton of her shirt. Taggart's thoughts were a blur . . . So it's come to this . . . the DI hater, the lawyer-baiter, the TV lady, the sexy tomboy, the lovely desiring woman, all in one and willing, at this moment, to fulfill what had begun, when? On that night at World Famous? Their first motorcycle ride? The night Collins died? The day he got his order to WESPAC?

No question he'd sensed what had to happen unless something, and something strong, deflected the feeling they obviously had for each other. Now, holding Ronnie, feeling her move in response to each of his movements, listening as her breathing kept pace with his own, there were no questions, no reservations. . . . Now, for the first time, Cathy, the woman he'd known—and loved—for so many years, couldn't stop or divert what he was feeling. More than anything else, he wanted to *show* Veronica how he felt.

Watching, studying, intent, as if each was trying to see inside the other, they stood there. A drop of water fell from Ronnie's hair to her cheek and ran slowly down her neck. Mike traced its path with his index finger down to where it disappeared. There he stopped and unfastened the first of the three buttons at the throat of her jersey. Unhurriedly, deliberately, Ronnie responded, slowly unbuttoning his shirt, pausing as he lifted hers over her head. On and on the ceremony continued, helping each other, barely touching, spiraling the intensity between them. At last they knelt facing each other on the bed, and once again Mike swept ever so lightly over her cheek with his fingertips, leaving an unseen mark wherever he touched her. This time she followed his hand as he withdrew it, continuing on with him beyond any place either had ever been before . . . not a taking but a sharing, not a conquest but a mutual surrender.

Eighteen

THE DAYS that followed were filled with reconstruction of Loren Collins's last few hours. Mike interviewed, reinterviewed every witness who claimed to have seen Collins on the night of his death, with the exception of the uncooperative Dr. Nellis. He learned everything he could about the medical findings on the cause of Collins's death ... trauma, effusion, edema, hematoma, hemorrhage, all the terms of the report.

Taggart also defended Sugar Bear at his court-martial, and Veronica watched the trial in hope of gaining some further insight into the riddle that was Mike Taggart. She had seen Taggart at the Article 32 hearing, where he had said very little, but as yet not in a trial. What would be the book on him, she wondered, as he and Jerry Hill, the prosecutor, fenced with each other during the selection of the court, the counterpart of a civilian jury.

Sugar Bear had been charged with assault and desertion, and Taggart's defense to both was compulsion, or self-defense. The prosecution decided not to spend the money to bring the victim of Sugar Bear's assault back to San Diego from wherever he was now living as a civilian, so the assault charge was dropped. The government was apparently confident it could put Sugar Bear away on desertion alone.

The government's case was easy. The custodian of Sugar Bear's

Service Record Book simply verified the entries indicating the day of Sugar Bear's departure and the day of his return, and the prosecution rested.

Taggart opened with a records custodian of his own, presenting evidence that before Sugar Bear's two-day stay in recruit training Sergeant Voorhis, who had been Sugar Bear's platoon sergeant, had been convicted of one count of maltreatment of recruits.

Next came Sugar Bear. Veronica was amazed. Dressed in a crisply laundered uniform, his hair neatly trimmed, he snapped out "Yessirs" and "Nosirs" to Taggart's questions. He was one of nine children. He'd grown up in the streets of Detroit without knowing his father but had known the Man from childhood: the landlord, who never fixed anything and threatened the family with eviction; the shopkeepers who would never give him a job, who called the cops if he and his friends hung around in front of their stores; and the cops—fearful, hate-filled second-generation Poles and Czechs—who floated like corks on the sea of black and went home at the end of their shifts to ghettoes of their own, the cops who called him "punk" and "boy" and prodded him with their nightsticks to move on. He also knew the winos and the fences and the pushers and the pimps, who were his neightbors and friends. He'd enlisted in the Corps while he'd been stoned, and when his head had cleared he'd thought why not, nothing could be worse than Detroit.

But it had been worse. The Marines took away his clothes, they cut his hair, they wouldn't let him talk; everything they handed him they threw; and everything they said they shouted. "Fall in" line up "asshole to belly button . . ." The first night Sergeant Voorhis put Sugar Bear's platoon in their racks at attention, Sugar Bear lay rigid in his bunk for more than an hour before he fell asleep. On the second day everything fell apart.

Q. "What happened on that second morning, Private Collinwood?"
A. "The Sergeant . . . Sergeant Voorhis . . . he come in first thing an' he was yellin' 'bout we have five minutes to get outside."
Q. "What happened then?"
A. "Ah couldn't fall out 'cause ah'd forgot my locker combination

an' ah couldn' get dressed. There was a lot of shoutin' about git outside and the res' of the platoon, they run out, an' ah'm still standin' there."

Q. "Did you go find the sergeant to get help?"

A. "He foun' me. Sergeant Voorhis come in an' he's lookin' aroun' and he sees me and he starts yellin'. Ah'm back up against my locker an' he's got this stick an' he's askin' questions an' evertime ah say I don't know he pokes me wi' his stick."

Q. "Show the court where he poked you."

A. "He poked me right here under mah ribs." Sugar Bear stood up and demonstrated.

Q. "What did you do?"

A. "Ah said, 'Don' poke me wi' that stick, man,' and he went crazy. He say he poke me wherever he wan' to an' he jab that stick up under mah chin, he say mah soul belong to God but mah ass belong to him."

Q. "What then?"

A. "Ah fired his ass up."

Q. "You mean you hit him?"

A. "Yessir, ah hit him."

Q. "How many times did you hit him?"

A. "Nuff so's he don' get up an' come after me, 'cause ah know ah'm in trouble as soon as ah hit him the firs' time."

Q. "Private Collinwood, you'd been hit before, you'd been yelled at before, what made you hit Voorhis this time?"

A. "Ah was scared. We was alone an' that's when things happen. That's when the Man do his worst, 'cause they's nobody around to see."

Q. "Is that what you learned in Detroit?"

A. "That's what ah learned in Detroit."

Q. "What did you do next?"

A. "I forced da lock an' got dress', and then ah made mah bird, 'cause ah know ain' nobody goin' understan' 'bout what happen."

Q. "Made your bird? Took off?"

A. "Ah got outta there, ah did"

* * *

185

Veronica couldn't help but think of Collins and Markey. And how Taggart was on the other side now. . . . If Loren Collins had fought back maybe he'd still be alive.

Taggart's next witness had gone through a transformation toward respectability even more remarkable than Sugar Bear's. It was Mark Levinson, the head of VICTEM, the group staging the wake for Loren Collins outside Gate Two, the authors of the graffiti that Taggart found such bitter reminders of her decision to report his client Markey's Da Nang court-martial. Levinson was now in slacks and a corduroy sport coat, and wearing a necktie and his beard and hair were neatly trimmed. He introduced himself as a Ph.D candidate in psychology at Stanford University. He told the court he'd been a Marine lieutenant and infantry platoon leader with the Ninth Marines in Viet Nam. That made the court take some notice.

Levinson testified about how difficult it was for inner city youth—he'd written his master's thesis on the subject—to be integrated into the armed forces. After all, many of the officer and nonofficer personnel they came up against were from the rural south and midwest, where minorities such as Sugar Bear belonged to were neither familiar nor popular. He also leaned on the fact that blacks from the inner cities had to fight for survival, that ordinary family discipline was rare with so many fatherless homes. It was unreasonable, he said, to expect such young people to adapt to military life. Officers, NCOs—they were just more cops to someone raised in the ghetto. Taggart anticipated the prosecution's response that some inner city kids did well, Levinson fielded it easily by saying that there were, of course, exceptions, and, in fact, that the exceptions tended to be as extraordinary in their successes as the rest of the group tended to be the opposite. He said the corps's recruiting standards had been relaxed during the social experiment known as McNamara's 100,000 and that Sugar Bear was a victim of that. He was being asked to risk his life in a war against other nonwhites and to do it in the name of the people who had persecuted him all his life. It didn't make much sense.

The court deliberated only a half hour before finding Sugar Bear guilty of the lesser included offense of unauthorized absence. Technically unauthorized absence differed from desertion in that it implied that Sugar Bear hadn't intended to remain absent. After an absence of two years, and apprehension while joyriding in a stolen car in his hometown, that was ridiculous. It was a bone thrown to the defense for a nice try. Taggart figured his gamble of trying the case to a full court instead of a military judge alone was lost. The sentencing portion of the trial followed and was very brief. Sugar Bear had no record of good time to point to as giving promise of potential for rehabilitation. Levinson's well-intentioned testimony had undercut the credibility of anything that could be said along those lines. Mike had explained to his client that courts were notoriously more harsh than military judges when it came to sentencing. Sugar Bear should bend over and grab his ankles, because the Corps was about to put it to him. It was no more than Sugar Bear expected.

This time the court stayed out over an hour in its deliberations. Sugar Bear waited outside the defense hooch rapping with some of the other brothers from the brig who were waiting to talk to their lawyers. From a distance, the chasers kept a wary eye on the group.

When the court returned everyone filed back into the courtroom and the verdict was read by the senior-ranking member of the court, a sour-looking major. Taggart guessed from his demeanor that the sentence was not unanimous and the major was in the minority. A good sign? Sure enough. Sugar Bear was volleyballed back to the civilian world whence he had come with a bad conduct discharge and forfeiture of all pay and allowances. But no brig time. Sugar Bear behaved as if he had won, haughtily informing his chaser that his services were no longer required.

"Capt'n Taggart," he said, "you an' me, we both know Sugar Bear can't be no Marine. That fella you brung in, he say so himself. You be a good lawyer, capt'n, an' when you make your bird outta the Corps you come to Motown and look up the Bear 'cause I get you all the clients you ever need."

Taggart smiled. "Sorry I couldn't have made that an admin discharge instead of a BCD. It was all set if we just could have skated that court-martial."

"I know it was, but the only way they can hurt me wi' those discharge papers where I'm goin' is if they wrap a brick in 'em." With that he stuck out his hand and shook Taggart's. "For you, skip, I'll do it the paleface way." He grinned, distinguishing by his reference the elaborate black power salute and handclasp that was popular among the brothers.

"Stay out of trouble, okay?" Taggart said, without any real hope that the Bear would be able to manage that.

It was late afternoon by the time Sugar Bear left, and Mike and Veronica stopped at the Officers' Club for a drink. Taggart was doing his post mortem of Sugar Bear's trial when Veronica suddenly interrupted.

"What amazes me is that in one breath you can argue that that DI's assault ought to be seen as an excuse for what Sugar Bear did, and in the next breath defend someone like Markey."

Taggart didn't answer. He didn't feel like arguing at the moment.

"Loren Collins..." Veronica went on. "You needed him as your witness today. He was a real expert on boot camp brutality."

Taggart's fists tightened. He didn't disagree. The difference between them was that he didn't believe Markey was the assailant. He looked at her, shook his head and ordered another drink.

Nineteen

PRUDHOMME LOOKED up at the sound of someone entering his office unannounced. It was his friend Jim Browning, Hotel Company's first sergeant.

"I just stopped by to check and see how my fugitive drill instructor's doin'," Browning said as he settled into a chair opposite Prudhomme's desk.

"Fugitive?"

"Staff Sergeant Markey."

"Oh . . . I wouldn't call him a fugitive."

"Well, he's sure in a hum, whatever you call him." Browning stretched and looked around the room. "How's he doin' up here anyway?"

It shouldn't have seemed an unusual question. Under ordinary circumstances Markey was one of Browning's men, and that's where he might be returning if he got off, although Prudhomme wasn't so sure. But the way Browning asked it made Prudhomme think twice about his answer. Browning's nonchalance was too studied, and his casual reference to Markey as a fugitive didn't square with a drill sergeant's typical attitude about another DI charged with maltreatment, especially murder. It was no joking matter.

"He's doing all right, under the circumstances," Prudhomme said guardedly.

"What do you think's gonna happen?" Browning wondered.

"How should I know?"

"Word is they got him by the balls," Browning probed.

"Who says so?"

"It seems to be what everybody's sayin'.'"

"Jim, who you been talkin' to?"

"Well, I got a call from this Captain Steiner this morning. He's the prosecutor in Markey's court-martial."

"You talkin' to the prosecutor?" Prudhomme winced.

"Hey, relax. He called me, okay?"

"What's he want?"

"He said he'd heard I was gonna be a character witness in Sergeant Markey's court-martial and he wanted to know how well I knew Markey and what I was going to say."

"Are you gonna be a witness for Markey?"

"I don't know." Browning shrugged. "He asked me a while back an' I said I would, but now, well, I ain't so sure. I mean, if it ain't gonna do him no good... The captain said they got him pretty good ... welts all over the private's belly like might of been made by a rifle butt and the guide sayin' he saw Markey hit the kid with the rifle. John, that ain't like some shitbird sayin' it. How many times can you remember a guide testifying against a DI?"

Prudhomme had to admit he couldn't remember that ever happening before.

"Besides," the first Sergeant went on, "I been thinkin' about it... Markey ain't nothing special. I mean, he's gonna want me to go in there and say he's the best damn DI on the field, or somethin' like that. I don't think that's true. He's no better than average—"

Prudhomme broke in, "Jim, you know Markey's fitness reports better than I do, but I've seen 'em. They're outstanding straight across, and you know it."

"Big deal. So's everybody else's. Sayin' somebody's only excellent is like sayin' he ain't worth a shit. But that ain't the point either, John. Captain Steiner says the CG's right on top of this one, that the Chief of Staff wants daily reports on everything that's goin' on in the case. Who knows what they're thinkin' up there. No sense riskin' pissin' somebody off when it ain't gonna do no good anyway."

Prudhomme was on the point of asking what Browning was afraid of, being sent to Viet Nam, but decided against it. Browning had always been more of a politician than a soldier, he wasn't going to change now. "Well, if that's the way you feel, Jim, Markey and his lawyer probably don't want you anyhow. No room for half-steppers in a case like this."

The message was received. "What about you?" Browning asked as he stood up to leave. "Since you think Markey's such a great Marine, are you gonna be a witness for him?"

"He never asked me," Prudhomme said.

He didn't add that Taggart, after talking to him, decided that he would make a poor witness, for all his good sentiments. He wasn't about to stick his neck out either, it seemed. The supreme law was in effect—C.Y.O. Cover Your Ass. Amen.

Tom Horn was six feet, three inches, but Taggart never thought him particularly strong except when he was trying to rebound against him. "Like now," Taggart thought, vainly trying to muscle Horn away from the basket as they jockeyed for position in the ongoing one-on-one battle they'd been waging ever since they met during their first year of law school.

From his superior position in the lane Horn snatched the ball out of the air and canned a three-footer, despite being blasted as Taggart leaped into him in an attempt to block the shot. Tom wobbled out from underneath the basket holding his ribs in mock pain.

"That's game, isn't it?" Taggart asked, retrieving the ball and bouncing it as he talked. "Go for another?"

They were both drenched, and Tom had his right shoe and sock off inspecting the sole of his foot. "This asphalt eats up my feet," he grumbled, and then, answering Mike, "Nah, I'm beat, need a beer. Where's Cathy with her two tall cold ones when we really need her—"

He bit off his words in mid-sentence. Tom had known the Taggarts

191

for six years, and with the exception of the year in Viet Nam, Cathy had always been there, on driveway courts, playgrounds, ball diamonds, football fields, from Ann Arbor to San Diego, watching, ready with a couple of brews whenever he and Mike finished trying to kill each other.

"I'm sorry, Tags," he said, reaching out and touching Taggart's shoulder as he spoke. "It just slipped out. Force of habit, I guess."

Mike shrugged. "I wonder where she is too."

They sat silent for a while on a concrete picnic table beside the court, soaking up the Saturday morning sunshine in the nearly empty park. Beyond them sailboats frisked on the bay in the light breeze.

"What're you going to do if she comes back?"

Coming from anyone else that question, with its implied reference to Veronica as well as Cathy, would have been out of line. Coming from Horn, a friend, it was less Tom Horn wanting to know what Taggart was going to do then wanting Taggart to know himself.

Mike looked at Horn. "Don't know, old buddy. Things are real strange right now." Taggart was spinning the ball between his palms, feeling its grain, bouncing it now and then between his feet on the concrete bench.

"How you coming with Markey?"

"The cards are all on the table, I think. It's going to be a GCM, that's clear. As for the outcome . . . Did you hear about Katkavage's staff briefing yesterday?"

Horn nodded. "I was there. Go-Go sent me in his place."

"I heard he announced a full investigation of recruit training instructional procedures. That right?"

"That's right. Battalion commanders to submit reports in thirty days. Kat says the command is going to 'root out' maltreatment. That's what he said."

"That'll stir things up down at RTR. Of course the timing's just a coincidence."

"Of course."

"C'mon"—Taggart threw a sharp bounce pass at Horn's feet and jogged out onto the court—"one more for the World Championship. And watch out for paybacks."

192

* * *

Being Sergeant Major Prudhomme's assistant turned out not to be such a bad job for Roger Markey after all. A couple of days after he'd bitched to Taggart, there came a growled half-request, half-command from Prudhomme's office. "Markey, get your ass in here."

Markey put down the book he was reading and walked in. Here goes another run for a Top Secret morning newspaper, he thought. But the sergeant major had something else on his mind.

"Marine Corps ain't payin' you to read novels, Sergeant Markey."

What's eating him? Markey wondered. He'd been reading novels at his desk right outside Prudhomme's door for three weeks now, ever since his thousandth request for something to do failed to produce any result. The sergeant major knew what he was doing, maybe one of the officers had complained. Markey couldn't tell whether Prudhomme was really angry, because the man's normal voice was about the same as a disgruntled lion's.

"Since you're such a bookworm," Prudhomme went on, "I'm gonna give you a special assignment. We been teachin' these recruits the same tired bullshit in Marine Corps history since Chesty Puller was a teenybopper. I want you to go over to the base library and read everything you can get your hands on about Marine Corps history and tradition and I want you to put together some recommendations on how we can make it all a little more...uh, motivational."

When he was sure Markey was on his way Prudhomme called the defense hooch. "Hello, Captain Taggart. This is Sergeant Major Prudhomme. I just thought I'd pass the word that Professor Markey's been launched."

"Thanks. He may surprise you with what he comes up with."

The first time she saw Sergeant Markey in the base library, Veronica was astonished. His presence was hardly consistent with her ideas about drill instructors, particularly this one. He sat almost motionless on the hard wooden chair like the proverbial ramrod, his back never touching the backrest. He wasn't just reading he was studying, taking notes. Evidently he had even devised some kind of crude filing system, because his papers were arranged in several separate piles in front of

193

him, and when he finished with one, he sometimes seemed to ponder in which pile to put it before setting it aside. Apparently it made a difference.

For three mornings now Sergeant Markey had been in the base library, in the same place, when Veronica came in to work on her preparations for interviews or to organize the notes she'd taken in earlier sessions or just to read the literature of this spartan subculture she'd so unexpectedly become involved with. Finding Markey was an unexpected bonus. She wanted to ask Taggart what Markey was doing there but was afraid that if Mike knew the huntress was so close to her quarry he'd alert Markey to have nothing to do with her.

As it was, the staff sergeant wasn't exactly breaking down any doors to get acquainted. Other than the librarian they had been alone in the library most of each morning. Veronica was sure Markey recognized her from their introduction following the Article 32 hearing, but other than a brief nod as she walked past him on entering the facility each morning, he paid no attention to her.

Ronnie noted that each morning, precisely at 10:15, Markey would go outside for a smoke break. She made up her mind that if he followed the pattern on the fourth morning she would take the initiative.

At 10:15 on the fourth morning Markey got up and went outside. Veronica watched him leave, intending to follow in a couple of minutes. As Markey moved out the door, though, he was greeted by someone walking by and they stopped to talk. Damn, Veronica thought, pressing so hard on her pencil as she watched them through the window that she broke the lead. Why did he have to see someone he knew today. But Markey's conversation with the passerby was brief, and as soon as the other person went off Veronica made a beeline for the door.

Markey was leaning against one of the columns of the arcade that ran the length of the east side of the drill field. He was smoking and staring out at the various platoons drilling in the heat on the merciless asphalt plain. "Column left; column right; keep your cover and dress; keep your cover and dress..." The singsong commands of the DIs floated through the morning air, punctuated occasionally with shouts of "Halt, you dumb sonsabitches" and a variety of other expletives from exasperated noncoms trying to mold mobs into fighting machines.

"How do they decide which one gets to carry the flag?" Veronica asked as she came up to Markey's right.

The sergeant turned and looked uneasily at Veronica. Still, the question seemed harmless.

"The flag's called a guidon, the man carrying it is called the guide," he told her. "In recruit platoons the guide is usually the number-one-performing recruit in the platoon." He said it like a lecture.

So that's the guide, Ronnie thought, remembering the guide selection process in Loren Collins's platoon. Could this be the DI standing beside her now who had sicced those recruits on each other on the night described in Collins's letter?

Markey had lapsed back into silence.

"Whew, I thought it was hot in there," she tried again, indicating the library behind them, "but it looks even worse out there where they are."

"Probably why they call it the grinder, 'cause its grinds you down."

Ronnie took a chance. "Has it ground you down, Sergeant Markey?"

He turned his head back a quarter in the direction of the drill field. "It's tryin' to."

"You know who I am, don't you, Sergeant Markey?"

"Yeah."

"I mean, you know what I do, that I'm a reporter?"

"Yeah, you talked to Sherill one time."

"Would you mind if I asked you some questions? You wouldn't have to answer any you didn't want to, but would you let me at least ask them?"

He looked at her. "You mean like why did I beat that recruit to death . . ."

"Excuse me, sarge, you gotta light?"

Markey and Veronica turned and came face to face with Corporal Litzinger, whom they both recognized as one of the clerks in the legal office.

"Sure thing." Markey reached into his sock for his cigarettes and took out some matches from the cellophane wrapper.

Veronica studied him as he did so. Markey was obviously feeling

195

the strain of waiting. "No, no loaded questions," she said when he turned back to her after Litzinger had disappeared into the library. "I know you're pleading not guilty and have always denied having anything to do with it. Sergeant Markey, I won't try to trick you, I promise you that. I'd like to know about your background, why you joined the Corps, your experiences since you've been in. General stuff. Okay?"

She could imagine Markey considering the question along with Taggart's direction not to talk to her.

Finally he said, "All right, but no questions about the night it happened."

"Fair enough." She wondered if she dared to take notes, decided not to. She didn't want to spook him. Just keep it simple, TV lady, she told herself, borrowing Taggart's name for her.

The sun was directly over the drill field and the recruit platoons had marched off to their noon meal before Markey and Veronica finished talking. Markey discovered that she was a good listener, and her questions sounded pretty sympathetic to him. So he told her why he came in the Corps, where he had been, what he had done, his feelings when he'd received orders to the field, and, even though he was no philosopher and usually refused to be drawn into discussions about the war, he had an answer when she asked him his feelings about Viet Nam.

"The first time I came into country the plane landed at Da Nang Airbase. It was a gray day, a light rain falling, at least light for that place. The NCOIC, that's the noncom in charge, lined us all up and we stood in the rain waitin' for transportation. I was at the end of the formation nearest this shed or shelter, what it really was was a roof on poles without no walls and it was filled with a line of marines waitin' to get on the plane we'd just come in on, when it turned around and flew back to Okinawa.

"They were yellin' and jeerin' at us. 'Just wait,' they'd yell, 'jus' wait' and 'hey, look at the fresh meat. You fuckers are goin' to be sorry! You don't know how sorry you're gonna be!' and other stuff too. They were offerin' to give our last regards to people back in the world. The strange thing was, they kept it up and kept it up until it dawned on me they were only half-jokin', and they really didn't give a shit about us or about scarin' us more than we were already scared. They didn't give a shit about anything, not after what they'd been through. The whole idea of not givin' a shit took a new meanin' for me that day. It wasn't the way I thought it was supposed to be, especially not in the Corps, and that was the way the war stayed for me, with all the rules that didn't keep you from gettin' killed, but kept you from ever havin' any real chance of winnin', with all the hatred it's caused back here in the states . . . But I tell you what"—his eyes narrowed and the angles of his face hardened—"I never quit carin', I never did, even if it seems like nuthin' is the way it's supposed to be anymore."

"Including the drill field?"

"Yeah, includin' the drill field, but I don't want to get into that. I already told you—"

"What about the court-martial in Da Nang? What happened there?"

"What do you mean 'what happened?'"

"Did you kill the other marine?"

"I hit him one time, he died. Let's talk about something else."

"What do you think's going to happen with your court-martial and the charges against you?"

Markey stared out at the drill field, then said, "I think they'll say I'm not guilty. Even though I tell myself it can happen, I still can't convince myself that an innocent man can get convicted of murder. And Captain Taggart's a good lawyer, a good man too . . . The trouble is, the more I think about it, the more I wonder whether it's gonna make any difference?"

"What do you mean by that?"

"I ain't sure. I mean, I know if I get sent to prison it'll make a big difference to my family, but so far as my life in the Corps, maybe it's already over. It's for sure that if I get convicted, even if I'm sentenced to no punishment, I'll never be allowed to reenlist. Where does that leave me and my family? For eight years I been a foot soldier, nothing else. I don't really know anything else. But there ain't a lot of demand for foot soldiers on the outside, so it's gonna be a pick and shovel for me, or maybe boxing groceries somewhere, or sweeping out some-place. Nothing' wrong with those jobs, except if you got a wife and two kids to feed, then they don't look like much, do they, especially after havin' been in the Corps and havin' really been good and taken pride at somethin' you liked, really liked. Even if I win, somebody's always gonna remember, and come promotion time or time to choose someone for a duty assignment, that person's always gonna be around to ask what if that court was wrong? Why take a chance on Markey, there's others just as good. Win or lose, I got a feeling it's gonna be a long time before anyone lets me or Sherill or the kids forget what's happened."

Markey bent over and kissed his daughter goodnight.

"Goodnight, daddy," she called after him as he went out of the room. Sherill was just coming out of their bedroom, where she had put the baby down in his crib. They almost bumped into each other in the tiny hallway.

"Oops, excuse me, lady," he said stopping short.

"Some drill instructor" she said, straining to be light. "Looks to me like you've got two left feet."

"Well, if so, it probably won't make any difference, not after today anyway," he said glumly.

Sherill turned and looked at him as they walked into the living room. "What's that supposed to mean?"

"Aw, I think I did something really stupid this morning, and I been kickin' myself ever since."

"Rog, what'd you do?"

"You know that woman, Veronica Rasmussen, the one Captain Taggart brought out here?"

"Yeah..."

"Well, the last few days she's been in the library out at the base where I been doin' that project for the sergeant major that we talked about. Anyway, I was outside havin' a cigarette this morning and she came out and started talking. Pretty soon she asked me if she could ask me some questions and... I, well, I said she could. We wound up talkin' for about an hour, maybe more."

Sherill felt sick. "Oh, Rog, not after everything Captain Taggart told us about not talking to anyone but each other and him."

"I know, I know. I told myself I shouldn't do it, but, Jesus, I was goin' crazy. I thought I was gonna bust tryin' to keep still, the way everybody's been throwin' charges around and me sayin' nothing. Everything that's written about it, everything you read, it's all written as if there's no doubt in anyone's mind I killed that Collins kid. Oh, sure, they throw in an 'alleged' now and then, but how many people even know what that means? I didn't before this thing all started. I just had to try to make at least one person besides you and Captain Taggart believe that I didn't do it, and even then I didn't tell her nothin' about the night it happened. We talked about a lot of things, but I told her I didn't do it, that I was innocent . . ."

They were sitting half sideways, facing each other on the couch. Markey was shaking his head at what he'd done.

"How could I do somethin' like that?" he went on. "Tuckin' Deb in just now I was thinking what a chickenshit way to behave. Takin' chances with our whole future together and goin' back on my word to Captain Taggart after all he's done. Shit, maybe I deserve all this—"

"Stop it, Roger, *stop* it." She put her hand over his mouth. "Don't you ever say such a thing, don't even think it. Anybody would have done what you did. Everything's been so awful, and you've kept it all inside until now. It's only natural. This whole thing's just been one big stupid mistake, but don't you *ever* say you deserve it, Rog. Please don't think that anymore."

"I don't know what to think, Sher, sometimes I think everything will be okay and other times I get real scared." Markey leaned back against the back of the couch and drew her to him. "You're the one who holds this show together, I know that much. A little of your backbone's what I need."

"You have plenty of backbone, Roger Markey," she whispered in his ear. "What you need is something to take your mind off your troubles."

At least we're together this time, she was thinking. She looked up at her husband, the Indian, the stoic, sitting there condemning himself for having briefly yielded to the temptation to speak out in his own defense. "Rog," she said, "let's go to bed early tonight."

Twenty

FEODOT WAS camped out a short pounce away from the charcoal grill, ready to recover in case someone fumbled the steaks she could smell broiling. Ronnie was casually monitoring their progress, and Taggart had assumed his best leaning-rest position against the patio fence, working on a beer.

In the living room, just inside the sliding screen door, the television droned the news of the world. Ronnie had hoped Taggart wouldn't turn on the news this evening. She had succeeded in having her coverage picked up by the network for the second time since she began to report the Markey case. Here goes, she thought, as he flipped on the television, then walked out to the patio. The anchorman began the story: "In San Diego today . . ." emphasizing the name of the city in a way that caused Taggart to stop in the midst of what he was saying and cock his head to listen. ". . . the doctor in the case of Staff Sergeant Roger Markey, the marine drill instructor charged with murdering a recruit in his platoon, said that the marks he observed on the victim on the night of his death looked like they could have been made by a rifle butt." The report then switched to Veronica in San Diego standing with Dr. Nellis outside Balboa Naval Hospital. . . . "This is Balboa Naval Hospital in San Diego, California, a medical facility that handles marine and navy personnel wounded in the fighting in Viet Nam. On the night of February 7, 1971, it was the scene of the death of Private Loren Collins, an eighteen-year-old recruit who was beaten to death during Marine boot camp. With me is Dr. Stephen Nellis, who treated Collins and was with him at the time of his death. Dr. Nellis, why did Loren Collins die?"

Taggart walked to the doorway and stood watching. Veronica watched through the screen from where she was standing. Nellis looked straight into the camera.

"In medical terms, he died of a rupture of the superior mesenteric artery. In short, he bled to death."

"Was there any indication what might have caused the injury?"

"When I examined his abdomen I found a series of red welts and abrasions and the beginnings of significant swelling and discoloration in the area. The marks appeared to me to be consistent with the type one might expect to be made by the butt of a rifle."

Veronica picked it up. "An eyewitness has reported seeing the defendant, Staff Sergeant Rober Markey, strike Loren Collins in the stomach with a rifle butt shortly before he was discovered near death. In an exclusive interview with this reporter, the defendant has repeated his denial of the charges against him. He did, however, admit striking a blow which killed another marine in Da Nang on Christmas Eve, 1968. Pretrial motions are scheduled—"

"Son of a bitch," Taggart muttered through clenched teeth. "When did you manage that?"

"I talked to him yesterday morning." She tried to sound matter-of-fact about the interview.

She had always thought that seeing how a man she cared for handled himself when he was really angry was need-to-know information, and had she not been the object of Mike's wrath on this occasion, she would probably have given Taggart a high grade for deportment. He didn't shout and, after his first surprised curse, he didn't swear at her. He stood regarding her silently, which made her feel damned uncomfortable in spite of her conviction that she'd been doing her job.

He kept a stony silence, then went inside the apartment for another beer.

She followed him in. "Mike," she said, "you're not just defending

Markey. You seem to care more about him, to be antagonistic toward anyone even presuming to question his innocence. You don't do that with your other cases, not with Sugar Bear—"

"Sugar Bear wasn't being used. He didn't have the antiwar people pointing at him like he started the war. He didn't have everybody who happened to feel sorry for the victim automatically calling for his conviction, turning his past inside out to find more to hand him with."

"Meaning me, I suppose." She was getting angry.

"I do. I didn't see you wearing out Sugar Bear's record book when you found out he beat a drill instructor senseless."

"Mike, be fair. That DI wasn't defenseless, and Sugar Bear *admitted* he did it."

Taggart shook his head. "Well, Markey says he *didn't* do it. Mad Dog's got his career on his mind, Mark Levinson's got his protests, and you've got a couple of grieving parents . . . everybody's got their own brand of tunnel vision."

Including you, she was about to snap back when she caught a whiff of burning meat. She ran out to the patio, where the main course was beginning to curl around the edges.

Muttering, at the steaks and Taggart, she stabbed and threw them on the plate beside the grill. "What'll we do with these?" she asked.

"Wash 'em down with enough beer and you won't know the difference," he said, taking the plate from her and placing it in the middle of the table where the rest of the meal waited. No more was said about Markey or Veronica's interviews or Nellis. But Ronnie couldn't avoid thinking on what he had said about her being influenced by the grief of Loren Collins's parents. Was she letting her emotions prevent her from seeing all that there was to see? She experienced her first serious doubt about the only thing she had been sure of since Mike Taggart.

Taggart was now spending many of his off-duty hours with Veronica, playing racquetball, jogging and walking on the beach. But most nights he spent pouring over his Markey notes, devising and revising, testing different versions, themes and arguments as he tried to come up with the key that might secure Markey's defense.

It occurred to Ronnie she had never detected in Taggart the pretense usually present in her relationships with men. He didn't seem to feel it necessary to impress her, or want her to go through hoops for him. Was it because he'd been married and knew from experience that two people couldn't get away with posturing in front of each other for very long. If so, at least there was one good thing about the fact he was married. Whatever, it made him easy to be with. As for Taggart, he was aware of the irony of doing with this woman so many of the things he'd thought of doing with Cathy during his year overseas. Was this a kind of payback?

Ronnie thought increasingly of Mike and Cathy's marriage, wondering what had driven them apart. Not since their walk back to the car on the evening after Beeson's blast at the Marine Corps' preoccupation with haircuts had Taggart even mentioned Cathy's departure. To know that they were separated had been sufficient then. Now it was no longer enough.

Ten days after Sugar Bear's trial they decided to go camping in Mexico, to Punta la Bunda, a spot on the map of Baja twenty miles or so below Ensenada.

Once through the squalor and commercialism of Tijuana, the road south was spectacular. Starting as a freeway paralleling a vast empty beach, it eventually narrowed, creeping up and clinging precariously to steep mountainsides, writhing along cliffbanks high above the rocky coast. Veronica was grateful they weren't on the motorcycle; even in the car there weren't enough handles to hold on to. The farther they drove, the more the countryside became in keeping with Veronica's midwestern notions of what Mexico ought to look like. Even the roadside pottery and produce stands disappeared after they left the main road, replaced by ramshackle houses dotting tiny cultivated plots, with children riding or leading worn-out-looking donkeys, and chickens wandering in the road.

"How far are we from San Diego?"

"About sixty miles."

"Seems like six thousand," she said.

"Miles or years?"

"Both."

The car bumped and jarred over a rutted track behind some grassy sand dunes as Taggart made his way among the potholes. "Pick a spot," he said.

"This is it? No campsites or anything?"

"This is it, campers. You were expecting KOA, perhaps?"

They parked in the lee of a large sand dune, leaving the gear in the car. Basking in the sun and sheltered from the wind by the drifted sand, they were warm enough, but if the sun went under a cloud it became instantly cool. They drank a little wine, listened to the pounding of the waves. No one else was in sight in any direction.

In the afternoon they walked far down the beach and, after more than a half hour, they came on an old man, an American, fishing in the surf and drinking tequila.

"Catching any?" Mike asked.

"No luck so far." The old man's skin was leathery and wrinkled and, taking off the battered red baseball cap he was wearing, he revealed a close-cropped head of gray hair. The emblem on the cap was the Marine eagle, globe and anchor.

"You a Marine?" Mike asked.

"Used to be, for almost thirty years."

"My name's Mike Taggart," Mike said, extending his hand. "This is Veronica Rasmussen."

"Bill Wilson, Gunnery Sergeant Bill Wilson, Gunny to people who still know me." The old man shook Taggart's hand, nodded to Veronica. "Here, let me set this pole down and offer you a drink." He slid the end of the rod he'd been holding into a notch on a stake he'd driven into the sand and offered his bottle first to Veronica.

Ronnie took the bottle, glancing at Mike. She pulled the cork out of the long neck and tipped it up to her mouth. Her first tug of the clear, oily-looking fluid almost knocked her flat, and it was all she could do to keep from coughing and spitting as she passed the bottle to Mike.

"Sorry I don't have no lemon for you to suck on." Wilson grinned.

"I'm in the Corps too," Mike told him. "Do you miss it?"

Wilson nodded. "The tough part is when ya retire. You've given up family for it . . . at least I did . . . and then you know the Corps goes on without ya, just like the rest of the world. I didn't feel old until the day after I got out. Maybe that's the final payback, you think?"

"Maybe so . . ." Taggart wondered to himself if there was any place worth a lifetime of belonging to.

"I got me that trailer over there"—Wilson pointed to a small green trailer parked in the distance behind them that Ronnie hadn't noticed before—"and I just sort of float around. Spend a lotta time down here though. It's cheaper, and after livin' so long in foreign countries this place's more like home than up north."

As they talked, the bottle went around each time more smoothly than the time before. Bill Wilson remembered the wars the Marines had returned from to parades instead of riots and demonstrations. Haiti, Iceland, the South Pacific, Japan and Korea, unrecorded brushfires and historic conflagrations. Hey diddle, diddle, right up the middle, Bill Wilson was a walking page of Marine Corps history.

A stiff offshore breeze had sprung up, and Ronnie could feel it chap her cheeks and lips. Now and then drops of spray would sting her face as the time, the place, the people, the stories from so far away fanned the glow she was already feeling. She had never felt quite so far away from Independence, Missouri, as she felt at that moment. She looked at Taggart. Did this beach, these stories . . . did *they* seem as unreal to him as they did to her? Go slow with this man, she'd told herself, only to find she was unable to take her own advice. But Taggart seemed like something out of her imagination sometimes, sent to test the things she thought she believed in. . . .

Suddenly Wilson's fishing pole was almost ripped from its stake by some unseen force just below the placid surface of the sea.

"Looks like you've hooked a whale," Mike said, jumping to his feet and breaking the spell Veronica had fallen into.

First Wilson, then Mike, then Wilson again wrestled with the strike, playing it out, pulling it in, leaning back with feet planted wide apart, the light tackle bent almost in two. Twice they thought they'd lost whatever it was as the line appeared to slacken, but each time it became taut again as soon as they began to reel it in.

Finally they could see the exhausted fish, still fighting as it was dragged into the shallow surf. Wilson had the pole, so Taggart grabbed the gaff and, kicking off his shoes, ran into the low surf, following the line with his left hand, holding his right arm out for balance. Struggling to stay upright against the force of the tequila and small waves, he reached for the catch, then jerked his hand away as a dorsal fin broke the surface of the almost waist-high water. Reflexively he jammed the gaff at the creature, catching it somewhere just behind the head. The water was immediately red and roiled all around him as he strained to keep the length of the short pole between him and the writhing fish. "Keep the line tight," he shouted over his shoulder to Wilson, all the time hauling against the stick in his effort to drag its load ashore.

It was a sand shark, no more than three and a half feet long. It battled on, thrashing about and gasping as it slowly drowned in the fresh sea air, its tiny black eyes staring blankly in the midst of its fury. Taggart watched it die as he tried to swallow away the sour taste of fear from the back of his mouth. He felt no elation at the successful landing. Rather he felt a curious mixture of pity for the death of the wild thing and regret at having been part of it.

Bill Wilson had no such compunctions. "I won't have to buy groceries for a week," he said, prodding the carcass to make sure it was dead. He offered them another drink to toast his good fortune, but both declined. They said their farewells and continued to walk slowly down the beach, arms wrapped about each other's waists, silently sharing their emotions until a huge gray building loomed darkly from behind the dunes silhouetted in the late afternoon sun.

Changing course, they veered in the direction of the structure, crossing dunes they discovered to be the shells of half-constructed beach houses drifted full of sand. Behind these ghostly outriders, across a spit of sandy mud overgrown with weeds, the concrete skeleton of an abandoned, uncompleted hotel rose three lonely stories above them. Inside, each footstep, each word spoken echoed from the high unfinished ceilings. Dark holes yawned into black basements to which there were no stairs. They wandered about, peering down holes, exploring shadows—

The snarl came without warning as they approached an especially dark corner of a cavernous room. Ronnie jumped a foot and caught her breath at the sound, drawing herself even closer to Mike as they both froze. Mike nodded in the direction of the sound. "Back up slow, don't turn around," he whispered sharply.

As Ronnie's eyes adjusted to the dimness of the corner, she saw a large mongrel dog about twelve feet directly in front of them, its lips curled showing its fangs, ears back, hair along its spine on end.

Step by step they walked slowly backward as the animal continued its gutteral grow. When they were finally well away from it, Veronica began to breathe again for the first time in almost a minute.

"Let's get out of here, Tags. We've antagonized enough wild creatures for one day. I think they're trying to tell us something."

On the way back they collected driftwood, and while Taggart built a fire Ronnie took the gear out of the car. Mike had a tent, but the night that was falling was so clear and beautiful, the stars so undimmed by any artificial light that they decided not to use it.

"How do these work?" Ronnie asked, holding up one of two identical sleeping bags.

"Depends on whether you want to make two one-person bags or one two-person bag."

"I think we better go with one two-person bag."

Later, wrapped in the downy cocoon and in the crook of Taggart's arm, she felt his lips move on the nape of her neck. She wanted to be reassured, she wanted to be told there were no more sharks, no more angry dogs, and Taggart wanted to tell her so, but in truth he didn't know.

She thought she could feel what she couldn't hear, that the uncertainty she felt was a two-way street, that Mike was as much in need of reassurance as she. Before when they'd made love she'd felt as if they were at the center of their world, as if things revolved around them. Not now. With the universe in sight directly above her, she saw them small and alone, about to be flicked into some kind of black hole in space. She could feel herself melt with tenderness, or was it him, or was it them, two becoming one once more, without effort, with one motion, leaving no seam...

In the morning she opened one eye and shut it again quickly against the sunlight. Where was Taggart? He certainly wasn't where she last remembered him. The scent of coffee brewing told her in which direction to look, and she turned toward the fire, where Mike sat watching her across the low flame.

"How did you sleep?" he asked.

"Terrific. What kind of bird nests in the sand, a sandpiper? I must have been a sandpiper in one of my other lives."

"Skinny legs, long beak, little round body, that'd be about right."

"If I had my clothes on I'd make you take that back."

"Don't come outside without your clothes, TV Lady, you just might freeze something off." He looked around and picked up a bulky hooded sweatshirt lying beside him and tossed it on top of the sleeping bag. "If you want to sit up and put this on, I'll pour you some coffee."

Like an Indian he watched, silent and impassive, as Ronnie slid halfway out of the sleeping bag, sitting and stretching without self-consciousness, naked in the cold morning air. She reached for the sweatshirt and shivered as the cool cloth touched her skin. Behind his mask, Taggart hoped that whatever happened to him during the rest of his life he would always carry with him the image of this lovely woman stretching and pulling on that sweatshirt.

"Cup of mud?" He handed her the coffee.

In the morning stillness they sat and watched a pelican fishing beyond the breakers. Finally she said, "Mike will you tell me what you meant when you said Cathy was gone? Why did you break up? If you have..."

"There's a saying, 'the only thing harder than being a Marine is being a Marine's wife.' That's especially true for Cathy. She grew up in the house her father was born in and married a man...me...she'd known since she started high school. Having a home and family and neighbors and roots have been extra important to her. Those are in short supply in the Corps. We've been married six Christmases now, and we've never had a tree. We were always on the way to somewhere. Living for that brief time in Chicago really affected her. She had a glimpse of what she wanted, and then the Corps slammed the door in her face.... But that's not all there was to it. There wasn't much choice about going in the service, and the Corps was the choice we both agreed on. I doubt she'd have left if she'd been happier with me ...As much as she liked Chicago she could see I hated it, and I think she began to wonder if I'd ever find anything I really liked, or maybe she was afraid I liked the Corps too much, although I can't believe she ever thought I'd stay in. Sometimes I think she married me as much for what she thought I'd become as for what I was . . . am. Anyway, that's some of what made her go. I think she's afraid I'll wind up some kind of a gypsy, like the old guy we met yesterday."

"Want to stop by my place before I drop you off?" Mike asked as they left the freeway at the exit marked "Beaches."

Ronnie agreed. "How about I cook something for dinner. You have something besides beer in that refrigerator, dont' you?"

Mike unlocked the door to let them in. Veronica went to scramble some eggs and he began to carry in the gear. The phone rang while Mike was outside, where Ronnie didn't know if he could hear it. As it rang again she reached to answer it, then stopped. She couldn't bring herself to pick up the receiver. Taggart finally answered after the fourth ring.

"Hello . . . Cathy, what's the matter? Are you all right? Where are you?"

At the sound of Cathy's name Veronica looked around for some place to go. She took the eggs off the stove and headed for the stairs, but Mike shook his head and motioned her back.

"Rape? . . . tried? *Cathy,* I can't understand half of what you're saying. Slow down, try to stop crying. Are you hurt? What's *happened?* . . . Don't be silly, you were right to call. Now tell me what happened." A pause, and then, "You have a job?"

Mike listened intently. Veronica watched him, his head was bowed, and he was pinching the bridge of his nose between his thumb and forefinger as he concentrated on what he was hearing.

"I'm glad I was home too, Cath," he finally said. "You're going to be all right now. Sleep, that's what you need right now more than anything. Are you by yourself in the house now? . . . Well, is there someone nearby you can call? When will Carol be home?"

Another long pause. Veronica offered a prayer of thanks she'd not answered that call.

"Yeah," Mike was speaking again in the same low, comforting voice as before. "Yeah, I think it's crazy too, Cath, but I can't answer any of those questions, at least not right now. I have about a million of my own, but now's not the time to try to sort it out ... you've had a rough day. Please try to get some sleep and call me tomorrow night, okay? We argue the pretrial motions in Markey's case tomorrow so you probably couldn't reach me there if you tried. The trial starts on Tuesday ... Me too, Cath ... now go to bed ... right ... well, good-bye."

Taggart settled the receiver back onto its hook and slowly turned to face Veronica. "Guess who?"

Ronnie didn't know whether to laugh or cry. It was all so foreseeable. She asked what happened.

"She's got a job and an apartment too, I think, although she didn't say so. She went out with some guy from work this afternoon, and when they got back to her place he didn't want to take no for an answer. Her screaming scared him away."

"Is she all right? He didn't hurt her, did he?"

"She's all right now, still upset but all right."

Along with her relief, came a flood of resentment toward Cathy. She couldn't help it. She looked at Mike, who was standing opposite her, looking at her but seeing instead a blonde woman crying alone in an apartment fifteen hundred miles away. Her date attacks her, so she calls the husband she left for sympathy. It was a call Veronica hoped she would never make.

She looked at her watch. It was almost eight o'clock. "Maybe we better call it a night. I don't feel much like eating anyway. I'm pretty beat. I just want to go back to the motel and wash off the ten pounds of Mexico I brought back with me. Can we go now?"

"Yeah," he said, "that's probably the best idea."

When they pulled to a stop in front of Ronnie's room she paused for a moment before getting out, taking Mike's right hand in both of hers. "Thanks for the lessons in scouting, Tags. Did I earn any merit badges?"

"A couple I'm sure the Girl Scouts of America haven't invented yet." He said it without much of a smile. "Goodnight, TV lady, I had a great time . . ." His voice trailed off, and then he added, "One of the best of my life."

Telling Mike not to bother getting out, Ronnie walked through the car's headlights, searched for her key and let herself in. She leaned back against the door as it closed behind her, listened to the sound of him driving off. Now it was her turn to let go. She fought back the tears, but couldn't make the pain go away. No matter how much she'd tried to fortify herself against the possibility of Cathy's resurfacing, it hurt and hurt badly actually to witness the depth of Mike's continuing involvement with another woman. Even—and at the thought she had to smile for a moment through her tears—if the other woman happened to be his wife.

Twenty-One

COLONEL MO was the ideal judge for a court martial. Years of duty behind a desk had allowed his stomach to catch up and surpass his formerly barrel chest. He moved with a slowness and deliberation that befitted his size and belied the quickness of his mind. There was none of the jolly good humor people usually associated with fat people in Colonel Frank Modelewski. He was a cold, hard skeptic who put up with no nonsense in his courtroom.

Taggart had tried cases in front of him on Okinawa and knew him as a fair man who would take a drink or two at the noon recess. Whether that would make a difference when, as now, there would be a jury to decide Markey's fate, Taggart didn't know.

Now Colonel Mo sat ponderously turning his head from Taggart to Steiner and back, as if watching a slow-motion tennis match, while the two of them argued Taggart's motion to prevent Dr. Nellis from testifying that in his opinion the marks on Collins's stomach could have been made by a rifle butt. It was not a medical issue, it was for the jury to decide, Mike insisted. Nellis's speculation about what made the marks would be given undeserved weight because Nellis was a doctor and testifying as an expert. And, in any case, there was nothing unique about marks left by a rifle butt. Predictably Steiner cited Nellis's medical training as the very reason why he should be able to give his opinion. Physicians treated wounds daily; wounds differed, depending on how they had been inflicted. The members of the court were entitled to the benefit of Nellis's expertise.

Taggart's motion was denied. He felt flat. He needed a better result on his next motion.

"Sir," he said to Colonel Mo, "the defense moves that all reference to a certain incident between the accused and an individual named Gilpin and the court-martial that resulted from such incident be barred from this trial."

The colonel shifted his eyes in the direction of Steiner without moving the rest of his body.

"Sir, the prosecution does not oppose. Evidence of findings of not guilty and prior bad acts are conceded to be inadmissible."

Mo was about to grant the motion when Taggart spoke again.

"Sir, the defense asks that the exclusion it requests extend to any evidence tending to indicate that Staff Sergeant Markey has a reputation for violent conduct or the equivalent."

Markey had sworn to him the fight with Gilpin was the only one he'd ever had in his life, but reputation-evidence was the only way Taggart could think of for Mad Dog Steiner to point the court-martial in the direction of Da Nang.

It was immediately obvious that he'd hit a nerve. Mad Dog shot out of his chair like he'd been goosed with a cattle prod. He assured Colonel Mo that he had never heard of such a thing. A man's reputation for violent conduct was certainly relevant to any determination of whether he had committed a violent act. Defense counsel was trying to extend the inadmissibility of the fight itself to legitimate and admissible evidence by grouping the two together.

"Not so," Taggart shot back. Even though reputation-evidence was usually admissible, it really amounted to nothing more than gossip, and in this case its tendency to focus the court members on events that even the prosecution conceded were inadmissible clearly outweighed its probative value.

"Nonsense," Steiner countered. "Nothing need be said about Da Nang."

"Sir, I have reason to believe the fight with Gilpin in Da Nang was the only one Staff Sergeant Markey has ever had in his life, but if I try to show that the witnesses have no knowledge of any specific acts to support the violent reputation they are assigning to Sergeant Markey, reference to Da Nang will be inevitable."

All was quiet. Each side had had its say. Colonel Mo sat like a huge, imperturbable Buddha, staring down at the floor in front of the bench, silent for more than a minute. Taggart could see the judge's chest move beneath his military blouse. He was twirling a pencil between his thumb and index finger. The slim cylinder was dwarfed between the meaty fingers. There we are, Markey and me, Mike thought, momentarily transfixed by the parallel.

Mo put down the pencil and raised his heavy-lidded eyes to the level of those of Taggart and Steiner, heaved a sigh as if it was an effort to speak, and ruled.

"The motion of the defense is granted. All reference to what has been referred to as the Da Nang incident, including any evidence attributing to the accused a reputation for violent conduct, is prohibited.

"Gentlemen, are there any other matters that need to be considered at this time?"

"No, sir."

"No, sir."

"Very well, further proceedings will commence at 0830 tomorrow morning. This court is in recess."

All right, all *right,* Taggart thought exuberantly as he walked out of the courtroom, followed by Markey. The old competitive juices were beginning to flow. He'd won one.

Veronica watched them leave. Thank God, Taggart won that motion, she thought. Maybe he wouldn't be quite so upset about her reporting of the incident.

In this she was disappointed. When she congratulated him that evening his only response was, "Now if we could only do something about what they already know."

"Everybody's here but the fucking commandant," Margolis muttered over his shoulder as he walked into the courtroom ahead of Taggart and Markey.

It was true, or nearly so. Mad Dog Steiner was already in place, nervously shuffling papers at trial counsel's table. In the front row of the visitor's gallery directly behind Steiner sat Go Go. Taggart had never seen him in court before. Beside Guinn sat Katkavage, the chief of staff. Mike knew the Kat would rather walk through fire than hobnob with a bunch of lawyers.

Nah, the command doesn't think this case is anything special, he thought, as he walked up the aisle and stepped in front of the bar. Not much . . .

Sherill Markey was sitting on the aisle in the front row behind the defense counsel's table, dressed for church, as Taggart had instructed. Veronica was sitting beside her. She saw Roger Markey brush his wife's hair with his fingertips as he walked by, and follow the gesture by clenching his fist as it hung at his side in a signal for Sherill to take heart. Taggart walked by without any sign of recognition.

In addition to Guinn, Katkavage and other base personnel who had found time to come in to watch the trial begin, there were others, like Veronica, with note pads on their laps, newspeople. There was also one middle-aged couple, also dressed for church: Frank and Martha Collins had come to see the trial of the man who'd killed their children.

Taggart wasn't paying attention to the crowd. He carried with him a looseleaf notebook containing a step-by-step breakdown of the case he intended to present—voir dire questions for potential court members, requested instructions to be given the court members, case citations in support of points he expected to become important, outlines of his opening statement and final argument, questions for the direct and cross-examinations of witnesses. It was all there in black and white. Step by step, the dances Taggart expected the various dancers to perform. And he was the choreographer, the director, who had to make the words, the steps, the dances come off the page, freeing themselves from the lifelessness of ink and paper, assuming tone and color and personality of their own. By inflection, phrasing, timing, by doing but not overdoing, Taggart had to make the court members forget they were mere listeners to accounts of past events. They must become observers, watching with their minds' eyes the unfolding of the events that had led to trial as if they were taking place for the first time. Taggart was standing at the core of the case as he stood waiting for the judge and then the panel of prospective court members to take their places. The importance of forging that link between the book on the table in front of him and the minds of the court consumed him. By now a veteran of over a hundred trials, he was so nervous he was afraid he might throw up.

The manual given to all the new lawyers at Morgan, Miller & Richardson informed them that at the end of the jury selection process not only were all of the panelists' prejudices supposed to be identified and the unacceptable eradicated, but the jurors were supposed to be indoctrinated with the theme of one's case in the process. Taggart wondered whether any of the mossbacks who had authored that manual had ever been faced with a jury drawn from a fifteen-hundred-person community being asked to deal with the first murder charge in its history and an accused who was known to have another homicide in his past even if not on his record.

Steiner began the voir dire with more ingenuity than Taggart had given him credit for. Once he disposed of some unimportant preliminaries, he asked, "Colonel Simmons, are you aware of the extraordinary amount of publicity this case has received?"

A. "Yes."

Q. "Have you read accounts of the case in the newspapers?"

A. "Yes."

Q. "Have you seen accounts of the case on television?"

A. "Yes."

Q. "Would the fact that the eyes of the whole country are on this case prevent you from giving both sides a fair trial?"

A. "No."

Q. "Would you feel that because of the publicity the case has received that you would have to decide the case in a particular way in order to vindicate the Marine Corps?"

A. "No."

Q. "Do you think you would be capable of finding the accused should be punished if the evidence, coupled with the judge's instructions, indicate that he is guilty, despite the fact that he's a fellow Marine?"

A. "Yes."

Under the guise of eliciting the colonel's promise not to be swayed by all the publicity, Mad Dog was reminding the whole court that they were seated in the eye of a storm, one in which the command had a strong interest, and he was evoking the sense of sacrifice on which the Corps was founded. He was subtly suggesting that whatever the evidence, the good of the Corps just might require Sergeant Markey's conviction. The questions were phrased in favor of the accused; the message they conveyed was anything but favorable.

When it was Taggart's turn he ran through his standard set of questions intended to give the panel members a chance to air their prejudices. No one took the bait. They all promised that if selected they would presume Sergeant Markey innocent until proven otherwise and would await the presentation of all the evidence before making up their minds. They would follow the military judge's instructions and, if after the presentation of all the evidence there was a reasonable doubt in their minds about whether Staff Sergeant Markey had caused Private Collins's death, they would vote to find him not guilty. It was boilerplate: standard questions, standard answers; nothing to cause even a ripple of interest, nothing at least until Taggart asked his final question.

"Colonel Simmons," Taggart addressed the senior-ranking member of the panel, "in the event the evidence reasonably indicates to you that Sergeant Markey did not strike Private Collins, would you vote not guilty?"

"Yes, of course."

"If the evidence reasonably indicated to you that Private Collins died as a result of a beating by someone other than Sergeant Markey, would you vote that Sergeant Markey be found not guilty?"

"Yes, I would."

"Now, a witness named Private William Johnson will testify for the prosecution in this case. He will be Sergeant Markey's principal accuser. Are you acquanted with Private Johnson?"

There wasn't one chance in a thousand that Colonel Simmons or any of the other panelists would know Johnson, but it was a chance Taggart couldn't take. Johnson would impress any Marine officer who knew him. Besides, it gave Taggart a chance to draw out his introduction of the defense theory of the case to the court in the voir dire process. Go slow, let it sink in, he reminded himself.

"No, I don't know Private Johnson," the colonel said.

"Do any of the other panel members know Private Johnson? Please raise your hand if you do."

Taggart scanned the row of panel members from end to end. No hand was raised.

"Colonel Simmons, if at the close of all the evidence you believed there was a reasonable possibility that Private Johnson, *not* Sergeant Markey, beat Private Collins to death, would you then vote to find Sergeant Markey not guilty?"

Like a single pebble tossed in a quiet pond, a murmured ripple spread through the courtroom and disappeared without Mo having to call for order. Taggart didn't even hear it, so intently was he watching Colonel Simmons, waiting for his response.

Colonel Simmons squared his shoulders. "Yes, Captain, I would."

Mike queried each panel member in turn, and each echoed Simmons's response.

"So, if you believe at the close of evidence that a beating by Johnson caused Collins's death, you will then have a *reasonable doubt* as to whether Sergeant Markey is quilty, is that right, sir?"

"That's right."

The other panel members agreed.

"Private Johnson was the Guide at Hotel-1. Now if you believe at the close of the evidence that he beat Collins out of some misguided notion of leadership, of soldierly discipline, will you vote to find Sergeant Markey not guilty?"

"Yes."

"And if you conclude that after beating Private Collins, Johnson accused Sergeant Markey, his drill instructor, to cover up his own guilt, will you vote to find Sergeant Markey not guilty?"

"Yes." A trace of impatience had seeped into Simmons's voice at

what was beginning to seem to him to be the same question asked a half dozen different ways.

Steiner picked it up immediately and objected that Taggart was "wasting the court's time with needless repetition."

"I doubt the court members will object to my being thorough in defense of a man's whole military career," Mike countered. "However, I have no further questions."

Steiner had no more questions either, and the challenges began. Now it was a numbers game. Conventional wisdom in maltreatment cases called for the defendant to exercise his right to have at least one-third of the court members be enlisted personnel. Most enlisted men had themselves survived maltreatment in boot camp and were reluctant to convict one of their noncommissioned brethren, or so went the strateic thinking. Next to enlisted men, those court members most cherished by the defense were mustangs, officers who had formerly been enlisted men. They too had been to boot camp; they knew what it was supposed to be like, and like lawyers after they pass the bar exam most thought it wasn't tough enough.

Ironically, Taggart's attempt at the Article 32 hearing to get the charge reduced to involuntary manslaughter for lack of premeditation appeared to have boomeranged. The charge had not been reduced, but Gerneral Fitzroy had ordered that it be tried as a noncapital offense. Theoretically this meant they were playing for lower stakes, because the death penalty could not be imposed, but as a practical matter there was absolutely no threat of a death sentence on this evidence, even if there was a conviction. What trying the charge as a noncapital offense really meant was that the prosecution needed only a two-thirds vote to convict, instead of the three-fourths required for capital cases. Conviction was easier. Taggart realized he had outsmarted himself.

There were eleven persons on the panel, including four enlisted men, all senior staff NCO's, and two mustangs. The minimum number of court members for a general court-martial was five. Taggart was guaranteed at least one-third would be enlisted. It took a two-thirds vote to convict. He and Steiner had one peremptory challenge apiece. Steiner went first.

"Sir," Mad Dog addressed Colonel Mo, "trial counsel challenges Captain Truesdale for cause."

Truesdale was one of the two mustangs. During voir dire he'd admitted being a former drill instructor. Taggart argued half-heartedly that this was not inherently prejudicial, but he'd known Truesdale was as good as gone the minute he'd revealed his former status. Mo excused Truesdale. Now there were ten members, and it was Taggart's turn to challenge for cause. Hastily he redid his math on a piece of scratch paper. Would Steiner have any more challenges for cause? He didn't think so.

"Sir," he responded to Mo's look of inquiry, "the defense has no challenges for cause."

"Very well, Captain Taggart." Mo knew exactly the game both counsel were playing. "Captain Steiner?"

"Sir, trial counsel has no more challenges for cause. However, I do wish to exercise my peremptory challenge."

"Proceed."

"Trial court peremptorily challenges Gunnery Sergeant Bates."

Mo excused Bates.

Taggart hated to see him go. Inquiries he had made on learning the identity of the panel the week before trial had identified Bates as a hard-drinking, brawling field marine, the sort Mike expected to be most sympathetic to Markey. Of the four enlisted panelists, Bates was Taggart's favorite, but he was powerless to prevent his departure. Apparently Mad Dog had made the same inquiries.

Steiner's challenge of Bates had been his last; it brought the panel to nine members, exactly one-third of whom were enlisted. Mike fully intended to use his peremptory challenge, but on whom? Not on Colonel Simmons; Taggart had liked the resolve in his voice when he'd answered Mike's final voir dire question. He was a strong man. If he could be convinced, his strength along with his rank might sway others. Mike thought he could convince Colonel Simmons. That left Major Lewis, about whom Taggart knew nothing other than that he was a career marine; First Lieutenant Young, a reservist who worked in the adjutant's office at Headquarters Battalion; and First Lieutenant Giles, a woman who was the assistant CO at the WM Company on base. She too was a reservist.

In Taggart's mind it was a question of which of the two reservists should go. Evidently neither intended to make the Corps a career. It was unlikely either of them would equate conviction of Markey with the softening of recruit training and, therefore, a threat to the Corps. But which of the two was most likely to be sympathetic to Markey. Mike had never had a woman marine on any of his courts. He had no book on them. Old stories about Indian squaws torturing their captives rattled about in his brain, competing with his conviction that most woman wouldn't put up with a lot of the initiation-hazing bullshit that college fraternities engaged in. Was boot camp that much different? Taggart stood pondering his choice until Colonel Mo found it necessary to clear his throat to prod him into action. Taggart didn't like Lieutenant Young. It was Young who kept assigning the lawyers weekend and holiday duty. Not, Mike suspected, because he disliked lawyers but rather to make points with his CO. Taggart decided to keep Lieutenant Giles. She looked like she might enjoy torturing captives.

Mo excused Lieutenant Young and ordered a recess until after lunch. The court was set, and Taggart was reasonably pleased. He had explained the selection process to the Markyes the day before, but now he recapitulated.

"We've got eight members, more than a third are enlisted. That means the prosecution's got to convince at least one of the enlisted you're guilty while holding on to all the officers," he said, primarily for Sherill's benefit. "Lieutenant Colonel Williamson's a mustang, so that can be an added plus. There's no guarantee, but all things considered this looks like a pretty good court."

Twenty-Two

AFTER LUNCH Steiner began his opening statement, supposedly what the prosecution expected to prove, but not an argument. Mad Dog, however, had only one gear, high: one speed, flat out. For openers he promised the court members that at the conclusion of his proof there would be no doubt of Markey's guilt. Obviously, he intended to argue until Taggart objected and Mo told him to stop. As he paced in front of the court, pinning each member in turn with his eyes, he told the jury the story as he saw it. Private Collins confronted by Sergeant Markey for some minor infraction in a lonely barracks passageway shortly after taps, face to face, nose to nose, frightened as only a recruit can be frightened when confronted by an angry drill instructor, the recipient of a short, sharp butt stroke whith his own rifle in the hands of Staff Sergeant Markey . . . "It was a textbook delivery," Steiner assured the members, "just the way it was taught in bayonet training, just the way a veteran of two tours in Viet Nam would strike when face to face, nose to nose with the enemy. It was the eighth week of training; Collins should have known better than to do whatever he did. No one else was around, maybe this would make Collins remember; it surely would do more good than harm." Mad Dog mimed the delivery of the blow, pausing for effect.

At the "more good than harm" remark, Taggart objected. Steiner was speculating, this was argument.

"Sustained, stick to the facts, Captain Steiner," Mo growled.

"Except for two things," Steiner continued, paused and then went on. "Except for two things. Markey and Collins were not alone in that passageway, there was a third person who saw what happened, who saw the blow, the blow that caused the harm, the blow that killed Private Loren Collins."

Steiner went on to describe Private Johnson, his eyewitness, his testimony, and the medical evidence evidence relating to the cause of death. There were no surprises. Taggart watched Steiner closely. Mad Dog had the intensity of a sprinter. His mouth was twitching slightly by the time he finally sat down.

The courtroom was filled with tension. It was oppressive. This trial was not a one-hundred-yard dash, it was a marathon. Taggart hoped the court members would find Mad Dog's nonstop intensity tiresome after a while.

Technically defense counsel could reserve his opening statement until the beginning of his own case. As a practical matter Mike couldn't imagine any reason for doing so. It meant forgoing his chance to interrupt the flow of the prosecution's presentation, forgoing his earliest opportunity to get Roger Markey's account of what took place into the minds of the court members. As Steiner sat down, Taggart stood up, as if they were on a teeter-totter.

He reintroduced himself, then asked Markey to stand up as he introduced him to the court members. Seated directly behind the defense counsel's table, Veronica wished she could see the look on Roger Markey's face as he nodded slightly to the members and sat down.

Although it was not an analogy Taggart would ever suggest to the court, it occurred to him that the roles of the two sides were like the war. The prosecution was like the U.S. forces; it had all the big weapons: the dead boy, his abdomen covered with welts on the outside, filled with blood on the inside, the eyewitness pointing the finger of guild directly at the accused; but it also had more ground to cover and, like the U.S., the prosecution had to hold every foot of it to win. The defense was like the Cong. It was guerrilla warfare, hit and run. As long as the defense was alive on a single issue, as long as it held one foot of ground, the prosecution couldn't win. With that in mind Taggart conceded the obvious. He agreed that something tragic had happened to Loren Collins and, whatever it was, had involved some kind of terrible blow to the boy's stomach. Mike's voice was quiet and sad and filled with regret about what had happened . . .

"However," he said, "the evidence will show that there were others present in the Hotel-1 barracks on the night Private Collins died, others with the opportunity to strike him, others with the motive to strike. There were almost fifty people in the barracks that night, fifty people with eight weeks' accumulation of grudges, jealousies, prejudices, all borne of living packed together, bumping into each other constantly, in conditions where fatigue, uncertainty and sometimes fear predominated. Any one of those people could have struck the blow that killed Private Collins, and the only way that Roger Markey can be convicted is if you, the members of this court, decide that there is *no reasonable doubt* in your minds about who, from among the fifty or so people present, did whatever was done. If there is a reasonable doubt in your minds you must find Staff Sergeant Markey not guilty. Staff Sergeant Markey will take the stand and swear to you, his fellow marines, his peers, that he did *not* do this thing. He will be backed up by the physical evidence which will show that Staff Sergeant Roger Markey should be found not guilty."

Taggart sat down. There were many details he could have discussed, but he wanted the court members to be their own detectives; he could imagine them congratulating themselves at picking up things from the evidence that he'd failed to mention. The discrepencies would mean more if, by the time he pointed to them in final argument, the members had already figured them out for themselves. It would make things a little more believable, more natural, a little less the contrivance of some lawyer. He sat down.

The most remarkable thing to Ronnie about her battles with Mike over pretrial publicity had been Mike's faith in Markey. It was truly difficult for her to understand based on what she knew of the case, and yet it was so strong that it had begun to chip away at her own conviction of Markey's guilt. She had been sure Taggart's opening statement would finally supply the key to his belief in the man he was defending. It was one thing to argue about the uncertainty of choosing one of fifty possibilities when all were equal. To do so in the face of an eyewitness account was quite another. Veronica felt she knew no more than she did before. How, she wondered, as she watched Mike walk back to his chair and sit down, how could he think my reporting so prejudicial when he apparently has so little to say on Markey's behalf?

Evidently Steiner was of the same opinion about the strength of the defense's opening, because Ronnie was sure she saw a taut, thin-lipped smile on his face as he stood to call his first witness. Mad Dog had decided to sart with a bang. Ignoring, at least for the time being, Lieutenant Cavanaugh and the corpsman, Steiner immediately called Johnson to the stand.

Johnson was summoned into the courtroom. He was wearing his dress blues. It wasn't Private Johnson any more, it was Private First Class Johnson. He strode into the crowded room without hesitation, his white barracks cover tucked under one arm, looking every inch a marine.

Steiner started slowly. Johnson was a powerful, compelling witness. No sense in rushing through it. Better to let the court members soak up the impact of the prosecution's story. Words alone did not create credibility. Little by little, Steiner drew from Johnson the information he wanted the members to hear.

They learned that Johnson had been the guide at Hotel-1 since the first day of training, that he had been promoted to Private First Class upon graduation, for his excellent performance, and had been awarded his blues as the class honor man. He had been counseled to eventually try for OCS through the enlisted commissioning program by none other than Staff Sergeant Markey.

Veronica throught of Sugar Bear as she listened to him, and of Mark Levinson's testimony about minority kids in boot camp. Pfc. Johnson, a black man, had certainly taken a different path than Sugar Bear.

Next, Steiner turned to the incident itself. Hotel-1 had been the duty platoon on the night it happened. Johnson had been busy just before taps supervising the posting of the first guard watch, one of whom was Private Collins. He'd had no chance to go to the head. After the final evening muster and lights out, he had gotten out of bed to go. The head was down the passageway and around the corner from the squad bay, in the vicinity of the duty office. As he entered the passageway he heard Sergeant Markey's voice around the corner. Johnson did not want to interrupt anything the platoon commander was doing so he slowed and peeked around the edge of the wall.

Q. "What did you see, Pfc. Johnson?"
A. "Sergeant Markey was standing by the door to the head with his back to me, and Private Collins was on the other side of him, away from me, but facing me, standing at attention."
Q. "Did Private Collins see you?"
A. "I don't know, I don't think so."
Q. "What happened next?"
A. "Sergeant Markey was saying something, but it was in a real low voice, like he usually talked, so I couldn't make out what he was saying. All of a sudden, Collins shouted yessir, and then Markey talked some more."
Q. "How close was Sergeant Markey to Collins?"
A. "Real close, like the DI's get sometimes. No more than six inches between them."
Q. "Was Sergeant Markey holding anything in his hands?"
A. "Yessir."
Q. "What was he holding?"
A. "A rifle, an M14, like the one issued to each of us privates in training."

From underneath the trail counsel's table Steiner produced an M14 rifle and handed it to Johnson.

Q. "Does this look like the rifle Sergeant Markey was holding that night?"
A. "Yessir, it looks just like it."
Q. "Show me how Sergeant Markey was holding the rifle."

* * *

227

Johnson stood up. The witness stand was raised about six inches above the floor of the courtroom, and Johsnon was at least 6'4". He towered over the 5'10" Steiner as he stood there, the rifle dwarfed as it hung horizontally across his body at arm's length, one hand around the narrow part of the stock just behind the trigger guard, the other just behind the front sling swivel.

Q. "What happened next, Pfc. Johnson?"
A. "Staff Sergeant Markey was still talking quiet to Private Collins. Then all of a sudden Sergeant Markey hit Private Collins with the rifle."
Q. "With what part of the rifle?"
A. "With the butt, sir."
Q. "What did Private Collins do?"
A. "Well, he staggered backward, all doubled up, and then he kind of raised his head and looked at the platoon commander, and Sergeant Markey come up to Collins and draped the rifle around his neck by the sling so it just kind of dangled there in front of Collins's face as he was standing there all bent over."
Q. "Step down here, Pfc. Johnson, bring the rifle. Stand facing me at the same distance that Markey was from Collins."

Johnson stepped out of the box and positioned himself as instructed, still holding the rifle loosely in his huge fists. Veronica had once met one of the professional football players on the Kansas City team. Johnson's bigness, the sense of relaxed readiness and physical confidence and grace he exuded reminded her of her earlier meeting with the player.

Looking up, Steiner told Johnson, "Without actually striking me"— he smiled winningly—"demonstrate to the court how the blow you saw was struck."

Johnson swung the butt of the rifle in a short vicious arc with his right hand, freezing with the corner of the butt plate a hair's breadth from Mad Dog's stomach.

Gesturing with his hand for Johnson to hold his pose, Steiner turned slowly to the court. "How many times did Sergeant Markey strike Private Collins?"

A. "More than once, sir. Three or four times, I think. It happened fast..."

"No further questions."

Colonel Mo wasn't finished nodding to Taggart to begin before Mike had bounded into position in front of Johnson. "Hold it, Pfc. Johnson, hold your position. You can relax, but don't move for just a minute."

Q. "That butt stroke you just demonstrated, you were pretty quick with that."

A. "Sir?"

Q. "That's how it happened when you saw Sergeant Markey do it, correct?"

A. "Sir?"

Q. "The blow you say you saw my client use against Private Collins was just as quick as the one you just demonstrated, wasn't it?"

A. "Yessir..."

Q. "And Sergeant Markey was holding the rifle exactly the way you're holding it now, correct?"

A. "Yessir."

Q. "You're sure?"

A. "Yessir."

Q. "Of course you know how to deliver a butt stroke, you were taught the technique in recruit training, weren't you?"

A. "Yessir."

Q. "That was before you went to the range, correct?"

A. "Yessir."

Q. "One of the things they teach you is to hold the butt of the rifle in your strong hand, isn't that right?"

A. "You mean like if I'm right-handed, to hold it in my right hand, sir?"

Q. "Yes, they teach you that, don't they?"

A. "Yessir."

Q. "That way you can put more force into your blow?"

A. "Yessir."

Q. "You're right-handed, aren't you?"

A. "Yessir."

Q. "That's why you're holding the butt of this rifle in your right hand, correct?"

Johnson looked down at his hands holding the rifle in front of him. "Yessir..." he answered a little more slowly.

Q. "It's more natural to hold it that way, isn't it?"

A. "Yessir."

Q. "Sergeant Markey is left-handed, isn't he, Pfc. Johnson?"

There was a moment of silence as Johnson attempted to recall the image of Markey to his mind. "I don't know," he finally said.

Q. "All right, hand me the rifle. You can sit down."

Taggart put the rifle out of sight as Johnson took the stand once more.

Q. "When you first saw Sergeant Markey and Private Collins in the passageway, Markey had Collins at attention, right?" '

A. "Yessir."

Q. "Collins was facing you?"

A. "Yessir."

Q. "Sergeant Markey was standing between you and Collins?"

A. "Yessir."

Q. "The sergeant's back was to you?"

A. "Yessir."

Q. "The sergeant was talking to Collins?"

A. "Yessir."

Q. "Then Sergeant Markey hit Private Collins?"

A. "Yessir."

Q. "With a rifle butt?"

A. "Yessir."

Q. "Hard, just like you demonstrated a moment ago?"

A. "Yessir."

Q. "Collins was struck somewhere in the stomach area?"

A. "Yessir."

Q. "Collins immediately doubled over?"

A. "Yessir."

Q. "And it's your testimony that Sergeant Markey struck Collins three or four times like that?"

A. "Yessir..."

Q. "All in the stomach area?"

A. "Yessir."

Q. "If Collins doubled up immediately from the first blow, his stomach area was protected from any later blows, wasn't it?"

A. "I don't know, sir."

Q. "Well, did Sergeant Markey pause between blows and straighten up Private Collins and then hit him again, is that what happened?"

A. "No, sir."

Taggart was tempted to spell it out, to ask how Markey could have hit Collins in the stomach with later blows if Collins was still doubled up from the first one, but he thought he'd pushed things far enough. There was no telling what Johnson might say. One unforeseeably plausible answer could wreck all the implausibility Mike had managed to create. Leave well enough alone. Taggart shifted to a different line.

Q. "Now, Pfc. Johnson, do you remember talking to me down in the Hotel-1 duty office shortly after the incident occurred?"

A. "Yessir."

Q. "We talked about what happened the night Collins died, didn't we?"

A. "Yessir."

Q. "You signed a statement for me about what happened that night, didn't you?"

231

A. "Yessir."

Q. "This is the statement you signed for me, isn't it?" Mike handed a single sheet of paper to Johnson who read it.

A. "Yessir."

Q. "That's your signature on the paper, isn't it?"

A. "Yessir."

Q. "That statement was true when you signed it, wasn't it?"

A. "Yessir."

Q. "And it's still true today?"

A. "Yessir."

Q. "In this statement you only mention Sergeant Markey hitting Collins, isn't that right?"

A. "No, sir, in this statement I don't say how many times I saw Sergeant Markey hit Private Collins."

Taggart took the paper back, looked at it, handed it back to Johnson.

Q. "That first sentence reads, 'On the night of 5 February I saw Staff Sergeant Markey strike a blow to Private Collins's stomach area.' That's what the sentence says, doesn't it?"

A. "Yes, but—"

Q. "But nothing, Pfc—"

"Objection"—Steiner was up—"counsel is interrupting the witness."

Taggart studied the court members. Did they understand his point? One wrathful blow, maybe, but it would have been madness for Markey to keep it up on the helpless Collins, especially with a rifle. Detection would be inevitable. What drill instructor, even the most vicious, would be that stupid? The court members, he thought, must be asking themselves the same question . . . he'd better make sure of it in his final argument.

Q. "That sentence you just read only mentions one blow, doesn't it?"

A. "A blow . . . I wasn't counting, sir."

Q. A smart kid. "The next sentence reads, 'Sergeant Markey was standing between me and Collins, so I don't know exactly where the blow struck him.' Did I read that right?"

A. "Yessir."

Q. That sentence also mentions only one blow, isn't that right? It says *the* blow."

A. "Yessir."

Q. "You read this statement before you signed it, didn't you?"

A. "Yessir."

Q. "You signed it on 10 February?"

A. "Yessir."

Q. "Just five days after you claim you saw Sergeant Markey hit Private Collins?"

A. "Yessir."

Q. On February tenth you only mentioned one blow. And now you say three or four?"

A. "Yessir. I wasn't paying special attention to numbers when I signed that statement..."

Taggart walked back and pretended to look at his notes. He wanted a long, empty silence, a kind of unspoken exclamation mark.

Now he picked up the thread again.

Q. "So you were the guide in Hotel-1 during the entire training period, is that right?"

A. "Yessir."

Q. "That meant you were the number one man, correct?"

A. "Yessir."

Johnson's answers to the last two questions fairly crackled with pride.

Q. "You understood during recruit training that being guide practically insured your promotion at the end of training, correct?"

A. "Yessir."

Q. "Sergeant Markey even told you to think about applying for OCS, didn't he?"

A. "Yessir."

Q. "He explained to you that leadership was important for OCS, didn't he?"

A. "Yessir."

Q. "Among the privates in Hotel-1, you were the leader, weren't you?"

A. "Yessir."

Q. "Others in the platoon had more trouble with training than you did, didn't they?"

A. "Yessir."

Q. "Part of the leader's job is to help others with their problems, would you agree?"

A. "Yessir."

Q. "You helped the other privates in the platoon with some of their problems, didn't you?"

A. "Yessir."

Q. "Of course the DIs helped a lot with these problems, didn't they?"

A. "Yessir."

Q. "It was the performance of the platoon as a whole that was important, correct?"

A. "Yessir."

Q. "One man's bad performance brought down the whole platoon's performance, correct?"

A. "Yessir."

Q. "Sometimes recruits had motivation problems, didn't they?"

A. "Yessir."

Q. "That's when they're not trying hard enough, isn't it?"

A. "Yessir."

Q. "They had to be encouraged to try harder."

A. "Yessir."

Q. "Sometimes the DIs had to kick some ass to encourage privates to try harder, to get motivated, right?"

A. "Yessir."

Q. "As the guide, you sometimes encouraged people to get motivated, didn't you?"

A. "Yessir..."

Q. "There was also something called Motivation Platoon to help privates get motivated?"

A. "Yessir."

Q. "The platoon was told that privates with attitude problems would be sent to motivation platoon?"

A. "Yessir."

Q. "And some members of Hotel-1 were actually sent to motivation platoon, weren't they?"

A. "Yessir."

Q. "Those privates had attitude problems in your opinion."

A. "Yessir."

Q. "Private Collins was sent to motivation platoon, wasn't he?"

A. "Yessir."

Q. "You believed Private Collins had an attitude problem."

A. "Yessir."

Q. "You didn't think Private Collins was trying hard enough."

A. "No, sir, I didn't."

Q. "Now, I listened very carefully to the account you gave Captain Steiner. Was that the truth, what you told Captain Steiner?"

A. "Yessir."

Q. "So Markey was standing close to Collins, who was standing at attention when you first saw them, correct?"

A. "Yessir."

Q. "At that point there was nothing about the scene that indicated to you that Collins had been hit before you arrived, is that right?"

A. "Yessir."

Q. "And when Markey finished talking, he hit Private Collins with the rifle?"

A. "Yessir."

Q. "Private Collins immediately staggered back and doubled up?"

A. "Yessir."

Q. "And then, without hitting Collins again, Markey hung the rifle around Collins's neck and went into the duty office, correct?"

A. "I don't remember exactly, sir. I told you, my best recollection is that it was more than once."

Q. "But you now concede it may have been only a single blow, correct?"

A. "No sir, I think it was more than one."

Q. "Sergeant Markey was standing between you and Private Collins as you watched this take place, correct?"

A. "Yessir."

Q. "So you couldn't actually see Private Collins's stomach, could you?"

A. "No, sir."

Q. "You couldn't see the exact spot where the rifle butt hit Private Collins, could you?"

A. "No, sir."

Q. "You just assumed he was hit in the stomach from the way Collins doubled up and staggered back, isn't that right?"

A. "Sir, I know he was hit in the stomach."

Q. "I'm not saying you don't, Pfc. Johnson, I'm just saying that the reason you know it is not because you saw the actual impact, but for some other reasons. You don't have x-ray vision, do you?"

Steiner objected that Taggart was harassing the witness. He was overruled.

Q. "I'll rephrase my question. I certainly have no desire to harass you. Because Sergeant Markey was standing in the way, you did not actually see the blow land, isn't that right?"

A. "Yessir."

Q. "You don't know whether it landed above or below Collins's navel, do you?"

A. "No, sir."

Q. "Nor to the left or the right of it?"

A. "No, sir."

Q. "Now, later the same night you reported to Sergeant Markey that Collins was sick."

A. "Yessir."

Q. "That was about an hour after you saw the blow struck?"

A. "I helped him to his rack and went to get a new guard posted. I figured he'd be okay when he got his wind back. Then about an hour later his bunkmate woke me up and said Collins was barfin' blood, so I went to the platoon commander."

Q. "So between the time Sergeant Markey left Private Collins in the passageway and the time you went to report Collins was sick, Collins was in the squadbay with the rest of the platoon, right?"

A. "Yessir."

Q. "Including yourself?"

A. "Yessir, once the guard was posted."

Taggart looked at his notes resting on the corner of the defense table. He checked off items he had covered, flipping pages in the process. When he finished he tossed the pad onto the center of the table and turned once more to face Johnson.

Q. "Pfc. Johnson, you saw Sergeant Markey chew Collins out that night."

A. "Yessir."

Q. "But Markey went back to the duty office without ever striking Collins, didn't he?"

A. "No, sir."

Q. "After Sergeant Markey left, you approached Collins, didn't you?"

A. "Yessir."

Q. "You were thinking Collins had fouled up again as you walked up to him, didn't you?"

A. "No, sir."

Q. "So you hit him with his own rifle just to teach him a—"

"OBJECTION." Steiner was on his feet. "Pfc. Johnson's not on trial here, Sergeant Markey is. Captain Taggart is badgering the witness. There is no evidence to support such a question."

"Overruled."

Before Taggart could repeat his question, Johnson answered it. "No, sir, I did not hit Private Collins that night."

"No further questions."

Steiner hastened to patch up the damage to his witness.

Q. "Pfc. Johnson, when you first saw Sergeant Markey and Private Collins in the passageway, did you expect to see Sergeant Markey hit Private Collins?"

A. "No, sir."

Q. "Did it startle you?"

A. "Yessir."

Q. "Were you a little frightened by what you saw?"

A. "Yessir."

Q. "Did you pay any particular attention at that time to how many blows were struck?"

"Objection, leading question."

"Overruled."

A. "No, sir."

Steiner asked Taggart for Johnson's statement.

Q. "Pfc. Johnson, I notice the handwriting of the statement is different from that of your signature. Did you write the statement?"

A. "No, sir, just the signature."

Q. "Who wrote the statement?"

A. "Captain Taggart, sir."

Q. "And then he asked you to sign it?"

A. "Yessir."

Q. "Did he say anything about how many blows were struck at the time he asked you to sign this statement?"

A. "No, sir."

"No further questions."

Mo glanced at his watch. "Gentlemen, it is time to secure. We will reconvene tomorrow at 1000."

Next morning Steiner began by attending to some housekeeping chores, calling Lieutenant Burnquist, the series officer, to testify that Markey had been the duty NCO on the night Collins died. He also testified that the platoon had not run the obstacle course during the week before Collins died, in an obvious attempt to head off any defense contention that Collins's injuires were suffered on the obstacle course. Burnquist was followed by Lieutenant Cavanaugh and the corpsman, both of whom testified about their observations in the Hotel-1 squad bay on the night in question. Of each, Taggart asked only who was present in the vicinity of Collin's rack in addition to themselves.

"The government calls as its next witness Dr. Stephen Nellis," Steiner then announced.

Lieutenant Nellis took the stand. A slightly built pale man in his late twenties, with curly brown hair cut in a decidedly unmarinelike fashion, Nellis gave off an impatience with court-martial proceedings consistent with the antipathy Mike had seen him show toward other things associated with the Corps. Instead of simply saying "yes" on administration of the oath, Nellis answered "of course," and sat down without waiting for instructions.

In response to Steiner's questions, Dr. Nellis told the members of the court of being summoned to the Hotel-1 squad bay at approximately 2300 on the night of February 5th.

Q. "What did you find when you arrived?"

A. "I found the deceased, a boy approximately eighteen years of age, doubled up on his bunk in obvious pain and in a state of deep shock."

Q. "What was it that caused you to conclude he was in pain?"

A. "The patient was moaning weakly, low in his throat, and clutching his midsection."

Q. "And what caused you to conclude Private Collins . . . it was Private Collins, wasn't it?"

A. "I was told his name was Collins. I have no idea of his rank."

It was hearsay but not in dispute. Taggart did not object.

* * *

239

Q. "What made you conclude Private Collins was in shock?"

A. "He displayed virtually all the symptoms of hypovolemic shock, that is, shock resulting from actual loss of blood. The boy was very pale and wringing wet with sweat. He was barely conscious, indicating possible decrease in his cerebral blood flow. I attempted to listen to his heartbeat and found it extremely faint and very rapid."

Q. "Why would his heartbeat have increased under the circumstances you've described?"

A. "Well, the heart is really just like a pump. Its job is to pump blood through the entire body. When the blood supply is diminished the heart has to make what remains do more work, so it responds by pumping faster and faster. This situation is aggravated by the collapse of the vascular system, the system of arteries, veins and capillaries that are tubes of various sizes the blood flows through. When the supply of blood is reduced there is less internal support for this vascular tubing and it collapses, thereby increasing the resistance through which the heart must pump the remaining blood, forcing it to work still harder."

Q. "What did you do when you found the boy like this?"

Taggart noticed that Steiner had adopted Nellis's reference to Private Collins as "the boy," probably in the hope of making Collins seem even more defenseless to the court. Nellis was an effective witness. He'd already displayed the knack of making complex, unfamiliar concepts understandable. And somehow he had the idea that by screwing Markey he would be screwing the Corps. Mike hoped that in his eagerness he would stumble into overkill.

A. "After listening for the heartbeat I attempted to question him but received no response or sign of any kind acknowledging that he heard me, so I administered a capsule of ammonia, like smelling salts."

Q. "What was the reaction?"

A. "He reacted to the smell and looked up at the group of us looking down at him and he seemed very afraid..."

* * *

Taggart tensed, ready to object. Nellis could testify about what he saw, but not about what was going through Collins's mind. Nellis couldn't tell the difference between pain and fear just because he was a doctor. Afraid of what? Clearly the inference Steiner wanted to create was that he was afraid of Markey, but wasn't fear of Nellis an equally reasonable assumption? Or Johnson? On the other hand, to object to testimony about fear would have exactly the opposite effect from the one Taggart wanted in the minds of the court members, emphasizing it instead of erasing it from their minds. In the instant he had to consider all these things, Mike studied the court members. They didn't seem more intent on this testimony than any other, so he let it ride. Better to deal with it on cross-examination.

Q. "What makes you say Collins was so afraid?"

A. "His eyes mostly. They'd been shut tight, contorted, and suddenly they were wide and staring right at us and he was mumbling something about being motivated . . . and he was crying."

There was a rustle among the spectators, who had been silent during this part of the testimony. Ronnie was also listening closely to Nellis, but out of the corner of her eye she saw Martha Collins get up and leave the courtroom. Frank Collins remained where he was, staring blankly at Dr. Nellis but no doubt seeing his son cowering near death in an unfriendly bunk in front of strangers far away from home.

Q. "What did you do then?"

A. "With the help of the corpsman I straightened the patient out. He resisted briefly and then lapsed into unconsciousness. I examined his abdomen and found bruises, the beginning of discoloration and swelling, as if he had been hit by a sharp blow to the stomach, for example by a rifle but . . ."

Taggart knew it was coming. He'd tried and failed to prevent it at pretrial, but he objected anyway. It was speculation, and he said so. If any of the court members had an ounce of objectivity they'd resent that smug son-of-a-bitch of a doctor telling them what caused the injury when he hadn't been there to see it inflicted. Or at least he hoped they would.

"Overruled, proceed Captain Steiner."

Q. "All right, you had just examined Private Collins's stomach. What did you do next?"

A. "I ordered an ambulance and called Balboa Hospital to make preparations for our arrival."

Q. "What kind of preparations?"

A. "I told them the patient's blood type, it was on his dog tags, and asked to have as much whole blood as possible ready for transfusion on arrival. I also asked them to have a vascular surgeon there when we got there."

Q. "Why a vascular surgeon?"

A. "The shock, the heartbeat, sharp decline in blood pressure, the marks and bruises, it was clear to me that the boy was badly battered internally, that he was losing a lot of blood and that whatever internal wounds he suffered had to be closed immediately."

Q. "How serious did you think Collins's condition was when you boarded the ambulance with him?"

A. "Captain, I was afraid he'd die on the way to the hospital."

Q. "Did he?"

A. "No. On the way to the hospital I attempted to initiate transfusion but I couldn't find a vein. They were rapidly collapsing to nothing. As soon as we arrived I made what is called a cut down, that is, an incision in the vicinity of the vein so that it could actually be seen. As a result we were finally able to begin blood replacement."

Q. "Did the surgeon assist you?"

A. "No, no surgeon was available. It was 12:30 A.M. on a Saturday morning—there was nobody, no specialist . . . nothing."

Nellis's voice itself trailed off as he finished his answer. Taggart was reminded of the leadership-training films in which a situation would fall completely apart, and at the peak of the crisis the question would appear, "What now, lieutenant?" End of film. What now, doctor? Taggart was forced to admit that doctors too had their tight spots, and Nellis had been in one that night.

Q. "At that point what did you see as your alternatives?"

A. "In my mind, there were none. I was no longer able to detect the patient's blood pressure. It was gone. The transfusions were no answer if we didn't stop the bleeding. He was quickly prepared for surgery and I opened him up in an attempt to find and correct the problem."

Q. "What did you find?"

A. "I made my incision in the abdomen, just above the navel, thereby entering what is known as the peritoneal cavity, the space where the intestines, among other things, are located. It's like a sack, it also contains the stomach, the liver, the spleen, and certain other internal organs. I found it filled with blood, a great deal of blood, far more than would normally be found. The first place I examined was the aorta, which is the principal artery carrying blood out of the heart."

Q. Wouldn't it have been better to x-ray him first, so you wouldn't have to search?"

A. "Captain, let me stress once more, there was no time. *No time.* Given the boy's condition and the relatively short time it had taken him to reach that critical stage, I was reasonably certain that the source of the hemmorrhage was in the vicinity of the aorta."

Q. "Was it?"

A. "It was. At the point where what is known as the superior mesenteric artery branches off from the aorta I found a tear approximately one-half inch in circumference, which was obviously causing the problem, or at least part of it."

Q. "Part of it . . . what else did you find?"

A. "Nothing, but of course it was impossible after finding the first rupture to be sure that others did not exist."

Q. "What did you do?"

A. "I attempted to close the wound as fast as possible. Throughout this surgical examination the patient's vital signs continued to be closely monitored. At intervals of every few seconds blood pressure and pulse were announced. I was aware as I worked that they were becoming

243

steadily weaker. I can tell you my own heart beat was running away with itself, that the temptation to act with more than deliberate speed was very great."

Q. "Were you able to close the wound?"

A. "I'm afraid it became unnecessary to continue to try. At a point when I was less than halfway through, I was advised that all vital signs had disappeared, that the boy was dead."

Q. "Do you have an opinion as to the cause of death?"

A. "Private Collins bled to death as the result of an internal hemorrhage from a large tear in his superior mesenteric artery at its point of origin from the aorta, a tear probably induced by a sharp blow to the abdomen with a heavy object wielded with a great deal of force, judging from the marks on the outside. The loss of blood prevented a sufficient supply of oxygen from reaching the brain and it killed him."

Steiner had no further questions. Veronica wondered if Taggart would have any. During his cross-examination of Johnson, she could see where he was going. He'd redeemed himself some from what to her was a rather mild opening statement. She could see, at least in theory, how Johnson might have had a motive to strike Collins, as well as the opportunity, but weighed against Johnson's convincing eyewitness account of Markey's assault . . . Ronnie now watched Taggart stand up slowly, head down, still immersed in his notes. What could he do to build his theory of defense beyond what he'd already done with Johnson? Certainly nothing with this witness . . . what did Nellis know about the atmosphere that prevailed in the platoon, about Johnson's attitude toward Collins? He was the medical expert testifying about his field of expertise.

If Mike Taggart had been asked for his own view of his prospects at that point, he'd have seconded Ronnie. Nellis had been very effective. He'd even managed to shed his pompous, smart-ass demeanor for a few minutes and appear sympathetic. Back on the farm his father used to say that if you couldn't chase the bull into the barn, well then, let him chase you. Hoping there'd be a way out on the far side, Mike proceeded to ask his first question.

* * *

Q. "Private Collins was lying in a bottom bunk when you first saw him, correct?"

A. "That's right."

Q. "When he opened his eyes in response to your ammonia capsule, you were bent over him, correct?"

A. "Yes."

Q. "Lieutenant Cavanaugh was standing there with you?"

A. "Yes."

Q. "Sergeant Markey was also present?"

A. "Yes."

Q. "And the corpsman?"

A. "Yes."

Q. "The corpsman was also bent over Private Collins?"

A. "Yes."

Q. "Private Johnson, one of the recruits, was also in the group standing behind you at Collins's bunk, wasn't he?"

A. "One of the recruits was there, yes."

Q. "I asked about Private Johnson specifically. You've seen him here in court, I believe. You know what he looks like. I ask you again, was Private Johnson there?"

A. "Yes, I believe so, though I don't see—"

Q. "You were paying close attention to Collins, right?"

A. "Yes, of course..."

Q. "But you don't know precisely what he saw when he was administered the ammonia."

A. "Well, the lights were on, we were all standing there..."

Q. "Then he might have seen all of you?"

A. "I suppose he did."

Q. "But you and the corpsman may have at least partially blocked Collins's vision of those behind you."

A. "It's possible."

Q. "The top parts of the people standing behind you might have been obscured from Collins's view by the top bunk, isn't that right?"

A. "...Yes, I suppose so."

Q. "You didn't actually see Private Collins struck, did you, Dr. Nellis?"

A. "No."

Q. "So when you suggested that he had been hit by something like a rifle, you were just using that by way of example, isn't that right?"

A. "Yes, but a very good example."

Q. "The marks you observed on Collins's stomach could also have been made by a pugil stick, couldn't they?"

A. "Yes..."

Q. "Or by a fist?"

A. "Yes."

Q. "Or by a boot?"

A. "Yes, although I imagine few recruits went to their bunks with their boots on."

Taggart shot back. "Yes, sir, I've noticed what an active imagination you have."

Nellis reddened. Mad Dog was on his feet, but before he could open his mouth Colonel Mo had admonished Nellis to answer the questions asked, and Taggart to stick to questioning.

Mike was glad for the pause the exchange had provided. The first few questions had been easy, but from here on it was uncharted territory. He had read the medical report and the autopsy report and he knew how he *thought* Nellis would testify to the next line of examination but he couldn't be sure. Steiner had skirted the issue on direct. Had he explained the reason to Nellis and set a trap, or had he simply rehearsed Nellis without sharing strategic considerations with him? It was his last chance, Taggart knew, to sit down and play it safe; but he also knew that whatever doubts he'd managed to raise so far would not get the job done. He had no choice, it was chance-taking time. He took up the autopsy, which had already been put into evidence.

Q. "Dr. Nellis, there were no pictures taken of Private Collins after he died so far as you know, is that correct?"

A. "Not that I know of."

Q. "Well then, I'd like you to paint a picture for the court members, if you will. Please direct your attention to the condition of the exterior of Private Collins's abdomen as you found it when you examined him in the squad bay. I now show you the autopsy of Private Collins, which is Prosecution Exhibit 4. Does it correctly describe the condition of Collins's abdominal area?"

Nellis scanned the autopsy.

A. "Yes, it seems to."

Taggart walked slowly to the side of the defense table farthest from the witness stand and took from behind it a poster that depicted the front view of a male torso, which Nellis identified as such, adding in response to a question by Taggart that, absent the welts, abrasions, bruises and swelling, it looked substantially as Collins's abdomen had looked.

Q. "For reference purposes it's the custom and practice of the medical profession to divide the abdomen into nine regions or sections, correct?"
A. "Yes."
Q. "Please take this marker and step up to the poster and section off the nine regions so the members can see where they're located."

Nellis stepped down from the stand and approached the tripod the poster was displayed on. The audience leaned forward for a better view. Nellis stood contemplating the poster, then neatly and carefully sketched two horizontal lines across the abdomen, bisected by two vertical lines, so that a large tic-tac-toe grid was superimposed on the drawing. Then he turned toward the court and, using the marker for a pointer, pointed to each of the regions and gave its name.

Q. "Thank you, doctor. Now, if you will take this red marker and remain standing a moment longer, the autopsy states that 'elongated and irregular bruises and abrasions were present on the left hypocondriac, left lateral, umbilical, left inguinal, pubic and right inguinal areas.' Do you recall seeing abrasions such as those described on Private Collins's abdomen on the night of his death?"

A. "Yes, I do."

Q. "These abrasions appeared to be fresh, that is, recently inflicted?"

A. "Yes."

Q. "Please draw on our friend here," Taggart indicated the poster, "the location of the abrasions you observed on the left hypocondriac region of Collins's abdomen."

Nellis drew a red line across the upper left-hand square of the grid in the vicinity of the lower left rib cage. Slowly, inch by inch, Taggart walked him through every welt and bruise he had seen. When he had finished there were at least twelve red lines on the torso, some overlapping. If a diagonal line had been drawn from the left rib cage to the right hip, virtually the entire area below it was covered with red lines, some of which extended well above the imaginary bisecting line.

Q. "In your opinion, doctor, does this poster drawing, as you have filled it in, accurately depict the location and extent of the welts and bruises you observed on Private Collins on the night in question?"

A. "Yes."

"Sir, I ask that this poster, Defendant's Exhibit 1 for Identification, be admitted inevidence."

Mo looked to Steiner.

"No objection."

"Very well, it will be received."

Q. "Now then, the superior mesenteric artery that you found to be torn, it's located beneath the umbilical region, is that correct?"

A. "Yes."

Q. "Please write superior mesenteric artery with this marker on the spot on the abdomen that artery is located beneath."

Taggart handed the doctor a blue marker, and he wrote "superior mesenteric artery" across the center square on the tic-tac-toe grid. Two heavy lines ran through the words. The rest did not.

"All right, doctor, please take you seat on the witness stand."

Q. "Doctor, you testified in response to questions by Captain Steiner that in your opinion, judging from the marks on the outside of the abdomen, the tear was probably induced by a sharp blow to the abdomen with a heavy object, wielded with a great deal of force. Do you recall that testimony?"

A. "Yes."

Q. "It's also true, is it not, that, judging from the marks on the outside of the abdomen, that Private Collins was the victim of repeated sharp, forceful blows with a heavy object?"

A. "I would say so, yes."

"No further questions."

Taggart was pleased. If Nellis had said *no* to that last one, no matter how illogical, everything that went before might have been meaningless. Every panel member was looking at the poster as he sat down. So was Veronica, so was Colonel Mo, so was everyone else in the courtroom.

Taggart leaned over to Sergeant Markey. "At least that's got 'em thinking," he whispered.

"I hope so," was Markey's quiet reply.

Mike was sweating even though it was a cool day. So was Markey.

Meanwhile Joe Steiner did a quick status-check of his case. The autopsy suggested there were several blows; Johnson said there were several blows; now Taggart had extracted from Dr. Nellis the opinion that there were several blows. Deciding he couldn't improve on Taggart's cross of Nellis, Steiner waived further examination.

Twenty-Three

AFTER LUNCH it was the defense's turn. Taggart called Prudhomme as his first witness. Meeting Colonal Simmons's gaze head on as he spoke the sergeant major's name, Mike thought how he'd anguished about who to call first. It was important to start strong, it was important to finish strong. Would the court expect to hear Markey right away or would it be more effective for his denial of guilt to be the last thing it heard before beginning its deliberations? What kind of witness would Markey be? If he saved Markey until last, who should he lead off with?

Ronnie watched as Prudhomme took the stand. Approaching it, he'd paused to nod in respect to the judge and the president of the court. None of the other witnesses had done that; it was a nice touch. Knowing the amount of thought Taggart had put into the presentation of his witnesses, she wondered whether the gesture had been Mike's idea or Prudhomme's.

To be young and big and strong and straight and hard was one thing. To be almost fifty years old and still be all of those things was another. The sergeant major's back hardly touched the back of the witness chair, and his bearing was so natural that he looked perfectly comfortable and at ease sitting there unselfconsciously with the decorations of three wars meticulously arranged above his left breast pocket.

Taggart's first question was how long the sergeant major had been in the Corps.

"Longer than you've been alive, sir, almost thirty years," came the reply.

"Have you been in combat?"

"Objection." Steiner was on his feet, saying that Prudhomme's combat record was irrelevant.

Taggart countered that the sergeant major was a character witness. The court members were entitled to know something about the witness whose opinion they were about to hear.

"Overruled," said Mo.

The chronicle that followed measured up to expectations created by the witness's appearance. It began with an eighteen-year-old wading ashore on Peleliu and Okinawa and ended there in the courtroom almost thirty years later, after stops in Korea, Lebanon, and two in Viet Nam. Along the way Prudhomme had seen sea duty, embassy duty and three tours on the drill field.

The tone was set. He described his contacts with Markey and said that the sergeant was known in the battalion as a quiet, intelligent career NCO with a good imagination, who could be counted on to do an outstanding job whatever the assignment. But despite the routine content of Prudhomme's testimony, Ronnie realized as she listened to him that he was making a strong impression. It wasn't so much what he said as the force and energy with which he said it. The light of conviction was in his eye, and it gave extra force to the words he spoke so simply and directly. Prudhomme was someone you'd want on your side in a fight. The fact that in this fight such a man had chosen to be on Markey's side spoke in Markey's behalf.

Prudhomme concluded his testimony with a little speech directly to the court members ... "Most people think drill instructors are some kind of savages who like hurtin' people and bein' mean. What people don't realize is that patience and self-control are two things anyone assigned to the field has to have a lot of. There's long hours, there's the frustration of always bein' evaluated in comparison with other drill instructors, there's the poor quality of the bottom fifteen percent of the recruits. I won't kid you, some do it better than others—no two are alike, but I say that Sergeant Markey here ain't a mean or cruel man, and he handles his temper as well as anyone I've ever seen on the field. He's better than I ever was at that part of it."

"No further questions." Mike was relieved. Too often character testimony ended up sounding as if the witness was saying just what he thought the jury expected to hear.

Steiner wisely decided not to take on Prudhomme.

The next witness was Prudhomme's opposite. As small as Prudhomme was big, as young as Prudhomme was old and as frightened as Prudhomme was not, Private Eugene Morkowski was almost shaking as he took the oath and sat down.

"Try to relax, Private Morkowski," Taggart said gently. "I just want to ask you a few questions. Did you know Private Collins?"

"Yessir."

Q. "How well did you know him?"

A. "Our bunks were right next to each other, sir, and we kinda got to be friends because we had a lot of the same, well, problems."

Q. "What problems would those be, Private Morkowski?"

A. "Oh, with training mostly. Neither me nor Loren . . . Private Collins, I mean, were very good at training. He was better than I was, though. Sometimes he'd help me out when he could."

Q. "So you had a tough time with the training program?"

A. "Yessir, I was what they call a recycle. Hotel-1 was my second platoon after I'd been dropped from my first one. I'm not very good at P.T."

Q. "Private Morkowski, I'm not trying to embarrass you, but I want you to tell me your nickname in the platoon."

A. ". . . Goofy, sir."

Q. "Who gave you that nickname?"

A. "Sergeant Sanchez, the first day I was in the platoon, but everybody called me that except Private Collins . . . and Staff Sergeant Markey."

Q. "Staff Sergeant Markey is accused of hitting your friend, Private Collins while you were in Hotel-1. Did you form an opinion about Staff Sergeant Markey's character? I mean in the area of violence?"

253

A. "Yessir."

Q. "Please tell the members of the court what that opinion is."

A. "Staff Sergeant Markey didn't have to hit ya. He never hit me, and I was about the worst private in the platoon. I never saw or heard of him hittin' anybody until Private Johnson said that about Private Collins. The night before we qualified at the range Sergeant Markey took me aside, I was havin' lots of trouble, but he said that he believed I could qualify but not to worry if I didn't because so long as he could see I was tryin', I'd be okay."

Q. "I see you qualified."

A. "Yessir, sharpshooter." Morkowski looked down at the marksmanship badge he was wearing.

Q. "Do you know Private First Class William Johnson?"

A. "Yessir, he was the guide in Hotel-1."

Q. "While you were in Hotel 1, did you form an opinion about Private Johnson's character, for violence?"

A. "Yessir."

Mad Dog shot up as if to object, but then sat down.

Q. "Tell the court members your opinion."

A. "Private . . . I mean Private First Class Johnson was a . . . a bully. He was the best fighter in the platoon. As the guide, he figured it was his job to motivate us. He was always tellin' us to shape up. He's the one who gave me my blanket party—"

Q. "What do you mean, 'blanket party'?"

"Objection. Testimony about the basis of the witness's opinion is improper. I move to strike the witness's remark about the blanket party."

"Sustained. The court will disregard the witness's reference to a blanket party."

Taggard didn't mind Steiner's objection. In case any of the members had missed Morkowski's reference to the blanket part, they now had it firmly in mind, and every Marine in the room knew exactly what it was without needing Morkowski to explain.

One person in the audience was especially affected by the reference to Private Morkowski's blanket party. Veronica remembered Loren Collins's description of a blanket party in his letter to his parents. Ronnie glanced over to where Mr. and Mrs. Collins were sitting. Evidently Martha Collins was doing some remembering too. She was staring at her lap, where she held a packet of letters. Unmistakably they were her son's letters from boot camp, the ones Ronnie had seen. Just seeing the letters again reawakened the sadness and anger she had felt when she read them, but this time her feelings were more complicated. This time she was less certain about who to blame. When Linda Collins died, Ronnie had assumed that the tradegy was at an end, that it had claimed its last victim. Now she wasn't so sure.

Meanwhile Taggart had shifted to another line of questioning with Morkowski.

Q. "Where were you after taps the night Private Collins died?"
A. "I was in my rack, right next to Private Collins's bunk."
Q. "Did you know he was hurt?"
A. "Uh-huh, I saw Johnson bring him back to his rack. Then, after about a half hour, I told my squad leader I thought Loren was real sick and needed help."
Q. "Did you see Sergeant Markey do anything to Collins that night?"
A. "Sergeant Markey come in and asked Private Collins what was wrong, and Loren didn't say nothing, but just sorta kept groaning. Sergeant Markey went away for a minute and then he come back and told Loren that he'd sent for a doctor and that everything was gonna be all right. Then he took a towel and rinsed off Collins's face and cleaned the barf out of his rack, all the time talkin' real low, sayin' help was on its way and how Loren shouldn't worry none."

"No further questions."
Steiner was on his feet, looking eager to tackle this cross-examination.

Q. "Private Morkowski, you say Sergeant Markey never hit you, but he did jump on top of you out of a tree, didn't he?"
A. "Well, what he did was drop down behind me and pull me out

of the back of the formation. He scared me real bad but he didn't hurt me none. Afterwards, he explained to the whole platoon what happened, and how that's the kinda thing that happens in Viet Nam and how we gotta keep our eyes and ears open every second."

Steiner obviously wasn't too thrilled with that answer.

Q. "When I interviewed you the day after Collins died you told me he jumped on top of you, didn't you?"

A. "I don't think so, sir."

Q. "How many times have you met and talked with Captain Taggart?"

A. "Let's see . . . I think three times, sir."

Q. "When were they?"

A. "Once before graduation, once when he told me he was gonna put me on legal hold, and once last Friday."

Q. "And each time he reviewed your story with you, isn't that right?" Steiner emphasized the word *story.*

A. "Yessir."

Q. "Captain Taggart told you what questions he was going to ask you, didn't he?"

A. "Yessir."

Q. "He also told you what he wanted you to say, didn't he?"

A. "He said he wanted me to tell the truth, sir."

Making simple witness preparation look like the invention of testimony was a favorite tactic of Steiner's.

Q. "It was Captain Taggart who first suggested to you that Johnson was a bully, is that right?" Steiner made an inspired guess.

A. "Sir?"

Q. "I mean, you didn't begin to think of Johnson as a bully until you heard Captain Taggart use the word, isn't that right?"

A. ". . . Yessir, I guess so."

Q. "Pfc. Johnson was also the best runner in the platoon, wasn't he?"

A. "Yessir."

256

Q. "And the best marksman?"

A. "Yessir."

Q. "And the best at drill?"

A. "I guess so."

Q. "And the best at inspections?"

A. "Yessir."

Q. "And the best at learning his Marine Corps' knowledge."

A. "Just about, yessir."

Q. "You don't like Private Johnson, do you?"

A. "No, sir."

Q. "In fact, it would be accurate to say that you hate him, is that right?"

A. "Well, I . . . I told you he was a—"

"No further questions," Steiner said quickly, confident he'd discredited Morkowski's testimony.

"Private Morkowski"—Taggart was promptly on his feet—"when you first heard me call Pfc. Johnson a bully, what had you just been telling me about?"

A. "Telling you about Pfc. Johnson and the blanket party, sir."

"Objection. Move the reference to blanket party be stricken."

"Overruled. You opened it up this time, Captain Steiner," Mo told him.

Q. "What does the word bully mean to you?"

A. "Someone who picks on people who can't fight back?"

Q. "Does that describe Pfc. Johnson?"

A. "Yes, sir."

"No further questions."

Dr. Jekyll or Mr. Hyde, Taggart wondered how the court members would see Johnson. Their verdict on Markey depended on their verdict on Johnson.

* * *

Mike straightened up from his desk and stretched. "I need some sack time."

It was dark outside. The defense hooch was deserted except for Mike, who was shoving papers on his desk in different directions to make a space for the sandwiches and coffee that Veronica had just come in with.

"How much more do you have to do tonight?"

"Half an hour ... forty-five minutes, maybe." He unwrapped his cheeseburger and began to eat. "Have you eaten already?"

"Not hungry tonight."

Several minutes passed in silence, broken finally by Mike saying, "Ah, good grease!" He wiped his hands on a napkin and drained the last of his coffee. "Thanks for the grub ... and the dazzling dinner conversation."

"I don't feel very dazzling tonight, I'm afraid," she said. "I keep thinking about what that private ... Morkowski ... said today about Johnson and the blanket parties."

"Yes ... ?

Ronnie was still feeling unsure ... Morkowski's account of life in Hotel Company's first platoon, along with the sight of Martha Collins holding onto her son's letters that told about what Ronnie now saw as a very similar account ... it all made her at least ask herself for the first time, What if Markey really didn't do it?

Did such thoughts amount to "reasonable doubt"? Should she tell Taggart about the letters? She hated to think of involving Martha and Frank Collins in the trial. On the other hand she'd had no hesitancy about reporting the Da Nang court-martial or Dr. Nellis's opinions. Should she be more solicitous of the Collinses' feelings than of Markey's? Was Loren Collins's death a greater tragedy for his parents than Roger Markey's conviction would be for his family ... especially if he didn't do it?

"Mike ... there are some letters you should know about. Loren Collins wrote letters to his parents that are like echoes of what Morkowski testified to today."

"What? How do you know about them?" Taggart's voice was tight. "Do you have them?"

258

"No, but I've seen them. Martha Collins has them with her. She had them in court today."

"I want to know everything you can remember about them," he said, giving her no chance for second thoughts.

Thursday morning, following Veronica's disclosure of the existence of Loren Collins's letters, Mike was in the courtroom with Roger Markey almost two hours before the trial resumed. Today it was Markey's turn on the stand and, barring the unforeseen, he would be the last witness. Together they went over and over Mike's questions, Mike standing at the far corner of the counsel table to cut the angle between himself and the court members, Markey on the witness stand getting the feel of it. Rehearsal time.

"Remember, look 'em in the eye," Mike repeated for the nth time. "This has to be an eyeball-to-eyeball denial. If it comes off sounding the least bit evasive or like an excuse, we're cooked. Those court members have to *believe* you didn't do it. Understand?"

"Yessir, I understand. It's my as . . . sir."

His client was rising to the occasion. Good. But how to get at least one of those letters Veronica had described into evidence? He would have to call one of the victim's parents, but which one? And how could he do it without being condemned by the court for the insensitivity of forcing them to testify?

The courtroom began filling with spectators. Taggart paid no attention as he sat pondering the steps he'd be forced to take as soon as Colonel Modelewski called the court to order.

By the time Veronica Rasmussen arrived, the spectators' gallery was nearly full. So, instead of the front-row seat beside Sherill Markey that she had occupied on the previous three days of trial, Ronnie took a seat in back beside Tom Horn, who nodded to her as she sat down. Ronnie surveyed the by now familiar scene. All except the judge were in their places, including the repeat spectators who tended to sit in the same places time after time. It was as structured as a formal wedding, she thought. Go-Go, Colonel Katkavage, Mr. and Mrs. Collins, all those who might be expected to sympathize with the prosecution sat on the right side of the center aisle behind the prosecution's counsel table. Sherill Markey, Taggart's close friends such as Margolis and Horn, and even Prudhomme, who had stayed to watch following his testimony, all sat on the left side behind the defense table. Only the news people chose seats at random. Ronnie wondered into which category she now fell—news people or friend of the defense. Had her status changed after last night? The decision to tell Taggart about the letters had been a wrenching one, and she was still uneasy about what she had done. Looking at Frank and Martha Collins sitting ahead of her across the aisle, she had an impulse to warn them to leave, to hide Loren's letters or burn them, to protect themselves from further anguish.

Veronica looked away quickly to stifle the temptation. As she did so she noticed for the first time an attractive young woman sitting by the wall on the defense side of the room. She was fairly sure the woman hadn't been in court before. And no note pad, so not a reporter. She really was very pretty . . . The reporter in Veronica began to take over, she was instinctively curious.

"Who's the blonde sitting over by the window?" she whispered to Horn.

It was obvious Horn knew who she was talking about. Without a glance in the other woman's direction he gave Veronica a long look, then said, "Cathy Taggart—"

Just then Colonel Mo walked in and the clerk ordered all to rise. On her feet, Veronica was thankful for the diversion of Mo's arrival. It wasn't guilt that she was feeling. It was more a realization that the inevitable time for decision had arrived.

Sitting down she wondered if Mike knew Cathy was back. He hadn't mentioned it the previous night when he'd dropped her off at the hotel. Had Cathy been waiting for him when he arrived home minutes later?

Taggart's voice broke into her thoughts.

"The accused calls as his next witness Mr. Frank Collins."

Taggart braced himself as he said the words. The surprised reaction they provoked made him, for a moment, feel like a Perry Mason. The gallery buzzed. Steiner did his part by beginning an indignant prosecutor's speech about the defendant having already put these people through enough. He was interrupted by Colonel Mo ordering both counsel to approach the bench. Meanwhile, in the midst of the uproar, Frank Collins sat staring straight ahead, numb.

Like most of Colonel Modelewski's side-bar conferences this one was short. Once Taggart had explained the reason for his calling Frank Collins, he was told to go ahead. Counsel returned to their places, and Colonel Modelewski turned to Frank Collins.

"Mr. Collins, you have been called as a witness. Will you please step forward and be sworn."

Martha Collins's hand was on her husband's arm as he got up. He stared straight ahead as he stepped forward and her hand dropped to her side.

Solemnly he took the oath, sat down and waited for the first question. Facing him, Mike was reminded of many of his neighbors when he was growing up . . . thick men with calloused hands, ruddy lined complexions, weathered looks out of keeping with the sit-down, indoor world of a courtroom. Farmers, horizon-watchers, hoping for the best, expecting the worst but never . . . never the nightmare that had clouded Frank Collins's horizon.

"Mr. Collins," he began, "my apologies for the necessity of these few questions. I'll be brief. You are the father of Loren Collins, is that correct?"

A. "Yes."

Q. "While your son was in recruit training, did he write to you?"

A. "Yes, to me and my wife."

Q. "What did you do with those letters, sir?"

A. "Do?"

Q. "Did you save them?"

A. "My wife did."

Q. "Does she have them with her in court today?"

A. "Yes."

"Mr. Collins, will you ask Mrs. Collins to give you the letters? I'd like to examine them."

Out of the corner of his eye Mike could see that Martha Collins was now holding the packet of letters in her hand, waiting for some sign from her husband. Frank Collins gave none. He sat in silence, staring at Taggart, and in Frank Collins's glazed stare Taggart got a glimpse of what a horseshit world it was. For one moment he no longer gave a shit about Markey, no longer cared about the outcome of the trial. He just wanted to step off the train that had run over this man's children and was now bearing down on him as well.

Taggart endured the silence as long as he could, not insisting, out of fear of antagonizing the court members. He looked at Colonel Mo, hoping to get his help without having to say anything.

Mo saw the predicament. "Mr. Collins," he said quietly, "give Captain Taggart the letters. They will be treated with respect."

Frank Collins shifted his gaze from Taggart to Colonel Mo. The courtroom was silent. "Sir, I was a Marine. I was in the war. I was proud when my boy joined. Scared a little, but mostly proud. Now I don't understand anymore. Loren's dead. Linda's dead. My wife and I spent the money we'd saved to see Loren's graduation to come here instead. And now I'm supposed to show my boy's letters to his mother and me? I'll do it, sir, if you say so, but I don't understand. I don't understand anything anymore."

He stood and walked slowly over to the bar, took the letters that Martha handed across, gave them to Mike and resumed his seat on the witness stand. As he did so Mike could feel the defense he had so carefully prepared running between his fingers like sand. He doubted that any letter could possibly salvage the case from the sympathetic reaction that even he was having. He feared he had made a critical mistake.

Colonel Mo called a twenty-minute recess to allow time for both sides to review the letters. Mike was grateful for it. When court reconvened Mike handed Mr. Collins one of the letters.

Q. "Mr. Collins, I give you what has been marked Defendant's Exhibit 2 for identification. Will you identify it for me please."

A. "It's one of my son's letters."

Q. "What is the date on it, sir?"

A. "4 February 1971."

Q. "Is that your son's handwriting?"

A. "Yes."

Q. "Is that his signature at the bottom of the page?"

A. "Yes."

Q. "Did you receive this shortly after the date that it bears?"

A. "Yes."

Taggart asked that the letter be admitted into evidence. Steiner objected it was hearsay. After a brief argument Colonel Modelewski ruled that only the first five sentences of the second paragraph could come in. They included evidence of Loren Collins's state of mind shortly before his death.

"Mr. Collins, I'm going to read a passage from this letter, Exhibit 2, and I'd like you to tell me whether I've read it accurately.

> While we were at the range, some of the others in the platoon threw a blanket over my bunkmate's head after lights out and beat him up in order to motivate him because he wasn't shooting very well. That's called a blanket party, or EMI—extra military instruction. Private Johnson, the guide, is the one behind it. He's worse than the DIs. Everyone in the platoon's afraid of him.

Q. "Did I read that accurately, sir?"

A. "Yes."

"I have no further questions."

Now it was Steiner's turn, if he took it. Taggart very much hoped that Steiner would cross-examine, and in so doing share some of the onus Mike was feeling for having subjected the victim's father to the ordeal of taking the stand. Taggart decided that if it were his choice, he wouldn't have done it. Steiner, however, stood up, holding another of Loren Collins's letters.

"Mr. Collins," Steiner began, "I'm sorry this has become necessary, but I need to ask you one or two questions in light of those asked by the defense counsel. First, please examine Prosecution Exhibit 3. Is that a letter you and your wife received from your son while he was in training?"

A. "Yessir."

Q. "What is the date on Exhibit 3?"

A. "December 25, 1970."

Q. "Christmas Day."

A. "Yessir, Christmas Day."

Q. "Please read the second paragraph of Exhibit 3."

Frank Collins read in hoarse monotone:

> I'm almost too sore to write. Yesterday we fought with pugilsticks, which are long bars with padded ends. We fight with them like Little John did in Robin Hood. I got knocked down by another private's first blow. For a minute I couldn't see but I could feel him pounding me. I was on my face when my eyes cleared, but all I could see was the boots and legs of the others as they gathered around. They were yelling kill, kill and cheering. The platoon sgt. kept yelling go for the gut, go for the gut and get up, maggot—

Q. "That's enough, Mr. Collins. I have no further questions.

"Read the *rest* of the paragraph, Mr. Collins," Mike said, and with scarcely a pause Collins continued:

> I was trying, but the other guy was standing right over me. I thought I heard the whistle, which is the signal to stop, but he wouldn't stop until the DI pulled him off. Afterwards the sergeant told me that if I let that happen six months from now my ears are going to be nailed to the wall of some VC hooch. He's probably right.

Collins's voice cracked as he finished.

Taggart could only hope that at the end he'd offset some of the impression from the part of the letter Steiner had had Collins read that Markey had somehow condoned Loren Collins being beaten when he was down.

Instead of further drills during the noon hour recess Taggart took Roger and Sherill to lunch, pointedly avoiding any talk about the trial. Instead they talked about the Markeys' children and Taggart's experiences with kids, which were limited to summers spent coaching little league while he was in college. Between tales of 140-foot home runs and accounts of how Deborah Markey was painstakingly coloring an entire coloring book just for Mike, the time somehow slipped past. Taggart was even able to keep down the unease caused by Cathy's reappearance that morning. The three of them were still in this suspended state as they returned and Sherill left them to take her seat.

Mike and Roger slipped into the defense hooch so Taggart could pick up some papers.

"Okay, sarge, you ready to go?"

"All set."

"Then let's whip it on 'em. Remember, if Steiner asks about those other incidents we talked about, let him have it with both barrels. Got it?"

"Yessir, locked and loaded."

Taggart nodded to Markey and even allowed himself a slight grin. At least his man was going up to bat in as good a frame of mind as he could have hoped. They entered the courtroom together, just before two. Colonel Mo and Steiner were already in their places.

It was a hot afternoon. The windows of the courtroom looking out across the drill field to the south were open. Once in a while the faraway sound of cadence being called would float in, but only rarely, because there was no breeze. The loops at the end of the cords on the shades hung perfectly still. There weren't any interruptions by the planes taking off from the neighboring airport. The wind, the airlines ... it seemed as though everything had paused to listen to Roger Markey speak in his own defense.

Taggart quickly tied up a loose end left dangling from the cross-examination of Johnson by establishing that Roger Markey was left-handed. Then he backed up. . . .

It seemed to Veronica that from the beginning of his testimony Markey dominated the courtroom that afternoon and that Taggart had dropped from sight, leaving only his disembodied voice occasionally to nudge his witness in a new direction.

Speaking slowly, in the slight drawl Ronnie remembered from her interview with him, Roger Markey spoke briefly of growing up in Alabama and of his decision to join the Corps. Then, at greater length, he told the court members where he had served and of his decision to make the Marine Corps his career. He spoke simply and directly. For the first time in his life, he said, he was judged on what he did, not on being poor and part Indian. So he had stayed.

When he came back from his second tour in Viet Nam he volunteered for the drill field and was accepted. That had been almost two years ago, and until being relieved the night Collins died his performance, his judgment, his obedience to orders governing drill instructor conduct had never once been questioned.

Ronnie noticed his voice soften a little at the mention of Collins's death, but he left the impression that, like any other hard fact, he wasn't going to shrink away from it.

Q. "Describe your contacts with Private Collins prior to 6 February."

A. "I saw him every day as a member of First Platoon. His performance wasn't good or bad—just average. I talked to him sometimes about improving his performance. I thought he had more potential than what he was showin' us. Sergeant Warthun and Sergeant Sanchez and me, we all discussed it and agreed that his head was someplace else, and if we could just get him to concentrate on the training he'd be one of the better recruits."

Q. "How did you try to improve his concentration?"

A. "Well, first thing, I took him aside and told him I didn't think he was giving it everything he had and that he better start, 'cause he was probably going to Viet Nam, where it would take everything he had just to come out with his skin. It didn't seem to do no good though. He just went on markin' time, making stupid mistakes, even though I knew from his GCT and just the way he carried himself that he could do better. At one time or another each one of us was on him to try harder. Finally I sent him to motivation platoon for a day for half-steppin' during pugilsticks. I told him before he went that maybe motivation would show him how much tougher things could get. I thought maybe that helped, 'cause not long after he got back we went to the range and shot Expert.

* * *

266

"One thing I have to explain. Talkin' about Private Collins like this makes it sound like I spent all my time thinkin' about him. That ain't the way it was. Every recruit has his own problems. Every one of 'em is in shock from bein' dumped into recruit trainin' and havin' it soft on the outside. Some handle it better than others. Private Collins was somewhere in the middle. There were lots with worse problems than he had. Private Morkowski, who testified earlier, he was one who did. I tried to teach 'em what they needed to do their best and get ready for what was facin' em, but I swear to you I never hit one of 'em. Not even once in almost two years did I ever hit a recruit, and that includes Private Collins.

Q. "Did you have a confrontation with Private Collins like the one Pfc. Johnson described?"

A. "No. First platoon had the weekend duty the weekend Collins was hurt. I seen him walking fire watch in the passageway between the head and the door to the duty office just after taps. Pretty soon after that I heard someone drop a rifle out in the passage while I was in the duty office. I looked out. It was Private Collins. He was just straightenin' up from havin' picked up his piece when I come out. I chewed him out. Ya don't just drop your weapon when you're walkin' post unless you're daydreamin'. It was the kind of mistake Collins had made all during the program"

Q. "You say you chewed him out. What'd you say and do?"

A. "I told him I was tired of his stupid mistakes, and if he didn't shape up I wasn't gonna graduate him. Then I put him at shoulder arms an' sent him on his way. That was the last time I seen him until Johnson shows up about an hour later and tells me Collins is sick."

Q. "Did anything else happen between you and Private Collins during your conversation about the dropped rifle?"

A. "No."

Now Marky paused, turned away from the court members, pivoted a quarter turn in the witness chair and looked straight at Frank and Martha Collins. There were tears in Martha's eyes.

"I didn't kill your boy, Mr. and Mrs. Collins," Markey finally got out. "I didn't kill your son. I was tryin' to keep him alive."

"No further questions."

Anxious to dispel the good impression that he sensed Markey had succeeded in creating, Steiner stood up quickly.

Q. "Pfc. Johnson was the First Platoon guide, wasn't he?"

A. "Yessir."

Q. "That meant he was the best man in the platoon, didn't it?"

A. "It meant I thought he was at the time—"

Q. "You even went so far as to counsel him to try for OCS, didn't you?"

A. "Yessir."

Q. "You thought he would be a good officer?"

A. "Yessir."

Q. "You think it's important for an officer to be truthful, don't you?"

A. "Yessir."

Q. "You wouldn't suggest that someone you considered a liar go to OCS, would you?"

A. "No, sir."

Q. "You testified earlier that you never hit any recruits, is that right?"

A. "Yessir."

Q. "It was a violation of orders to use force against the recruits in your charge, wasn't it?"

A. "Yessir."

Q. "Was that why you didn't ever hit a recruit?"

A. "Yessir."

Q. "But you frequently used force against the recruits, didn't you?"

A. "No, sir."

Steiner stopped, looking surprised at the answer.

Q. "What was that? Did you just tell me you did not use force against recruits in your charge?"

A. "Yessir."

Q. "You jumped out of a tree onto Private Morkowski, didn't you?"

A. "That was different. That—"

Q. "Just answer my question. Sergeant Markey, you jumped out of a tree onto Private Morkowski, didn't you?"

A. "Yessir . . . just behind him . . ."

Q. "And you dragged him backward out of the formation?"

A. "Yessir."

Q. "You sometimes bit recruits?"

A. "I once bit a recruit, yessir."

Q. "As a matter of fact, you violated other orders regulating the conduct of training, did you?"

Taggart could hardly sit still. Markey wasn't on trial for other order violations. The question was irrelevant, but he thought Markey could handle it. If he objected he might appear to be trying to hide something. He decided to let it ride and clear things up on redirect if he had to.

A. "Sometimes, yessir."

Q. "You made the recruits miss regularly scheduled meals?"

A. "Sometimes, yessir."

Q. "You made them go out in the rain when they were supposed to be in their racks?"

A. "Yessir."

Q. "You knew these things were violations of orders when you did them?"

A. "Yessir."

Q. "You did your best to scare the recruits in your platoon, didn't you?"

A. "In a way, yessir, but for a reason."

Q. "Of course . . . now, on the night you confronted Private Collins about the dropped rifle you were standing with your back toward the direction of the squad bay, is that right?"

A. "I think so, yessir."

Q. "The squad bay was around the corner from where you and Private Collins were standing?"

A. "Yessir."

Q. "So if Pfc. Johnson was watching you and Private Collins from around that corner, you would not have seen him would you?"

A. "No, sir."

Q. "You thought dropping a rifle was a stupid mistake, didn't you?"

A. "Yessir."

Q. "You thought it was typical of Private Collins, didn't you?"

A. "Yessir."

Q. "You thought it was the kind of mistake that should never be made after the first week of boot camp, didn't you?"

A. "Yessir."

Q. "Yet here was Collins making the same stupid mistake at the end of the eighth week, right?"

A. "Yessir."

Q. "That must have been terribly frustrating for you as a drill instructor."

A. "It was more frightening, sir. I was scared."

Steiner's surprise at the answer was genuine, and he dropped his guard a little.

Q. "Frightened? Why frightened?"

It was the first question Steiner had asked that couldn't be answered with a simple "yes" or "no." It called for an explanation, and it was all Mike could do to keep from yelling "stick it to him, sarge."

Markey turned from Steiner to the court members. "I mean I was scared for Collins, for every other marine who had to depend on someone like Collins, who couldn't seem to get it together, for every recruit I ever graduated outta training. I'd been two tours in Viet Nam when I come on the drill field, been wounded three times, watched my best friend take ten hours to die after the guy next to him stepped on a boobytrap, watched dozens of men get killed or maimed, most of 'em by an enemy they never saw. I stayed awake for thirty hours at a time, too sick from malaria 'n dysentery, too tired to eat, too wrung out from fear of not knowin' where the next step would lead to even care anymore. I seen men go insane from the fear of not

270

knowin', men who could take the heat and wet, sores, leeches, dust, but who were just so scared of the ambushes, the boobytraps that they finally ambushed themselves.

"I'd been through the trainin' myself, I knew how unprepared I was for what I found. I grew up sleepin' in a dry warm bed and eatin' reg'lar most of the time, but not Charlie, he grew up in the jungle, eatin' rice and sleepin' on the ground and never bein' safe against nothin'. The VC's got a big headstart in this war—"

"Sir"—Steiner interrupted the testimony—"I move to strike all of the witness's current answer as unresponsive."

"Overruled," Modelewki said. "You asked him why he was frightened. He's telling you. You may finish your answer, sergeant."

Steiner sat down, shaking his head, and Markey went on with his story.

"Before I'd been on the field very long I began to feel, well, sort of haunted by the people I trained and sent over there. I felt like I was killin' 'em myself by not trainin' 'em, by turnin' 'em loose without bein' ready. But there wasn't much I could do. I just made up my mind to try and give 'em the mental toughness to put up with the fear and tough time they was gonna find. That's why I tried to scare 'em— to make 'em wonder if I'd be around the next corner, to keep 'em alert. That's why I sometimes made 'em go hungry, without sleep, made 'em stand in the rain. That time we bit that private, me and Sanchez, we didn't leave no marks. Didn't have to. It was the fear that came from us knowin' he'd called Sanchez a spic when he thought we didn't . . . we was trainin' that kid never to take nothin' for granted. What I done I done because I wanted to help 'em live. I didn't hit Private Collins, I was scared for him."

Q. "So you substituted your personal judgment for that of the Marine Corps in these matters, isn't that right? Taggart put in that last to anticipate and defuse Steiner's rebuttal.

A. "Sometimes I guess I did, sir."

"No further questions." It had gone as Taggart had hoped. The testimony had ended on an upbeat note for the defense. Taggart rested.

"Does trial counsel have any rebuttal?" the judge inquired.

Taggart leaned back, allowing himself to relax just a little now that the evidence was all in and, he figured, the proceedings ended for the day. He was wrong.

"Yessir," Steiner replied, "for its first witness in rebuttal, the prosecution calls Corporal Victor Litzinger."

"Litzinger?" Mike straightened up, trying to conceal his surprise. "What did Litzinger have to do with the case?"

Markey shoved a hastily scribbled note in front of Mike as Litzinger entered the courtroom and walked to the witness stand. "Who's Litzinger?"

"One of the legal clerks. He works for Colonel Guinn," Mike whispered and then was on his feet.

"Sir, may counsel approach the bench?"

"You may."

Taggart and Steiner gathered to Colonel Mo's right, opposite the court members. They spoke in whispers.

"Sir," Mike said, "I was not advised of trial counsel's intention to call this witness as required by section 44(h) of the Manual. I request an offer of proof regarding the testimony trial counsel expects this witness to give."

Colonel Mo shifted to Steiner for a response.

"Sir, the witness will give impeachment testimony and, as such, the decision to call him was not made until the accused testified. That's why the defense was not informed."

"What's his testimony?" Mo rumbled in the world's loudest whisper.

"Corporal Litzinger will testify that he overheard the accused admit he killed Private Collins."

Taggart's shock was surpassed only by his rage. "Sir, Captain Steiner must think you and I are fools if he expects us to believe he has a witness to an admission of guilt whom he has only now decided to use. Why didn't he use him as part of his case in chief? So he would have an excuse for concealing the witness from the defense, that's why. To prevent any investigation of the purported admission. I move the witness be excluded."

Every time he said the word "admission," Taggart almost gagged.

Veronica watched the trio at the bench intently. Colonel Modelewski sat pondering the decision he had to make while Steiner bounced impatiently on his toes and Taggart stood planted like a linebacker in the path of whatever story Victor Litzinger had to tell. Although they had scarcely moved as they talked it had obviously been a contentious exchange, not mere housekeeping. Taggart in particular had spoken intensely. Veronica wondered what the court members must think of this pantomime. What was it the lawyers didn't want them to know?

Whatever, the colonel had made up his mind. "Motion for exclusion denied," he said. "Captain Taggart, if at the conclusion of the direct examination you feel that you need a continuance, you may so move and the issue will be decided at that time."

Taggart and Steiner returned to their tables, and Taggart asked for time to confer with his client.

"Stand by for a shock," Mike muttered. "Remember, keep a poker face. Steiner says this guy overheard you admit you killed Collins."

The look of mute surprise and dismay that flickered across Markey's face at the news would not have served him well at cards, although Taggart doubted it wa detectable by the court.

"No way, captain. There's never been anything to admit. You got the whole story. I don't even know this guy."

Taggart nodded. "Well, let's see what he has to say." As if he had an alternative.

Steiner hurried through the introductory phase of his examination, then settled down to the main course.

Q. "Corporal Litzinger, are you acquanted with the accused, Staff Sergeant Roger Markey?"

A. "I know who he is."

Q. "How do you know that?"

A. "I work at Base Legal. Staff Sergeant Markey's become pretty well known up here. Someone pointed him out to me a little while after the case began."

Q. "That would have been back in February?"

A. "Yessir."

Q. "Have you ever overheard the accused discuss the subject matter of the charge against him?"

A. "Yessir."

Q. "When was that?"

A. "On April 1st."

Q. "Where did it take place?"

A. "Outside the base library."

Q. "Describe what happened on that occasion."

Litzinger was a company man all the way. He had made rank by being smart enough to carry out orders and adhere to prescribed routine, and never to question either one. If the Marine Corps said it, it was so. There was no room for doubt. The Corps had charged Roger Markey with murder. Taggart knew that Litzinger's attitude from the moment charges were filed had been hang the guilty bastard. Whatever Litzinger had heard Markey say had filtered into his brain through an already-in-place veil of hostility. Taggart dreaded hearing his answer.

A. "Well, I was on my way to the library for Colonel Guinn and I wanted to have a smoke while I was there, but I didn't have any matches. Then I saw Sergeant Markey standing beside the pillars opposite the library door talking to Captain Taggart's friend, that woman right over there."

Litzinger pointed at Veronica, and she felt as if his finger were boring right into her chest. Somehow Litzinger's testimony concerned her interview with Markey. Veronica racked her brain. They hadn't even discussed Collins. What was Litzinger going to say? What was Taggart thinking?

Steiner interrupted Litzinger's narrative. "Let the record reflect that the witness pointed to Veronica Rasmussen."

Q. "Go on, sergeant."

A. "I saw that Sergeant Markey was smoking, so I went up to ask him for a light. They had their backs to me, looking out at the drill field, so they didn't know I was there and could hear them talking as I came up to them."

Q. "Was it your intention to eavesdrop, sergeant?"

A. "No, sir. I just wanted a light, and I just happened to overhear what Sergeant Markey said."

Q. "What was that?"

A. "As I approached them she was saying something but I didn't hear what. Then Sergeant Markey began to talk and he said, 'I beat that recruit to death.' Those were his exact words."

Q. "Sergeant Litzinger, are you sure of what you heard?"

A. "Yessir, I'm positive. I mean, working at Legal and all, I know the charges against Sergeant Markey, and there was no mistaking—"

"Objection." Taggart was on his feet. "The witness's opinion of the sharpness of his hearing is irrelevent. Move the answer be stricken."

"Sustained."

Q. "By the way, Sergeant Litzinger," Steiner affected nonchalance, "where are you from?"

A. "Atlanta, Georgia, sir."

Q. "Before coming in the Marine Corps what was your job?"

A. "I worked for the Atlanta Police Department."

Q. "What was your job?"

A. "Undercover surveillance."

Q. "So you've had experience observing and reporting criminal activity?"

"Objection, leading question." Taggart knew Steiner didn't care about the answer. The question answered itself. Steiner was just driving home Litzinger's apparent special qualifications for the court members.

"Sustained."

Steiner was standing behind his counsel table staring down at his notes. He studied them for a few seconds more. He started to ask another question, changed his mind.

"No further questions."

Taggart, looking for straws, thought that at least there was a third party witness . . . he wouldn't have to rely solely on Markey's naked denial to refute Litzinger.

He glanced at the notes he'd made as he sat listening to Litzinger. One-word reminders of possible areas of attack: "bias," "misunderstanding." Taggart itched to stand up and go after that conniving son of a bitch on the witness stand, to demonstrate with the immediacy of his attack the obvious flaws in what Litzinger was saying, but he resisted the temptation. Make haste slowly, his dad used to preach. Better to ask for a recess and think things through, talk to Markey and Veronica, put a little more distance between Litzinger's direct testimony and the time the court had to start deliberations. Taggart asked for a recess.

Veronica's exchanges with Taggart during the recess were near-unbearable. He spoke to her as though she were a stranger. She told him Markey had never admitted anything to her, but wasn't sure he accepted her word. And he was apparently so focused on his immediate need to meet the challenge of Litzinger's testimony that he didn't seem able to accept her attempt at showing how sorry she was to see her interview misused against Markey. It was, in a word, a lousy half hour for all, and she was glad when the recess was over and everyone was back in his place.

The first rule of cross-examination, Taggart well knew, was never ask a question if you don't know what the answer will be. But Litzinger's claimed law enforcement experience was too intriguing to ignore, so Taggart was about to break the rule, even though he felt like he was walking through a mine field. By asking small, modest questions he hoped to detect danger areas while he was still able to back away. Maybe he would only get blown up a little bit.

Q. "Corporal Litzinger, how old are you?"
A. "Twenty-three."
Q. "How long have you been in the Marine Corps?"
A. "Five years."
Q. "So you were only eighteen when you enlisted?"
A. "That's right."

Here goes, Taggart thought, taking his first step into enemy territory.

Q. "You weren't a policeman when you were eighteen, were you?"

A. "No, sir, I didn't say I was a policeman. I said I worked for the police department."

Q. "Did you have a badge?"

A. "No."

Q. "Were you given a weapon?"

A. "No."

Q. "A uniform?"

A. "I was undercover."

Q. "You didn't have a uniform?"

A. "No."

Q. "Did you receive a regular salary from the department?"

A. "I was paid by the department."

Q. "But not a set amount at regular intervals."

A. "No."

Taggart took another step.

Q. "Were you what the police call a snitch?"

"Objection, argumentive," Steiner called out.
"Sustained. Rephrase your question, Captain Taggart."

Q. "You were a paid informant for the police, is that right?"

A. "Yes..."

Q. "If you provided a useful piece of information the police paid you what they thought it was worth?"

A. "Yes."

Q. "An informer for hire—?"

"Objection..."
"Sustained. Counsel, approach the bench."
Taggart knew when he asked it that the question would provoke Mo's anger, but he had to plant the seed. Marines were law-and-order people, and he had to strip away all dignity from Litzinger's claimed law enforcement experience.

"Captain Taggart," Mo said, "one more like that and it's going to cost you a month's pay for contempt. Understood?"

Taggart met Colonel Modelewski's level gaze head on. His words were angry but his eyes showed respect. He knew what Taggart had to do. Mike wondered how Mo would have handled Litzinger when he was trying cases.

"Yes sir, understood."

"Sergeant Litzinger," Mike resumed, "at the time you overheard this bit of conversation between Sergeant Markey and Miss Rasmussen, you knew that Miss Rasmussen was a television news reporter, didn't you?"

A. "Yessir."

Q. "You were at the library on an errand for Colonel Guinn, right?"

A. "Yessir."

Q. "Did the colonel want you to look something up for him?"

A. "No, sir, he wanted me to get him a book."

Q. "What book?"

A. "I don't remember. The colonel wrote the title down for me."

Q. "He wrote it down for you so you wouldn't forget it?"

Litzinger paused.

A. "Yessir."

Q. "You approached Sergeant Markey and Miss Rasmussen to ask them for a light."

A. "Yessir."

Q. "So it wasn't your intention to be an eavesdropper."

A. "No, sir."

Q. "As you approached them you didn't care what they were saying to each other, did you?"

A. "No, sir."

Q. "So you weren't paying any particular attention to what it was they were saying?"

A. "Well, I know what I heard."

Q. "That's not my question, sergeant. You heard what you heard without really intending to, isn't that right?"

A. "Yessir..."

278

Q. "You weren't paying any particular attention to what was being said. Correct."

A. "Well, yes, sir, but—"

Q. "Apart from what you testified to in answer to Captain Steiner's questions, you didn't hear anything else Sergeant Markey said to Miss Rasmussen, did you?"

A. "No, sir."

Q. "So you have no idea what *else* was said between them, isn't that right?"

A. "What else? No ..."

Q. "You don't know in what *context* Sergeant Markey spoke those six words you've testified you heard?"

A. "Context?"

Q. "You don't know what he said immediately after you heard him say those six words, do you?"

A. "No, sir ..."

Q. "And you don't know what he said immediately after you heard him say those six words, do you?"

A. "I guess not ..."

Q. "You don't know whether those six words you heard were even a full sentence, do you?"

A. "No, sir."

Q. "Working in base legal you immediately understood the possible significance of those six words, didn't you?"

A. "Yessir."

Q. "You didn't stop and think, for example, that those six words might have been part of a denial by Sergeant Markey?"

A. "No, sir, I only know what I heard ..."

Q. "It could well be that what Sergeant Markey said was 'You're wrong if you think I beat that recruit to death.' Do you agree?"

A. "I don't know, sir."

Taggart could think of more innocent ways the six words might have been used, but he'd pretty well gotten the testimony he wanted from Litzinger. He decided to save the rest for argument.

* * *

Q. "You didn't ask Sergeant Markey how he was using those words, did you?"

A. "I didn't think it was any of my business."

Q. "Instead you simply assumed Sergeant Markey was standing there admitting his guilt to a television news reporter, is that right?"

"Objection, argumentative."

"Overruled, answer the question."

A. "Sir, I didn't assume anything. I just went back and told Colonel Guinn what I heard."

Q. "Have you worked in legal administration the whole time you've been in the Corps?"

A. "Yessir, ever since I finished training."

Q. "Colonel Guinn is the staff judge advocate here at MCRD, right?"

A. "Yessir."

Q. "Your primary duties are to provide Colonel Guinn clerical assistance?"

A. "Yessir."

Q. "You're aware that one of Colonel Guinn's duties is to advise the command about legal matters?"

A. "Yessir."

Q. "At the time you reported those six words to Colonel Guinn, it was your understanding that Colonel Guinn had recommended that the command bring charges against Sergeant Markey, is that right?"

A long pause Litzinger looked up at the ceiling and back again at Taggart.

A. "I don't remember."

Q. "You've been in the Corps for five years, so you must have reenlisted, is that right?"

A. "Yessir."

Q. "You intend to make the Corps your career?"

A. "Yessir."

Q. "A career in the Corps depends on your ability to earn regular promotions, wouldn't you say?"

A. "Yessir, I suppose it does..."

Q. "Colonel Guinn writes your fitness reports, which determine whether you'll be promoted, doesn't he?"

A. "Yessir, he writes mine...and yours too."

Mike decided to cut it off. He'd done his best to call this 'smart ass' credibility into question. But the guy wasn't backing off.

"No further questions."

Steiner quickly tried to rehabilitate Litzinger by having him repeat the six words Taggart had so carefully kept him from repeating, and Litzinger left the stand.

"Prosecution rests."

Now it was Taggart's turn once again. It was time for a counter-attack.

"Defense calls Veronica Rasmussen."

Veronica's stomach was turning over. No amount of on-camera experience had ever prepared her for this. But bad stomach or not, it was show time, and acting nervous and upset on the witness stand wasn't going to help undo the harm she'd so unintentionally made possible.

Q. "Miss Rasmussen, who do you work for?"

A. "I'm a television news reporter for Monarch Broadcasting Company in Kansas City, Missouri."

Q. "What brings you to San Diego?"

A. "I'm here on assignment to report on this court-martial. Loren Collins's family lives in my station's broadcast area."

Q. "Do you recall talking to Roger Markey outside the MCRD library on April 1st?"

A. "Yes."

Q. "What was your purpose in talking to him on that occasion?"

A. "I asked if I could interview him, I wanted to get a story."

Q. "Had you ever talked with Sergeant Markey before?"

A. "I had been introduced to him once, nothing more."

Q. "Have you ever spoken to him since?"

A. "No."

Q. "During your interview with Sergeant Markey, what did he tell you about the charge that he killed Private Collins?"

Veronica turned to face the jury.

A. "Nothing. He said nothing about it. One of the conditions of the interview was that we not talk about this case . . . and we didn't."

Q. "Do you recall the interview being interrupted by Corporal Litzinger?"

A. "Someone asked Sergeant Markey for a light, I don't know who."

Q. "At what point in the interview did that occur?"

A. "At the very beginning."

Q. "Miss Rasmussen, if Sergeant Mark had admitted his guilt to you at any time during the interview would you have reported it?"

A. "I would have. It would have been a scoop. Front page material."

Q. "Did you report the interview?"

A. "Yes."

Q. "Did your report contain any mention of any admission by Sergeant Markey?"

A. "No, it did not."

"No further questions."

Throughout her testimony Veronica could feel Joe Steiner's black eyes on her, and now stared back as he stood up to cross-examine.

Q. "Miss Rasmussen, you took no notes of your conversation with the accused did you?"

A. "No."

Q. " . . . You're pretty well acquainted with the defense counsel, aren't you?"

A. "Yes . . ."

Q. "You've been seeing him socially?"

A. "Yes..."

Q. "You and he are on...intimate terms?"

"Objection, the witness's personal life is irrelevent." Taggart knew better than to object. He knew that by doing so he just circled Steiner's whole line of questions in red in the court's mind, and in Cathy's too for that matter. He'd even told Veronica during the break that it was coming, but the nasty, leering way Steiner had gone about it was more than he could take.

"Counsel, approach the bench," Modelewski said.

Mo had a question. "Why aren't Ms Rasmussen's feelings for you relevant to show her bias, captain?"

"Trying to show possible bias is one thing, sir...trial counsel's made his point. Now he's just harassing the witness—"

"Nonsense," Steiner interrupted. "Bias is a matter of degree. I'm entitled to show the extent of their relationship."

"Objection overruled, but, Captain Steiner, don't dwell on this. Move on."

"One more question, sir," Steiner promised as he and Taggart turned to leave the bench.

Veronica watched them go back to their counsel tables. She wished Taggart hadn't prolonged the ordeal by objecting, but at the same time she was glad he'd put in some protest. She also couldn't help wondering how much of it was to protect her, how much for Cathy's benefit...

Steiner broke into her thoughts with a vengeance.

Q. "Miss Rasmussen, isn't it a fact that you have been sexually intimate with counsel for the accused?"

Taggart's warning to her that it was coming didn't make it any less jolting. The embarrassment, having her relatioship with Taggart used against him and his client, of having it paraded in front of Cathy Taggart, all combined to prevent her from challenging Steiner with a so-what-you-son-of-a-bitch, which would have been true to her feelings. Instead she came back with a barely audible "yes" and hated herself for it.

"No further questions," Steiner announced in a voice whose tone called her a whore.

"Just one more question, Miss Rasmussen," Taggart broke in. "Is there anything about your friendship with me that would cause you to lie under oath?"

"No, nothing."

Markey approached her on his way to the stand as she was coming off. Veronica ached to somehow communicate that she was sorry, to gauge how he was taking the afternoon's events, but she was afraid that even a glance might be misconstrued and so she turned away as they passed.

It was the end of the fourth day of trial. Roger Markey had now been fighting a murder charge for more than three months. It showed. His normally sharp features were drawn as he sat down after being reminded that he was still under oath. Staring at Taggart, waiting for the first question, Markey's eyes were more intense than Mike had ever seen.

Until Litzinger's testimony, the trial seemed to be fought in the middle of the ring. Now they were fighting from the corner. Now there was a shade of desperation in Markey's bearing. It was as if the first time he had begun to believe he might be convicted, and with that realization had come the loss of the grim, quiet confidence that he had consistently shown ever since recovering from the publicizing of the Gilpin incident in Da Nang.

Q. "Sergeant Markey," Taggart began, "you heard Corporal Litzinger's testimony this afternoon?"

A. "Yessir."

Q. "What's your recollection of that interview?"

Markey slowly began to shake his head.

A. "Sir, I never hit Private Collins. I already told you that, and I never told anybody, not Miss Rasmussen or anybody else, that I did

... If those words Corporal Litzinger mentioned were said, then they were said as part of something else."

"No further questions." Mike sat down.
Steiner took up the questioning.

Q. "Sergeant Markey, you agree with Corporal Litzinger that you were talking to Miss Rasmussen outside the base library on April 1st?"
A. "Yessir."
Q. "You agree with Corporal Litzinger that he interrupted your conversation?"
A. "Yessir."
Q. "You agree with Corporal Litzinger that he asked you for a light?"
A. "I don't remember what he wanted."
Q. "You don't deny saying *I beat that recruit to death?*"
A. "I don't remember saying those words."
Q. "You don't remember one way or the other?"
A. "I don't remember."
Q. "So you don't deny making the statement."
A. "I don't remember, but I—"
Q. "Corporal Litzinger's memory may just be better than yours?"
A. "I don't think so."
Q. "You're not saying Corporal Litzinger is lying, are you?"
A. "I don't know whether he's lying or not."

"No further questions."
Trial recessed until the next morning when, Mo announced, counsel should be prepared for final argument.

It was 5:30 when Taggart and Markey returned to the defense hooch from the courtroom. The hooch was deserted and, after just a few words Markey took off too leaving Taggart alone with his headache.
Wearily Mike began to collect material he would need that night at home to put the final touches on his argument for the morning, when someone knocked on the door.

"Come on in."

"Michael, can I talk to you for a minute?" It was Cathy. "I know we agreed this morning to wait until the trial is over to discuss us, but there's one thing I want you to know now."

Taggart felt the vise holding his head tighten about three revolutions. "Sure, Cath, what is it?"

"Michael, I knew you'd been going out with that reporter... but it still hurt to hear her say it today on the witness stand. But hurting the way I did, well, Michael, it made me know again how much I love you, how much I want for us to try again..."

Taggart felt like he weighed a thousand pounds. "Cath," he said, forcing himself to his feet, "I can tell you I had no way of knowing that whole scene was going to be played until Litzinger testified. Once that happened it was inevitable, Steiner had to say what he did. But I'm truly sorry that it happened, that you had to hear it that way. It's easy to say, but believe me, I never wanted to hurt you."

"I know... If I didn't believe that I wouldn't be here. I guess I'm more to blame than you... Anyway, let's not talk about it any more now. The trial's almost over. Let's wait until that's behind you like we agreed.

"I just wanted to tell you I understood, to ease any strain you might feel. You don't need any more distractions now... Maybe we can get together this weekend? I'll be at the Moreheads..."

Fortunately she had already walked out the door before he could put together an answer.

Twenty-Four

"TAGS, I need a lawyer. Are you too busy to talk?"

Mike was relieved to hear Veronica's voice. When the phone had rung he'd been afraid it would be Cathy. Having spent the last four hours getting ready for the morning's final argument, he didn't think he was up to another session with Cathy tonight.

"Sure, I can talk. One more time through this argument and I'll come unglued. How about I come over and we take a hike?"

"Great—see you in a few minutes then."

Ronnie promptly came out of her room and got into the car as soon as Mike pulled to a stop.

"How about going over to Mission Beach?" she said.

Mike turned the car around and drove toward the beach. One look at Veronica told him he'd been foolish not to think that Cathy's appearance would force a reexamination of his relationship with her as well as Cathy. It was a bridge he'd always known he'd have to cross, but since the trial had started he'd been able to concentrate only on Markey's problem. Which in a way was a welcome escape.

Surf sounds and salt smells flooded into the car as they opened the doors to get out. Above them the skeleton of a darkened amusement park loomed, the empty rides mute in each other's shadows.

"That place gives me the creeps." Ronnie shivered as they walked across the lot toward the sand.

"A clown without its makeup..." Taggart began with mock solemnity, nudging her gently at the same time. Veronica did not smile.

It had been overcast and foggy by sundown, so there were no stars. From far out on the sand at low tide the lights along the promenade did not reach each other in the fog and appeared only in dim isolation ringed with the mist's encroaching darkness.

"We've spent some time on the beach, you and I, these past few weeks," Taggart said, breaking the silence in hopes of inducing some response from Ronnie, but the pause that followed was a long one. He decided to keep quiet. By this time he knew that Veronica would speak up if, and when, she had something to say.

They walked on, each trying to frame questions and answers now so near the surface. Finally they came to the south end of the beach where the jetty reared above them as it stretched across their path out into the water, thousands of huge pieces of concrete piled one on top of another to protect the ship channel into the bay.

"I haven't been down here since that night we went to World Famous," Veronica spoke at last. "Is there a place to stand out there?" she asked, pointing in the direction of the light on top of the seaward end of the barrier.

"Sure, there's a path of sorts. Follow me." Mike scrambled up the pile and helped Veronica, who was at his heels, up the last few feet. At a spot midway between the shore and the light they sat on one of the flatter chunks, Veronica in front of Mike, leaning back against his chest.

"I saw your wife today in court..." Veronica began.

"Yeah, I know ... that was quite a surprise."

"Mike, I don't mean to push things, but it's time to look at this ... situation. Even with the trial you must think about it..."

And what even during their most intimate moments he'd been unable to say now came tumbling out.

"Once in high school a girl I dated asked me why I never told her I loved her. It seemed all the guys her friends went with told them

288

they loved them. I could only laugh and say I didn't know what it meant. Now I know . . . This is going to sound corny but to hell with it . . . being with you is magic to me, something right out of the Arabian Nights. Just keeping up with you has made me better than I am—"

She started to protest this testimony to her magical powers, but he put his finger over her lips.

"Wait a minute, TV Lady, at least let me finish my speech. All that wouldn't be enough to make me feel what I'm talking about. There's an effortlessness being with you that I've never felt before. I can be with you doing something completely apart from you and still feel that there's something going on between us. All the posturing that usually goes with male-female relationships doesn't seem to have happened with us, and this is in spite of our having been on opposite sides of this case . . . Which says something in itself about what's going on." He paused a moment. What he had to say next was tough . . . "I'm not altogether naive, Ronnie. I know it's possible to be deeply involved with more than one person . . . I don't know if I still love Cathy. She and I, we've been hard people for each other for quite a while now. Can you *remember* how much you loved someone without still loving them? Because I do remember, and I still have strong feelings. I just don't know what they are . . . We've been together so long."

Veronica was crying. He felt like joining her.

Beneath her tears Veronica thought to herself how it was all so damn foreseeable. There she was, Veronica Rasmussen, odd woman out in the eternal triangle. They'd never believe it back in Kansas City, not modern woman Veronica Rasmussen. But the truth was she was no more in control of her feelings now than she'd been after their first night at World Famous. Taggart was being so damned *honest*, which was admirable, she guessed, but it hurt like hell. Okay, buck up, TV Lady.

"Tags, you make me out to be more than I am—but I'll accept it. I feel like you do, I've loved our times together, they've been better, more, than any ever with anybody else . . ." She looked up at him, she took his hand, pulling it down, caressing it between her palms, holding it against her breasts. "You touch me without trying. It's just there . . ."

289

Neither of them took the next step, neither said what was on their minds.

As they got up to go, Veronica, still holding his hand, couldn't help adding, "You know, Tags, if we ever do get together, we'll be one hell of a team."

Twenty-Five

Taggart could sleep like a baby before such as job interviews, the bar exam, even his wedding, but in the hours before any important direct, open competition, he inevitably felt awful. He knew as he set his alarm before shutting off the light that he would have no need of it that night. He lost count of the times he glanced at the luminous dial as it crawled toward morning, never coming any closer to sleep than a restless dozing, eventually getting up feeling weak and empty. There had never been a big game or a big trial without this queasy prelude. Just as during high school wrestling matches, when he felt so weak during warmups it was difficult to imagine actually wrestling, today he felt almost too weak to kickstart his bike when he left for work.

Was Steiner feeling the same way this morning? Mike hoped so. He always tended to think of his opponents as cool and self-assured, summoning whatever knowledge, strength and poise they would need to win with the ease of pushing a button. It had been a great boost to his own confidence when once, after an important game, an opponent admitted going through much the same ordeal. Still, he had to keep reminding himself that nobody had that kind of magic button.

With an aggressiveness he did not feel, Taggart muttered, "Let's get this show on the road," to Markey, who was waiting in the defense hooch when he arrived. They made their way into the courtroom, where a full house awaited them. At his place at the counsel table was a handwritten note. "No guts, no glory. Whip it to 'em, Tags." It was signed "The Defense Hooch." He wondered whether he would encounter that kind of camaraderie when . . . if . . . he returned to his civilian firm eight months from now.

He shoved the note over to Markey as Colonel Mo called the court to order, and the sergeant smiled for one of the few times all week. "My sentiments exactly," he said.

Steiner proceeded to live up to his Mad Dog moniker. Maltreatment was not the grand old Marine Corps tradition, he thundered, this was not the Old Corps, it was the *Marine* Corps, where decisions were based on hard facts, not obsolete myths, and the hard fact was that *an eye-witness had seen Markey smash Loren Collins in the abdomen and leave him gasping and staggering in the passageway, his insides suddenly awash with his own blood.* And another hard fact was that, in an unguarded moment, *Markey had admitted his crime.*

Steiner further emphasized Private First Class Johnson's outstanding record in boot camp and the fact that Markey himself had suggested Johnson for OCS. And then he began to trace the events of the night Collins died . . . Collins was walking his post, he was confronted by Markey for having dropped his rifle, they had stood eyeball to eyeball in the passageway, Collins at terrified attention, Markey with his back facing the direction of the squad bay. "Every detail," Mad Dog hammered away, "every detail, every detail of Johnson's account meshes perfectly with that given by Sergeant Markey . . . every detail but one. Every detail, every detail of Corporal Litzinger's account of the conversation in which he overheard Sergeant Markey say 'I beat that recruit to death' meshes perfectly with that given by Sergeant Markey . . . every detail but one . . . Markey *admits* his confrontation with Loren Collins on the night the boy died. Markey *admits* that someone interrupted his conversation with Miss Rasmussen to ask for a light. He *admits* that the prosecution witnesses' accounts of events are accurate . . . right up, of course, to the point of anything harmful to his case, and then he quickly says, Oh no, it didn't happen *that* way . . .

"Who are you going to believe? Is it really likely that two Marines, witnesses to independent events which Markey *admits* took place, would twist those events in a way likely to convict another Marine of murder? Given the fact that the events occurred, ask yourselves who has the motive to lie about the one detail in which the accused differs from the accounts of Pfc. Johnson and Corporal Litzinger."

Steiner then reviewed Dr. Nellis's opinion that the injury had been caused by a blow delivered with tremendous force by something like a rifle butt... "As for the defense's farfetched theory that Pfc. Johnson was Private Collins's assailant, well, I'm not going to dignify that with a response. You've heard Johnson, you can see with your own eyes the kind of Marine he is. The accused himself recognized Pfc. Johnson's caliber when he made Johnson the Hotel-1 guide, when he suggested Johnson try for OCS. If Pfc. Johnson was trying to hide something, would he have admitted to the defense counsel that he thought Collins had an attitude problem? Believing someone had an attitude problem is one thing, beating him to death for it is quite another. If Collins had an attitude problem, for whom did he represent a more serious problem...Pfc. Johnson, who would graduate and never see Collins again, or Sergeant Markey, whose career was graded on the basis of his platoon's performance? It's easy to see how Collins's attitude problem could have become the source of enormous frustration for Sergeant Markey, so much so that finally one night he just lost control, and Loren Collins died.

"Consider Pfc. Johnson and then consider Private Morokowski— Goofy, another attitude problem, another nonhacker, someone who in one breath says Pfc. Johnson was the best Marine in that platoon and in the next admits he hates him. Jealousy? Envy? Which man do you want to believe?"

Steiner had to be persuasive. It was the members' duty to put any sentiment or kinship they might feel for Markey as a Marine, as a professional soldier, to one side. Well, Collins too had been a Marine, and his death was a blot on the honor of the Corps. Now, perhaps more than at any other time in its history it was the duty of the military to see to it that justice was done and not to fuel the critics' fires with any legitimate basis for criticism. Steiner thought this hopefully, but of course did not give any of it voice.

"You've heard the expression shooting fish in a barrel," Steiner concluded. "Ask yourselves whether hitting a man with a rifle while he stands before you, at attention, defenseless, under your thumb, is any different. Staff Sergeant Roger Markey killed that boy, he has *admitted* it, and justice demands that he not be allowed to get away with it."

Taggart stood up now, drew a deep breath to settle himself, and addressed the court in a low, even voice.

"Loren Collins's death is a tragedy that has marked every person that it has touched. His family certainly, the lawyers who have had to try the case, you, the members of this court who will have to decide it. But the most indelibly marked is Roger Markey, sitting before you now, fighting to prevent the tragedy from consuming yet another victim. The trial counsel has just told you his view of what justice demands. I ask that you let the military judge tell you what justice demands. The Colonel will instruct you that if you have a *reasonable doubt* about whether Roger Markey did as he is charged, then you *must* find him not guilty. *That* is what justice demands. Contrary to the assertion of the prosecution, there is reason-a-plenty to doubt the charge against Roger Markey. Weigh for yourselves what you've seen and heard these last few days. Consider who has been doing the talking.

"But first I want to clear up this alleged admission." Taggart rolled a large blackboard to a position where it could be clearly seen by the court while he let his announced intention sink in. "Here we have the six words Corporal Litzinger claims he heard Sergeant Markey say." Taggart wrote, "I beat that recruit to death" in the middle of the board.

"Corporal Litzinger has told you that Sergeant Markey was talking as he approached, but that the only words he heard were those six. Litzinger doesn't even know whether those six words were Sergeant Markey's full sentence.

"As members of this court with a man's fate riding on your decision, I ask you to consider the possibilities."

Mike turned back to the board and wrote three words immediately to the left of the six. The board now read, "The command thinks I beat that recruit to death."

294

"Is that an admission?"

Taggart erased the first three words and wrote, "How could anybody think that..."

"Is that an admission?"

Again he erased the words he had added and this time wrote, "There's no way..." and then he very emphatically chalked an exclamation mark at the end of the resultant sentence.

"Is *that* an admission?"

Taggart left his new sentence on the board to give out—he hoped—its message to the court as he plunged ahead.

"I suppose Captain Steiner is going to stand up on rebuttal and tell you that clause I added is speculation, but is it any more speculative for me to add it than for him to take it away? Remember, please, this conversation was an on-the-record interview with a reporter. Is the prosecution asking you to believe that while steadfastly maintaining his innocence in this court-martial, he was simultaneously admitting guilt to a reporter? Is the prosecution asking you to believe that Sergeant Markey admitted guilt to a reporter whose only purpose for being in San Diego was to report on this trial, and that she didn't report it?" Were they remembering Steiner's claim that Ronnie didn't report anything so damaging to his client because of her relationship to his defense counsel? He couldn't dwell on it...

"Under the circumstances, you may safely assume that *if* those six words were said, they were surely part of a longer statement that was perfectly consistent with Roger Markey's vow to you that he is innocent."

Taggart paused, looked at the board, back to the court, and quietly repeated the words, "There is no way I beat that recruit to death!"

At this point Taggart reviewed for the court all of the rungs of the ladder up which Markey had climbed in his career. Boot camp, ITR, promotion first to the NCO ranks and then to staff NCO, each time in the shortest possible time, each time with the highest possible fitness reports. Two tours in Viet Nam, wounds, decorations, leadership, followed by the selection for Drill Instructor School with all its character screening and evaluation. The man they were judging had spent nearly two years on the field without any suggestion of improper

295

conduct until now. "At each step of the way Roger Markey has demonstrated courage, loyalty, intelligence, dependability, and has earned the respect of people with and for whom he has worked. Sergeant Major John Prudhomme has high standards, he does not lightly vouch for someone under oath."

Taggart invited the court to weigh the word of people like Markey and Prudhomme against that of the prosecution's witness, suggesting by his tone that Johnson was a liar. Who else had a motive in striking Collins? Who else was on the scene and knew that Collins had dropped his rifle that night? Who else felt it was his duty as a leader of the platoon to whip the recruits into shape? Pfc. Johnson, of course! The prosecution was asking the court to convict Roger Markey of murder on the testimony of Collins's most logical assailant.

"It doesn't take much imagination to picture Johnson coming around the corner as Sergeant Markey left Collins standing there and walked into the duty office. Johnson testified he was on his way to the head. Did he drag Collins in with him and work him over? If you think it's reasonably possible that that's what happened, then you must find Roger Markey not guilty.

"I suggest that it is indeed reasonably possible that Johnson, the giver of blanket parties, is the person who beat Loren Collins to death. Blanket parties. Talk about shooting fish in a barrel!"

Taggart again dragged out his chart depicting Collins's torso. "As court members you need look no farther than Johnson's own testimony for proof that he's lying. Remember, he was very clear that Collins was standing at attention in front of Sergeant Markey when he first saw Collins that night. If Collins had just been hit in the stomach with a rifle, would he have been standing at attention?

"Then Johnson says Markey hit Collins three or four times. Is Johnson suggesting that Markey hit Collins, Collins doubled up, Markey straightened Collins up, and then Markey took aim and hit Collins again, and that Markey repeated this process three or four times? Because that's how it would have to have happened if you believe Johnson. Otherwise how could Sergeant Markey have struck Collins in the stomach with the rifle with the later blows when Collins was jackknifed in front of him. That process of stiking, doubling, straightening and striking hardly sounds like a blow struck in a flash of anger by a frustrated drill instructor, as the prosecution would have you believe.

"Remember Johnson's written statement to me when I interviewed him. He mentions only a single blow, and when questioned, he says that he 'doesn't remember.' Now, it's one thing not to remember how many blows you saw when you say you saw several. It's quite a different matter to say you don't remember whether you saw one or more than one. That's a difference that's difficult to forget.

"The truth is that Johnson wrote that statement before he was made aware of this brutal roadmap—" Taggart indicated the chart depicting the marks on Collins's torso—"he wrote it the way he thought it would be believable, mentioning only one blow. Then he learned what Collins's stomach looked like and he changed his story, but it was too late to change his statement."

Taggart picked up the chart and began to parade it slowly from one end of the row of court members to the other, talking in a matter of fact tone as he walked. "I haven't been stationed at MCRD very long. I'm sure many of you have been here much longer. Does it strike you that what the prosecution is asking you to believe just isn't the way maltreatment takes place? Don't you believe that most of the times when some DI loses his temper and strikes a recruit that it's out of frustration over the private's inability to perform? It's a blow struck for emphasis, to make whatever the lesson more memorable—that certainly doesn't make it right, but the point is that it's just one blow! Drill instructors don't pummel people senseless with a hailstorm of blows, especially with a rifle butt. A serious injury would be inevitable. It would be impossible for the DI to escape detection. The prosecution is asking you to believe that Roger Markey, a drill instructor with a spotless record during his two years on the field, stepped completely out of character and committed virtual suicide.

"All the evidence is that there were repeated blows, and that means Sergeant Markey did not commit this crime."

As he spoke, Mike pinned each court member in turn with his eyes. They knew it was true, they had to...

Replacing the chart, Taggart zeroed in. "This flaw, this discrepancy

297

between what's charged and what our common sense and logic tell us in view of the condition of Collins's body following the attack is the most eloquent clue to what really happened. Johnson watched Markey chew out Collins, and he took over from there when Markey finished. But this time Johnson went too far. *This* time he didn't have a blanket. Johnson may have been able to intimidate the rest of the platoon out of reporting his brutality, but he couldn't intimidate Collins out of dying . . . he couldn't frighten those marks on Collins's stomach into keeping silent. And now they have revealed Johnson's lies.

"Gentlemen, ma'am"—Taggart looked from member to member on the court—"even if you completely disregard Roger Markey's sworn testimony that he did not hit Private Collins, the fact remains that Johnson's testimony, the only testimony in the entire case linking Markey to Collins's death, is impeached by the indisputable physical evidence in this case."

During his argument Taggart had moved only to show the court his exhibit and when writing on the board. Otherwise he stood riveted to one spot, letting his hands, arms, eyes and tone of voice animate his remarks without becoming a distraction. Now, however, he came several steps closer to the court members. Veronica sensed he was coming to the end of his presentation. He spoke in a low voice, so low that the spectators strained to hear.

"Every morning since this case began, when I come to work, and every night when I go home, there's a person marching up and down outside Gate Two carrying a sign that reads 'The Marine Corps eats its young!' I'm sure you've seen it too. I know that it's intended to refer to Private Collins, but I think it has particular significance for Roger Markey. Staff Sergeant Markey has written a record of honor and dependability across his entire Marine Corps experience. In years of service he has never given you reason to distrust him. His leadership and experience, and that of young staff NCO's like him, will be the life blood of the Corps for the next twenty years. Don't be too anxious to assume that because a recruit has died, a DI must be at fault. Do not be quick to accept the word of his single accuser, so at odds with the objective facts of the case, over the word of someone who has

298

served the Corps so well. Do not let this grim tragedy consume yet another innocent victim."

Taggart sat down amid a hush in the courtroom. At least, he told himself, he had said the things that needed saying.

Steiner spoke in sharp rebuttal for nearly ten minutes. He reminded the court again that Markey's testimony was the same as Johnson's and Litzinger's right up to the point it became hurtful to Markey, and then . . . "Suddenly Markey has a very different story to tell."

Steiner cleverly asked what Johnson had to gain by lying. Other than Taggart, no one had ever suggested Johnson was the guilty party. No witnesses had ever come forward to testify against Johnson. No one had ever pointed a finger at him. To believe Johnson had a motive to lie against Markey, the court first had to believe Johnson had some reason to think that unless he lied he would be accused. There was not a shred of evidence to suggest that. Yes, Johnson had pride in his leadership role . . . did that make him a murderer? Or did that make him a good Marine?

And Litzinger . . . what was his motive supposed to be? To curry some unspecified favor with his commanding officer? The court should compare that with Sergeant's Markey's motive for lying—to save his neck—and then decide who was telling the truth.

As for Taggart's speculation about the context in which the six words were used, was it any more speculative simply to believe that the six words were intended to convey exactly the message they did? The defense was asking the court to believe that something else *might* have been said. The prosecution was asking the court to believe only what *was* said. Not even the accused could deny those six words were said.

"Lastly"—Steiner's voice rose, then lowered slightly—"you need only believe Sergeant Markey intended to strike Private Collins to convict. There is no need to believe that he specifically intended to kill the private. All this defense talk about such an attack being suicide for a DI assumes that the DI was thinking rationally. If he'd been rational he wouldn't have hit Collins at all. No, what you have here is a flash of rage at an admittedly inept private who's at the end of his ninth week and still can't hang onto his rifle. Sergeant Markey is thinking to himself that this is the kind of guy that his fitness report is riding on, this is the kind of guy who's going to get people killed in Viet Nam, and he blows up. And when he calms down again, the damage has been done.

"Who, by the way, says Collins was ever so doubled up that Markey could not strike more than one blow to his stomach." Steiner grabbed up the rifle off the exhibit table and held it in position to deliver a butt stroke. "Maybe Markey never moved the weapon far enough away from Collins's stomach to allow him to double up completely until after he delivered several blows." He executed five or six short, quick, vicious jabs with the rifle butt, none moving in an arc of more than six inches, to demonstrate what he was talking about. "It boils down to this"—Steiner's voice was taut—"either you believe a first-rate eyewitness or you swallow the web of speculation and innuendo the lawyer for the accused has spun. I'm confident in your ability to choose between the two.

"Thank you for your attention."

Colonel Mo gave the court members their instructions, and they were left to deliberate.

As Taggart and Markey emerged from the courtroom into the crowd milling in the passageway, Margolis, Beeson and Horn were waiting for them.

"Looks good, Tags," Margolis said.

Beeson agreed.

Did they mean it? Taggart was afraid to believe. Eyewitness testimony was tough to disregard. He eyed the taciturn Horn standing, as always, at the back, catching his eye.

He nodded in apparent agreement.

"How long do you think it will take them to decide?" Markey asked once they were in the defense hooch.

"Probably not very long"—Mike shrugged—"what they've got to decide may be hard, but it isn't complicated. I'd guess a couple hours."

A couple of hours, Taggart thought to himself, wondering how he'd be feeling when it was over.

Sherill Markey came in and Mike talked some reassuring small talk.

Then Veronica came in as the Markeys were drifting out. "I'm not interrupting any technical discussions, am I?" she asked.

"No," Mike said in a deliberately offhand manner, at the same time glancing to make sure the Markeys were out of hearing, "just trying to build some bad-news bridges."

"Do you really think he's going to be convicted?" Ronnie asked.

Taggart shrugged. "I've been over the ground so many times now I can't see the forest for the trees. Better to hope for the best and prepare for the worst."

"Well, I'm glad I'm not on that court." She meant it as a signal to Mike of how far she had come from her pretrial conviction of Markey's guilt. But Mike's mind was elsewhere, and if he caught it he gave no indication.

"It's almost noon, Tags. Beeson, Margolis and some of the others wondered if we wanted to go to lunch. The court won't come in before we get back."

"You go, I'm not in the mood," he told her, cutting her off when she started to protest. "Really, go ahead. I'm not going to be any kind of company until this is over anyway."

"Okay," she finally agreed, "can I bring you back something, a cup of hemlock or—?"

"Get outa here," He almost smiled. "I'm just not very good at waiting, that's all."

She left, and Taggart was by himself in the defense hooch. Everything was so quiet that he was reminded of the night he sat there waiting to confront Markey over Gilpin's death in Da Nang. He tried to pass the time by writing a letter to his mom, he couldn't remember the last time he'd written to her. He tried to remember if she knew about Cathy's leaving. He tried to put down what he was feeling, but half an hour later the page was filled with cross-outs and he crumpled it and threw it away. Mom would have to take a raincheck.

He watched as cars crept by on the sunny street outside, past Roger and Sherill Markey walking back from wherever they'd been. Markey had mentioned where as they left, but Taggart had forgotten. He wondered whether the drivers of those cars knew that decisions were being made at that moment, less than a hundred yards from the street, that might completely tear apart the couple they'd just passed. Of course they didn't, but even if they did, would it make a difference? People were constantly getting torn apart, and even those who were aware of it usually didn't do anything about it. He thought again of the people, maybe some friends, dying in Viet Nam as he sat there doing nothing about it. He was no special case.

For a couple of hours after lunch people filtered in and out of the office in their usual routine, ignoring Taggart except for a greeting. Horn came down to say that Steiner was making life unbearable for everybody at the other end of the hall. Mad Dog wasn't very good at waiting either.

By 1530 the court had been in deliberation more than four hours. "What the hell can they be doing in there?" Mike fumed. "They either believe Markey or they believe Johnson. After this long, more time isn't going to help them decide."

"Maybe they've decided to take turns humping Lieutenant Giles before they come out," Margolis said in his best—or worst—Groucho Marx impersonation from his adjacent desk.

Taggart laughed in spite of himself before turning back to his file. He reviewed the brief presentation he planned in the unhappy event of conviction. There was little in the way of extenuation and mitigation of sentence that he hadn't already presented in the guise of character evidence. Markey couldn't testify . . . having denied the blow he couldn't very well now say he'd learned his lesson, nor would it profit him to repeat his denials to this court. It would amount to an attack on their judgment and would only antagonize them. Sherill Markey was all that was left. Taggart would put her on to tell how her husband's presence was vital to the family's well-being, and then he would remind the members of Markey's record again, and they would decide the sentence. God, how he hoped it would never get that far.

By 1630 the defense hooch was again deserted except for Taggart, this time in favor of Friday night's Happy Hour. Orders had been left with the duty clerk to call the club if the court was coming in. Taggart gave up even the pretext of working. He just sat distractedly, hopping from one day dream to another, never staying in one place for long, thinking what a pretty shadow the sun through the pines outside his window made on the opposite wall. He was aware of the passage of time only when the shadow finally disappeared. He was still sitting there half entranced in the darkened office when Markey came in from wherever he and Sherill had been waiting it out to say that she'd gone home to relieve the babysitter. If she could get a replacement, she'd be back later.

Taggart merely nodded. By now he was beginning to doubt himself. He needed some fresh air but could hear people out in the passage and knew the crowd was back from dinner to take up its vigil again and he was in no mood to talk. He phoned the clerk to say he'd be right outside the main entrance of the building and slipped out the side exit of the foyer leading to the defense hooch. If anyone saw him, they decided to let him go.

Once outside he stood alone in the dark, breathing deeply and listening to the crickets on the general's lawn across the street.

"Excuse me, captain, you got a light?" The voice came from behind Mike, startled him, and he turned to see a figure step toward him from the shadows of the pines beside the building. They were face to face before they recognized each other. It was Frank Collins.

Taggart's heart sank. What could he say to this man? He fumbled through his pockets and for once came up with some matches, which he handed to Collins.

"Nice night," Mr. Collins said after a couple of seconds.

"Yessir," Taggart managed to get out.

"I didn't know it was you when I asked for the light," Collins went on, squinting at Mike through the smoke. "Feels kinda strange to be talkin' to you like this after watchin' you all week and with everything that's happened."

"Mr. Collins"—Mike reached back for strength to get the words out—"I hope you don't think anything I've ever done or said is any sign I'm not deeply sorry about your son's death."

"No, I don't think that," Collins replied slowly. "My wife and I talked about it some the night after you called me to be a witness and some more again this afternoon. I think we're both kind of sorry we come out for the trial. We thought it would make us feel better

303

to see the man who killed Loren convicted, but I know we ain't gonna feel any better if your sergeant there's convicted. Maybe what the preacher's been hammerin' inta my head all these years about turnin' the other cheek has finally got through . . . or maybe it's that we're just not sure they got the right one . . . I don't know what it is but readin' Lauren's letters about what went on and knowin' myself from when I was in, well, it almost makes me think it wasn't no one man behind Loren's death . . . maybe it was what they call the system . . . except you can't put a system on trial, can you? . . ."

"No, sir, not in here you can't," was the best Mike could find to say in reply to this remarkable man's comment, "but it's going on out there every day," and he pointed in the direction of the demonstrators huddled outside Gate Two.

"I know," Collins said, perhaps remembering his other lost child, and then he took a deep breath and let it out real slow. "But I reckon they ain't got all the answers either. . . . Anyway, I got no hard feelin's toward you, Captain Taggart," and he held out his hand.

Mike took it, turning slightly so the light from the headquarters entryway wouldn't reflect any dampness in his eyes.

After that they stood talking quietly for another half hour about the midwest and farming and the differences between raising the corn and soybeans Mike had grown up with and the wheat and oats Frank Collins grew. They were fifteen hundred miles from San Diego when they were interrupted by the duty clerk leaning over the second floor railing.

"Excuse me, Captain Taggart, the court is returning in five minutes."

The Markeys were waiting at Taggart's desk at the opposite end of the defense hooch as he entered. Taggart sucked in his breath and smiled what he hoped was reassurance.

"Captain Taggart"—Sherill put her hand on his sleeve—"I'm so scared."

Roger too looked pale and drawn but said nothing.

Mike paused. He loved these people. His heart ached at the fear of betrayal he knew they must be feeling. "The Marine Corps eats its young! The Marine Corps eats its young!" The words drummed in his brain.

He put his arms around their shoulders. "We'll deal with whatever comes."

Spectators were filing back into the courtroom as the three of them approached, and the crowd parted to let them through.

Taggart felt distanced from everybody, detached, as though he were looking through the wrong end of a telescope.

Ponderously Colonel Mo took his place. How many times, Taggart wondered, had Mo reenacted this scene in his career? What did Mo expect to happen here in the next few minutes?

"Court will come to order," Mo grunted with a preemptory bang of his gavel. "Summon the court members."

Heads turned as the clerk led the members into the courtroom. They walked with eyes downcast, as if by meeting someone's gaze they feared to betray their verdict or, perhaps their feelings about the verdict.

"Mr. President," Mo addressed Colonel Simmons, the president of the court, "have you reached your verdict?"

"Yes, sir, we have."

"May I see it, please."

Simmons passed a folded sheet of paper to Colonel Modelewski.

Slowly Mo's blunt, sausagelike fingers unfolded the thin slip. He studied what was written there without saying anything, then looked up at the court members.

"Do you agree that this is the verdict of the court?"

Heads nodded in assent.

"Very well," he said handing the paper back to Colonel Simmons. "You may read the verdict, sir.

"Accused and his counsel, stand and face the court."

"Staff Sergeant Roger A. Markey," Colonel Simmons began, "It is my duty as president of this court to inform you that the court in closed session and upon secret written ballot, two-thirds of the members present at the time the vote was taken concurring, finds you guilty ..."

The room exploded with reporters scrambling, bumping into each other in their anxiety to get to a phone. Colonel Mo's demand for order was lost in the momentary clamor.

Colonel Simmons went on reading ... "of the specification and charge of murder."

305

It didn't matter. "Markey killed the Collins kid, the court confirms . . ." The stories were already formulating in their minds as they rushed for the door. All but Veronica, who never moved, who sat staring at the backs of the two men standing in front of her, no longer wondering whether she was there as a reporter or friend of the defense.

She put her arms around Sherill Markey, who was sobbing beside her. Taggart seemed to her to be moving woodenly, a toy soldier. His voice was barely audible as he made a motion that Sergeant Markey be allowed to remain free pending sentencing, which was granted. He sat down, stood up again as the court was dismissed. . . .

26

MIKE TAGGART loved Washington, D.C.

When he was in OCS and Basic School at nearby Quantico he had spent his few precious days off in Washington wandering from shrine to shrine, overdosing on the history that he'd been told about and read about since he was a little boy.

The Court of Military Appeals was one shrine he had missed on all his earlier visits, and the only history Taggart had in mind as he climbed the courthouse steps this cold January day was the ordeal of the last twenty-one months, which had seen Roger Markey go to Leavenworth Penitentiary, Cathy go back to Chicago without him, and the rest of his life go pretty much to hell in the process.

Today, though, he felt better than he had in many months. Step by step he remembered . . . Prudhomme dragging Private Morkowski into the defense hooch on the Monday following Markey's conviction; Morkowski sobbing, saying he'd heard Johnson beat Loren Collins to death in the platoon head on that terrible night, that *he'd* been in the head when Johnson dragged Collins in and struck him over and over, that he'd heard the blows land, heard Loren groan and recognized his voice as he begged Johnson to stop, recognized Johnson's voice as he told Collins to "shut up," heard Johnson half drag Collins back in the direction of the squad bay. Morkowski said he'd been so scared then that he drew his feet up so Johnson wouldn't see that anyone was in any of the stalls; so terrified of Johnson that he hadn't been able to make himself tell Taggart what he knew, hoping against hope that Markey would be acquitted. Taggart shook his head in angry frustration at that memory of Morkowski, fucking up his chance to avenge the death of his only friend, fucking up his chance to save an innocent man, just like he'd fucked up practically everything else he'd ever tried to do, making, finally, his confession to Prudhomme two hours after Markey had been sentenced to twenty years in prison.

"Newly discovered evidence" was what the law called such extraordinary developments. "Bullshit" was what Joe Steiner called it when he first heard what Morkowski had to say. And the command agreed. They had finally convicted a drill instructor, a significant inroad on the much publicized alleged maltreatment of recruits had been made, something they could *point* to. The very fact the case had received so much publicity reinforced the command's reluctance to retry it. So the command opposed Taggart's motion for a new trial. Morkowski was mercilessly cross-examined by Mad Dog Steiner at a hearing in front of Colonel Mo. The fact that he'd already testified at length without saying anything about what he'd heard, that he'd testified about his blanket party while not mentioning the assault, that he hadn't actually seen anything—all these "facts" were raised by Steiner to support his argument that Morkowski was just trying to get even for his blanket party, that the whole thing was just a last ditch, concocted defense trick, that in exercise of due diligence the defense could have discovered this evidence in time for the original trial if it were real, and that it was so implausible that it had no weight in changing the outcome.

Colonel Modelewski agreed. Taggart's argument that he wasn't at this point asking for Markey's acquittal but only for the chance, *the mere chance,* to have a court consider Morkowski's additional testimony, testimony that did not conflict with anything Morkowski had testified to earlier, fell on very deaf ears. Motion denied.

The months that followed were a haze of string-pulling for Taggart to be allowed to handle the appeal, long hours of research, brief-writing and cold coffee, conferences about the appellate process, grounds for reversal, review of the trial transcript. Mike could no longer remember any of his other cases. They'd just happened, had come and gone. But the Markey case stayed in his head, and guts . . . along with the memory of his promise to a little girl in a swing. . . .

By the time Taggart's date for release from active duty arrived he no longer felt he owed Cathy anything. It was as if she'd sat tapping her fingers waiting only for his enlistment to end. All of the tenderness she'd shown right after the trial had quickly eroded as she saw that Taggart was even more at odds with the world than before, that he was obsessed with the Markey appeal.

"You know, I'm not so sure you even care all that much about Markey," Cathy told Mike during one of their many arguments. "I think he's just your way of trying to pay back the Corps for all your terrible imagined losses. Funny thing is, Mike, it's you who's being paid back instead . . ."

Taggart had not answered her. Two months before his release date they went home to Iowa for Christmas. Cathy did not return to San Diego. A month later she moved to Chicago, and filed for divorce.

So now it was Michael Taggart, civilian. No more rank, no more uniform, a partner in the San Diego firm of Taggart & Horn, attorneys at law, specially retained counsel in the case of *United States of America v. Roger Markey,* on appeal to the United States Court of Military Appeals. Taggart reminded himself of the ancient mariner in Coleridge's poem, a relic with a dead bird tied around his neck. The image occurred to him again as he topped the steps and entered the appeals-court building. This was the end of the road. Win or lose, would he at least be able to untie himself from this legacy of the Corps?

Inside, all seemed hushed. Each step Mike took echoed in the otherwise empty corridor. The walls were hung with battle flags and portraits of soldiers, a courthouse theme more appropriate than most jurists liked to admit.

Taggart paid no attention to the decor. He had visited the building the day before, had sat in the empty courtroom trying to imagine it in session. He had already argued the appeal over and over in his mind, now he wanted his final mental rehearsals to be played out in the setting where the argument would actually take place.

309

The courtroom was empty when he entered it. *United States of America v. Markey* was the only matter on the morning's schedule. Taggart sat at the table assigned to appellants, dwarfed by the huge room and high ceiling, shadowed by the dark paneled walls and the tall bench where the judges would sit. He arranged some papers on the table for ready access but did not look at them. He knew them almost by heart. He sat in silence, legs crossed, trying to anticipate any new scenarios that might confront him once the argument began, trying to push away any thought of Roger Markey in a Kansas prison fifteen hundred miles away. He felt very scared and alone.

When Veronica Rasmussen told Eddie Logan that the Markey appeal was being argued in Washington, D.C., and asked to go there to cover the story, he quickly surrendered. He knew anything else would be a waste of time.

In the months since Veronica had returned to Kansas City after the Markey verdict Eddie had watched her go through some changes, subtle changes missed by people who didn't know her as well as he did. She was still the station's main attraction, its ratings star, but she seemed to have lost her edge. For months she had made too many trips to the mailroom, and even now she would sometimes act startled by a ringing phone, as if it was jarring her out of some other distant place. Oh, she still brought verve and intelligence to most any story she handled, but they didn't seem to give her the same excitement that they once had. In fact, Veronica Rasmussen seldom got excited anymore. Eddie knew she'd gotten involved with Markey's lawyer while she was in San Diego, that the guy was married, and that he'd gone back to his wife . . . but Ronnie was too smart a lady to still be carrying a torch after nearly two years for any guy.

What Eddie did not know, what none of her friends knew, what even Taggart didn't know was that every Sunday afternoon she would drive across the river to Kansas, to Leavenworth prison to visit a certain inmate she knew there. In the year and a half he had been there, she'd never missed a single Sunday. . . .

* * *

310

Taggart watched now as one by one the various court personnel began to file in as the time for the argument drew near. The clerk and the reporter chatted as they organized for the hearing. Captain Swearingen, the navy captain who was the commanding officer of the defense facility, arrived and sat down at Taggart's table. He was accompanied by Lieutenant Clyde, the military lawyer assigned to the case. The two officers exchanged greetings with Taggart, then left him alone.

On the opposite side of the lectern where people addressing the court stood, the prosecution team began to assemble around the table designated for appellee's counsel. Joe Steiner was there. Like Taggart he had managed to wangle a special assignment, to argue against the appeal. Taggart had met the other two officers at Steiner's table but couldn't remember their names.

Veronica was among the last to enter the courtroom. She knew Taggart's tendency toward early arrivals and wanted to come in after he did to avoid distracting him. She had waited almost two years to be with him again, she could wait another hour.

When she saw him sitting with his back to her, she badly wanted to run up to him, to tell him how much she had missed him, that she had been lonely, that she'd continued to follow the Markey case and, indirectly, Taggart's life through her visits with Roger Markey in jail. Instead, she stood in the aisle and studied him for a moment. Same guy, same tall, lean, loose-jointed figure slouching slightly in his chair, waiting. He was even wearing a dark green suit—no such thing as an ex-Marine, she thought to herself with a smile. She took a seat about one-third the way back, aware that the sight of Taggart was stirring a tempest inside her unlike any she'd known since their night together on the seawall two years before. She was not surprised.

"ALL RISE."

The command jarred Taggart out of his thoughts. He looked around, expecting to see the three judges on their way to the bench. Instead, a black curtain behind the bench was drawn and there the judges stood, like, it occurred to him, three new contestants for some kind of quiz show. After a moment they stepped forward and took their seats, and the senior judge, who was seated in the middle, asked Taggart whether he wanted to use his allotted time all at once or whether he wanted to reserve some for rebuttal. Taggart reserved seven minutes for rebuttal.

"Very well," the judge said. "You may proceed."

Taggart looked slowly from judge to judge, making eye contact with each man. "May it please the Court..."

And so began twenty of the longest minutes of Mike Taggart's life, not because the judges bombarded him with tough questions that because they asked him nothing at all. He asked at the beginning if there was any particular issue the court wanted him to address. Three negative shakes of the head were his only reply, leaving him alone at the lectern in the first appellate argument of his life, and with no sense at all of what the court considered key to the case.

Taggart had decided his main issue on appeal, the one he intended to devote all his time to in oral argument, was Colonel Mo's refusal to order a new trial on the basis of Morkowski's testimony that he overheard Johnson assault Collins on the night Collins died. In his appellate brief Mike had also raised the admission of Dr. Nellis' rifle-butt testimony and the inadequate notice he'd been given of the prosecution's intention to call Corporal Litzinger to testify, but both those issues were losers. He wouldn't waste time with them unless there was some indication of interest in them from the court.

Taggart began to feel his way by reviewing the standard for granting new trials on the basis of newly discovered evidence. The Manual for Court Martial required that the evidence really be newly discovered, not something counsel knew but held in reserve just in case of conviction. It had to be evidence that Taggart could not reasonably have been expected to discover *before* the end of trial, and it had to be something which, in light of all the facts, would probably produce a substantially more favorable result for the accused.

Taggart was convinced that Morkowski's belated revelation met all tests. He had had no clue that Morkowski had been a witness to the assault at any time during the trial, despite two long interviews with the man. Morkowski was plainly terrified of Johnson; he had already been beaten by him once; he was by his own admission the worst private in the platoon, the weakest and most scared. Everyone called him "Goofy." Johnson was the guide, the strongest and most imposing. Morkowski's fear of him had been understandable. There was just no way the defense could have known "Goofy" Morkowski's secret until he was ready to tell it.

The murder conviction of an innocent man, plus his own guilt, had forced Morkowski to overcome his fear. But psychological motives aside, it had *happened*. In the transcript of the hearing on Taggart's motion for a new trial Morkowski had said he heard Johnson beat Collins to death. He had been *no more than five feet away* when it happened. It made no difference whether the prosecution believed it, whether Colonel Mo believed it, whether the Commandant of the Marine Corps believed it, the court members at Sergeant Markey's murder trial might *reasonably* have believed it, and *that* was what was important.

"Remember," Taggart told the judges, "all that's required for an acquittal is reasonable doubt of guilt. Who can say that hearing a witness' testimony that someone *other than* the accused committed the murder would not create at least a reasonable doubt of the accused's guilt?

"This was an exceedingly close case. Private Johnson, the prosecution's principal witness, was a proven bully with the greatest motive of anyone to strike the victim. His account of what he saw was seriously impeached by the examining physician's testimony about the way the beating must have happened. Sergeant Markey had spent two exemplary years on the drill field without any suggestion of brutality. He denied ever striking the victim. It took the court members eleven hours of deliberation to decide the single issue of guilt or innocence. Even without Private Morkowski's testimony, the decision between guilt and innocence in that court martial hung for hours in a delicate balance. How can anyone say that Private Morkowski's account of what he heard that night in the head could make no difference?"

Taggart sat down just as the red light signaling that he had one minute remaining of the time alloted for his opening argument flashed on. They had still not asked a single question. He studied the faces of the judges. They revealed nothing.

313

"Counsel," the senior judge nodded in Steiner's direction.

"May it please the Court," Steiner began, "one of the major issues on appeal is whether the *alleged* newly discovered evidence would make a difference in the outcome, if presented. In that connection I think opposing counsel misspoke when he described Private Morkowski as a witness. A more accurate description of what defendant is contending is a claimed *ear* witness, someone who actually testified for the defense at trial but said nothing about even hearing the victim assaulted until some time after conviction and sentencing. There is strong reason to believe that his belated account of overhearing an assault is nothing more than an attempt to avenge—"

"Excuse me, counsel," the judge on the right interrupted Steiner, "don't you think the witness' motives are something better left for the court members to decide?"

"Not when the witness fails to come forward until after the trial is over," Steiner said quickly. "When that happens the judge is entitled at least to consider the motives of the witness when deciding whether the evidence might reasonably affect the outcome."

"And you say that because Private Morkowski was beaten by Private Johnson earlier in training, Morkowski is now falsely accusing Johnson of murder?" the judge said. "Isn't it also likely that Morkowski was terrified of Johnson, both because of his own beating and because of what he heard Johnson do to Collins?"

All Steiner could manage was that the judges had to look at all the circumstances of Morkowski's testimony, and that on balance it clearly was not believable.

The judge on the left spoke up. "What about the prosecution's surprise witness? Do you feel concealing that Corporal Litzinger claimed to have knowledge about the case until the moment you were ready to use him meets the standards of fairness required by the Manual?"

Steiner said that he did, repeating his argument at trial that Litzinger's testimony was used only for impeachment.

"I disagree," the left judge said. "Regardless of the label you put on it, Litzinger's testimony, if believed, constituted an admission by the accused, and for trial counsel to have failed to disclose a known possible admission constitutes prosecutorial misconduct."

Veronica told herself she didn't have to be a lawyer to understand what those sentiments meant for Markey. She wondered what Mike's reaction was. Mike's reaction was that he hoped at least one other judge agreed with the guy on the left.

"I want to get back to the matter of the newly discovered evidence," the senior judge said. "Is it the prosecution's position that the accused should reasonably have been aware at time of trial that Private Morkowski witnessed the assault?"

"Yes"—Steiner was emphatic—"if in fact he did witness it. Most recruits aren't very sophisticated witnesses. Morkowski less than most. Any skilled attorney would have known within a few minutes of interviewing him that he was hiding something, if he was."

"You interviewed Private Morkowski, didn't you, Captain Steiner?" the judge said, echoing the very question Taggart was silently asking.

"Yes, sir."

"Did you know Private Morkowski was withholding that he had witnessed Johnson's assault on the victim?"

There was a pause that made Taggart shift his gaze from the judges to Steiner. Was it possible that Mad Dog had known from the beginning that Morkowski had witnessed Johnson beating Collins?

"No, sir," Steiner finally said. "The government believes he invented the story at a later time."

All three judges had now been heard from. Steiner's time was about up. The green light signifying three minutes to go had already flashed. Maybe, Veronica thought, her Sunday afternoon visits to Kansas were nearing an end...

"Your Honors," Mike began, "there's not too much I can add to what I've already said and to the thoughts expressed by Your Honors' questions. The Marine Corps court-martialed Roger Markey because it claimed he broke the law, and then it proceeded to break the law itself... in its eagerness to convict him. The law requires an accused be given notice before trial of probable witnesses. This was not done. The law requires that a new trial be granted in the event of discovery of new and significant evidence. This was not done. If the government is not going to play by its own rules, why bother to go to a trial at all? It's a much smaller step than any of us likes to believe from denying a man a reasonable opportunity to present all the evidence that exists in his favor to just dragging him out and shooting him. The court is the only safeguard any of us really has against such abuse. All through his Marine Corps career Roger Markey gave everything he had in the performance of his duty, and *this* is the way he's been paid back—twenty years in prison and a dishonorable discharge, while all the while a known witness to the actual killing sits unheard. On behalf of Staff Sergeant Roger Markey, and his family, I respectfully request that this conviction be reversed."

Taggart hoped he had won. The thought brought a sense of relief, but not real joy. He was sure Markey would never be retried, but maybe, like the war itself, the case had taken too long, too much had been lost. He hoped to hell not.

Taggart picked up the unused notes he'd brought, stuffed them into a folder and turned to leave. Veronica now stood in front of him, smiling and crying at the same time. "You did it, Tags," was all she said.

And as it turned out, he had.

He knew when he saw her that he should have expected her to be there, but he hadn't. He'd only daydreamed about it, wanting so badly to see her again but tearing up the letters he started after Cathy left, putting down the phone with her number half-dialed, waiting for his own life somehow to get squared away.

She looked the same—shorter hairstyle, but that was all. Just like he'd been remembering her every day for the last two years ... on beaches, in cars, in courtrooms, anywhere and everywhere. No place or person could divert him for long from his thoughts of her. His remembrance of her had become his best, his most treasured possession. She'd become his invisible companion, his friend who was there but wasn't ... he even *talked* to her sometimes when he was alone ...

"What's next for you?" Veronica asked when he didn't say anything.

"Going to Mexico for a week or so. Want to come along?"

She studied him hard for a few moments. It was a question she'd been ready to answer for nearly two years.

"I'd love to."

There was a cool breeze. The sound of their feet going down the courthouse steps reminded Taggart, God help him, of the recruits marching at MCRD.

A newsstand headline caught his eye. "CEASE FIRE SIGNED." The war that had torn the country apart was officially over, but with uncountable battles still to be fought, by the blameless as well as the blamed. Maybe fifty years from now the last forgotten booby trap, the last unexploded shell would go off, killing some child who had not yet been born. Had it really mattered which side you were on? Now, for those who remained, the long and painful comeback could at least begin.